honey trap

A NOVEL

TONY BRENNA

Honey Trap

Published by Pacific Press Interational

All rights reserved.

Copyright © 2022 by Tony Brenna

ISBN 978-0-98521-091-5 | eBook ISBN 978-0-98521-092-2

www.pacificpressinternational.com

info@pacificpressinternational.com

DEDICATION

I dedicate this novel to Elena Rodriguez Brenna, my wife of 33 years and valued writing partner. She did much of the heavy lifting (including editing) to get this novel to press.

My thanks, also, to journalist and friend Gwen Carden, who tackled the first edit of *Honey Trap*. I'm grateful for her many useful suggestions to improve the plot.

CONTENTS

honey trap

CHAPTER ONE:

IRAQ 2003

The glare of noon turned to terrifying darkness when a black hood slammed over journalist Mike Delano's head as he left shell-torn Erbil's only remaining internet café where he'd just filed that day's story.

The adrenaline surged as he sought to tear the suffocating cowl from his face. But a gun barrel rammed painfully into his spine made him freeze.

He was seconds from death if the weapon's owner pulled the trigger.

"What do you want?" he gasped, his lungs laboring against the stifling hood. "I got money if that's what you're after."

The pistol pushed harder into his back.

"Do as we command, filthy infidel, or you die," warned a voice thick with lethal menace.

Now Delano understood. It was a kidnapping. Angry but not suicidal, he didn't resist when they ripped his computer and phone away. Seconds later, he was shoved into a car waiting with its engine running, ready for a rapid takeoff.

Within, strong hands flipped him over like a broken doll, binding his wrists with cords so tight they cut into his flesh. Then another body landed, knocking his breath out in one long, angry gasp.

"Mike, is that you? Who the hell are they?" protested the muffled voice of Bill Bryant, Delano's photographer, who'd been nearby snapping shattered homes and fleeing Iraqi refugees.

"Shut the fuck up," Delano replied fiercely, thankful the Special Forces veteran hadn't put up a fight as his hands were bound.

Within seconds, the car sped over cobbled streets, its front seat occupants chatting victoriously. It had been easy grabbing the journalist unbelievers they'd watched at the internet cafe since early morning.

Blind and bouncing about on the ripped, urine-stinking back seat, Delano and Bryant swore under their breath as the car hit bumps and dodged shell craters.

Struggling to breathe in the heat and stench, they felt humiliated by the unforeseen trap. Neither had any clue who'd taken them hostage; it could be any one of a dozen vicious terrorist splinter groups.

Delano wished he'd never demanded to cover the conflict between the US-led coalition and Saddam Hussein's Iraq as well as Islamists fighting among themselves. He and Bryant had been idiots to trust their local interpreter. He'd sold them out to militants who ransomed foreigners for the cash needed to strengthen their cause.

Although they had value if returned alive, both journalists feared their chances of survival were slim as the car raced onward pitching them painfully into one another, slamming them against the roof.

Shell bursts outside sent up an ominous rattle of sand and pebbles. Bitter cordite fumes penetrated their hoods – and the snap of machine gun rounds made them cower deeper into the tainted upholstery, trying to be as small a target as possible.

Cursing in Arabic, their abductors were as scared as the captives. Often, the driver's evasive maneuvers came close to running them all off the road.

Finally, they stopped on the outskirts of Kupri, near the Kurdish border. The Arabs hastened out of the vehicle, pulling their captives out of the back, yanking the stifling hoods from their heads.

"Get out, pigs," ordered the taller of the two. More militants with partially covered faces and menacing eyes swarmed around, shoving them into a multi-storied building, a former police station. They'd soon learn that it now functioned as an interrogation center and prison. It housed 50 or 60 prisoners held for ransom.

Interrogators held the pair at gunpoint, demanding passwords so they could examine their prisoners' laptops and phones, as well as their British passports.

Delano was lucky: nothing damning appeared on his computer. Bryant was less fortunate. On the photographer's laptop were pictures of dead Muslims killed by coalition troops occupying the country. His papers showed he'd served in Britain's Special Forces, a death warrant.

Delano watched in stunned horror as a single pistol shot to the photographer's head killed him. The bearded executioner holstered his gun, smiling at the quaking reporter with almost genial approval.

"You no problem, Delano, sir," he said in unexpectedly formal English. "You not like the dead dog. He helped kill Muslims, took pictures. I let you live. In time you learn – Allah is the true God. Could save you while you with us."

The strangely affable executioner nodded briskly at two orange-clad wretches leaning against a nearby wall trying to be invisible. They shuffled forward, heads down, leg-manacles grinding over the blood-spattered Moorish-patterned tiles. Each grabbed one of Bryant's legs, dragging him to a rundown garden used as a crude cemetery.

Through the briefly open back doors, Delano saw more men in orange jumpsuits digging graves. It appeared there was plenty of work for them.

Relieved to be alive, Mike felt shocked and guilty for failing to save his friend and colleague. He wondered if he'd survive this horror.

His mind flashed on the folks back home: his aged bipolar mother in South London whom he loved but rarely saw; the guys in the pub where he drank when home from assignments; fellow reporters in the bustling newsroom.

What would they make of his disappearance? In just a few hours, his world had changed – and certainly not for the better.

* * *

Alone in the humid darkness of his cell nearly two years later, Mike Delano prayed not to be next to die. He was still alive in late 2005 only because his newspaper, *The Daily Chronicle*, had trickled money to the Caliphate while haggling over the full price for his release.

Already, the paper had paid over half a million pounds – and his captors believed they could get still more. But time was running out. If the other half million pounds demanded to pay his ransom in full were not forthcoming, they would take him to the desert and behead him.

The cash coming in small separate payments had aggravated his Islamic captors. Although an excellent newspaper, the Chronicle had financial problems and the owner was stingy. Delano thought uneasily, "If he doesn't pay up soon, I'm dead."

Twice before, these sadistic thugs held a knife to his throat and filmed his terror as he awaited the grisly cut that never came. Each time they roughly pushed him back into his cell alive, his jumpsuit soaked with the piss of fear.

Filming their captives wetting themselves at the touch of the beheading blade amused these executioners. They calculatedly recorded sham executions and sent the videos of their terrified kneeling victims – along with cash demands – to relatives, employers, governments.

Without another monetary infusion from London, Delano knew he wouldn't get a third reprieve.

Similar mock executions had preceded the killings of his cellmates, Ben Sandys, a talented British helicopter mechanic, and Joe Walsh, a witty Irish Catholic charity worker. The end had come for them when, after two years of imprisonment, their governments had refused to pay more blood money.

They knew their deaths would become propaganda promoting Islamic terrorism. Beheading infidels was dramatic. The idea of this manner of death had been hard for them and Delano to bear. It recruited more Muslims eager to shed Christian blood.

Slumped alone in the corner of his cell, Mike recalled the sequence of events that landed him in captivity. He'd been a fool to ask for this assignment. Why hadn't he listened to fellow reporters who'd warned against increasingly dangerous Middle Eastern reporting?

"But no," he thought, "I wanted to be where the action was." He could have stayed in his job at the United Nations. Life was sweet in New York: diplomatic parties; attractive, educated women from all over the planet; and a comfortable apartment in Manhattan.

But diplomacy bored him. The real story was where the fighting took place, not in the air-conditioned black tower by the Hudson River.

Delano prided himself as a reporter who always got the story others missed – moreover, foreign correspondents filing from war zones made big names for themselves.

He asked to cover the hot Iraqi war in 2003 with nearly a million killed and thousands more fleeing their homes.

"I thought it would advance my career," he mused bitterly. "But now I'm in deep shit."

With nothing but time for self-reflection, he realized he'd been overly ambitious. He'd wanted to be the best from his years as a youngster training on local weekly papers in the London suburbs until the day he triumphantly clawed his way onto major British dailies as a foreign correspondent.

His constant search for headlines had brought him to the brink of a painful and humiliating death. The last survivor of the threesome, he couldn't stop thinking about his lost cellmates. They had become like brothers, the siblings he never had.

Delano's upbringing as the only child of an aspiring but failed actress hadn't been easy. Growing up, his feelings had seesawed along with her bipolar behavior. Sometimes he took pride in her good looks, other times he burned with embarrassment at her uncontrollable emotions. He'd also suffered from her disastrous taste in men. As a teenager, Mike spent more time straightening out her tangled affairs than she devoted to him.

He had never known his father, who died when he was young. His stepfather, a violent ex-Royal Navy drunkard, gave him good reason to leave home and start work as a teenager. In contrast, his former cellmates Ben and Joe had enjoyed peaceful childhoods with parents they adored. Mike envied the happy memories which they recounted, even while he enjoyed hearing them.

By now, Delano knew censored versions of their beheadings would have appeared on American and European television networks. Most Western TV dared show only the condemned kneeling moments before the knife slashed into their throats – but not the aftermath of severed heads placed on dead chests.

Commercial networks had no stomach for the reality of Islamic atrocities. They feared offending advertisers, the life-blood of their operations. By contrast, internet depictions of beheadings were gorily direct, drawing a vast audience of young men waiting to be radicalized.

Delano especially detested the jihadist jailer in charge of executions who'd murdered his friends. Raised in Britain, this terrorist thug was a Pakistani who spoke fluent English and reveled in running the prison death squad.

Mike had never seen his face, only his dark cobra eyes glittering with menace through the gap in his kufiyah headdress. The jailer cloaked his identity, fearing retaliation against his relatives in London's emigrant community.

Brought up in a ghetto, he loathed the British for their centuries of mistreating Muslims. Barking orders in a cockney accent that sounded bizarre in these surroundings, he had become master of this Iraqi dungeon – and loved the job.

Beatings from him were frequent. And when he beheaded a captive, he considered it payback for the racism he had suffered growing up.

Delano nicknamed his tall, skinny black-robed nemesis "the Pervert" for the way he peeped through the cell door slots at his prisoners, especially those marked for death. He fed on their terror and enjoyed whipping the condemned days before they died, a sure signal their time was up.

Mike had heightened his jailer's hatred by refusing to read English translations of the Koran. Punishing this heresy, the Pakistani and other guards hung the reporter naked, upside down, and whipped him until he passed out. Most prisoners avoided such torture by pretending to accept Islamic indoctrination. Delano refused.

Three days after his friends were beheaded, the reporter glimpsed the Pervert peering through the peephole at him.

"You're next, Delano," he sniggered nastily. "You wrote lies about Muslims. Your vile newspaper didn't pay up. Your bosses don't care about your ugly head. I'll take care of it…as I did for the others…"

Through the slot in the door, the Pervert shoved ugly proof of his actions: photos of bodies stretched out on the sand, the heads of Joe and Ben grotesquely placed on their chests. The terror on their dead faces chilled Mike. His jailer's obscene pleasure ended in profanity when Delano tore up the photos and dropped the pieces into his slop bucket.

Mike flinched when the cover slammed shut over the steel door's slot. Alone in the darkness, his brain was a swirling haze of anger, loneliness, and fear.

Misery had been tolerable when shared with his friends. They'd played games, talked about their past lives, romances, wives, children, and buoyed one another's moods. Delano tried unsuccessfully not to think about the horrible death awaiting him.

Without the others, he was more alone than ever before in his life. At 32, he had no wife or children. Tall, auburn-haired with penetrating blue eyes, two years of imprisonment had destroyed the muscular tone of his once athletic body.

Women in London and New York had gone for him in a big way. But he had never wanted more than brief affairs. He lived for his work – and had seen no reason to change.

Tears wet his face unchecked as he recalled the last vision of his friends, handcuffed and dragged away, kicking and protesting, by guards. Now it was his turn. He dreaded going to pieces, giving the Pervert extra pleasure when the knife sliced into his throat.

Rats scurrying along pipes above his cell broke the silence. Then a distant scream from another prisoner reminded him that soon his misery would end. He felt almost thankful. As a distraction, he mentally framed the story he would have written about life in an Islamic prison.

It would have shown how prisoners became shadow people, starved to skeletons, crippled by beatings and disease, burned by electric cattle prods, enduring a daily struggle to survive. He changed his mind. He would not continue with such thoughts. They served no purpose now.

Delano rolled over on the straw-filled mattress, falling into a fitful sleep.

* * *

Just before dawn, an enormous noise returned him to consciousness, making him sit bolt upright. It sounded like bees swarming. The buzz grew angrier, closer, and soon a rumble loud enough to penetrate his basement cell was followed by explosions.

From above, American and British warplanes loosed laser-guided bombs at desert targets packed with jihadists. They destroyed everything in view, not caring who died: civilians, rebels, foreign fighters – anyone still occupying the town.

Delano's terror of a beheading in front of the cameras faded. The bombardment had shaken him, but now it uplifted him. Better to die by bomb blast than to be decapitated by the black-robed sadist.

"Bring it on!" he screamed at the ceiling. "Blow the fucking place to pieces! I don't care. Kill us all."

Hopelessness gave way to optimism. Maybe he had a chance to escape this dungeon. As if in answer to his plea, a mighty blow blasted him across the cell. Pieces of concrete rained down, knocking him senseless. Everything went black.

He came to, opening stinging eyes on a world of crumbled masonry and twisted rebar. White dust covered everything, hanging in the air as thick as snow.

His brain felt raw, his ears rang. His nostrils filled with the smell of explosives. A collapsed steel support beam lodged inches above his body, protecting him from concrete slabs that could have smashed him flat. Blood flowed from a jagged cut on his right cheek.

Not one to pray, he mumbled: "Alhamdulillah" – praise be to God. These words of gratitude he'd learned but refused to speak for his captors. Crawling out from under the beam, he saw the steel cell door hung from twisted hinges, leaving a gap.

Bleeding and bruised, he crawled through the opening into the corridor. Parts of the roof remained intact; elsewhere, gaping holes revealed puffy clouds and a sky clear of jets. Instead, support choppers hovered overhead machine-gunning escaping jihadists.

Around Delano at the dungeon level, guards and prisoners lay dead or dying. Lethal pressure waves from the blasts had flashed down the stairs, destroying everything in their wake. The force had tossed victims like rag dolls, sucking their breath from them.

Miraculously, the closed cell door had shielded Mike from the explosion's full impact. Astonished to be alive, he forced himself to focus on his surroundings.

Hearing freedom's call, he crawled into the corridor and pried a knife from the hand of a dead guard. He was on the move. He prayed the stairs leading to the street remained intact as he lurched along to the north side of the shattered building.

Reaching the stairs, through swirling dust he saw another ghostly shape with the same idea. The figure staggering up towards the light was the Pervert, wounded but alive. Blood lust coursed through Delano's veins, his exhaustion disappearing.

Fury moved the knife in his hand into a stabbing posture. The energy of long-suppressed hate propelled him in a murderous rush. The Pakistani, sensing danger, began to turn and reached too late for his pistol. Air whooshed from his lungs in one long sigh as Delano pounced.

His knife repeatedly sank between the Pervert's thin shoulder blades. Not fatally stabbed, the black-clad jailer squealed in agony at each piercing, desperate to wrench free.

"I'll kill you, Delano," the detested voice snarled. "I'll cut you to bits."

"Not this time, motherfucker," Delano roared maniacally, his murderous rush lasting as he turned his enemy over, ripping the black hood from his head and exposing the executioner's face for the first time.

A shaft of sunlight revealed a young, thin, and sallow visage, distorted by rage, pain, and terror. A long nose angled down to a thick black beard. Familiar, once-horrifying snake eyes pleaded for life.

"You took my friends' heads. Now yours comes off!" Delano bellowed, his blade slashing at the guard's skinny throat. Blood pulsed over him; the deluge pleased his soul.

The freakish creature's dying convulsions brought the journalist a savage pleasure he'd never known before. He hacked through bone in a murderous frenzy until his prize – the Pervert's head – hung by strands of stubborn sinew, the face a twisted mask of horror.

More bombs exploded nearby, but Delano didn't care. He must have this trophy. He slashed again and again until the stubborn head came free.

"Who's the man now?" he crowed triumphantly, tugging on the luxuriant beard. He held the grisly prize up until he was eye to eye with it, babbling in frenzied delight.

"You won't be taking any more heads, you vicious bastard," he told the lifeless face through clenched teeth, pausing as if awaiting an answer.

When it didn't come, Delano tossed the knife and picked up the Pervert's World War I revolver in one hand, the dripping head in the other. He clambered over the rubble and into the street.

Delano was a fright to behold in the brightening dawn light. His unkempt beard had become a canvas for grotesque spikes of blood and dust. Gore had turned parts of his orange jumpsuit a ghastly purple. Emerging from the ruined prison, he looked demonic but had never felt more angelic.

He'd avenged the deaths of Ben and Joe. He wished they could somehow know he'd slain the jihadi dragon and survived. Nothing would stop him from getting home now. He would kill anyone who tried. Clutching his bloody keepsake by the hair, he limped along the dusty road. Kupri was an unrecognizable wasteland of flattened buildings, many aflame.

He took one final look at the Pervert's head, a symbol of his recovered pride. He longed to keep this gruesome souvenir of revenge, but knew it would impede his escape. He dropped the head, letting it rest for a moment in the sand. Then he kicked it with all his might.

Like a bloody soccer ball, it landed in the flames of a burning house, the hateful face sending up a shower of reproachful sparks. Delano watched for a few moments as it smoked and sizzled in the white-hot heat, the beard burning first. It was like having a seat at the Devil's bar-b-que.

"There's no Allah where you're going. Burn in hell!" he roared.

Refugees streaming away from the burning buildings studied the blood-drenched lunatic nervously as he joined them.

None dared question him. He followed behind prams and carts carrying the few possessions the runaways had salvaged from the wreckage of their homes.

Armed with the ancient pistol and a knife, Delano intended hijacking a car or commandeering a ride to the Kurdish border, 25 miles away.

Limping along for hours, he told himself, "No one will ever intimidate me again. God help anyone who tries – I'll destroy them."

His mind turned back to the story, the one he hadn't believed he'd live to write. He would memorialize his slain friends: the photographer shot through the head, the beheaded cellmates.

Delano would tell it all in a book, including how he killed the Pervert – even his joy in beheading him. Then what? He could never go back to an assignment as stodgy as covering the UN.

He struck war correspondent off the list. He'd had more than his share of terror and violence.

Hurrying along the road towards safety, he wondered what remained for him in journalism, the only work he'd ever cared to do.

CHAPTER TWO:

FAME AND BLAME

In London a year later, Delano had scored with a best-selling book about his captivity in Iraq. His earlier reports as a correspondent had won him Britain's coveted Reporter of the Year award. But his admission to killing his Anglo-Pakistani prison guard made him a controversial figure.

While he disliked the limelight, the promoters of his book, *Prisoners of Islam*, insisted Delano engage in print, radio, and TV interviews. His actions during the Iraq nightmare drew both praise and condemnation. Liberal interviewers called them barbarous; enemies of Islam applauded.

During one major TV interview, the journalist caused an uproar.

Roland Standborough, a sleekly pompous personality known for his bitchy interrogations, relished humiliating the targets of his disapproval – and it was obvious Mike was one of them.

"Isn't it true, Mr. Delano, you're a racist? That you hated Muslims after Islamic terrorists attacked your beloved New York on 9-11; that you became obsessed with revenge against Muslims. Isn't it true your experiences in Iraq provided a perfect opportunity to vent your hatred by brutally murdering a young radicalized British citizen?" he asked with an insinuating smile. "It's my opinion, you've exploited your gruesome beheading of a London-born Islamist of Pakistani heritage to callously sell more books."

Angered by the malicious attack and weary of hostile inquisitors criticizing his intentions, Delano reacted to the interviewer's brow-beating words.

"I'm tired of people like you judging me. I was heartbroken when Islamists shot my photographer. They murdered two beloved friends. They extorted more money for their evil cause. The guard I killed was the son of a bitch who decapitated my cellmates and intended giving me the chop, too."

Loud applause for Delano's retaliatory remarks annoyed Standborough, his face reddening; studio audiences usually hung on his every word and supported him.

His audience had turned on him. Along with the show's viewers at home, they liked what they saw and heard from this gutsy, outspoken reporter.

Delano was an imposing figure glaring at his tormentor. The scar on the right side of his rugged face made him roguishly appealing to women. He was six feet tall, trim, and muscular again from months of daily workouts since returning from Iraq. He impatiently brushed wavy reddish hair out of his gray-blue eyes as he stared defiantly into the camera.

"But hacking off the guard's head makes you as barbaric as him, doesn't it?" Standborough persisted. "Wasn't kicking his skull about like a bizarre soccer ball ghastly? You make much of these macabre and brutal actions in your book. Now you ask why people condemn you for killing that wretched man so hideously?"

Suddenly Delano was out of his seat, fists bunched, eyes blazing. He leaned over Standborough, snarling, "You critical bastards couldn't endure one day of what I went through. I'm sick of cowards here at home moralizing about my actions. They don't know what they're talking about…nor do you."

Now the studio audience stood, too, cheering and shouting "let him have it" and "tell him to go to hell."

Standborough's face had gone from red to white. No interview subject had ever presented such a threatening posture in his long experience, nor provoked such an audience reaction; he cringed away, intimidated.

Delano spat his final damning words: "My book is about brave men who died, not about me. I avenged their deaths. It's about the barbarism of a radicalized British Muslim, who paid the price for his cruelty. And if you must know, yes, I enjoyed cutting the bastard's head off."

Unclenching his fists, disgusted with the interviewer, the journalist stalked off the set as the audience continued to roar approval, wanting more.

The next day's papers headlined the televised clash. Photographs showed Delano, fists balled, menacing Standborough.

"TV Punch-up Narrowly Averted!" screamed the *Daily Mail*. "Killer Journo Ready to Strike Interviewer!" said the front page of the *Sun*.

While *Prisoners of Islam* was flying off bookshop shelves in Britain and America due to this incident, Delano turned down further interview requests while continuing with book signings. Readers eager to buy his book were easier to handle.

Having to justify his actions exhausted him. Nearing age 34, he was at a professional crossroads – with no idea what he wanted to do with his life.

He wouldn't go back to war reporting – or the UN. He wondered whether his success with this book was a one-off sensation, unrepeatable. He pondered whether to try his hand at novels – but fiction posed a new challenge. Was he up to it?

His personal life was not rewarding either. He was lonely, ready to settle down but hadn't met anyone with whom he wanted to make a lasting commitment. For the first time in many years, he had no plan. He wished someone would come along to help solve the problem.

CHAPTER THREE:

HIS LORDSHIP

Lord Max Rothenberg snapped off the laptop video he'd been watching and gazed moodily out of his armored black Bentley Arnage as it glided almost soundlessly through gloomy rain-slicked City of London streets.

He pondered the Roland Standborough interview he'd just seen. This Delano fellow might be the answer to one of his business problems. Two concerns occupied his ever-scheming mind this day. One was here in London: finding a new editor for his largest-circulation tabloid Sunday newspaper, where sales were slumping dismally.

The other was in Los Angeles, where a predatory union thug was delaying filming at his cherished Paragon Pictures studio – and costing him a fortune in lost revenue.

He might have left these headaches to others, but Lord Rothenberg was a hands-on tycoon. Meticulous attention to detail had made him one of the world's richest men. Nothing of importance within his media empire happened without his knowledge or involvement.

He'd gone over the list of people available for the editorship position and didn't like any of them. As for the union tough guy holding Paragon for ransom, Rothenberg had finally decided to accept a solution suggested by his brutal security chief and fixer, Gil Ackerman.

His Lordship's Bentley arrived at 400 Leadenhall Street in the heart of London's financial district. First out of the front seat was Ackerman, a burly disgraced former CIA agent. As well as handling Paragon security, he often acted as his Lordship's bodyguard.

After studying the passersby, Ackerman nodded to the liveried chauffeur who leaped out smartly to open the door for their master.

Rothenberg, heavyset at five foot eight, emerged in a military-style tan overcoat, his wide-brimmed black Homberg hat pulled down. It shaded darting inquiring eyes, bushy dark brows, and hedonistically fleshy features, all inherited from his Hungarian Jewish father.

He had reason to be cautious; his Lordship had enemies. An opponent of organized labor, he'd been instrumental in breaking the backs of print and film unions in Britain and America. His right-wing publications, TV, and radio stations in both countries crushed opponents without mercy.

The tycoon's support of right-wing Zionists through his media outlets also drew the wrath of militant Islamists. Radicals of various political and religious persuasions on several continents would celebrate his sudden death. Several had already made unsuccessful attempts on his life.

His Lordship hastened into Global Media International's white Carrera marble entrance hall. Six nervous GMI commissionaires snapped to attention. The headman had already summoned the executive elevator for the Boss.

Its high-speed car sped him to his 70th-floor aerie. From there, the British-born media chieftain gouged competitors, ruled foreign companies, and hired or fired those pleasing, or displeasing, him.

Editors in five countries sent opinion pieces, magazine covers, and newspaper front pages daily for his approval. Banks of screens carried feeds from his television stations in Britain, the United States, Canada, Australia, New Zealand, and Asia.

Media executives everywhere dreaded his disruptive displeasure. Rothenberg ordered front pages scrapped or changed at a moment's notice. He pulled programs off the air arbitrarily when audience ratings slid.

Presidents and prime ministers were wary of Max Rothenberg, too. Without his support, British politicians lost elections. Press power had earned him a life peerage from a subservient UK government.

In Washington, his cash donations and right-wing media outlets swayed US policy. White House officials put him straight through to the Oval Office when he called. He had a similar influence in Australia and Canada, and he was extending his broadcast empire's clout to China.

Apart from print and TV, Rothenberg's passion was movies. Paragon Pictures in Los Angeles was his prized possession. Its Oscar-winning films featured a globally admired stable of superstars, the best known of which was Morgan Masterson.

Elizabeth Hightower, Rothenberg's elegant executive vice president, and most trusted employee, greeted him as he stepped out of the elevator, followed by Ackerman. A tall, chilly blonde Alfred Hitchcock would have approved, Liz was visiting London from California, where her primary responsibility was running Paragon.

Like Rothenberg, she divided her time between GMI's executive offices in London, New York, and Los Angeles. Liz took Rothenberg's hat and coat, hanging them up. He gave her a fond kiss on the cheek and seated himself at an expansive desk in front of a battery of monitors.

Once settled, he lit a full-bodied Cuban cigar, savoring the flavor as he studied front-page and cover proofs from GMI publications around the world. A speed-reader, he scrawled caustic comments on them in red ink. He was the one person in the company allowed to use that color. Anyone else caught wielding a red pen – from executives to errand-boys – he fired.

"I watched that Delano clip you sent me," Rothenberg growled from amid a cloud of aromatic smoke, the nicotine pleasantly increasing his respiratory rate and already strong critical capacity to razor-sharp level.

"A journalist who cuts off Arab heads? I find that interesting. It took chutzpah escaping those vile Moslem murderers. We need a spirited operator like him working for us. He could provide what I'm looking for."

"You're right, chief," Liz replied, pleased she'd been correct in thinking he would admire Delano. "Thought you'd like the guy's audacity..."

Rothenberg turned to both Hightower and Ackerman: "Get hold of this Delano. Bring him to the plane on Sunday, Gil. I'll talk to him; see if I can interest him in joining us. He could be just the man to bring *News of the Planet* up to snuff."

Ackerman was unhappy. While it was short notice to find Delano and convince him to travel with Rothenberg to California in the next 48 hours, he was confident they could pull it off. But from what he'd heard, he didn't like the sound of this maverick journalist. He kept those thoughts to himself.

"I'll have him on the plane Sunday, boss," he answered dutifully. "You can check him out during the flight."

Rothenberg grunted approval.

"Now, what about this Quinton Werner problem in LA? What do we do about him?" Ackerman asked while he still had the boss's attention.

"I think your solution has become the only answer," Rothenberg replied grimly. "He's delayed by more than six months two movies I green-lighted for Morgan Masterson. He's held up filming the action scenes in Mexico, that could have saved us millions."

Liz Hightower smiled bleakly as she buttoned up the conversation: "He's bled us enough. For five years we've been paying him off. He received a couple of hundred thousand bucks to get out of Paragon's way last June. Now he wants millions more to pull his unions off our backs."

"That settles it. Werner values himself far too highly. Call your Chicago friends," Rothenberg said quietly. "We can settle the union problem with others to get production moving again."

Using a scrambled satellite phone, Liz placed the call. These specialists took care of critical corporate problems when all else failed. Their services were expensive and discreet. When their Chicago contact answered, Liz turned away, though Rothenberg and Ackerman could still hear her side of the conversation.

"Yeah, it's me…. We've got a job for you. Uh-huh, the whole deal. In LA…. As soon as possible…. How much…? Hold on."

Liz turned to the mogul: "They want 300K for a rush West Coast job."

"Fine, fine. I don't care about the details. Run it through your budget for studio security," he said huffily.

"OK. It's a deal – half now – the rest on completion. You'll have full details within the hour." She disconnected and smiled at Rothenberg reassuringly, her perfect white teeth gleaming like an alpha she-wolf.

Max sighed contentedly. People should know when to stop gouging him. This union schmuck deserved what was coming. There would be no fuss. Police and local media contacts on Paragon's payroll would handle that. It would look like a burglary gone wrong, hardly newsworthy – no ugly headlines.

Pleased that postponed filming would soon start, he expected one of the new films to become a blockbuster. Morgan Masterson needed a hit. His last film was a box office disappointment. Max was proud of Morgan's career. He had nurtured it personally.

The actor was a gold mine, but his raging libido often caused problems. If he could just keep his dick in his pants, it would be better for everyone all around. Ruffled by thoughts of past Morgan troubles, Rothenberg stood up, stretched, and walked away from his desk.

Max wanted to be at his London mansion. He had a delectable and ambitious young actress who sought a Hollywood career waiting for him there. He paused at the floor-to-ceiling windows to stare down at the streets far below.

His skyscraper was a landmark, towering over its nearest glass and steel competitors. Atop the tower, the GMI logo blinked in huge red neon letters radiating corporate power to all four points of the compass.

The chill October rain was drenching Londoners heading home. From this height, they looked like a stream of ants. These morons read his papers, watched his ad-packed low-brow television output, and made him rich.

GMI hosts, stars, and journalists told them how to look, how to vote – and how to live their trivial little lives. He liked having the power to manipulate people everywhere.

Rothenberg headed toward the elevator, preparing to go. Liz was immediately at his side with his hat and coat.

"The car's waiting to take you home," she said. "Have a good flight Sunday. I'll be joining you in LA in a few days. Good luck with this Delano character..."

CHAPTER FOUR:

SPIKED

Charlie the Spike, a dapper shaven-headed African-American, didn't let the killings he did for a living weigh on his conscience.

He rarely lingered on memories of previous hits. Once he completed jobs, he hardly thought about the marks again. There was no point.

The past was history; he lived for the day. On odd occasions, when he did think about them, he felt nothing more than professional pleasure. He prided himself on his skill at silencing challenging targets, offing them with speed and efficiency.

Short with tender brown eyes, his appearance was always faultless. His English-tailored suits of worsted wool were perfection, cloaking a frame made powerful by pumping iron.

His silk shirts came from Singapore, his hand-painted ties (containing a wire for garroting) from Paris. His expertly crafted footwear, custom-made in Milan, included steel toes. When necessary, he could kick a man to death.

Ever the dandy, Charlie carried a silver-topped cane containing a sword forged from the most exquisite Japanese steel. With this, he occasionally skewered victims – thus his alias in crime circles, the Spike. Elsewhere, he was Charles Treven Johnson, a successful business consultant.

Raised on Chicago's South Side, his first murder paid 25 bucks for slipping a stiletto between the ribs of a rival gang member who unsuspectingly befriended the likable 12-year-old. By his 48th birthday, he'd made hundreds of hits.

He carried all of them out with precision. The Spike left nothing behind to haunt him or his clients later. Superbly professional, few knew his true occupation.

On every hit, he worked through third parties. Charlie rubbed out mobsters, liquidated crooked lawyers, and killed corrupt investment bankers. He reluctantly accepted domestic jobs for the right price: cheating wives, unfaithful husbands, and troublemaking mistresses.

His success provided a healthy bank account. Depending on the complexity of the work, he received between $150,000 and $300,000 a hit. He demanded payments deposited directly to a Swiss bank.

When word came that a movie unionist had pissed off someone with $300,000 to spare, his ears pricked up, and he took the assignment. His mob bosses said it would be a smooth hit. The mark lived alone on a private ranch property at the end of the San Fernando Valley. It sounded easy.

* * *

The Spike's Dodge Viper made the 2,020-mile Chicago to LA drive in 46 hours. He stopped eight times for food and gas but not for sleep. Dexedrine tablets kept him sharp on long runs, and driving gave him time to think.

It was an excellent year so far, with six contracts fulfilled. That meant another million or so bucks in Charlie's Swiss bank account. The Spike reckoned he'd call it quits on his fiftieth birthday, only two years away.

With ten million dollars banked, no debts, his house paid for, why push his luck? The game wasn't what it used to be. A depressed economy brought amateurs into the field – young roughnecks kidnapped, tortured, and slaughtered at cut rates. These wild men took appalling risks and were themselves either killed or caught. He had no time for them.

Traveling by road was a wise precaution for Charlie. He left no paper or electronic records of his movements from town to town. He only flew on the rare occasions he traveled abroad. Driving avoided airport security. They'd want to confiscate his prized sword cane.

Irrational though it was, he felt naked on a job without it. He was firm in his superstition that his sword must kill three times a year to continue bringing good fortune. He would use it for the crucial third time this year on Quinton Werner.

The Spike swapped cars when he reached the San Fernando Valley. He put his beloved Dodge Viper in a covered parking garage and rented a Mazda under an assumed name, presenting a false driver's license.

At dusk, Charlie drove the Mazda up the dirt road leading to Quinton Werner's secluded home. He parked 500 yards from the building and completed his journey on foot. Waiting for darkness, he checked out the property and took a position at the back.

Lights were on in the ranch-style house. A television played so loudly he could hear a cheerful local weatherman delivering that night's favorable forecast. Good, the sound would cover his approach. He decided to enter through the back door.

Charlie mentally rehearsed his next moves. He would burst inside, gun in one hand, sword in the other. With surprise on his side, he'd skewer the mark in a flash with his favorite kill – a stab through the heart. The sword temporarily plugged the blood, stopping it from spurting onto his fine clothes.

He was agile and would step aside when he withdrew his steel. He'd done others like that. Quick and final, there would be no noise or mess. If he missed the heart, there was always the pistol to finish off the victim – one slug to the head.

When done, he'd snap quick pictures with his phone. Later, he'd print out the best, sending several copies to the "cutout" people for whom he worked. Often, clients wanted pictures for confirmation. Some liked to gloat over downed enemies.

The Spike tiptoed to the back door. Luck was still on his side; light streamed from a crack between the unlatched door and the doorframe. Moving soundlessly, he approached, intending to climb the three steps. At the first step, however, he felt searing pain and heard an angry snapping sound. Steel teeth had clamped down to the bone, holding his right leg as agony enveloped him.

"For Christ's sake, a bear trap," he thought in disbelief, shuddering with shame at being trapped by something so primitive.

The back door flew open as Charlie sought control over his misery and shock. Quinton Werner's six-foot-two frame stood starkly outlined against the light coming from the house.

"Welcome to my humble abode," the extortionist sneered. "As you can see, I was expecting you."

The Spike dropped the cane in his left hand. Working on instinct and experience, the .38 in his right hand came up fast, aimed for the center of Werner's forehead.

But he wasn't speedy enough. Werner slammed the heavy door.

"Jesus," Charlie moaned. He knew the motherfucker was going for a gun. Werner would butcher him like a trapped coyote.

Opening fire at the closed door where the mark had stood, Charlie prayed his shots would penetrate, hitting the target. The retorts echoed off the canyon walls of the Chatsworth Mountains, but there was no sound of a body crashing down behind the door.

The ringing silence intensified the terrible throbbing in the hitman's leg. Through the pain, he regained his calm. Straining for the slightest sound, he heard a door open and close. It sounded like it came from the front of the house.

Is this creep running? Charlie thought he detected a figure flitting through the starlit shadows to his right.

Again, he opened fire, but his gun flashes revealed no target. Were his eyes playing tricks? He gasped with desperation. "I gotta get my leg out of this trap."

Where the teeth had gone in was an aching fireball; he feared the bone had shattered. What if this job left him limping, in real need of his cane?

A fresh surge of anger gave him the strength to lean forward far enough to recover the sword-cane. He'd never suffered such torment.

He tried prying open the trap with the cane, but the hardened wood surrounding the hidden blade began to crack.

The jaws wouldn't surrender his shattered leg. Built to hold bears two or three times his size, it needed enormous strength to break the cruel grip.

In mad desperation, Spike drew his sword, slashing at the darkness around him. But there was nothing to cut or stick.

Then came rapid footsteps. The Spike couldn't tell from which direction they were coming. Terror made his heart pump madly when he heard mocking laughter.

He felt ashamed, weak, and humiliated. This jerk's going to kill me, he thought, suppressing a moan. He'd become the mark.

The blow knocking him senseless came from behind. Breath rushed from his throat in an unuttered curse. The cerebral fireworks display faded fast to blackest black.

* * *

Cold water drenched the Spike. He came around with a start to see Werner standing there with an empty bucket. He had no idea how long he'd been out. A bright light shone in his confused eyes. He was in a carpentry shop on the property, he supposed. There was no escape; Werner had tied him to a wooden chair.

His attacker had bandaged his mangled limb enough to stop him from bleeding out. For seconds, he ridiculously lamented the ripping of his expensive suit. The agony of the pain in his leg partially drowned out a throbbing bump on the back of his head.

"What the fuck, man!" he exclaimed, finally able to speak. "I need a doctor."

Werner leaned in close. Spike could smell his garlicky breath, sense his merciless disdain.

He flinched at the blankness of the man's angry dark eyes blazing from a face chiseled from granite.

"Yeah, right. You need a doctor," Quinton said, amused. "Doubt you were about to extend me that same courtesy when you stuck me with this…"

He waved Spike's beloved sword under his nose. Then he ran his finger lightly along the blade. His touch was slight, but a trace of blood misted the razor edge. He whistled in admiration.

"Japanese steel, I'd say. And costly, right? Impressive. I'll enjoy using it. First, a few questions. Who sent you, and how much are they paying?"

The Spike wasn't answering questions. As soon as he did, there would be no reason for this hellish prick to keep him alive.

"Fuck you," he snarled, his lips drawn back like a furious and frightened feline. "Now, are you going to let me out of here? If not, all hell will break loose on your stupid fucking head. When my people find out, they'll send an army to destroy you. You made a big goddamned mistake – let me go, and that's the end of this. I'll get fixed up and forget it ever happened."

Werner walked around the chair, gently placed the sword's blade parallel to the right side of the Spike's head, and pressed down. His ear flopped onto the floor like a wet leaf. Spike screamed as Werner stepped away, avoiding the crimson spray.

"Who sent you? I assume it's Max Rothenberg. Rather spend money having me killed than fork up what I deserve. I've been expecting you or some other piece of shit since he refused to pay," he sneered, stepping behind Spike again. "Tell me what I need to know, or lose the other one."

Spike felt the anticipatory kiss of his sword's edge against his left ear. His world was upside down, a horrific nightmare. No mark had ever interrogated him before. When necessary, he did the questioning.

"Don't," he begged. "Don't cut me again. I'll tell you what I can.…"

Werner moved in front of Spike to sit on a stool facing him.

"Go on then, tell me," he said, waving the blade under Charlie's flinching nose.

"I don't know Max Rothenberg. I work through cutouts. Nobody said who ordered the motherfucking job. I never know. It's the truth, I swear it."

"Where you from and who sent you? It's your last chance."

"Chicago. I got word to come here from a connection. Syndicate people I work for there..."

Werner viewed the Spike with contempt. But he needed to know more.

"You aren't giving me the answers I want. I'm getting angry. Stretch your pinky finger out, unless you want me to take the other ear.…"

Anchored to the wooden chair by industrial tape around his wrists, waist, and feet, the Spike could barely move, blood ran down his injured head, dripping on his right shoulder. Reflexively, his hand balled up to avoid what was coming.

"Jesus, man. Don't do this. We can make a deal – cash," he sobbed.

Werner's eyes narrowed. He needed money to get out of town. Rothenberg would keep trying to kill him.

Watching his interrogator's reactions closely, the Spike grasped at his only chance to escape this fouled-up job alive.

"If you let me go, I can get you big bucks. I know we can agree," Charlie begged.

"What kinda agreement?"

Charlie spoke without hesitation.

"I'll pay a million if you let me live. You can have my Viper, too. I parked it at the Chatsworth shopping mall," he offered. "I'll sign it over, give you the keys. Better than the jalopy you got out front…"

"Stretch out your pinky. Or didn't you hear me?"

When the Spike didn't move, Werner walked around behind him. Delicately he rested the Japanese blade where the remaining ear joined the head and sliced.

The ear flopped down. Werner picked it up, waving it like a trophy in front of Spike's horrified face.

"Now, Mr. Hitman, before I take you apart piece by piece, tell me. You offered a million, but I need to know how much you've got."

"I'll give you two million, just stop cutting on me!"

"Wrong answer. How much dough have you got in the bank? The truth or I start on the fingers; especially that trigger finger."

He looked at Spike quizzically. The man was fading fast from loss of blood and shock. He needed to speed up the interrogation. He circled his victim, sword poised.

"Nearly $10-million," the Spike gasped out hastily. "You get it all if you let me go. Just stop cuttin' on me. I swear I'll never come back…"

In the next hour, the Spike lost pinky fingers from both hands as Werner forced him to reveal details of his Swiss bank account: routing and account numbers, passwords, everything needed to withdraw millions.

His torturer sat in front of Charlie, using his cell phone to call Switzerland, assuming his identity – confirming he had access to the Spike's wealth.

Satisfied, Werner smiled coldly.

"You ain't so good at your job, are you?" he said.

"Now you got my money, you gonna let me go?" Spike's words escaped in a feeble whisper.

Even as he mumbled them, he knew the answer. People had posed the same question to him. About to die, they clung to the slightest hope. Now he was one of the damned.

"Come on, man, you're a pro. You know the answer," Werner said as he lined up Spike's beloved sword with his heart. "Goodbye, Mr. Hitman, have a good trip to hell. All those folks you offed will be waiting to greet you…"

"Fuck you, asshole!" Spike screamed in a last act of defiance.

Werner pressed forcefully with a twist, and the Japanese steel stopped its owner's throbbing heart.

Charlie the Spike had been right. It was the best kill, even for the victim. So quick, he hardly felt a thing.

Werner cut the dead man free from the chair. He dragged the corpse through the workshop doors to the rear of the property. Breathing hard, he pushed the mutilated hitman into a previously dug grave.

With dawn's light rising, Werner stripped and burned his bloody clothes. He went into the house to shower, pack, and reserve an airline ticket to Geneva.

He'd draw on the Spike's millions, then go on to Beirut where he knew family on his mother's side would take him in. They had jihadi connections that made his activities look positively innocent.

Killing Rothenberg's hitman would provide more cash than he'd demanded from the studio boss. The irony pleased Werner. Paragon had paid him well over the years but never well enough. The additional money he'd asked for didn't compare to the value of the dirty work he had done for Rothenberg. He'd used bribery and violence to keep movie trade unionists in line. He'd had resisting troublemakers beaten, killed if necessary.

His Lordship should have known better than to take out a hit on him. He'd make the SOB and his studio pay.

CHAPTER FIVE:

A JOB INTERVIEW

Mike Delano, weary from his book tour, took a break from author signings around Britain to enjoy the hospitality of friends in their historic Thames-side home near Windsor. It was the perfect place to relax, even while he wrestled with what was next for him professionally.

It was late Friday evening, and he was looking forward to spending Saturday sailing on the river. As he sipped a nightcap of Imperial Ale, the chords of an old English hunting song sounded from his phone.

"Who's calling me this late?" he grumbled, putting down his chilled pewter mug. He considered not answering, but after years in newsrooms, he was incapable of resisting the demanding lure of a ringing phone.

He answered and heard a calculatingly warm and pushy American voice: "Mr. Delano, my name's Liz Hightower."

Without pausing for a response, she added, "I work for Max Rothenberg. His Lordship's keen to meet you. He liked your TV interview. Also, we've read the yarn about your escapades in Iraq. Of course, you're familiar with Lord Max and GMI?"

The woman put Mike's teeth on edge. Of course, he knew who Rothenberg was. Everybody did, especially journalists. Her dismissal of the horrors he'd suffered in Iraq as "escapades" annoyed him.

"What does he want?" he asked. "I'm on holiday."

"Lord Rothenberg needs to meet you," Liz sniffed, picking up the petulant tones in what she considered his snotty British voice.

"Why?" Delano replied churlishly.

He wasn't an admirer of the press lord. He used his media to bludgeon opponents and ruin politicians opposing him. Coercive yellow journalism made Rothenberg media successful but offensive to Delano.

"It's not for me to say, but Lord Rothenberg has you in mind for an important post," Liz answered, now eager to set the hook; she felt he could slip away at any moment.

"What position may that be?" Mike asked.

Despite his dislike of Rothenberg, job offers were always an intriguing way to gauge one's professional worth.

"I can't say more, but I think you'll miss a unique opportunity if you don't meet my boss," the American replied, moving ahead before he could object. "I'll have my associate Gil Ackerman join us on speakerphone. He'll arrange the details."

Ackerman had been listening in and sensed problems with this guy. CIA training gave him a nose for troublesome people. Hightower may already have said too much. If the two of them didn't deliver Delano, they'd both get an ass-kicking from Rothenberg.

Fired from the CIA for being too savage an interrogator and a sexual harasser of female suspects, Ackerman prized his position at GMI. He needed to reel in this journalist for Max. He switched on his limited charm.

"Michael, his Lordship's offering a pleasant gratis trip to California on his private jet. You can stay in his mansion if that appeals to you – or we can put you up in a hotel."

"I'm not free until next weekend. I could make time then," Delano conceded, aggravated by the man's easy familiarity.

"That won't do, Mike. Lord Rothenberg's leaving tomorrow morning. You need to come to the airport early and fly with him to California."

ner, but don't miss a big opportunity because it's short notice," Ackerman
chided. "It's the way Rothenberg operates. At least find out what he wants."

Delano's mind raced; God knows, he needed a change of pace.
Perhaps this was it. Maybe this manipulative mogul with global clout
might provide the next step in his career. And a few days among the west
coast palms couldn't hurt.

"OK. I'll be at Heathrow tomorrow morning. That OK?"

"That's excellent," Ackerman rejoiced. It was easier than expected.
Jesus, he'd considered knocking the guy over the head, kidnapping him if
necessary. He hated failing his master.

"Come to Hangar Four, Northside, private aircraft service area. Be
there at 9:00 am. I'll let the guard at the security gate know you're coming.
You can park your car there until your return. You can't miss our plane.
The red and gold GMI logo is on the fuselage and tail. Don't let us down."

* * *

Arriving early, Delano quickly found GMI's gaudy jet. A steward with the
bulk of a professional wrestler welcomed him aboard the 747 with courtly
grace. A gun bulge under his left armpit suggested he was also a bodyguard.

"Welcome, Mr. Delano. My name is Frederick," he said. "You won't
mind if I pat you down? It's routine. We do it until we get to know our
guests. I'm sure you understand."

Delano flushed but didn't complain as Frederick ran practiced hands
over him. He also examined the contents of a briefcase Mike carried. It

33

contained his laptop, resume, passport, a copy of his book, underwear, and toiletries.

Frederick led Delano along a thickly carpeted corridor into an astonishing stateroom containing brushed gold Edwardian chairs upholstered in red velvet, similar couches, and a sturdy mahogany table. Logs flickered like burning wood in a realistic fireplace. It seemed like a country mansion great room rather than a giant aircraft cabin.

He instantly recognized Lord Rothenberg sprawled in an armchair, legs outstretched, studying spreadsheets.

The mogul looked up, a faint smile playing over his fleshy lips. He waved a negligent hand, inviting his guest to take a seat in a facing ornate red and gold chair.

"Welcome, dear boy. So, you're coming to California. Excellent. It gives us time to get to know each other, discuss what I have in mind for you," he said in plummy British tones.

"You'll be comfortable in LA. Stay at the cottage on my estate, or book yourself into a good hotel – your choice. GMI will cover any expenses you incur. You're welcome to visit my movie studio, meet some of my stars. You can return to London on this jet later in the week."

Quite a genial host, Delano thought. But he still needed to know about the offer, and why him? The answers arrived when Rothenberg resumed speaking.

"I see you standing at the crossroads professionally, and I can provide splendid new opportunities for you. I need an editor who's talented, determined, and uniquely individualistic. You fit that bill."

Uncertain how to reply, Delano nodded. He'd never considered working for a right-wing provider of print and broadcast trash.

GMI had a few respectable newspapers in London and New York, but its British daily and Sunday tabloids were the big moneymakers with millions of readers.

Their broadcast divisions provided similar stuff: gossip, celebrity interviews, reality shows, and unashamedly slanted political reporting.

Mike was surprised the mogul wanted him. He'd always worked for ethical media where factual reporting was the standard. Delano puzzled over how Rothenberg had detected his current career indecision. The mogul was right: he was at the crossroads.

Newspapers in the digital age were losing their appeal – to him as well as to readers. Computer nerds and university-trained corporate toadies had replaced the old-school shirtsleeves journalists Delano knew and admired.

The new breed, journalism school grads, saw electronic media as supreme, not print. It was why Delano had begun to think his future was in books, not newspapers. Reporting talent was no longer enough to gain entrée to journalism's ruling class.

Moreover, the new breed of technocratic editors viewed Delano as a dangerous, show-boating upstart. Some had spread the slanderous accusation he'd exploited the beheadings of his friends – and of the Pervert – just to sell a book. But he almost took it as a compliment, that they still feared him as a competitor.

While there was some truth to their smears, he wouldn't accept the put-down from despicable upper-class deskbound detractors just out of university. He considered them too timid to go anywhere near a war zone.

Deep in thought, Mike flinched when Rothenberg pressed a button, and seatbelts snapped around their waists from hidden slots in the gilded chairs bolted to the aircraft floor. Engines fired up, and the 747 began its takeoff roll. There was no getting off now.

His Lordship lit a cigar and looked at Mike calculatedly as his jet lumbered into the sky. He was among the privileged few in the world still smoking aboard an aircraft. Max Rothenberg was a person who broke the rules all the time. And for a moment, Mike liked him for that.

Searching the mogul's hooded eyes for clues as the plane leveled off at 30,000 feet, Delano asked, "Why exactly am I here?"

"I need you to edit *News of the Planet*, my Sunday property," Rothenberg declared, rubbing his baby-smooth manicured hands together enthusiastically.

"You're my pick for this job. Sales are sliding under three million. Two years ago, they were four million weekly. I'll give you £1.8-million a year as a start, bonuses when sales bounce back – shares in the company, plus a GMI directorship."

Impressed but not sold, the offer interested him. It pleased him to think how foppish toadies within GMI's corporate hierarchy would react to an outside hire for a job they all coveted.

Seeing reservation in the younger man's eyes, Rothenberg continued: "There are excellent benefits, too. You'll have a chauffeur-driven SUV, generous expenses, membership in London, New York, and LA clubs, and a six-week annual vacation."

The mogul paused, adding: "I need an editor with guts. An attack dog. Someone willing to crush our enemies. I also want the editorial department re-staffed; get rid of weaklings. I need men with balls and the kinds of resourcefulness you've displayed."

Delano envisioned a new future. Five years in this job, and he'd have a nest egg giving him life-long security. He'd also be one of the best-paid editors in the business. Idealism fought with morality; should he edit this scabrous publication?

The Sunday tab ran pictures of nude women, exposés of royalty, movie stars, and politicians, with a smattering of real news in the mix. But the offer was an excellent one. His journalistic principles were becoming early casualties in this ethics battle.

Rarely, nowadays, was a lower-class lad who had made his name on fearless reporting and sheer talent allowed to rise to edit one of Fleet Street's most successful tabloids.

Mike warmed to the idea that accepting the position would anger the university crowd who'd come to monopolize most of the industry's highly-paid top jobs. That alone was motivation enough for him.

Rothenberg looked at him, eyes quizzical, his voice demanding as he rammed home his message: "You're right for this job. I know it, you know it. I need someone like you, not afraid to…" He paused, and then with a smile, continued, "not afraid to lop off a few heads…"

Delano didn't welcome the snide inference to his Iraq experience but considered it wiser to ignore His Lordship's poor-taste pun.

Dismissing Mike's hesitation, Rothenberg continued laying out his needs: "And of course, you'll personally supervise special assignments for me. I've political enemies, and I need them rendered harmless. That wouldn't be a problem, would it?"

When Delano appeared ready to ask what exactly "rendered harmless" meant, Rothenberg snuffed out the question with more mind-boggling enticements.

"There's a signing bonus of £50,000 on your five-year contract. There's also a small but comfortable Mayfair townhouse with housekeeping service twice weekly. All part of the package."

Delano's resistance was fading. He could take the bait. However, if he later regretted it and wanted to return to mainstream media, the shame of Rothenberg's brand of yellow journalism would stick. But what the hell; he would be wealthy by then. It wouldn't matter.

What price his integrity? That was the question.

"May I have some time before giving my answer?" he asked.

Rothenberg agreed. The 747 was an hour into its 11-hour flight.

"Go get some rest. We'll resume our little talk over dinner," Rothenberg urged, moving towards the desk at the other end of the stateroom.

On it sat a satellite-linked computer. Mike presumed it provided up to the minute information from Rothenberg's media properties worldwide. The mogul was never out of touch.

"Incidentally, you'll find some files on a terminal in your cabin. Take a look at them," Rothenberg suggested. "They'll give you some idea of the breadth of our information-gathering. We get to know nearly everything about everybody."

Frederick, who had a near-psychic ability to appear precisely when required, showed Delano to his cabin.

There, beer and wine chilled in ice buckets. Brunch was also waiting: turtle soup, freshly-caught Scottish salmon, salad, warm rolls, and a selection of desserts. A computer screen and keyboard sat in a corner beside a double bed.

Delano was hungry and ate eagerly. He'd wait until later to study whatever was on the terminal so conveniently set up next to the bed. After the meal, weary from his early start, he climbed under the luxuriant sheets for a catnap.

Doubts about the job offer kept him awake. Was this the right move? He'd specialized in diplomacy and wars in foreign countries, not domestic politics or movie stars. He had no contacts in such glitzy spheres. This job required contacts in both.

He had barely closed his eyes when an insistent buzzing from the bedside computer woke him. The screen blinked out a message: "Welcome to GMI Michael Delano – Please feel free to browse." A list of files appeared on the monitor.

The first one that caught his eye, he could not resist opening: "Mike Delano Journalist." It was a detailed account of his life. There were pictures of him playing soccer as a schoolboy; shots taken of him in the newsroom of a South London weekly, his first job.

Surprisingly, there was an image of his first girlfriend. Details of his expulsion from St. Joseph's Catholic school for disrupting religious instruction classes were there too. The file even included a note from the principal, Brother Nicholas:

"Michael Delano mocks the doctrine of the Immaculate Conception and questions the infallibility of the Pope. How can a boy from a good Catholic home behave like this? I am ordering his removal from St. Joseph's."

Astonished, Mike read distressing details of his mother Daisy Louise's mental instability. They covered years during which she received electric shock therapy and psychiatric treatment requiring lengthy hospitalization.

There were also snapshots of his bipolar mother and drunkard stepfather, Robert Brooks, whom Mike detested as he grew up. Their relationship was argumentative and violent. Brooks was the reason he left home at age 17 to work in local newspapers.

The detailed summary of his career was a trip through Delano's memories. It included the newspapers he'd worked for, stories he'd covered in the Middle East and at the United Nations, the salaries he had earned. The file also listed the financial details of his book deal with the publishers of *Prisoners of Islam*.

It astounded Delano. How could they have gathered such comprehensive material on him? He now understood GMI wasn't just a media organization. It was a spy network using all the tabloid trade tricks: phone tapping, computer hacking, private investigators, and paid informants.

Further examination of other files confirmed his suspicion. The meticulously gathered content was both chilling and surprising. And it was surreal being 30,000 feet above the Atlantic, getting the low-down on the lives of renowned men and women in Britain and America.

Especially surprising was the exhaustive dirt GMI publications had on British royals. It was material only obtainable from those working within the palaces – and in several cases from members of the royal family itself. Other folders covered captains of industry, superstar actors, pop stars – and, of course, politicians.

Unusually detailed was the data on Roderick Morley, a Conservative member of Parliament for Cheshire. Delano wondered why Morley was significant enough to merit so much attention.

Mike shut down the computer, having seen enough. He tried to sleep but couldn't. He understood: his lack of connections didn't matter. GMI had all the investigative tools he could use to probe anyone of editorial interest.

The big question persisted. Should he edit a trashy Sunday paper and get rich or stick with his desire to become a novelist? Hours before the plane touched down in LA, Mike decided.

As the jet crossed America's "flyover states," Frederick arrived to announce, "Lord Rothenberg is looking forward to seeing you at dinner."

Delano followed him to the mogul's table in the main salon. Small talk ensued as they dined, but just as the chocolate mousse cake appeared in front of them, Delano gave his answer.

"I accept your offer."

The prospect of wealth and power had won out over scruples. The job might even be rewarding in non-financial ways, he thought. Exposing hypocrites could well be both satisfying and necessary.

"Glad to hear you made the right choice," Rothenberg boomed enthusiastically. "Welcome to GMI!"

CHAPTER SIX:

JUNKYARD DOG

Roderick Morley's first realization of pain as pleasure came during a youthful game played with his Aunt Edith's tiger skin rug. The moth-eaten fur was a relic of the British Raj, when they shot Bengal tigers as trophies.

Roderick was eleven years old and enjoying his third holiday at his aunt's Cheshire mansion in northwest England. He had a crush on Annie Mercer, the blonde-haired daughter of the estate's head gardener. Annie, two years older, boasted a curvy, athletic silhouette, honed by helping her father dig, plant and prune.

Annie liked sadistic horseplay with Roderick, a timid boy from a titled southern English family. Their play included her smacking the submissive Roderick's behind until he screamed. To her delight, he always came back for more.

Their favorite game involved sneaking into the mansion's rarely used drawing room to play "tiger." She was Shere Khan, the big cat terror of Kipling's *The Jungle Book*. Roderick was Mowgli, the Man-Cub raised by wolves.

Annie would hide behind the Georgian furniture or under the grand piano with the tiger skin draped over her shoulders. When Roderick walked by, she'd pounce, snarling, and pull Roderick to the floor. Sitting astride him, Annie sank her sharp, white teeth into his arms, legs, and neck – leaving bite marks and bruising.

The more vicious she became, the more painful the attack, the more he squealed with delight – and the more quickly his penis stiffened. Though he didn't fully understand what was happening, Roderick knew he liked it.

These early erotic experiences ended abruptly when Roderick's mother, Lady Priscilla Morley, noticed bruises and scabs on his arms and legs. Under questioning, Roddy treacherously blamed Annie for the injuries.

Wanting to mask his connivance, he claimed he couldn't stop her from playing so roughly. His lies resulted in Annie receiving a thrashing from her father. Roddy's family banned the children from "playing" together.

Despite the interruption, Rodney never forgot his early experiences with the young disciplinarian. Later, his pleasure in pain grew to be a compulsion that would haunt him to the end of his life.

* * *

Mistress Giana Gallina, a full-bodied blonde reminiscent of Tiger Annie, was an expert with whips for lashing and paddles for spanking. She knew just how much to hurt clients without scarring or injuring them.

The Reverend Roderick Morley, acclaimed preacher, Conservative MP for a Cheshire ward, father of three, prospective cabinet minister, could testify to Giana's practiced arm – and hand. He was grateful for the way she massaged away wheals on his scrawny buttocks with a special cream—a small but pleasant reward after discipline.

Tall, thin, and wiry with limp brown hair and dull blue eyes, he avoided getting naked in front of Jemma Morley. His too plump and excessively godly wife believed sex was for reproduction, not pleasure. His mournful face took on a hangdog look every time he was in the same room with her. His gut tightened like a closed fist at the sight of her naked.

Busted for bite marks as a youngster, Roderick, now 54, feared any questioning about damage to his alabaster white skin. In truth, his worries were overblown; Jemma paid far more attention to the televangelists she worshiped than she did him. He dreamed of being free to live his secret life without fear of discovery – and without Jemma.

Were his perversions to be exposed, his Westminster colleagues would ostracize him. They valued his reputation as an up-and-coming Parliamentarian of unblemished character.

After sharing three lines of cocaine with Mistress Giana, Roderick relaxed on the sofa, watching as she slid out of her black leather bustier, freeing soft swinging breasts. Naked, she sat beside him, allowing "baby" Roderick to suckle her nipples.

After masturbating him to climax, she caught his ejaculate in her hands, rubbing his semen into her face and blonde pubes. Roderick, who sometimes had impotence issues, sighed contentedly.

His conscience was clear. He wasn't cheating on Jemma. As much as he wanted to, he'd never penetrated Giana during their many liaisons. She was his irreplaceable indulgence, well worth the £1,200 he paid twice monthly for three hours of careful "discipline."

When family life chafed, submission and punishment were essential to his well-being. It became uplifting at troubled times, notably when Parliamentary legislation he'd backed and presented failed.

Failure, however, was not an option for his next act. In his long battle against Max Rothenberg, his forthcoming antimonopoly bill would stop the GMI conglomerate's hostile takeover of its most potent rival, Wellington Broadcasting Corporation.

In gratitude, Roderick expected Wellington to provide him a well-paid seat on their board. He detested Rothenberg and his deviant-bashing tabloids. They sensationalized and exposed behavior that sadomasochists like himself wanted to keep well under wraps. The antimonopoly bill would be his vengeance on GMI.

Roderick felt incredibly contented driving his white Jaguar through London's crowded streets to his Hampstead home, replaying memories of his session with Giana. He had all the votes needed to obstruct GMI's hostile takeover of Wellington Broadcasting. He intended to present damning information against the conglomerate from the Conservative front benches of the House of Commons within ten days.

Roderick, a consummate politician, expected his bill blocking the publisher who'd angered so many parliamentarians would earn him a cabinet post. It would thrill his sweet Giana to have such an influential man as a client.

* * *

Mike Delano looked at the pictures spread across his desk in his splendid glass-walled office. They showed a voluptuous blonde in a black bustier whipping and paddling the Reverend Roderick Morley's bony ass. Other photos revealed him naked, snorting coke through a straw with the dominatrix, her breasts spilling out of her revealing costume.

Pictures of her masturbating Roderick were too risqué, even for the Sunday Planet's bawdy audience. But Delano was confident his Lordship would insist on using some of the milder shots of them sharing cocaine. Exposure as a drug-using pervert would destroy the Reverend Morley's credibility and delay his bill, clearing the way for GMI's takeover of Wellington Broadcasting.

Warned their jobs were on the line if they didn't get dirt on the MP, Delano's team of reporters and photographers had followed Morley undetected for weeks.

Eventually, they discovered his visits to Giana Gallina's house of discipline. Mike's specialist photographer, Phil Pritchard, had snapped the "money shots" from a painter's cradle loaned when they paid off the building manager with five thousand pounds. The stealth team had lowered and moved the cradle undetected along the rear of Giana's Paddington apartment block.

Phil, a low-light expert, photographed Roderick's sexual shenanigans through a gap in the curtained third-floor windows. Pritchard's pictures were tabloid gold. Delano held the best one in his left hand and punched in the number to Rothenberg's direct line with his right. The mogul picked up immediately.

"Max, I've got the goods on Morley, pictures of him naked with a dominatrix whipping him. Better still, there are shots of the pair snorting cocaine together," he said.

"Excellent," Rothenberg opined. "They'll dishonor the bastard, stop them voting down my Wellington deal. He's history once this appears. Likely to resign from Parliament. I hope there's a second-day yarn, too. We'll run more of the pictures with it."

Delano waited for final approval. His Lordship seemed nervous about this one, not showing his usual confidence. He'd face accusations of destroying the MP to further GMI interests. After several silent seconds, Rothenberg spoke again.

"Outstanding work, Delano. Run it page one in *News of the Planet* this coming Sunday. Then pass it on with fresh copy and pictures to our magazines and TV stations. The readers and viewers will love this one."

"Will do, Max. You still want to see the pictures?"

"Yes, send 'em up – and pay all concerned a bonus."

Rothenberg disconnected without saying more. He rarely said hello or good-bye. It irritated Delano, just as these hatchet jobs on his boss's enemies had begun to make him achingly uncomfortable during the two years he'd worked for Rothenberg.

He'd done a bunch of them since becoming a top GMI editor, and his continued success depended on completing more of Max's personal "projects." Rothenberg had every reason to applaud Delano. He'd revamped the staff at *News of the Planet*, hiring an amoral crew of editors, reporters, and photographers.

They were men and women willing to charge through brick walls for a story. Some weeks, their scoops boosted Sunday circulation to six or seven million. Delano had made the paper the world's best-selling and most profitable tabloid. Advertising flooded in, the bottom line swelled.

The Morley story ran that weekend under the page one headline: "Sadomasochist Preacher MP Caught Using Coke After Whipping!"

Pictures showed the clergyman MP naked, snorting cocaine with bare-breasted Giana. Another photo, filling half the turn-page, showed Roderick leering wantonly as his leather-clad lover whipped his skinny buttocks.

Sunday Planet circulation soared to a near-record seven million copies with this tawdry tale.

* * *

A week after the exposé appeared, news editor Roy Sykes rushed into Delano's office, waving a wire service report. Thames police had hauled the Reverend Morley's body from the river. The report said his wife, Jemma, had difficulty at the mortuary identifying him.

Roderick had been in the Thames for several days. Boat propellers had mutilated him, and gulls had pecked out his eyes. Her children were shocked to see Jemma Morley carried out of the mortuary in a dead faint. Delano's eager photographers had taken pictures of Jemma as ambulance men transported her sobbing to Westminster Hospital.

"Jesus Christ, I didn't expect that to happen," Mike thought grimly, feeling slightly sick.

There'd been other stories too that set his teeth on edge, yarns that hurt and humiliated people. But, for God's sake, they didn't jump in the fucking river and drown themselves, he thought. There were still three years to go on his GMI contract. He was beginning to think he'd made a significant mistake accepting this job.

A ringing phone jarred Delano out of his guilt trip. His Lordship called to say he had learned of the MP's death and wanted a follow-up story on Sunday.

"Here's the headline," he barked, barely containing his glee. "Pervert Preacher MP Drowns Following Exclusive Planet Revelations of His Sordid Life."

"I'll get on it right away, Max," Delano said dutifully, hating himself for not voicing his utter disgust.

"Good operation, two page-ones for the price of one," the mogul announced before promptly disconnecting.

Delano wanted to throw the instrument across the room. The man was heartless. He put down the phone, his stomach in a knot.

His reporters hacked phones, bugged celebrity bedrooms, and corporate suites. They exposed people with cancer, set up unsuspecting crown ministers with prostitutes and rent-boys, made British royals' lives miserable – but it was the first time Mike had been directly responsible for driving someone to suicide.

Delano reached into his desk drawer for a cigarette and lit up. He would never kick the habit while working here. At first, he'd enjoyed the never-ending hunt for exclusives – and the big paychecks. But this was getting too down and dirty for him.

Pictures of Jemma Morley and their children – two university-age boys and a teenage girl – at the MP's funeral served only to deepen his depression. It was getting harder to avoid the truth: he'd gone from idealistic and respected foreign correspondent to purveyor of titillating dirt served up with Sunday breakfast all over Britain.

He'd become Max Rothenberg's junkyard dog, a sell-out in his own eyes. He had joined a group of extravagantly paid media executives living in terror of losing their jobs to the mogul's displeasure. The money and power, hot women, nightclub life, first-class travel, chauffeur-driven limos all disappeared if you irked Rothenberg.

Delano's resounding success as an editor put him in line for more rewards and eventual elevation to GMI global management. The problem was, he didn't think he could tolerate the grueling, soulless years needed to climb to greater heights.

Was the daily quest to satisfy Britain's ignorant masses' prurient interests what he wanted out of journalism? He had no answer. All he knew for sure was, scavenging for dirt was making him miserable.

CHAPTER SEVEN:

FIRST MEETING

Delano felt flattered when invited to a luncheon thrown by Viscount Clarence Hamden at his country estate in Sussex. A close friend of Lord Rothenberg, the Viscount's newsprint subsidiary supplied much of the paper that passed through GMI printing presses.

Delano relished being away from the big city after his drive down from London. Two hours later, after shaking many hands, exchanging industry gossip, downing several glasses of champagne, and consuming a first-class lunch, he ventured out to the mansion's terrace for some fresh air.

As he relaxed and admired the rolling South Downs, an elegant brunette in an off-the-shoulder afternoon cocktail dress appeared at his side. They had not met, but he recognized Lord Rothenberg's daughter. He had noticed Rachel Mizrahi earlier, standing alone, looking bored amid the Boss's cronies who were doubtless boasting about their mistresses, golf scores, hunting, and fishing prowess.

He smiled, acknowledging her presence. Up close, she was stunning. Her body was shapely and muscular. Her face, burnished by the sun and framed by long ink-black hair, had an outdoorswoman's glow.

Rachel rode to hounds, was a crack tennis player, and a celebrated portrait artist with aristocratic clients. Her lips were full and inviting, her almond-shaped brown eyes mischievous. At five-foot-nine-inches, she was eye to eye with him in stilettoes. Her black designer dress provided a tantalizing glimpse of tanned breasts.

"Hello, I'm Rachel Mizrahi," she said, her voice husky and cultured as she extended a manicured hand.

"I saw you out here. It looked like a better place to be. These parties are all similar – dreary. I came because Daddy didn't want to come alone."

"It's a pleasure to meet you, Mrs. Mizrahi," he said. "I'm Mike Delano, one of your father's editors."

Rachel studied him. She well knew who he was. She had read his book and enjoyed his outspoken appearances on television, where he ably defended the Sunday Planet's muckraking. Also, he was the youngest and, without any doubt, the most attractive man at the gathering.

"So, you're Daddy's attack dog, the one that drives MPs to suicide. 'All the news that's shit to print.' Right? How can you do it, week after week?"

Delano's eyes sparked at the challenge. She went for the jugular. It was refreshing.

Not many folks openly disparaged Rothenberg's profitable tabloid, although, behind his back, they disapproved of the yellow journalism he used to crucify opponents and punish politicians. Most detractors, especially those with essential jobs or places in society, stayed silent for fear the paper would turn on them at the slightest provocation.

"Of course, I don't begrudge you your opinion," Delano replied. "But I don't believe your father will be using that promotional slogan, catchy though it is."

Studying him slyly from under long dark lashes, she admired his strong jaw, Roman nose, and thick wavy auburn hair. Rachel also liked the rascally smile that flickered across his face when challenged, creasing the four-inch scar that ran across his right cheek like a lightning strike. He looked piratical.

"Be honest. Bet you hate the fucking job. Aren't you in it for the money like the rest of Daddy's editors?" she said in mock accusatory tones, with an amused flutter of lashes used like weapons. "Is it satisfying shafting my father's enemies, doing his dirty work, destroying lives?"

Coming on top of career doubts that had intensified since the MP's suicide, Delano did not need this reminder of his ethical collapse. He did not have to take this crap, even from the Boss's daughter. No matter how well he performed, the paper received too many critical comments from Rothenberg himself.

"Giving readers what they want sells papers," he responded defensively. "Popular journalism's a grubby game with dark moments. Some say I sold out. But your father provided a big opportunity – and I took it."

Seeing the fiery flash in his eyes, she knew she had gone too far baiting him. She liked his restrained but truthful answer.

"I know your background," she said. "I read *Prisoners of Islam*. A really good read. What a nightmare you suffered. But digging dirt on the rich and famous is degrading, isn't it?"

Abashed, Delano hid behind a smirk. Deciding to take a different tack, he poked holes in her scornful comment.

"Don't be too rough on the Planet. Doubtless, it helped finance your expensive education, provided the many luxuries you enjoyed growing up. Want me to tell Max his Sunday rag offends his snobby daughter?"

She laughed, pleased to get a rise from him, yet sorry she'd pierced his armor. His candor intrigued her. He was not the least bit like the fawning, bleating upper-class twits usually occupying GMI's top jobs, Oxbridge types who curried favor with the Boss's daughter.

"Max knows how I feel about his tabloids – and doesn't care. He never listens to my ideas anyway. He's kept me out of GMI when I wanted a role there. He thinks I should be home having babies. Daddy can't wait for me to produce a grandson to inherit the crown."

Delano had heard rumors of the difficulties between father and daughter. Although she adored Max, who had raised her, she resented him running her adult life. Mike was surprised she was still badgering "Daddy" for a management role.

This was getting too personal; he did not need to know more. He suggested they rejoin the other guests. She demurred.

"Bunch of nasty old farts back there," she said. "I can't breathe with all their vile cigar smoke. Here's a better idea," she said, fishing a joint out of a tiny, bejeweled purse. "Let's go down by the lake and smoke. Then we'll go in. I can deal with those folk better when I'm a bit high."

Delano hesitated but followed. She was captivating; he wanted to know more.

Rachel kicked off her high heels and carried them. Her shapely legs moved apace. Following a step behind, he enjoyed the sway of her hips, the rhythmic motion of her toned buttocks descending the slope. Her perfume reached him on the late afternoon summer breeze ruffling her waist-long hair. He was smitten. Married woman or no, he wanted to hold this spirited, provocative sprite close, to kiss her fuchsia lips, know her body – an impossible fantasy.

By the lake, they sat on a bench shaded by a curtain of willows. The waning sun reflected crimson off the glass-smooth water as Rachel lit the joint, inhaling deeply. Fragrant cannabis fumes filled the moist Sussex air.

Delano took the joint readily. He had not smoked pot for years, not since his cub reporter days. Delano and other hard-up juniors on the local weekly lit up in the storeroom when they could escape their editors' attention – and had spare cash to buy weed.

The powerful dope revived good memories of incidents with the other young reporters he had not thought about for years. He smiled happily.

"What's so amusing?" she asked. "Let me in on the joke."

"I remember stories I cobbled together stoned as a junior reporter. Lucked out, keeping that job. Editor, crusty old buzzard, hated drugs. He was a boozer who smoked two packs of cigarettes daily. Didn't stop him writing editorials against 'the pot menace.'"

She giggled, figuring she had Delano pegged. He played the game, but at heart, rebelled. It was something they had in common: two rebels striving to appease her tyrannical father. She sensed she could trust him. It jolted her, realizing how swiftly she could become attracted to him.

Curiosity had drawn her out onto the terrace to join him – her interest aroused after seeing him interviewed on TV for his book and, later, in his role as a frequent spokesman for the Sunday Planet. She could not explain why, but she wanted him to trust her, to know he had a friend in her – primarily as her father so dominated both their lives.

Her thoughts came tumbling out as the pot took hold. She said she had been trying to please Daddy since she was a toddler when he parted from her mother, Gerda, a Belgian-born Jewish beauty, who would not tolerate her husband's serial cheating.

It was not until she was nine that Max allowed her to spend time with Gerda. Delano listened sympathetically – hoping Rachel would not come to regret sharing so much. There was no stopping her. From childhood, Max wanted to control Rachel's life. She received phone tirades over minor misdeeds while visiting with Gerda.

Brought up in strict Jewish tradition, he forbade her to have Christian friends when she became a teenager – a rule she broke once she entered art school.

Max refused Rachel a role in his business and threatened disinheritance if she did not accept his rulings. He claimed she was too soft-hearted, like Gerda, that she did not have the metal of a woman like Liz Hightower, who matched him for toughness.

Rachel suspected her exclusion from GMI also came from Rothenberg's fear of her discovering his dirty deals, and losing his grip on her. Friends she had calculatedly made within GMI hinted at some of the company's dark secrets.

Her becoming a successful artist had displeased Max. He demanded she marry a "nice Jewish boy" and produce a grandson Max could train to take over the conglomerate. She had wed Aaron Mizrahi to appease Daddy – but so far, she had avoided pregnancy.

Delano held up his hand to stop her, but the emotional floodgates had opened, revealing the scale of her resentment.

"Daddy married me off three years ago like I was some fucking broodmare. I was just 22," she said, taking an angry hit on the joint and breathing out pungent smoke.

"I'd be cut off with a pittance if I didn't go through with it. Aaron's ten years older than me, a Goddamned Israeli arms dealer. Who knows how many deaths and injuries he's been responsible for? He and Max expect me to produce a Rothenberg heir, but I've fooled them."

Delano did not ask how, nor did he want to hear more. They fired up the joint for a few more tokes inhaled in thoughtful silence. Rachel had moved in close, and it excited him when she ran a finger over the scar on his cheek.

"How'd you get that?" she asked.

As he started to tell her, she leaned in and kissed him gently on the lips. Savoring the nearness of her body, he held her momentarily in a gentle embrace. This show of affection was insane. How had this instant attraction developed? Nevertheless, like her, he felt its irresistible pull.

Rachel sensed Delano could provide the love missing from her life. She was a woman who went for what she wanted – and she wanted this man. They finished the joint, enjoying the pleasant buzz, and Delano took her hand gently.

"Shall we go back?"

Their absence could prompt gossip. Had Max noticed their departure? At last sight, he was downing Scotch and badgering Lord Hamden about the high price of newsprint.

"Yes, we'd better return. But I want to see you again – and soon," Rachel declared. "It's been such fun."

"I guess we can work something out," Mike replied, seeking a noncommittal tone, giving himself room to come to his senses later.

They took their time strolling up the slope towards the mansion. From the terrace, Delano saw Lord Rothenberg through the picture windows, gesturing animatedly.

It appeared their absence had gone unnoticed. Mike felt relieved Gil Ackerman was not on the guest list. The security snoop surely would have noticed and told the Boss they had walked the grounds alone for more than two hours.

* * *

At Rachel's suggestion, they met the following Monday at the Green Park Tennis Club in London for a few fast sets. Hot and sweaty after Rachel beat him by three games, Delano suggested they skip the locker rooms and go to his home for a shower and a midday glass of bubbly.

He ignored the alarm bells clanging in his brain. He was asking for trouble getting involved with the Boss's married daughter. Rachel, who was staying at Max's Shepperton mansion 30 miles away while having her Pimlico apartment refurbished, accepted his invitation.

At the townhouse, she showered while Delano put the Veuve Clicquot on ice, thrilling to the guilty knowledge of her closeness. Returning damp in one of his bathrobes, she looked on appreciatively as he popped the cork and filled two crystal flutes.

Although he did not show it, Delano was on edge, cursing himself for letting her park her bright blue Aston Martin outside. They should have left it at the tennis club and taken a taxi home. Various nightmare possibilities presented themselves. What if reporters from one of the rival tabs saw them arriving together – or ran the plates?

Would some eagle-eyed newshound notice her distinctive car parked outside for hours? It would provide a juicy scandal item for one of their rivals: "Is Tab Editor Romancing Rothenberg's Married Daughter?"

He imagined the possible headline and dreaded the devastating results. By the time they opened the second bottle, his concerns had abated.

Rachel was irresistible as she sat sipping champagne, her long dark hair bundled up, nipples thrusting against the damp fabric of the silk robe he had loaned her.

Delano was getting hard, the bulge in his tennis shorts challenging to hide. He could read the message in her eyes. The recklessness of the circumstances increased his ardor.

Nevertheless, he held back. Determined to overcome his indecision, Rachel stood and allowed the robe to part, displaying her toned and tanned body.

Seconds later, they were in a passionate embrace. Delano swept her into his bedroom as their unstoppable passions flared, and they made love on his king-sized bed for the next two hours.

Spent, they lay still afterward, locked together in languid, delicious contentment until the outside world began to intrude.

Dusk was approaching, and Rachel got into her Aston and left reluctantly for the drive on the Kingston bypass to Shepperton for dinner with Daddy.

Even the prospect of dining with her overbearing father could not taint the joy coursing through her body. It was a pleasure more thrilling than she experienced after seeing a portrait subject come alive at her hand.

Thank God she would not have to deal with her often-absent husband. Aaron was out of the country again selling tanks and guns, loyally providing Israel with needed hard currency.

Max admired his soulless son-in-law's work for Zionism and longed for a grandchild from the marriage he had arranged, but Rachel had secretly stayed on the pill. She was not in love with Aaron and did not want his baby. She had convinced Aaron that her failure to become pregnant resulted from his long absences.

Her fling with Delano was not the first time she had cheated on her husband. She disliked his humorless company and cringed when he touched her. She should never have let her father force her into a marriage with a man who sold tanks to dictators, weaponry to African revolutionaries, and arms to anyone planning to start a war.

Rachel disapproved of his weapons deals, and they argued fiercely over Middle Eastern politics. She especially disliked the Israeli treatment of the Palestinians.

With guilty tears welling, she had admitted to Delano she wished one of Aaron's customers would blow him away – a degree of cruelty that surprised Mike.

From early in their romance, Rachel considered Delano an antidote to what ailed her. Thoughts of him made her tingle. His strength was tender, decent, and fearless. He'd be a reliable ally in a foxhole.

A year later, what had started as a fling turned into a passionate love affair. Being in his arms as often as possible was heaven for Rachel. She wanted a future with him and even fantasized about having his child.

They met at his townhouse or out-of-the-way country inns. Both looked forward eagerly to Aaron Mizrahi's foreign trips; his frequent absences provided them more time together.

However, there were weeks when Aaron stayed home and sought to monopolize Rachel's time. Those occasions left Delano moody, restless, and unhappy.

The intensity of their feelings was more than either had experienced before. They longed for the day when they could go public with their relationship like an ordinary couple. For now, Rachel's loyalty to her father, and Mike's wish to keep his job, kept them sneaking around like thieves.

Something deep down in Rachel's makeup drew her irresistibly to Mike. To her, he was street-smart, creative, expressive – strategic in his thinking. Although she did not see it at first, these qualities were also ones she admired in her ruthless father.

Yet Delano was the shield she sought against her tyrannical parent. He was a warrior, unafraid to punish society's wrongdoers, a journalist who used brains and muscle to win battles. He had accepted dangerous assignments and famously proved willing to get his hands bloody when necessary.

Protecting the weak and facing down power was at his core. Mike resonated at her most profound level. He was not like other suitors who had sought to romance her because she was the mogul's daughter. Rachel harbored no qualms he was attracted to her station or wealth – the material advantages that appealed to her husband.

Aaron viewed Rachel as a trophy he'd won by marrying into one of the world's wealthiest Jewish families. She had wed him to please Max, thus preserving her inheritance and hope of becoming a part of GMI management one day. The longer she knew him, the more she viewed Aaron as a cynical user. She desperately wanted to end their marriage.

Now it was a question of picking the right time to reveal this to her father. He would be furious when he learned about her love for Delano, more so because Mike was a gentile – and an employee.

Working for Max's scandal rag was not a good fit for him; she knew it was a mistake. Mike needed to be where the action was: marching with protesters, covering battles, questioning deposed dictators.

Dishing the dirt on Britain's anachronistic royalty or exposing movie star decadence did not feed his soul. Nor did bringing down her father's business enemies. She had guessed from the start such assignments left Delano feeling cheapened.

The man she adored had taken the wrong fork in the road, but fortunately, it led him to her. Now she would never let him go. From the moment they met, there was destiny between them. She wanted his children, to spend her life with him.

However, when Rachel approached Aaron about a divorce, he brushed her off. Shrewdly, he warned, "Max will disinherit you, and you'll never be part of the family business. If you're wise, you'll make this marriage work."

His determined refusal stemmed from Max's promise of a GMI directorship when he left the arms trade and produced children with Rachel. Her father's hold on everybody's life made her more determined to escape.

Delano, too, was having difficulty deciding how to handle this problem. He wanted to find a strategic moment to leave his unhappy editorship. He did not plan to quit until Rachel gained Aaron's agreement to a divorce – which the Israeli was stubbornly resisting, knowing nothing of his wife's affair.

"We can expect a severe reaction when Max finds out I've come between you and Aaron, and that I'm quitting," Mike warned. "He's the most vindictive man I've ever known. He'll try to punish us both."

"What do you mean?" Rachel asked.

Delano did not answer immediately. He was unwilling to discuss his darkest thoughts about how harsh Rothenberg's response would be to such a double-barreled challenge.

"Forget I ever said that," he said. "I just want to marry you. I love you. We need to avoid scandal. When the time's right, I'll talk to Max, tell him the truth. He'll have to accept it."

Impatient to have her way and escape the marriage, Rachel became broody and abandoned birth control. Making love with the idea of having his child became her obsession. It added a new and exciting meaning to their encounters.

She formed a foggy notion that pregnancy would hasten the day she and Mike could marry. She fantasized it would be a lever she could use to force Aaron to free her. However, when the pregnancy occurred, she panicked.

"You're two months pregnant," her gynecologist confirmed.

It was Mike's child. She'd avoided sex with Aaron when he was last home. Rebuffed, he'd left for Africa – complaining she was breaking the tenets of the marriage her father had arranged.

Now, she feared the ugly scene with her father. She also worried about hurting Mike by putting him at the center of a scandal media rivals would mock in headlines.

Rachel needed to ease the pressure she felt by talking to someone not directly involved. Before telling Mike, she swore her best friend, Marjorie Levy, to secrecy and confided in her.

"It's not Aaron's child – the father's someone else I care for deeply," she told Marjorie, who convincingly hid her shock.

"I'll demand a divorce when Aaron returns. I'll tell him I'm in love with the man whose child I'm carrying," she said. Left unsaid was her plan to wait until then to tell Mike.

Within 24 hours, Marjorie broke her promise. She revealed Rachel's secret to her husband Phil, a GMI advertising executive whose company position was shaky.

Grateful for ammunition to save his job, Levy went to Gil Ackerman, Rothenberg's security chief: "I don't know how true this is, Gil, but I have heard a disturbing rumor. Rachel Mizrahi's pregnant, and Aaron isn't the father," he said.

Ackerman was cautious. What was the best way to exploit such intelligence? He wouldn't tell the Boss yet. Make a mistake about something so crucial to Rothenberg, and he would be out.

"Keep quiet about this while I investigate," he assured Phil Levy. "If it's true, his Lordship will be grateful for the information. You just might keep your job."

Ackerman assigned a private investigator to Rachel, who logged her every move. He needed to be sure of his facts before going to the Boss.

Two weeks later, the investigator returned with his report.

"She goes to a townhouse at 110 Bruton Place, Mayfair. She's there several times a week. She stays for hours, occasionally all night." Ackerman could not believe what he was hearing.

It was Delano's place. How did the SOB think he could get away with banging the Boss's daughter? What if Max's "golden boy" was the father?

He'd disliked Delano since the day Rothenberg hired him. If Delano had knocked up Rachel, it was the end of him – and good riddance. The security chief called for an urgent meeting with the mogul to break the news.

"Are you sure? There can't be any mistakes," Rothenberg thundered, his face crimson, his fists bunched like he was ready to punch someone out. Frantic, he paced his London office wild-eyed. His words became a long raging howl, jarring the nerves of those around him.

His deputy, Liz Hightower, in from LA, paced beside him, begging Rothenberg to sit down, to be calm. She handed him valium and water, urging him to swallow.

Ackerman watched the furor he had created with satisfaction. He had never seen the Boss so out of control.

"I'm going to ruin that son of a bitch if this is true. He'll never get another job in Britain. I'll see to that…"

Still disbelieving, he asked again, "Are you certain there's no mistake?"

Having got him seated, sipping ice water, Liz assured him patiently: Ackerman's finding was reliable. Gil had shown her the report just moments earlier.

Tears of rage ran down Max's cheeks. A senior executive had betrayed him, with his daughter a willing co-conspirator.

Losing Delano would cost millions. Now, he also faced having a bastard grandchild and the wrath of Aaron Mizrahi, who would doubtless exploit the situation to gouge more concessions out of him.

"So, tell me again what you know and how you found out," he commanded Ackerman.

"Rachel confided her situation to Marjorie Levy, who told Phil, who came to me. We've got pictures of her entering Delano's house with a key and leaving early in the morning."

He handed Rothenberg the file with time- and date-stamped photos. Disgusted, he flicked through the pictures of the couple kissing at the townhouse front door, at a local pub sitting in a corner, clearly lovers.

At the back of the folder was Ackerman's most damning evidence. His investigators had bribed a nurse at the gynecologist's office into copying Rachel's medical chart. It was there in black and white: the doctor confirmed she was pregnant.

Max's rage mounted as he read the report. The notes described an up-tilted womb "that could make delivery difficult, possibly dangerous." The doctor suggested she return with her partner to discuss prenatal care – but there were no further notes of a follow-up appointment.

He barked new orders at Liz Hightower and Ackerman.

"I want Delano removed from all company property, from the house, and my newspaper. I want him gone – today. There must be no trace of him. And destroy his reputation, too. You understand?"

CHAPTER EIGHT:

BRANDED A THIEF

A sanitation crew arrived with Gil Ackerman in charge to clean and disinfect the Mayfair house. Rothenberg wanted no lingering trace of Rachel's tawdry affair with Delano.

Satisfied he'd fulfilled the Boss's orders, Ackerman drove his Land Rover to the Sunday Planet's East London offices on Canary Wharf. There, two security guards stood by to escort Gil to the 14th-floor editorial department.

They stormed past the protesting receptionist to the editor's suite. Delano, evaluating feature copy on his computer screen, looked up just as one of the guards bent over and yanked the computer's power cord from the wall socket.

Delano rose from his desk, startled.

"Have you lost your frigging mind?" he yelled.

Then noticing Ackerman grinning mockingly, he demanded, "What's the meaning of this, Gil?"

Ackerman looked at the editor triumphantly. He'd waited a long time for this moment.

"You're toast, buddy. Fired, washed up. I'm here with a message from Lord Rothenberg. He wants your ass out of his newspaper office – right now."

His voice was taunting, high with malice. "Box up your stuff, and we'll escort you from the building. Don't think about going home. It's not yours anymore. I changed the locks. Your shit's in storage. I'll tell you where when I'm good and ready. Get a hotel room – find a friend to stay with – if you have any left by the end of today."

Word soon spread across the editorial floor: something weird was happening in the editor's office. Reporters, subeditors, and secretaries crowded Delano's doorway. Others stared through the glass walls trying to make sense of what was taking place.

The firing didn't surprise Delano, although he had no idea what specifically had triggered his dismissal. By falling for Rachel, he'd stuck his neck out. He'd known all along he'd have to pay for it. Though angered by the public way it was happening, he was not overly worried.

He had job offers from other tabloid papers – and could soon be working again if he wanted to stay in this dirty business– and he had Rachel. Presenting an unconcerned front for the onlookers, Delano asked sarcastically, "What happened? Did the Boss find out I used one of his red pens?"

With so many ears straining to hear every word, Ackerman didn't want to get the blame for gossip leaking about Rothenberg's daughter. He put his face close to Delano's and whispered menacingly: "No. He found out you knocked up his daughter."

Mike was stunned. Could it be true? He had to speak to Rachel urgently.

Ackerman backed off and resumed in grating tones: "You'll hear from our lawyers. We'll pay what's owed you up till today. Hand over your GMI credit cards – they're canceled. Call a cab – your car and driver's reassigned. Go, or my guys will pitch you onto the street."

"I have more than three years to go on my contact," Delano said. "I'll sue for breach of contract."

"Go ahead. Sue. You'll lose. We're about to make you look like shit," Ackerman sneered.

Delano looked at him with contempt. He knew Ackerman's history. From the start, he'd sensed Rothenberg's watchdog was a douchebag – a spiteful coward who'd happily do him harm.

"OK, Ackerman. Out of my way. I'll go see Max. You've exceeded your authority, treating me this way…"

Ackerman's bulky body blocked his way.

"You're poison with the Boss. He never wants to see or hear from you again. And I won't allow you to get anywhere near him."

Delano knew better than most how Rothenberg held lifelong grudges. His affair with Rachel wouldn't find forgiveness.

But what was this about her pregnancy? Was it his or Aaron's? Apprehension gripped him as he thought of her. Beneath her rebel pose, she remained Daddy's little girl, fearful of offending him.

Years of psychological conditioning had formed her. She submitted to her father's lesser demands, but not the big ones. Getting pregnant outside her marriage would send Max through the roof. She must be going through hell right then. He had to get to her right away.

Mike waved goodbye to his staff as he left his office. A popular editor, he could see some of them were tearful.

He carried his box of belongings to the elevator, head held high. The guards got in with him to make sure he went down to the lobby, not up to Rothenberg's editorial department lair.

On the street, Delano hailed a cab and checked into the Savoy Hotel. From a room overlooking the Strand, he called Rothenberg's direct number. Maybe he could appease Rothenberg, protect Rachel from his wrath.

Liz Hightower intercepted the call, ice in her voice.

"Lord Rothenberg wants nothing more to do with you, Delano. Further harassment of any member of his family will be cause for legal action, starting with a restraining order. You'll go to jail, understood?"

She disconnected.

Left holding the silent phone, Delano was more intrigued than intimidated, pondering the word "jail." What an extraordinary threat.

Ignoring the warning, he called Rachel. In a rush of words, she managed to say she was at her father's country home, under the involuntary "care" of a doctor and two strong-arm nurses.

"I can't get out," she sobbed. "I'm confined to the second floor. They've locked all the doors. They claim I'm having a breakdown. I can't reach Daddy. I can see security men in the driveway. It's ridiculous…"

Just as he was about to reply, someone snatched the mobile away from her. He heard her cries of protest while struggling to regain the phone. Then an unknown male voiced announced: "Mrs. Mizrahi isn't taking any calls – especially not from you, Mr. Delano."

Within 24 hours, the meaning of Liz Hightower's threat became apparent. GMI auditors accused Delano of fraud, asserting he'd stolen hundreds of thousands of pounds during his editorship.

They claimed he'd intercepted and pocketed payments that should have gone to Sunday Planet contacts and freelance writers. Delano's dismissal and the serious allegations against him made front-page news.

Rothenberg fueled the fire at a press conference the following day.

"I'm not comfortable discussing this. I provided Mr. Delano the editorship of my largest newspaper and every opportunity to succeed. I trusted him. But our accountants discovered he'd embezzled several hundred thousand pounds, possibly more. I don't employ thieves."

Striking a pose of leniency, the tycoon added, "His dishonesty has caused me great personal distress. But I'm considering his suffering in Iraq. For that reason, we won't bring legal action against him."

Delano's shattered reputation caused all British media opportunities to evaporate. He had become an overnight pariah. He knew it was pointless suing his accusers. GMI would produce the cooked books to prove his guilt.

Widely reported, the embezzlement allegations overshadowed Delano's former distinction as a heroic reporter who'd triumphed over a cruel terrorist. Media rivals enjoyed his fall, piling on with editorials expressing shock at discovering him to be "an editor whose dishonesty has disgraced the profession – a man to shun."

CHAPTER NINE:

A BIG LIE

All of Rothenberg's fury now focused on Rachel. There was no way he'd allow her to have Delano's child, fathered by a goy who'd deceived him personally and professionally.

He ordered his security staff to hunt down Aaron Mizrahi, who was selling weapons to rebels involved in the Sudanese civil war in North Africa.

"She's pregnant by Mike Delano!" Max screamed. "I've fired him, ruined him, but you must leave Sudan immediately to deal with Rachel. I have a plan to handle this and restore your marriage. Be on the next flight to Lucerne."

The cuckolding angered Mizrahi. But he knew better than to argue with his father-in-law – the man who selected him as a suitable husband for Rachel.

Aaron more than ever wanted the fat GMI contract Rothenberg had promised him for marrying Rachel. He was anxious to get out of arms dealing, which had become increasingly dangerous.

"I'll be on the next plane. But why Switzerland? Isn't she in England?" he asked, puzzled.

"Because Rachel's at GMI's private clinic in Lucerne. I'll explain later," Rothenberg replied.

He wouldn't go into the details with his son-in-law, that he'd ordered Rachel abducted and doped by a shady doctor and nurse in his employ. They took her in a company jet to his GMI-owned clinic, where Paragon Pictures sent stars for face-lifts, liposuction, drug detoxification, or abortions. The clinic's seclusion high above Lake Lucerne and its well-paid staff ensured strict confidentiality and exclusivity for high-profile patients.

"Your plan, whatever it is, has my full support. I trust you," Mizrahi said ingratiatingly. "I'll book a flight immediately. I'm stunned. Rachel's dishonored me. She's let us both down," he added hastily, knowing Rothenberg didn't give a damn about his son-in-law's honor.

In London, exasperated, Rothenberg put down the phone. He wondered now, had Aaron been the right choice? The Israeli had turned out to be spineless, unable to control Rachel when needed. Worse, he hadn't produced heirs.

The mogul had moved swiftly to avoid any embarrassment after Delano's firing. He feared if the pregnancy became known, the story of Rachel's adultery with a notorious tabloid editor would receive page-one coverage in rival gossip rags. Their owners, envious of his success, detested Rothenberg and reveled in putting him down. More humiliating would be if Max's enemies figured out the real reason for Delano's sudden firing.

* * *

When Rachel awoke, she had little idea where she was or what had happened to her. For the flight to Switzerland, doctors had injected her with Propanol, a drug causing loss of consciousness and lack of memory.

At the clinic, they terminated the pregnancy without discussion or consultation with their VIP patient.

Instructed by Rothenberg, upon his arrival in Lucerne, Aaron Mizrahi signed papers saying his wife had miscarried and he had authorized doctors to treat her.

Groggy and confused, Rachel awoke in a hospital gown. Seeing Aaron by her bed was a startling and unpleasant surprise.

"What are you doing here? I thought you were in Africa," she said unhappily. Looking around the room, she added, "Where is this?"

Mizrahi did his best to appear sympathetic as he lied about what had happened to her. "You're in Switzerland. You had a medical emergency. When Max told me you were unwell, I had you brought here. You were unconscious when I arrived."

He bent over to kiss his distressed wife's pale cheek, but she turned away.

"Max considered it wise you receive treatment in privacy, so we're at his company clinic in Lucerne. Your father didn't want the press getting hold of an embarrassing tale."

Rachel leaned forward, her voice hoarse and angry: "What are you talking about? What embarrassing tale?"

Aaron looked down. He couldn't face her accusing eyes.

"You miscarried. You lost the pregnancy. You were hemorrhaging," Aaron said, repeating the lie he and Max had agreed upon. "It's just as well, in the circumstances. I know you've been unfaithful to me. The baby couldn't have been mine."

Rachel tried to focus. She was beginning to suspect the origins of the betrayal. She'd made an enormous mistake confiding in Marjorie Levy.

She should have known her "friend" couldn't keep such news from her husband. That corporate weasel Phil had probably gone straight to Max.

"You're right. You've been away months. How could the child be yours?" she said, glaring at her unloved spouse. "I don't remember any bleeding. Suddenly, my pregnancy's over? How can that be? What have you done?"

She began to sob uncontrollably. Aaron felt desperate; this wasn't going well. Jesus Christ, she didn't believe him. His future depended on this marriage and remaining in the Rothenberg family. This cheating bitch could ruin everything.

"I know you had an affair with Delano," he said, his voice becoming shrill with anger. "Your father fired him. He's out of your life forever. We can get past this, Rachel. We can start over."

Rachel gasped between sobs. She'd lost the baby, destroyed Mike's career, and now they were cutting her off from the man she loved.

Seeing her verging on hysteria, Aaron sat cautiously on the edge of the bed, reaching for her hand. She snatched it away, disgusted. She was becoming convinced that Aaron had ordered the abortion.

"Naturally, I'm hurt," he went on, ignoring the disdainful hand withdrawal. "But I can forgive you. I'll be working for GMI soon. No more travel away from you. We'll have the children I want – we want. Think how happy you'll make your father."

Rachel sat up, tears of rage streaming. "You wicked bastard. You killed my child. Couldn't stand the thought of another man getting me pregnant…"

As he clenched and unclenched his fingers, he wanted to strangle her. Instead, his lean, tanned face became a mask hiding his rage. He again tried kissing her. Rachel recoiled as if he was venomous.

"Have a child with you? I cringe at your touch. I want a divorce. I'll put you in prison for kidnap, for inflicting bodily harm…"

Unexpectedly, she struggled out of bed, her long nails talons. She intended raking Aaron's eyeballs out. He hopped up from the end of the bed, stepping away hastily.

"You miserable swine," she screamed, advancing. "Why didn't one of those misled fucking Africans you're selling guns to shoot your arse? You don't know how many times I've prayed for that."

When he retreated still further from her menace, she grabbed a heavy water pitcher and, moving with surprising speed, smashed it against the right side of his head, showering the room with glass shards.

The blow sent him staggering backward, collapsing into a visitor's chair, shocked, bloody, and stunned. Two nurses hearing the uproar rushed in appalled at the sight of the bleeding visitor – and the raging woman about to slash his face with a jagged piece of the pitcher.

One burly woman grabbed the weapon out of Rachel's hand, pushing her back onto the bed. The other worked at staunching the flow from the gash in Mizrahi's temple.

"She's a madwoman!" he howled. "I don't deserve this. She's out of her mind."

Turning again to Rachel, now restrained, the truth came tumbling out of his mouth.

"Just so you know, Max ordered the abortion, not me. His people discovered your pregnancy. He called me, telling me to come. I didn't have you brought here. That was your father, not me."

"You're a liar. I hate you! Daddy wouldn't do that to me," Rachel screamed after her husband's fast disappearing form.

The door opened again, and Dr. Elias Muller entered, his hypodermic loaded with Lorazepam. Sitting beside his patient, he slid the needle into her arm.

"You'll feel better, Rachel," he assured, "You mustn't fight it. You need a long, long rest…"

* * *

Max Rothenberg flew into Lucerne a few days after Aaron returned to Sudan. He'd responded to frantic phone calls from Dr. Muller, the clinic's medical director, who skirted Swiss law on most issues involving the clinic's patients in return for a bloated salary.

But Rachel was becoming too problematic for Muller to contain – despite the fact they tranquilized her daily and excessively.

"She's threatening us with the Swiss authorities – she insists on leaving. She could be big trouble. Please, Lord Rothenberg, you have to calm her down. She's demanding a phone to call her lawyers. She wants clothes, airline tickets, money to return to England."

Rachel was barely awake when her father entered her sick room. Relief flooded her.

"Daddy, thank God you're here," she said, struggling against the sedatives to sit up and ask the questions he dreaded.

"You didn't tell them to bring me here, did you? Aaron said you did. He claimed you ordered the abortion. You wouldn't do that, would you? He's a liar, right?"

Rothenberg, feeling unaccustomed guilt, feigned ignorance and anger.

"Of course not! Aaron took charge when I told him you were pregnant. He claimed you'd started miscarrying before he got to London," Max lied.

"Not true! I never saw him in London," she protested. "All I remember is the doctor and the nurse who suddenly appeared. Did you send them, Daddy?"

"Yes, only because I was worried about your emotional health. I meant well. I suggested my people bring you here for privacy. Aaron said you were bleeding when he arrived."

"I don't remember any miscarriage," she protested. "Who permitted an abortion?"

"I can only tell you what I know. If that's what happened, it was Aaron – he's your husband. He had the authority to do that. Not me."

Rachel looked relieved. "I knew you wouldn't hurt me, Daddy. I just want to go home now."

He sat beside her on the bed, pulling her into his comforting arms. She felt reassured on the rare occasions when he showed her affection. Even during their stormiest disagreements, she adored him like the "daddy's girl" she'd always been.

"Aaron claimed you fired Mike for thievery. That's got to be another lie, and I'll tell everybody so. Where is he? I want to be with him, to be his wife. He didn't know I was expecting."

Rothenberg became rigid. He had to stop her: "He stole money from GMI. Do you want to wed a thief? He betrayed us both. He's finished in the business."

Rachel was sobbing now. "I don't believe it. I must go home. I'm divorcing Aaron," she insisted. "I want to be with Mike."

Rothenberg became cold and measured.

"Take my advice. Better to remain here until you're well. I'll be back soon to check on your progress."

A nurse arrived to administer another injection. It took the edge off, helped her feel better. She'd stopped resisting the shots; she was starting to look forward to the injections, to rely on them. Max kissed her cheek and left as she dozed off.

In the director's office, he ordered: "Keep her sedated. She can't leave. No one's to see her. I'll tell you when she can be released."

Dr. Muller, increasingly worried, nodded reluctant agreement.

* * *

Having learned from Rachel's mother, Gerda, that her daughter was at the Swiss clinic, Delano tried on three occasions to visit, but armed guards turned him away. When they caught Mike in disguise a fourth time, Dr. Muller summoned the gendarmes and initiated trespass charges against the journalist.

Eight months went by, and still, Rothenberg wouldn't agree to his daughter's release. He wanted to both punish and keep her quiet.

Aaron Mizrahi believed Rachel had suffered enough when during a visit it became clear to him that she'd become addicted to the drugs used to keep her quiet. He still hoped to salvage their marriage; it remained key to his safe, secure future as a GMI executive.

"Max, I want to give my marriage another chance and to assume the position you promised me," he said in a call after returning to Sudan.

But Rothenberg now considered Aaron a failed, gutless husband, and shocked him by replying, "There are no board positions open to you, now or in the future. Stick to selling munitions."

Another in the long line of people Rothenberg had double-crossed, Aaron wasn't accepting the brushoff. "Don't forget, Max. Rachel disgraced us both. Remember, I know why you hid the real reason for branding Delano a thief and firing him. You wouldn't want it known Lord Rothenberg abducted, drugged, and imprisoned his daughter in a quack clinic after having her lover's baby forcibly aborted."

It was a dangerous game going after Max Rothenberg, and Mizrahi wasn't a good player. Before he could make good on his threat, his jeep mysteriously exploded in flames as he entered it outside his Khartoum hotel.

Gil Ackerman called Rothenberg by satellite phone from Sudan: "That business here's taken care of, Boss. Nothing more to worry about."

Rothenberg media blamed terrorists for the attack on a man they painted as a hero:

"This brave Israeli gave his life aiding the Sudanese government in the struggle against terrorism in their country. Osama Bin Laden's followers built a network that took hundreds of lives. Sadly, Aaron Mizrahi became their latest victim."

A tribute from Lord Max Rothenberg to his son-in-law read:

"Aaron Mizrahi was one of Judaism's heroes. His loss is heartbreaking to my family. His wife, Rachel Rothenberg Mizrahi loved him dearly and has been hospitalized grief-stricken. That their short marriage should end like this is, indeed, tragic. Aaron will live on in our hearts."

CHAPTER TEN:

STUBBORN OPPONENT

The autopsy technician pulled out the drawer of the mortuary cooler and removed the sheet covering a middle-aged female body. Mike Delano gazed dolefully at the face of Carmelita Sanchez, once a housekeeper at the home of one of Hollywood's biggest stars.

Surfers had found her on an Oxnard beach, 62 miles northwest of Los Angeles, with her throat slashed. Black stitches were vivid on her sea-wrinkled neck skin, where the medical examiner had closed the gaping wound.

"Yes, that's Carmelita," Delano said, swallowing hard, his eyes glassy with sorrow and guilt. "When are you releasing her for burial?"

"That's up to the coroner. We got her yesterday, and there's a backlog of cases," the mortuary attendant replied. "I don't think there will be too much of a delay, though," he added. "Cause of death is obvious. Police are searching for suspects."

Yeah, and I don't think they'll find them, Delano thought bitterly. He had more than a hunch who'd committed this crime – and why.

Mike was glad to swap the chilled antiseptic morgue cleanliness for the sunshine warmth outdoors. He'd filed a missing person report when Carmelita disappeared three days ago. The police asked his help with the identification when what they believed were her remains washed up.

Speeding along the Pacific Coast Highway in his white Porsche convertible headed for his new beachfront Malibu home, Delano cursed himself for being the cause of Carmelita's death. He'd genuinely liked her, and she was crucial to a story he was writing.

The Mexican housekeeper, a single mother of two young children, had confirmed bizarre rumors about her movie idol boss and was the primary source for the latest exposé Delano was readying for publication.

It revealed how Lord Rothenberg's Hollywood studio, Paragon Pictures, covered up the drug-fueled decadence of its biggest star, Morgan Masterson.

In addition to confirming he sexually harassed female actors working with him, Carmelita had revealed the superstar had tried to force himself on one of his terrified adopted teenage daughters after a drink and drug session when his wife was away.

Delano pulled off the highway and called his partner, Dave Fuller, to stop the story's publication. With the primary source dead, it was no longer usable.

"It's her, been in the water for a couple of days. They weighted the body. Dumped it off a boat. It broke free and drifted ashore. I feel awful. Somehow Paragon found out she was talking to us."

"Who do you think did it?" Fuller asked.

"Don't know for certain. But I'd be willing to bet Gil Ackerman did the knife work. He's a sadist, enjoys inflicting pain."

"Without Carmelita as our main source, guess we have to hold the piece you wrote," Fuller said.

"Yes, hold it until I can find someone else to stand it up," Delano said before disconnecting.

Dejected, he continued the drive home. He'd been in California for just over a year – and not being able to contact Rachel continued to break his heart.

Disgraced in London by Rothenberg's smear campaign, thwarted in Lucerne by clinic guards, he had accepted an offer to partner in a new LA news agency with his journalist friend Dave Fuller – and business was booming.

While he hadn't shared his deeper motives with Dave, his dual purpose in America was to rebuild his career while avenging himself on Rothenberg by attacking his studio and its roster of big stars.

Before leaving Europe, he had contacted Rachel's mother Gerda in Belgium to explain the reasons for her daughter's plight. Surprised and deeply upset, she promised to pass on news about Rachel if and when she heard anything.

"That miserable man has banned me from writing or visiting her," Gerda complained of her former husband. "I'll do anything I can to help get her out of there and away from him."

"Don't worry, Gerda, I'll get her released. She's the woman I love and intend to share my life with," Delano promised.

It was a strong declaration coming from someone who'd always avoided commitment. But when Rachel arrived in his life, Mike had entered previously unexplored territory. For the first time, he wanted a permanent relationship. He had come to love Rachel with a passion and intensity he hadn't experienced with any other women.

* * *

After editing Rothenberg's Sunday paper, Delano was an expert in running a ruthless tabloid-style staff that pulled off the journalistic coups that earned millions and were published globally.

Eight staff reporters from his former London Sunday paper, plus brash paparazzi photographers from Latin America, worked freelance for the agency. They were tenacious men and women who would go to any length to get the best stories and pictures – and the big bonuses that went with them.

Celeb Scoops International exploited the global demand for all forms of Hollywood news and pictures, especially scandals – the dirtier the better. CSI gained rapid success with clients throughout the world.

Delano lost himself in the business, hoping to distract himself from Rachel's plight – but she was always on his mind. And even now in California, he wasn't free of her father's continuing malice against him.

Lord Rothenberg's first move against Delano in the US was to forbid his media worldwide from buying stories or pictures marketed by the agency. When that wasn't enough, the mogul sought unsuccessfully to widen the embargo to other publishers where he had influence.

"I want them driven out of the scandal business, blacklisted throughout the entertainment industry," Rothenberg thundered at an LA meeting of fellow movie magnates.

"Keep their reporters and photographers off your sets. Forbid them from interviewing your talent. Have them arrested if they trespass. These scum hacks and paparazzi working for CSI are untrustworthy, especially Delano. He's a thief. I'll remind you, he stole money from our organization when I employed him."

But Hollywood ostracism failed. Delano's cutthroat crew, with a big budget for travel and bribes, dug deep for stories, pictures, and videos that filled scandal magazines and TV entertainment everywhere.

Los Angeles was a town full of snitches. People who worked for actors, producers, or directors often went from worshiping to detesting their bosses. Motivated by greed or by the humiliating treatment they received, many revenged themselves on their narcissistic employers by becoming paid informants to the burgeoning scandal industry.

In CSI, Delano and Fuller had built Hollywood's premiere spy network. They harnessed the avarice of show business eyes and ears far and wide. Informants worked at all levels: publicity-seeking cosmetic surgeons promoted their skills, leaked the names of famous clients; mistreated house servants spilled the beans on unkind employers; money-hungry press agents and envious actors seeking to hurt rival thespians tattled on their enemies; corrupt cops sold information and tips for photo opportunities when they arrested criminal celebrities.

Word spread that Delano paid the most generously for scoops. CSI invested six-figure amounts in series that became blockbusters and paid hundreds for smaller news items.

Incriminating photos, love letters, or recordings that authenticated scandal were worth many times their weight in gold if they supported page-one stories that drew millions of hits on the internet and sold countless newspapers and magazines.

The agency went to extraordinary lengths to get exclusives. It bugged celebrity homes, hacked phones, and computers. Its reporters even picked over celebrity garbage for news leads.

CSI's photographers pursued stars on motorcycles, planes, and boats. Very little happened in Tinseltown – and in cities around the world – without Delano and Fuller learning about it.

Broken marriages, new romances, drug addiction, and celebrity illness provided the most salable stories. When stars fell sick, money-hungry nurses and orderlies earned extra cash by tipping the agency off.

Their newshounds chased ambulances, photographed actors arrested in drug busts, drunk driving incidents, even murder cases. They caught married celebrities with male and female prostitutes and in various other compromising circumstances.

It was all grist for the worldwide scandal mill that had become a multi-billion-dollar industry. Delano and his team had let the sleaze genie out of the bottle – and it was never going back. The celebrity media's editors relied on their pictures and reports.

Despite Rothenberg's attempts at smothering him, Mike revealed numerous secrets Paragon Pictures tried concealing from the public. But regardless of his new success, Delano remained a tortured man.

He felt degraded by the cash-for-scandal business, of which he was now a leading practitioner. Becoming part of Hollywood's destructive dream factory sickened him even more than his stint on Rothenberg's tabloid.

Mike yearned for his previous journalistic career, where he took pride in his work. And his inability to get Rachel out of the Swiss clinic tormented him, as did the thought that their romance was over.

Moreover, his cynicism grew as he hunted the rich and famous. He saw actors as addicts hooked on wealth, power, and fame. Unlike mainstream reporters who functioned as cogs in the Hollywood publicity machine, fawning over celebrities, Delano had no liking for them. He detested their exploitive studio bosses even more.

Above all others, he loathed Rothenberg. The mogul had seduced him into swapping quality journalism for muckraking – and although he was getting wealthy, he blamed himself for being weak enough to be drawn into it.

Nor would he ever forgive the media mogul for cruelly abusing and snatching away the one woman he'd ever loved. He held on to one shred of optimism – his belief that by squeezing Paragon Pictures and exposing its criminality, he could break the mogul's grip on Rachel's captivity.

Mike marked Paragon's top star, Morgan Masterson, as his main target for scandalous exposure. The globally renowned married actor was a skirt-chasing drug freak and child molester – his decadence hidden from his enormous fan base.

Women were crazy for Morgan's long-lashed liquid brown eyes and the way gray stubble outlined his chiseled jaw. At six-foot-two, with sleek dark hair and a classically-toned body, he was a Hollywood god.

Rothenberg's lawyers silenced scandal stories about Morgan with libel actions, injunctions, and threats. Starlets, who previously had been willing to talk about sexual harassment from Masterson, developed sudden amnesia.

Paragon paid them off with cash or promises of better roles. Under threat of banishment from Hollywood, they signed nondisclosure agreements and kept their mouths shut.

The murder of Carmelita Sanchez weighed heavily on Delano. The violent death of his source strengthened his determination to ruin Morgan – and through his downfall deal Paragon Studios and Lord Rothenberg a savage blow.

CHAPTER ELEVEN:

HIGH FLIER

No hint of grey appeared among the white clouds seen from the Airbus A321 flying from Los Angeles to New York. Nevertheless, Morgan Masterson was peevish in the comfort of his first-class seat.

Morgan demanded the best of everything – and griped when he didn't get it. He usually traveled in one of Paragon's Lear jets, but on this day, corporate brass had seized both company aircraft to attend a sales conference in the Bahamas.

The only worthwhile part of Morgan's enforced commercial flight concerned a honey blonde crewmember named Suzanne. This flirtatious flight attendant paid him thrice the attention she gave other passengers, cooing her admiration for his acting and movies.

Soon he was thinking how good it would be to bed her. Morgan became aroused when her breast softly nudged him as she leaned over to adjust his pillow. He read it as an invitation to easy seduction, and before they landed at Kennedy Airport, he had her phone number.

This latest flirtation annoyed Marilyn Gonzales, his battle-scarred assistant seated beside him. Keeping him out of trouble was the trickiest part of her job. It was always the same traveling with Morgan, and it disgusted her. He just couldn't leave women alone.

It happened on sets with ambitious starlets, at Hollywood parties, at fan club events. He even picked up attractive waitresses and barmaids. His dalliances cost the studio a fortune in hush money – and kept her employed.

Marilyn worked hard alongside Paragon's PR people to keep Morgan's name out of the worst gossip columns. In turn, his promoters buffed and polished his image with "tame" writers as a family-man superstar with one of Hollywood's rare lasting marriages.

Paragon exploited that image in photo features and interviews. His films earned hundreds of millions annually. Studio executives feared the world learning the truth about Morgan: his so-called "happy" marriage to country music superstar Delia LaBelle was contrived and phony.

Delia had given birth to two children, and then they adopted four more. He'd fought his wife each time she suggested another foreign adoption. He branded her obsession with taking in orphans "sick" and urged her to get psychiatric help.

The reality was his devoutly Christian wife and their demanding brats bored the narcissistic Morgan. He was a lousy father and stayed away from home as much as possible, but it didn't stop him posing with Delia and their brood for magazine covers.

Publicity about "Hollywood's Father of the Year" and the "Happiest Marriage in Tinseltown" boosted his popularity. Image and career success were all that mattered to him.

Ogling the attractive flight attendant diverted the superstar from brooding over career setbacks. His last two pictures had been OK, but not the smash hits he needed. He was banking on his next film, a Vietnam saga called *Mission Cyclops*, to restore him to glory. Shooting would start soon in Florida.

"We'll be landing shortly, Mr. Masterson," said Suzanne, her curvy body and Texas twang adding fuel to his already surging libido. "Time to buckle up. Bring your seat to an upright position."

He smiled up into her green eyes. Subtleties of their color changed every time he gazed into them. He could see her melting at his interest. It was difficult for her to look away. There was heat between them – and they both knew it.

"I'm buckling up, as requested," he said, giving her the full wattage of his superhero smile. "It's been an excellent flight, the service splendid."

When she tucked his tray table away, he spoke more quietly and rapidly into her ear.

"Thanks for giving me your number. I'll be in touch. Promise."

* * *

When Suzanne arrived at her West Side apartment that evening, she called Skip Henderson, a gay "entrepreneur" who lived mostly by dealing cocaine to wealthy clients, several of whom were his lovers. He also had a profitable sideline selling tittle-tattle to tabloid reporters.

"You'll never guess who was on board tonight!" she told him, giggling tantalizingly.

"I have no idea. Why don't you tell me?" Skip snapped. She irritated him with guessing games when all he wanted to do was return to a movie he'd paused on his DVR.

"I was working first-class, and there he was – *the* Morgan Masterson. He was wonderful. Such a gentleman, as mama would say. He took my number, promised to call. He's here all week," she said triumphantly, knowing Skip also had the hots for the tall, dark, and handsome actor.

"Of course, you know he's married," Skip said imperiously, nastily trying to bring her back to earth.

"Who doesn't?" she responded irritated.

"Was he with another woman, not his wife?" Skip asked. "We can make a buck out of that, you know, ‹Morgan Flies to New York with Mystery Woman.' That's worth a few hundred. I'll cut you in if I sell it."

It was her turn to be impatient. She'd been thinking of getting laid, not making money. And she wondered if Morgan could be the key to her new future. Modeling was one of her ambitions. Why not acting? Mama had also taught her well: never allow an exploitable event to get past her.

"Sorry to disappoint you. Morgan was with a dowdy Hispanic, his assistant," she said. "I'll let you know if he takes me out. I don't want money..."

She paused. "Just get my picture in the papers. I'm sick of flying. Time for me to move on – modeling, acting. Meeting Morgan could be the break I need..."

Skip saw real possibilities in their assignation – serious money possibilities.

"For sure, I'll get your picture in the papers if you date him. Make sure to give me all the details – before and after."

"I'll do that," she cooed. "Goodnight, Skip. I love you..."

"Yeah, love you too, doll."

They each hung up happy, each scheming how to exploit Paragon's biggest star.

Suzanne didn't trust Skip. She'd given him news tips on famous passengers before. The payment was often less than she expected, not the 50-50 split he promised.

Skip had a key to her apartment so he could take care of her cat when she was flying. Now he hatched a bigger plan – suggested by the reporter he called about selling the story – for if and when she bedded the superstar.

Once Skip knew when Suzanne was seeing Morgan, he'd slip into her apartment after she left for the assignation. He would hide a motion-activated video recorder in her bedroom – without telling her, naturally. Even knowing her greed for fame and money, he figured she'd balk at such a distasteful plan.

* * *

By Friday afternoon, Suzanne was on edge. She would be on a flight to Tokyo Sunday night, and still no call from Morgan Masterson. She'd just about given up on him when her cellphone rang.

"Sorry it took so long to call," Masterson said, assuming she'd know who was speaking. "I've been in meetings all week, promoting the new flick I'm doing."

"Oh, I understand. It sounds like you've been *real* busy," Suzanne said with just enough edge to her drawl to make her point: she didn't like such neglect, even from famous actors.

"You sound unhappy, but I honestly have been thinking about you. Just haven't had a minute alone," he soothed. "Let me take you to dinner tonight."

Her heart hammered. She struggled not to sound too eager before agreeing. When Morgan asked where they should meet, she suggested an out-of-the-way West Side Japanese restaurant.

"No one will bother you there. I know the owners. They'll give us a table in the back."

"Sounds excellent," he said, admiring that she understood his need to keep a low profile. "Fans can spoil a meal, much as I love them. Keeping our dinner private makes it even more special, being with you," he added while neglecting to say it also made it much less likely his wife Delia would find out.

Suzanne assured him she was on board with keeping their date discreet, adding: "I'm so looking forward to seeing you…"

"Me too. I want to see all of you," he said with a suggestive chuckle.

Her cheeks flushed. She might be hoping to get a shot at a new career from Morgan, but she'd also fantasized about him since her teen years. Hearing his seductive voice over the phone was a thrill; she was even more excited at the prospect of being with him one-on-one.

Most of Morgan's movies included at least one opportunity to show off his Olympian chest and muscular physique. He moved across the screen with feline grace. And his voice! The way he delivered his lines turned her on. She was the lucky woman who would have him exclusively – at least for this night. They agreed to meet at seven o'clock at the Asian Pearl.

Marilyn Gonzales heard only Morgan's side of the conversation. It was enough to tell his assistant that she'd be on her own that night. She'd enjoy some time alone in Paragon's penthouse on 56th Street and Park Avenue, where they were both staying and where he expected her to cater to his every whim.

The studio kept the Manhattan apartment for visiting VIPs. Morgan was in a spacious master suite with sweeping views of Central Park. Marilyn took a smaller but still comfortable room down a hall off the living room.

Marilyn knew he had arranged to see his airline pick-up. She prayed he'd be discreet. She'd share the blame if he got into trouble again. They'd both face the wrath of Rothenberg if a whiff of scandal attached itself to this promotional tour.

Morgan appeared from the master suite showered, shaved, and set for seduction. Though she'd never say so, Marilyn had to admit he looked good: hair gelled and styled, his grayish stubble trimmed to a fashionable length. His faded blue jeans were a perfect fit, molded to his tight buttocks, showcasing his long legs. The whiteness of his t-shirt contrasted nicely with a soft black leather jacket that set off his powerful shoulders. Daily work-outs and a personal trainer kept his 46-year-old body in good shape.

"How do I look?" he asked, his face purposefully composed in profile to look its most appealing as if cameras were rolling.

"Fetching," Marilyn noted sarcastically, putting down a glass of red wine, the first of many she planned for the evening. "So, you're slumming with the flight attendant tonight?"

He'd wanted to be rid of Marilyn's annoying presence for some time but couldn't fire her. He knew as long as she kept reporting his actions to management, her job was safe. She was the studio's leash on him, working under Liz Hightower's protection. If he went too far in any indiscretion, Marilyn yanked him back – and there was nothing he could do about that.

"For Christ's sake, Marilyn, don't go looking down your nose at me. I've been working my ass off. Don't I deserve some fun?"

He didn't wait for an answer. Marilyn looked happy enough, swigging her red wine. That should keep her quiet, he thought.

"It's been a boring fucking trip – all business," he snapped over his shoulder, heading for the elevator. But Marilyn was no longer listening.

Morgan spotted Suzanne waiting under the restaurant canopy. He had opted for the anonymity of a cab to get to the Asian Pearl, not a company limo.

The sight of her long blonde hair piled up on her head, and casual sweater dress that clung to every curve provoked a quiet whistle. The cab driver looked in the rearview mirror and grinned.

Her girl-next-door freshness appealed to him: tanned skin, great figure, and nectar-sweet lips. Her wide green eyes shone with pleasure at seeing him again, and Morgan knew he was in for an exciting night.

The Japanese meal turned out to be excellent, the restaurant the right choice. As Suzanne had promised, the owners seated them in a rear booth where he wouldn't attract attention. The media would pay plenty for pictures of him with a beautiful woman other than his wife, and everyone had a camera these days. Such photos appeared with snide headlines: "Where's Delia Tonight?" or "Morgan's Out on the Town Again!"

These "gotcha" images maddened Delia. There was always a row when she saw them. But Morgan secretly enjoyed tabloid attention; he believed in the adage that bad publicity was better than no publicity at all.

As he began aging, he was glad when the rags printed pictures that made him seem intriguing. He needed to keep fans hooked. He thought, to hell with Delia and her carping; he didn't divorce her because of the bad publicity it would attract, not to mention the millions a split would cost.

He fervently wished he were single and didn't have to answer to Delia, Marilyn, or Liz Hightower. They were a bunch of witches hovering menacingly over his love life.

Plum wine and sake smoothed the flow of conversation. Suzanne amused him with tales of her Texas childhood and adventures as a flight attendant. He boasted how he never looked back after swapping bleak Nebraskan farm life for California.

His brash self-assurance captivated her. Suzanne had been around many men, but Morgan was a particular turn-on. He radiated confidence. He was famous, amusing, and rich. Side by side in a booth, they held hands between courses, snuggled a bit, and before dessert arrived, they had kissed.

Morgan suggested they return to Paragon's penthouse, where he figured Marilyn would be in her room, curled up with her bottle of wine or already asleep. He thought the ambiance of the studio's opulent apartment would help get Suzanne into bed.

"You'll love it," he said. "You can see all over Manhattan from the terrace. It overlooks Central Park."

But she pointed out her place was much closer, only two blocks away, and she lived alone: "Let's go there for a nightcap. Maybe you'd like to smoke some hash?"

The prospect of getting high with Suzanne swung the deal for Morgan. He couldn't wait to screw her. Stoned, she'd be all the better, he thought. They walked to her Riverside Drive apartment with a sixth-floor view of the Hudson River.

Morgan wondered how she managed such a pad in Manhattan on a flight attendant's salary. Naturally, Suzanne never mentioned her two elderly married lovers helping to cover the mortgage.

This young woman gave nothing away; men who wanted to play had to pay, one way or another. Suzanne felt certain Morgan would help make the necessary introductions for a modeling career if she pleased him.

He sipped brandy and watched her deft fingers load a crystal pipe with hash. She explained how a colleague who flew with Air India smuggled the potent drug in from Afghanistan. Suzanne handed him the pipe, and he inhaled the pungent smoke deep into his lungs.

It lifted him from celebrity demands and blotted out thoughts of his unsatisfying marriage, making Suzanne a shimmering golden image of sexuality. She made him feel loose and free – like he was 18 again.

She went into the bedroom after saying: "I'll slip into something a little more comfortable." He was already high enough to find the cliché to be the height of wit and chuckled appreciatively.

The smile that first attracted him on the plane was full of promise when she returned. He couldn't wait to hold and stroke her firm breasts, tantalizingly visible under a lace-trimmed black negligee.

Her hair fell in a golden cascade around tanned shoulders. The sweetness of her perfume filled Morgan's nostrils. Aching to be inside her, he was hard immediately.

"I've wanted this from the moment I saw you," he whispered, following her into the bedroom, shedding his clothes, lying on the bed, throbbing with lust. Lifting her nightgown, she straddled him and guided him into her.

Their lips met as they locked together, each hungry for the other. This woman is no star-fucker, he told himself. The way she moved showed how much she wanted him. She far surpassed Morgan's usual prey of role-seeking starlets.

He relished the feel of her, the smell of her. His passion heightened in the next hour as they progressed from hashish to cocaine – which he snorted off her body.

Eager to keep his high going, he stumbled from the bed to search the inside pocket of his leather jacket. He reached in for the China white, mixed it with the hash, and offered it to Suzanne.

"What is it?" she asked.

"China white – pure heroin. It's OK to smoke when it's not mixed with a bunch of crap. I do it all the time," he said with a wink and an encouraging grin that had made so many fans swoon.

They both smoked, passing the pipe back and forth. Suzanne was up for anything Morgan wanted. They tried screwing again, but he kept going limp and slipping out of her. Angry, he pushed her head down for her to take him in her mouth.

With a desperate shake of her head, she turned aside feeling nauseous. Suddenly, she was vomiting off the side of the bed and began to shake uncontrollably. Only mildly concerned, Morgan slid over to the other side of the bed.

His eyelids heavy, his whole frame went limp as he fell asleep. He woke up hours later to find Suzanne hanging head down off the bed, her hair matted with puke, her breasts flattened against the rug, her buttocks stuck grotesquely in the air.

He shook her. No response. Panicking, he felt for a pulse. Thinking he felt something, though weak and fluttery, he thought with relief, "She's alive." But relief turned to terror: "What should I do?"

His hand flinched toward the phone until he thought better of it.

"I have to get out of here. Discovered with some overdosed bimbo? It'll ruin me!" He'd been in bad spots before, but nothing as terrifying as this.

Still drunk and high, he managed to struggle into his clothes. He left the building, thanking his lucky stars nobody had seen him.

He never spotted the lens poking through an opening in a basket of artificial orchids atop the bookcase where Skip Henderson had carefully focused it on the bed hours earlier. The extended play digital camcorder had recorded everything.

* * *

When Henderson phoned Suzanne the following afternoon, there was no reply. Concerned, he hurried to her apartment to check it out. What he found made him feel ill, faint with disgust and horror.

He discovered his friend as Morgan had left her, face-down in a pool of puke, hanging off the bed, buttocks stuck in the air, lifeless. Any chance of revival was long gone. Skip gagged, then pulled himself together.

Calling the paramedics now was useless. Skip figured she'd been dead for hours. He mourned his friend, but he wasn't leaving the recording device for the police to find. God knows what was on it.

After wiping his fingerprints from everything he'd touched, he picked up his recorder and left. His contact in LA was a journalist who scooped everybody with Hollywood stories. When called with tips, Mike Delano had always been polite, helpful, and fair. He paid well, more than anyone else. And Delano always had ideas to help a story along.

When Skip had told him the previous day about Suzanne's date with Morgan Masterson, Delano suggested placing a recorder in the bedroom to capture any possible action. "It'll provide backup to anything I may write about their affair," Delano had said casually. "A recording keeps the lawyers off my back. They can't argue with it."

Skip rejoiced in having taken Delano's advice. Sad as it was to have lost Suzanne, what he had in his hand now was like a solid gold bar. When he'd played the recording, it was clear Masterson had left Suzanne to die of an overdose after their marathon sex and drug session.

He was sure the actor could have saved her by calling the paramedics. Instead, the coward fled after feeding her a dose of heroin. Skip left a teasing voicemail message: "Mike, you want to buy a sex and death recording – involving the one person at Paragon you're especially interested in?"

He paused for a moment and added: "Your honey trap went wrong. My dear friend is dead, and that cowardly motherfucker ran out on her. You'll want this. Call me and let's talk money."

CHAPTER TWELVE:

LYING PATIENT

Back in Beverly Hills, Morgan Masterson sat squirming before Dr. Amie Abendroth, giving his version of the events causing him to flee the ugly scene in Suzanne's apartment.

He showed neither guilt nor sorrow for her death – only an overwhelming fear of losing his career if the public, or police, learned about his involvement in the flight attendant's overdose.

"The drugs were hers. I fell asleep. She was dead when I woke up," Morgan lied. "Amie, there was nothing I could do. I had to get out. If it became known I was present, the press would have crucified me..."

His voice trailed off as he stopped begging his psychiatrist's approval. Rather than the assurance he sought, he received a prolonged silence. Only the distant hum of Sunset Boulevard traffic six floors below penetrated the cozy office with its deep, body-hugging chairs, potted palms, and calming abstract art.

Dr. Amie wasn't in a generous, forgiving mood. Genuinely horrified by what she'd heard, disapproval furrowed her brow.

"I'd have thought your first concern would have been for Delia and your children – what your latest debacle would do to them if they learned about it," she said.

"Let's not forget a young woman died sharing drugs with you. Don't you care about that? Doesn't your lack of concern point to the repeated pattern of bad behavior we've discussed so many times?"

Morgan struggled to hold back angry tears. His reaction to censure was always fury and tears. He was an overindulged child who couldn't take any form of criticism. He pushed deeper into the wing-backed patient chair, where he'd sat through many similar rebukes for inexcusable behavior.

"Now *you're* turning on me," he protested. "Of course, I worry about my family. God knows, Delia might condemn me publicly if this gets out. Our marriage already hangs by a thread."

Dr. Abendroth hated his whining, his gutless protests, and often considered dropping him as a patient. Psychiatrists were supposed to remain neutral and non-judgmental, but she was struggling to do so with this client.

His latest stunt was gnawing away at her impartiality. She knew the truth: Morgan's wife bored him, and he cynically allowed their many adoptions to keep her occupied while he chased women.

Morgan would never change. He was a sociopath viewing himself as the only "real" person on the planet. Everybody else was a prop in his life story. Others didn't feel emotions or pain with the intensity he did.

He was the one who mattered. He was the only one who existed. His ego was a ravenous monster that needed constant feeding. Still, his psychiatrist tried to make sense of the impossible problems he brought her.

"You must shape up, Morgan. If you want your family to respect you, stop cheating. Go home more often. Show love. I thought you'd learned how to feel for others. It's not constantly all about you."

Her words offended him, but he nodded reluctant agreement.

"You're right. I must spend more time at home. I don't want them reading crap about me in those fucking tabloids."

Dr. Amie shook her head. Continued success made his behavior more toxic. He'd been a patient for eight years; they had barely made any progress. Therapy hadn't helped his addictions. He was a disappointment to everyone who got close to him.

She wondered why she'd failed so badly with this predator. He lied to her about everything – and she knew it. His show of personal weakness was in bizarre contrast to the strength he portrayed on the screen.

Dr. Amie wanted to slap him, tell him to stop behaving like a scared child. This time, evil had caught up with him, putting him beyond her help.

She'd had other clients like Morgan: impossible to fix. She knew he was unlikely to change, but she kept seeing him.

He paid promptly and, after treating him for years, she felt a responsibility towards him. After all, she was the only person who would confront him with the truth.

A tiny gray-haired woman with intelligent eyes focusing from behind bottle-thick glasses, Dr. Abendroth added more notes to Morgan's file as she asked: "What do you think you should do?"

"Keep quiet, go on with my life, and hope it dies down," Morgan responded more casually than he felt.

"Do you think that's a good idea?" she prodded.

"I dunno. What do you think I should do?"

"It's not my place to tell you what you should do. You tell me," she responded, knowing that the law in California would prevent her from reporting a crime confessed to her in therapy, though she wished she could.

"What other options do you have?"

"Call the police? Tell them I was there? That what happened wasn't my fault? That the woman had a fatal reaction to the cocaine she supplied?" he barked back, omitting any mention of heroin. "That's how it was!"

"The drugs were all hers," he repeated. "I panicked and left. I called 911 when I got back to the company penthouse. I gave them the girl's address and told them she'd overdosed."

"It was an anonymous call?"

Morgan shifted uncomfortably in his chair. "I didn't give any name."

It was another lie. Dr. Abendroth doubted he'd called anyone; he was too much of a coward. She knew him: he hadn't cared whether the woman was dead or alive when he fled.

"I couldn't tell the cops I was there," he said firmly. "It would get out. Delia would divorce me. Fans would desert me. Rothenberg would go berserk. Ax me from two important films I'm about to do."

The psychiatrist struggled to maintain her cultivated neutrality. Morgan exploited everyone, especially women. His pleas for help when his reckless adventures went wrong were tiring in their frequency.

"Well then, any other options?

"I supposed I could tell Max the truth," he offered with little conviction. "Warn him, just in case any of this blows back on me."

Morgan sank even deeper into his chair as he mulled over going to the boss. He recalled that the restaurant owners where he dined with Suzanne knew he'd been there, and he'd foolishly used a credit card to pay for dinner. Sooner or later, they'd find out he was the last person to see her alive.

"Goddammit," he snapped miserably. "I'm screwed!"

Dr. Abendroth couldn't stop herself from nodding in agreement. And she reproached herself for feeling glad he was getting his comeuppance.

Morgan was pale when he left the doctor's office, driving home in a daze. What else had he forgotten?

Luckily it hadn't happened in LA. That piece of shit scandal writer, Delano, would have gotten onto it. Then he'd be fucked for sure. The scumbag reporter seemed determined to find and publish dirt on him. Why?

He hadn't done him any harm. Thank God the studio had taken care of the problem with Carmelita Sanchez.

Perhaps confessing to Max was the best way to go. Maybe Max could make this go away, too. It was his best option.

He didn't care how they resolved it as long as this latest problem disappeared, like the treacherous Mexican bitch had.

Arriving at his Bel Air mansion troubled, Morgan put on a happy face for his wife and the kids. His friendliness made Delia suspicious. She wondered why he was being so nice. What was he hiding, now?

She decided it was a good time to announce the planned adoption of another child, a Nigerian orphan boy. Oddly enough, he seemed to take in stride the news that their brood would now number seven.

"The more, the merrier," he said, with only a hint of his usual bitter sarcasm.

Morgan had no doubt he'd married a lunatic. Delia collected brats the way other nut-jobs filled their homes with stray cats and dogs; in her case, it was boys and girls. Collapsing onto the bed in the master suite, he lit a joint to ease his concerns, wishing he had some China white, too.

He considered his session with Dr. Amie. It wasn't comforting, but she had pushed him towards reality. He must come clean with Max about the Suzanne debacle. The boss was in LA, but would soon leave for his Costa Rican Island. Best to get to him before he left.

Max would know how to handle everything.

CHAPTER THIRTEEN:

BOMBSHELL

A few miles from Morgan's Bel Air mansion, an ecstatic Mike Delano spun up the disk in his video player for the third time. He had paid Skip Henderson $150,000 for this recording. It was the most he'd invested in backup for a single story – but worth every penny.

It was the exclusive that would destroy Masterson and blow Lord Rothenberg's evil personage to smithereens. Delano pressed the play button for another viewing.

Morgan's cunning studio protectors couldn't defuse this bombshell. This video would leave Paragon's legal team speechless.

The screen flickered, and the pixels resolved into two lustful figures, images that filled Delano with malicious delight. The rutting superstar's performance was devastating – and this time, he wasn't acting.

Oblivious to everything other than his lust, his features stood out in all frames. Morgan's lawyers would never be able to claim it wasn't him. The sound was clear, too: the actor's animalistic grunts, Suzanne's orgasmic moans.

He could hear Morgan's famous voice, so powerful and gravelly that you'd think he had an extra testicle: "You got any blow, honey? Keeps me hard…"

Suzanne obediently produced the coke with a silver straw from a bedside cabinet. Grabbing the narcotic, Morgan ignored the straw and spilled white powder from the bag onto her waxed pubes in a streak of powdery white.

Then he went down on her like one of Italy's Lagotto Romagnolo dogs rooting for truffles. His fervor momentarily spent, Morgan sniffed his fingers. The aroma of juicy sex and drugs pleased him. It stimulated his libido, but his body let him down.

When he tried mounting her again, Morgan couldn't maintain his erection. Impotence frustrated this spoiled playboy. He twisted his features with ugly annoyance, preparing to throw a tantrum. The camera caught his usually picture-perfect persona in sordid disarray.

Sexual contortions had converted his gelled hair into a wild mop, and sweat cut snail trails across his coke-smeared face. His pupils looked enormous. Vexed, he staggered off the bed to his jacket to get a bag of white powder.

Grinning lopsidedly, he shook the plastic bag at Suzanne, saying, "China white, baby!"

The actor mixed his heroin with Suzanne's hash and cocaine with the knowledgeable look of a medieval alchemist.

Pleased by his concoction, he loaded the powerful mixture into the deep bowl of Suzanne's crystal pipe. They took turns smoking, refilling the bowl until his narcotic brew was all consumed.

Then, everything went wrong. When Morgan still couldn't get hard, he pushed Suzanne's blonde head down to his limp penis. Working with her lips and tongue she tried bravely to stimulate him but suddenly gagged. She freed herself from his grip and hung off the bed, vomiting the contents of her stomach into the thick shag carpet.

Morgan watched angrily, his drugged-out face registering only self-ish fury at her failure to get him off. When he tried pulling her limp form back, she was too heavy for him to lift.

Still retching, she slipped face-down and helpless into the pool of her vomit, her milky-white buttocks sticking up as if mocking Morgan's failed rescue. Discontented, he turned away, moving to the other side of the bed.

Delano sensed the actor wanted no further dealings with her. To him, she'd become a sickly lump of used and smelly flesh. Oblivious to her choking gurgles, instead of helping, he slugged down a shot of brandy and passed out.

Mike fast-forwarded through the recording, picking up the action again. It showed Morgan now awake, walking around the bed and urgently shaking Suzanne without response.

The actor shuddered with disgust at the stinking mess she'd become. Instead of turning her over, trying to save her, he was leaving. Moving around the room, he snatched up his clothes from where he'd dropped them hours earlier.

In his haste to pull on his skin-tight jeans, he fell backward. Sitting on the rug like some spoiled kid, he finally got his underpants and jeans on.

Standing, he gathered his t-shirt, leather jacket, and shoes, stumbling through the bedroom door to the living room to finish dressing.

He'd left the room without a second glance at the stricken woman who'd so fascinated him an hour before.

Delano couldn't believe what he had – it was dynamite. As they said in the business, this story "had legs," potential for dramatic follow-ups. He could keep various incarnations of this yarn going for weeks.

Every word would be another nail in Rothenberg's coffin. Morgan's career was over. The extent of his decadence would turn off the legions of female fans who'd made him into a box office champion. It would also shatter his marriage to deeply religious Delia.

To assuage any guilt he felt about his role in setting up the honey trap, Delano consoled himself with the thought: "I'm doing the wife and kids a favor, helping them get rid of this worthless son of a bitch."

But deep down, Mike feared he was kidding himself; another young woman had died, and he was destroying an entire family. He brushed aside the discomforting thought.

An avid angler, he grinned, congratulating himself with a loud whoop and cry of: "I finally caught the big one!"

At last, Delano had Rothenberg where he wanted him – and he savored his victory. It was a euphoria similar to what he'd experienced after beheading the Pervert.

Before destroying Paragon's biggest star, he would taunt the mogul by informing him of the imminent publication of an exposé that could withstand any legal challenge his studio cared to mount.

Vindictively, Delano made a show of employing fair journalistic practice by sending Rothenberg a copy of his text and frames from the video, asking for the mogul's comment before publication.

He knew he had the winning hand: unassailable proof that Hollywood's most famous star was a sex-addicted, drug-addicted adulterer. The story and video shattered the phony family-man persona Paragon had foisted on Morgan's fans for decades.

* * *

Rothenberg shook with rage as he studied the devastating demolition of his most valuable superstar property.

The headline screamed: "Movie Hero Abandoned Dying Blonde After Sex and Drug Orgy," by Michael Delano – EXCLUSIVE.

The as-yet-unpublished text followed:

"Paragon Pictures superstar, Morgan Masterson, left a Universal Airlines flight attendant to die after sharing a sex and drugs binge with her.

"The tragic victim was Suzanne Francis, 23, a former beauty queen from Amarillo, Texas. She died choking on vomit caused by a toxic mixture of drugs consumed with Masterson at her luxury Manhattan apartment.

"Paragon Pictures will no doubt seek to hide Masterson's role in Ms. Francis' untimely death. The studio has suppressed previous reports of his adultery and drug use.

"An exclusive video shows Morgan shared a potent brew of narcotics with Ms. Francis. It included heroin, which the screen star supplied and added to the lethal mix.

"Paragon has cloaked past accusations made by women working with Masterson. They complained about his use of drugs and persistent sexual advances.

"His movie set victims alleged the star threatened their dismissal unless they shared opiates or 'snorted' narcotics with him and engaged in sexual acts to keep their roles.

"The video shows Masterson having intercourse with Ms. Francis before she succumbed to a lethal mixture of alcohol, hashish, cocaine – and, more significantly, heroin the actor supplied."

The report went on to describe how Paragon bosses bought off angry starlets forced into having sex with Masterson, how they received cash settlements or substantial film roles in return for their silence.

According to Delano's story, the video proved Masterson supplied the heroin, which was the ultimate cause of the flight attendant's death.

Horrified, Rothenberg studied stills from the recording. They showed his superstar in the act of providing the heroin and mixing it with the other drugs before his lover fell unconscious, choking face-down in the thick vomit-soaked carpet.

There was worse to come as Lord Max read on. Dealing with Carmelita Sanchez's death, Delano's report alleged Paragon Pictures had the housekeeper murdered to prevent her from denouncing Morgan as a child molester.

"Surfers found Mrs. Sanchez, 43, with her throat cut on an Oxnard beach after working for Morgan Masterson's family. Police believe the divorced mother of two's body was weighted and dumped from a boat.

"Mrs. Sanchez told this reporter before she went missing that Masterson tried forcing himself on one of his adopted daughters, a 15-year-old he and his wife, Delia, had adopted from a Peruvian orphanage. Police are still investigating Mrs. Sanchez's murder."

Delano wrote: "In her interview with me, Mrs. Sanchez asserted 'Mr. Masterson, he no-good. His adopted children, the girls fear him. When wife away, he goes to their bedrooms drunk or high, with no clothes on. When they are scared about what he do, I chase him away with broom. He angry. Fires me after what happen with girl from Peru.'"

The story closed with a brutal indictment of Masterson by theatrical agent Skip Henderson, who found Suzanne Francis dead – and had also viewed the videotape.

"This video proves Masterson is both a lecher and a coward. He abandoned Suzanne when he realized she was dying because of the drug cocktail he prepared," Mr. Henderson charged.

"What man leaves a woman to die when he could have helped? It's not what you expect of a screen hero or any decent guy. If he had called medics, they could have saved her. His was an act of gross cowardice, abandoning her. All he cared about was saving his reputation."

Asked who placed the camera used to film the sex and drugs orgy, Henderson didn't admit to working at Delano's bidding.

Instead, he theorized: "I can only think Suzanne did. No doubt, she wanted a memento of their lovemaking."

* * *

When his phone rang an hour later, Delano knew who it would be.

"Rothenberg here," said the cultured British voice Mike knew too well. "I gather it's time you and I had a little chat. See if we can't settle our bad feelings."

Hearing that voice anew gave Delano cold shivers. It revived objectionable memories of his subservience to His Lordship's demands at the Sunday Planet.

Delano swung around in his swivel chair, firing up one of the five Marlboros he allowed himself daily. He had cornered his archenemy – and lit the fuse on the most explosive scandal likely to rock Hollywood this century.

"Hello, Max. I thought it might be you," he answered, forcing his voice to sound respectful, verging toward patronizing sympathy. "I'm fascinated to know your reaction to my story. As good a read as the gems I used to produce for you in the old days, I'd say. The fans will love it, right? What will they say when they learn Paragon cut a woman's throat to protect its biggest star's phony reputation?"

Rothenberg ignored the cynicism, apprehension goading him to get to the point.

"All right, Mike. You've finally got your boot on my neck. Congratulations. I recognize that, so let's get to the bottom line," he said, his voice quivering with rage. "Of course, we've had our differences. But now's the time to put hostility aside, to think in business terms. I want to make you an offer – a good one. But you must drop that story."

Delano laughed mockingly. "I don't know about that. You've put me through nasty shit. You branded me a thief, kidnapped your daughter, and aborted *our* baby – and much more. I'm sure you remember."

"So, what do you want to make this story go away?" Rothenberg interrupted harshly.

"Nothing, I'm just giving you a chance to defend your biggest star before I publish. Morgan's deservedly on the garbage heap when I print this. As for Paragon, there's big trouble coming. People will go to jail for the Carmelita Sanchez murder, maybe even you, Max."

Rothenberg did the calculations. He'd already invested millions in Morgan's yet-to-be-completed next film. He planned other projects starring Masterson. Avoiding his public shaming was Paragon's only possible response. He figured, too, the studio could buy off corrupt detectives investigating the Sanchez killing – but it was all going to look terrible for his studio.

"Why not drop by my office?" he said, breaking the silence, sounding conciliatory. "I know we can come to an understanding."

Delano twisted the knife. "I don't think that's possible. Morgan has to pay for what he's done. So does your studio. You've protected a predator, had an innocent woman murdered. No matter the excuses, I'll publish. I've got my recorder running. What do you want to say?"

"Publish that story, and you'll never see Rachel again. That's what I have to say," Rothenberg said, playing his trump card, steel in his voice. "Don't be a fool, Mike. Come over to my office and talk. There's big money involved, millions. You could benefit personally and financially. You're holding some good cards now, if you play them right."

Delano felt nauseous. It was like his interview on the plane: benefits dangled enticingly. Rothenberg's utilizing his own daughter as a pawn in this dirty game was despicable. But using the Masterson story could be Mike's means of freeing her. With His Lordship bringing Rachel into the equation, Delano felt less set on nailing her vile father – and far more interested in recovering the woman he loved.

His voice was husky as he replied: "When shall I be there?"

Rothenberg sounded relieved, replying: "Does eleven o'clock fit with your plans?"

Delano grunted agreement, putting down the phone. Again, he felt tainted. When would he free Rachel? How many millions were involved? Enough cash could buy them a new life compensating for what they'd suffered: her imprisonment and the abortion, his ruined reputation and lost UK career.

He could gain more from this than simply destroying Max and his depraved actor. At last, he had the power to make the tycoon pay for the misery he had caused. And there would be no deal unless he also rescued the woman he loved.

* * *

Liz Hightower welcomed Delano to Paragon like a long-lost friend, shaking his hand and embracing him fondly, murmuring she was glad he and Max were repairing their breach.

Delano smiled thinly. The two-faced bitch had threatened him with jail the last time they'd spoken. He remembered even if she pretended not to.

Regardless, he followed her lithe form into Max's office suite with its sweeping views of the San Fernando Valley.

His Lordship waited, wearing his poker face, the one he wore when dealing with a challenge. Mike knew what to expect – he'd seen it before.

Delano refused Liz's offer of an aperitif wine and sank into a chair opposite the tycoon.

"Let's get this over fast," he said. "I want Rachel released from your Swiss clinic. I want no more interference from you – and you'll pay generously for the upheaval you've caused in our lives."

"What do I get in return?" Rothenberg countered.

"As much as I hate spiking it, the Morgan Masterson story goes away – at least for now. You break any part of any agreement we make, and it's back in play, published globally – including the material about you having Carmelita Sanchez murdered."

Rothenberg paled with outrage as Delano continued with a warning: "You should know I've copies of the video in three separate bank vaults – as well as in my office safe. Should I inexplicably disappear or meet with an accident, they're ready for release globally with an affidavit attesting to the authenticity of the text."

Delano paused to let his threat sink in.

Rothenberg saw no easy way out of this unpleasant and expensive mess except to negotiate on Delano's terms.

He pulled himself together with difficulty. Everyone had their price, even this menacing hack. The man had betrayed him, ruined Rachel's marriage, destroyed her life, and he should have neutralized him long ago.

"How would you like to make ten million dollars, Mike? Half when you surrender the video – and I mean all copies. The rest when you sign a contract pledging not to write disparaging stories about Paragon and the people I employ?"

Delano rose to leave, moving towards the door. Rothenberg stood, too. "What's the problem? Where are you going?" he nervously inquired.

"Ten million, that's insulting. Do you think I'm still one of your corporate minions? That's the form of compensation you provide burned-out vice presidents when they've nothing more to offer."

"Well, tell me what you want." Rothenberg snapped. "I'll consider it."

"Fifty million dollars on signing our agreement. Another fifty million next year, the money delivered in cash to a Bahamian bank of my choosing," Delano said, still standing a few feet from the door.

Rothenberg looked stunned as he moved behind his desk to light a cigar and ponder this ultimatum.

With Morgan gone, his losses would be just south of $400 million. Buying off the Carmelita Sanchez investigation would cost millions more.

Delano remained standing, poised to depart. His heart hammered. He was about to get what he had come for, what he wanted most.

"And I expect to see Rachel in Europe, as soon as we've settled our business," he said, smiling tightly at Rothenberg. "Do we have a deal?"

Still agonizing about the price tag, Rothenberg hesitated. Bargaining over his daughter made the deal especially bitter. But he knew he couldn't keep her in the clinic much longer. People were questioning her absence.

"Agreed on Rachel. I guess there's nothing I can say or do about her misplaced affection for you," he sniffed miserably. "But I need some time to think about the money."

"What's wrong, Max? Are you getting cheap?" Delano asked. "I print that story, and Morgan's finished. Think about the lawsuits from women he's molested; they'll come out of the woodwork and sue the hell out of you. And then there's the Carmelita problem."

He paused, adding, "And that brings up another concern I have, about the Sanchez family."

"What's that?" Rothenberg asked sharply.

"I want you to send her relatives in Mexico $1.5-million and pay for educating her children. Now do we have the $100-million deal or not?"

Rothenberg nodded grimly, all resistance collapsing: "I'll have my attorney set it up. You'll get the papers by the weekend."

He pressed a buzzer on his desk, and Liz Hightower appeared. She could see from the boss's face the meeting hadn't gone well.

"Liz, show Mr. Delano out," the deflated mogul ordered.

CHAPTER FOURTEEN:

PLOTTERS

"Allah's blessing, my brother. Welcome to Beirut," said Basheer Hakim, warmly embracing and kissing Quinton Werner.

Werner had just stepped off a flight from Zurich, where he'd withdrawn a large sum of money from the Spike's purloined savings account.

"As-salaam," said Basheer's twin brother, Abisha. He added his embraces to the enthusiastic greeting, giving Werner the traditional three kisses, showing recognition, trust, and affection.

Werner responded politely, self-consciously kissing both men as Arab tradition required and speaking one of the few Muslim phrases he knew: "Wa Alaykum Salaam" – peace be unto you.

Basheer and Abisha were distant cousins on Werner's maternal grandmother's side. In the past, they'd visited him in Hollywood, posing as budding film students. In a way, they were. They had learned to produce slick documentaries for Hezbollah jihadists seeking recruits in their fight against Israel and the West.

Werner had dismissed them as a couple of nuts. But now they could be helpful to him. He recalled how they detested the American entertainment industry. The twins held Hollywood – especially Jewish directors, writers, and producers – responsible for the anti-Moslem sentiments pervading movies and television.

Back then, Quinton had scoffed at their intentions to wage jihad against Hollywood. Now, since his clash with Rothenberg and the hitman had left Werner a wanted man, the notion of joining a jihad attacking wealthy show business bosses appealed to him.

Quinton's main aim was to punish Rothenberg for taking out a hit on him. Thus, in return for his cousins' help, he'd agreed to join forces with them in a strike against the Academy Awards, designed to draw global attention by causing the deaths of many well-known people.

The conspirators left the airport in a battered jeep driven by Basheer. By the time they arrived at the twins' home, they had cooked up battle plans that pleased all three of them, with proposals to inflict maximum damage on their common enemies.

Their first crippling blow would be against a Paragon movie shoot in the Florida Everglades. Quinton said it would be a good practice run, knowing Rothenberg stood to lose millions if they pulled it off. Most of this Vietnam epic, starring Morgan Masterson, was already in the can. Paragon needed to film one more big action scene at the core of the movie to complete it.

The second mission would attack the Oscars, which concentrated many of the industry's highly placed people at a single location. They knew bombing the ceremony would draw worldwide attention, playing out on live television.

The twins valued and trusted Werner because he was "family," someone who'd proved he could keep their dark secrets. They respected his knowledge of the American entertainment industry and his contacts on the West Coast. Better still, he had promised to finance their next project.

"Did you bring the money," Basheer asked expectantly, speaking excellent English. "We've planned an onslaught against the Zionists for next month. We need explosives and timers."

"I've got $50,000 for you," Quinton replied, patting his backpack. "What's the target?"

"We're bombing a hotel on the Mediterranean coast. We're expecting it packed with Israeli dignitaries staying there before a political conference with Lebanese politicians," Abisha replied.

"Then we hide for a while in the mountains. Come with us if you like. Maybe a few weeks from now, we'll be ready to help with the American jihadi attacks."

The prospect of living in a cave with them appalled Werner, even if he was on the run after killing Charlie the Spike.

Quinton planned to remain quietly and comfortably in a small Beirut apartment where he would recuperate from cosmetic surgery. He intended to change his appearance and name before returning to the States.

"When are you going back?" Basheer asked.

"Not until I've had the surgery and have a new passport. I'm relying on you guys to help with that."

For an additional $15,000 to pay the cosmetic surgeon and the expert forger who would produce a new American passport under Roberto Costello's name, they agreed.

At the twins' apartment, Werner handed over $65,000 of the $250,000 he'd withdrawn from the Swiss account. With the cash, his cousins set up the arrangements that provided his new identity.

A week later, a nurse wheeled Werner into a secret surgery suite where the doctor usually worked on injured Sunni militants and shadowy Middle Eastern underworld figures. After a few hours he was bundled into a car to take him to recover in his apartment hideout, still groggy from the anesthetic, his head swathed in bandages and wearing dark glasses.

The surgeon had shortened his prominent nose and taken a bump out of the bridge. A silicone pad inserted in his chin removed the cleft and strengthened his jawline. Adjustments to ears, eyebrows, cheeks, and lips completed the job.

Of German and Lebanese descent, Werner, 45, was swarthy with the muscular build of a weight lifter. After his transformation, he could pass for Latin as easily as Middle Eastern. His eyes remained the same: dark, inscrutable, and cold.

Since his Louisiana boyhood, he had been a thug, having fled the South for Los Angeles after a family brawl. It involved a baseball bat and left his mother's lover in a wheelchair and her telling him hysterically, "You're no good. Never, never come back…"

Twelve years later, he emerged as a union leader, feared for his violence. But studio brass valued his heartless abilities – and paid him to solve their labor problems.

He did it by beating up fellow unionists who opposed him, with some rumored gone to early graves in the Mojave Desert.

Back in his initial Hollywood days, Werner had spent his spare time picking up attractive women in San Fernando Valley bars. That was how, years before, he'd met struggling young actor Morgan Masterson, for whom skirt-chasing was also a way of life.

Before Morgan got his first break, he and Werner shared a rental house – and many of the women they met. Their friendship took on a different and more practical turn when Morgan's star ascended, and he married Delia LaBelle.

Marriage, however, didn't curb Morgan's insatiable appetite for sex – and for a time, he relied on Quinton to use threats and violence to silence women boasting too loudly about affairs with him. Their friendship faded as Morgan became a superstar and Paragon's fixers began taking care of his extramarital problems.

Quinton still counted Morgan as a close friend, one of very few he cared about. He relived old times as he came out of the anesthesia, smiling when he thought about their long-ago womanizing.

"We had a lot of fun," he chuckled to himself while recuperating. "And I got him out of a lot of scrapes with women."

He planned next to see a cosmetologist who'd continue his transformation. She would dye his black hair blonde and crop it short. An optometrist would provide contact lenses that turned his brown eyes dark blue.

"Is that you, cousin?" and "I hardly know you anymore," the Hakim twins told Werner upon their return from the mission that killed dozens of Israelis.

"Now you're ready to have new passport pictures taken," Abisha smiled, giving Quinton the address of the forger's studio.

A week later, new passport in hand, Werner left for LA. He intended to hide out in a Van Nuys safe house he had rented.

He supposed Paragon still had a hit out on him; the Chicago mobsters would be looking for him, too.

They'd likely gone to his home and discovered the shallow grave where he'd buried their sword-carrying assassin. Werner was well aware of how these types worked. They'd seek vengeance for his killing of one of their own – and they'd never stop looking for him.

He had to stay hidden until meeting up with the twins in Florida for the movie set attack. Then he'd leave the country, possibly for good.

CHAPTER FIFTEEN:

"MORGAN MORON"

A traumatized Morgan Masterson was surprised to find he still had a career at Paragon. He had just spent a wretched hour with Max Rothenberg, who appeared ready at any second to tear up the contracts for his subsequent three films.

Morgan's sex and drugs binge had violated the morals clause of their agreement. He had tried brazening it out with the Boss, as usual, begging his forgiveness. But groveling seemed only to stoke His Lordship's fury.

Max had angrily shoved aside Morgan's embrace on entering the studio's executive office.

"Don't touch me. Don't speak. Shut up and sit down," Rothenberg growled.

Morgan ignored the warning. "I guess you know, I made a terrible fool of myself in New York," he murmured.

"Shut up, Morgan MORON. That's your new name as far as I'm concerned," Rothenberg snarled. "This latest debauch of yours will cost me more than $100 million in hard cash to pay off someone I despise."

Max's rare admission of failure surprised Masterson. Who had taken him for that enormous sum?

He started to speak: "I can explain…" But seeing Rothenberg about to explode, his ineffectual words trailed off.

"I know all about it," Rothenberg screeched like an eagle swooping on its hapless prey. "A woman's dead, overdosed from heroin you supplied!"

He saw Morgan's eyes go glassy with guilt – and fury at being caught.

"You'd better not start blubbering here, you disgusting creep. It's your worst escapade yet. Drugs. A dead woman! For God's sake, dummy – and all on tape."

Leaning against his expansive desk, looking at the ceiling in search of divine help, Rothenberg raved: "It's criminal. They could lock you up. You supplied heroin. That alone gets you jailed. You left her to die of an over-dose. That finishes you with fans. If it gets out, you're history…"

The suggestion terrified and puzzled Morgan. How could Max know all the details: the drugs, including his supplying the China white, how he ran out on Suzanne?

"Who's telling you these lies?" he asked in a feeble attempt to bluff.

Rothenberg's voice grew thunderous. His mouth was inches from Morgan's face. The actor flinched from each spray of spittle.

"Lies? The only liar here is you. I've seen the pictures. Delano's got the story. He can prove you brought the heroin and left the stupid bitch overdosing." He paused for a fiery drag on his cigar. "And he's got a video of you fornicating, snorting coke off her snatch, giving her heroin."

Morgan was ashen. Max always knew everything. This was it; he was out.

"A video? We weren't recording it."

"Because, moron, your dick led you into a honey trap, the oldest trick in the book," Rothenberg said slowly, contempt dripping venom-like from each harsh word. "Delano set you up, probably with her connivance."

Morgan moaned, tears wetting his cheeks. Head down in humiliated defeat, he made another fumbled try at a response.

"She seemed like a nice kid. I'd just met her. She was a flight attendant on the stupid fucking commercial plane to New York."

Deep sadness replaced the look of rage on Rothenberg's face. He shook his imposing, leonine head as though dealing with an imbecilic child.

"How many times must we save your moronic ass? It's getting so you're not worth it. I've put money and time into your career. You throw it in my face. I should be rid of you permanently."

The word "permanently" penetrated Morgan's terror. He was ready to do anything for one more chance. Career, money, fame, all he lived for lost. Rothenberg could toss him on the Hollywood scrap heap. Morgan had seen him do it to others when angry like this.

"Please, Max, I swear it'll never happen again. You've got my word. On my children's lives," Morgan begged.

Rothenberg snorted scornfully. "Your children? For God's sake, man, you tried screwing some of the girls. Wasn't there enough pussy in town without going after teenagers in your home?"

Then in a softer but more menacing tone, he added: "That's why I have the Carmelita Sanchez problem. Police are still looking into her death. Delano's on to that too…"

Morgan, shuddering at the reminder of his part in Carmelita's death, tried again: "I promise you, Max, no more women, drugs, or booze. I know you don't believe me, but you have my word."

"You must be joking. Your word's not worth the breath it takes to say it."

Relief flooded the actor as Rothenberg went back to sit behind his desk; it was a good sign. Calmer, Max selected a fresh Havana from the teak humidor and snipped off the end in one decisive movement. Like a fire-eating dragon, he drew in the flame from a jewel-encrusted lighter, exhaling a cloud of rich, fragrant smoke.

"Morgan, you do that film in Florida. You'd better make it a success: no crazy behavior, no tarts with cameras, no drugs or seductions. And, incidentally, you're working for scale on this flick, and several more after that. I'm not paying you another cent until I recoup the millions I spent silencing Delano."

"Work for nothing?" Morgan asked incredulously.

"It's not for nothing, *moron*. The things we did cleaning up after you were extremely costly. Don't you understand that?"

He shoved papers across the desk.

"Sign these. When your agent complains, you tell him this new deal is fine with you. He can just take it, or you'll fire him and find a new agent. He'd better not call here asking for more, tell him."

Morgan delivered a shaky signature across the flagged pages.

"I'm sorry, Max. Never happen again, believe me. All I want is one last chance to make good on my word."

Rothenberg looked at him scornfully. "Right, you're still with this studio. But foul up on this project, it's the end of you. Understand? Now go to Florida. You wanted Stuart Cohen to direct this flick. You said he's the finest in the business, that he brings out the best in you. I don't agree, but we got him for you anyway. The dailies so far look good. He's already waiting on the set. You'd better give him your best work. Any questions?"

Morgan shook his head.

Rothenberg pointed to the door.

"Get out. I still have to mop up evidence of your Manhattan fiasco. Paying off the restaurant owner, making sure he doesn't blab about you being there with that unfortunate woman the night she died."

Morgan couldn't leave fast enough. He still had a career; it was all that mattered. One hundred million. He shuddered. Far more than he'd make on the next movie. For Christ's sake, his salary plus more was going to silence that motherfucker Delano. Max could silence anyone, even that reporter douchebag.

A final question nagged as he packed his bags for Florida. What did Rothenberg mean when he warned, "fuck-up on this film, it will be the end of you"?

He knew how Max did business. Carmelita found out the hard way. With sudden foreboding, he knew he'd need to watch his step.

CHAPTER SIXTEEN:

CASH AND CROISSANTS

It took 18 large duffle bags to transport $50 million in cash to the Bahamas. Rothenberg had the money flown in on a studio jet. It landed for a brief time on a secret Bahamian estate runway belonging to one of Max's wealthy associates.

Under Gil Ackerman's watchful eye, the crew pushed the bags out to armed bank guards, and the plane left. An armored SUV ferried the cash weighing 750 pounds in $100 bills into town for clerks at the Freetown Trust Company to count.

Mike Delano had arrived in Freeport three days previously to sign for his cash and set up an account in the name of Anthony Sandys, the alias he had chosen for his offshore banking. It was a month since he'd made his deal with Rothenberg.

He still agonized over his decision to accept the enormous bribe in exchange for dropping the Masterson story. He knew in gaining this fortune, he had sunk further into the gutter.

It was his second day in Nassau, and he was meeting "Major" Ralph Clark-Hall, an unashamedly corrupt banker, for the first time. Clark-Hall was a peppery little man who spoke with the clipped tones of the British upper class.

He looked like a character from a Graham Green novel with a gray military-style mustache and spotless white tropical suit. In reality, the banker had never served in any branch of the armed forces. He was a financial parasite thriving on the dishonesty of others.

Strangely, Clark-Hall's utter lack of integrity made Delano feel less burdened by his plunge from journalistic grace.

"Delighted to make your acquaintance, Mr. Sandys," said the bank manager, using Mike's new alias.

Delano was a junior member of the "one percent club" with just $50 million (and the promise of another $50 million to come). Other depositors had billions stashed away on Caribbean islands, invested in foreign properties, art, and other assets. Their total wealth surpassed the budgets of small nations. Delano had entered a thriving underground economy made up of the shady enterprises he would have attacked when he was an honest reporter. Now he'd joined this gang of filthy-rich global scoundrels.

The Freetown Trust Company was into everything involving dirty money. While it laundered fortunes for drug traffickers, it mainly catered to corporations hiding billions stolen from taxpayers, company shareholders, trade unions, and governments.

Clark-Hall, sensing his new client's thoughts had drifted off, coughed politely to regain his attention. The man seemed perplexed, downcast, even unhappy – not like someone who'd just come into possession of a considerable fortune.

Jolted out of his gloom, Delano shook the manager's outstretched hand. "Yes, good to meet you, too," he said. "The money arrived in good order? It's all there?"

"Yes, it's all there," said the manager. "We've counted it, checked for counterfeits. As I explained in our phone conversations, there will be a three-percent counting fee. We pay no interest on deposits. We can wire you cash anywhere, and you can write checks for which there'll be a small fee."

Delano winced at the mention of the counting fee. "Three per-cent, eh? Guess that's normal," Delano said, accepting it as the high price demanded for handling tainted money.

He followed the manager into his oak-paneled office where fresh-ly-squeezed orange juice, hot coffee, and buttery croissants awaited them.

Delano signed, as Anthony Sandys, for his account. These Brits made tax dodging and unlawful transactions seem like any other honest deal. Clark-Hall was typical of the breed, stylish and polite.

As Mike prepared to bid his suave banker farewell, he cheered up, imagining the pain he'd caused Rothenberg. Max must have hated paying out so much of his own money – and in cash, too.

"Mr. Sandys, it's a pleasure doing business with you," said Clark-Hall. "And I understand there will be another $50 million coming soon. Correct?"

Delano looked at him, smiling as if uncertain of how to answer. "We'll have to wait and see. My benefactor's unpredictable, but I'll make certain he eventually coughs up everything he owes," he replied.

If the remark puzzled the bank manager, he didn't show it. Rothenberg's private attorney had assured him a second cash payment would arrive within six months. To Clark-Hall, this wasn't a big account, but still worth having.

Delano had barely left the bank when he wrote his first check on the account: $3.5 million to the Oceanic Yacht Company for a 53-foot Tartan yacht, a vessel he'd always wanted. He named it *Talespinner* and directed the yard to get her provisioned, ready for sailing within a month.

Leaving the yacht broker, Delano picked up his luggage from the hotel. He took a cab to the airport where he booked a flight to Brussels.

Not only had Rothenberg delivered the first payment as promised, but Mike learned in a phone call from Gerda that the Lucerne clinic had already placed Rachel in her mother's care.

Airborne, pondering his excellent fortune, Delano looked out the window from his first-class seat, down at the brilliant azure ocean with its spectacular clarity. He could see dolphins chasing schools of fish.

There were 700 tropical islands sprinkled over a 100,000-square-mile-archipelago for him to explore once aboard his sailboat. If all went well, he would not be alone.

CHAPTER SEVENTEEN:

TIME TO HEAL

After checking in to the Hotel Metropole in Brussels' historic center, Mike Delano called Gerda Rothenberg.

"Hello, Mr. Delano. Yes, Rachel's here with me. She arrived by ambulance a week ago. I have to tell you that I was shocked by her condition – the weight loss and dark circles under her eyes. My girl will need an abundance of time to recover."

Delano heard the anxious note in the mother's voice. He, too, was concerned about Rachel's health after a year of confinement and what he feared was medical abuse.

"I'm in Brussels, Gerda. I'd like to see her if you think it is advisable," he suggested.

There was an uneasy silence.

"Mr. Delano, Rachel's not as you remember her. They mostly confined her to bed, heavily sedated, for an entire year. She's thin and barely eats. It's like she's in a mental fog. I have arranged for a psychologist to visit her twice a week. She says my daughter's mentally and physically traumatized. She's helping Rachel with the withdrawal from the drugs they forced on her in the clinic."

Delano's rage mounted; his loathing for Rothenberg intensified. He'd never rest until he destroyed him – and again, he felt dirty after doing business with him. But if he hadn't bargained away the Masterson story, he was sure they'd have kept Rachel locked up.

"I realize it's a difficult time, but perhaps I could visit? If it doesn't help, I will leave. But please tell her I'm here. That I tried contacting her at the clinic, writing, phoning. That I couldn't get past security there. Rachel's been on my mind every day. I love her."

Gerda sounded indecisive, wanting what was best for her only child. "I don't want to cause her more stress. I've got your phone number. I'll call, Mr. Delano. Please, be patient. I promise to call, if and when she's ready to see you."

* * *

Two weeks passed and there was no call. Delano fought against his desire to phone again. He bought books to study the effects of long-term bed-ridden sedation. Victims suffered mental and physical damage, sometimes organ failure.

Depressed by what he had learned, Delano stayed in his hotel room, alternating fretfully between reading and watching TV, waiting for Gerda's call. He didn't intend returning to the Bahamas without the woman he loved.

During the fourth week of his long wait, the phone finally rang.

He snatched it up. It was Gerda.

"Hello, Mr. Delano. Would you like to speak to Rachel? She wants to talk to you."

The husky voice he remembered so fondly came through the phone: "Mike, I can't believe you're here. I thought I'd never see you again. Daddy had only bad things to say about you."

Delano saw no point in responding to Rothenberg's lies. Nor did he want to start on the wrong foot with Rachel, who could be extraordinarily loyal to her father.

"How are you?" he asked, his voice trembling, full of longing to communicate the depth of his feelings.

"I've been so confused, and so tired. I want to lose myself, bury myself in sleep, forget what happened to me. I'm no longer how you knew me. I'm in a wheelchair most of the day, I can barely walk; I'm that weak."

"I'm so sorry, Rachel," Mike murmured, his stomach churning at what he heard.

"I don't think I'll ever again be the person you once knew. I don't want to disappoint you when we meet. Maybe you're better off without me," she said, sounding broken.

"Nothing about my life is better without you. I swear it. I'm here to help. No matter what it takes. Or how long it takes to get you back on your feet. I love you."

"My mother says you've built a new life in America. That Daddy drove you out of England. He claimed you were after our money, that you stole from his newspaper. I didn't believe it Mike, didn't want to believe it, but I wasn't in any position to argue."

"All lies, Rachel. He hates me. He couldn't break me, though God knows he tried. I've got him where I want him right now. He won't bother us anymore."

He stopped when he heard sobbing. He could only go so far in discussing Rachel's father. The mogul still had the psychological grip on her he'd established from childhood.

Finally, she spoke again.

"Mike, I was pregnant. I should have said. I made a mistake confiding in the wrong people. They told Daddy, and he called Aaron. He had me kidnapped and the baby aborted. Aaron blamed Daddy for the abortion, but he lied. Bad as he can be, Max wouldn't kill his grandchild."

Delano didn't challenge her belief; he knew exactly who Max could be.

"Let's not go there," he said. "I want you back in my life. I'll leave if you don't feel similarly. Or if seeing me proves a setback."

"Of course, I want to see you, Mike. I need you now more than ever," she replied, her voice breaking. "Thinking about you is what kept me going at that horrible place. I wondered if we'd see each other again."

"Shush, we'll be together," he said, sensing how hurtful her memories were. "Don't worry. I'll help get you well. We'll face this together."

* * *

Mike started Rachel off with gentle strength training while she was still in her wheelchair.

"Let's do a few minutes of moving your arms up and down, holding them out with the weights on," he urged.

"Now the legs," he said, attaching a separate set of weights. "Lift those lovely limbs so I can see them."

It was hard going initially, but as weeks passed in the basement of Gerda's house, where Mike had installed the latest exercise equipment, Rachel gradually grew stronger.

Delano kept her company, exercising alongside her, providing the loving encouragement she needed.

She felt humiliated at no longer being the woman Mike had met two years back, when she beat him at tennis, jumped powerful stallions over six-foot Sussex hedgerows – and never missed an opportunity for passionate lovemaking.

At his encouragement, her lost appetite revived. A month under his tutelage, she gained enough strength to struggle out of the wheelchair without help. He applauded as she took faltering steps around the basement unaided.

Each day, Mike and Gerda were in the kitchen, supervising the cook who prepared the high-protein mini-meals their patient needed.

"For God's sake, I can't eat all this food," Rachel moaned when he brought her midday lunch, soon after midmorning fruit snacks.

"Come on, let's share it. I'll help," Delano said, selecting a juicy piece of steak and eating it with relish.

"It's so tender it will melt in your mouth," he tempted, bringing another meaty morsel to her reluctant lips.

Rachel knew he wouldn't stop treating her like a child until she chewed and swallowed. Five months of the diet and exercise program brought improvements.

Mike looked on appreciatively as the curves he admired so much in the past returned. She was again filling out her clothes admirably.

He'd practically moved into their home, arriving early each morning and leaving in the evening after having dinner with mother and daughter.

"I admire you so much for doing this," Gerda thanked him. "Without you, I don't think she'd have recovered."

The only pauses in the physical therapy Delano readily allowed were for Rachel's twice-weekly sessions with the psychologist.

"What's she telling you?" Mike asked after one of the therapy sessions. "Anything interesting I should hear?"

"Aren't you the nosey one? I guess it's why you're such a fine journalist," Rachel giggled. "And I'm sure you'll approve of what we decided today."

"What was that," he asked eagerly.

"That my love for you is healthy. That my preoccupation with my father is unhealthy. Especially, the unresolved anger I feel over his refusal to give me a role in the business. She says I've spent too many years appeasing a tyrant – that my deep affection for him does me little good."

"She's right about that," Mike grunted, hackles rising at the mention of Rothenberg. "It's no surprise to me he went crazy when he learned about us. His need to control people's lives – especially yours – verges on insanity."

Seeing Rachel's face starting to cloud, he stopped. Surely, she didn't need a shrink to tell her exposure to Max was toxic? That it would require life-long therapy to undo the harm he'd inflicted.

Yet still, she didn't accept her father could have been responsible for the abortion. She continued to blame the ordeal on her late husband.

But Delano didn't challenge her beliefs. He avoided adding to the psychological damage Rachel still carried from the abuse at Rothenberg's foul clinic.

"He's tried to run my life for too long, and I must break free," she finally admitted. "And, Mike, you're the only person on the planet who can help me do that."

Her declaration thrilled him and provided the proper moment for his proposal. He went to one knee, looking up at the woman he adored, declaring: "Rachel. I love you and always will. Please, become my wife?"

"Oh Mike, of course, I will," she responded shakily. "Are you sure you want to continue dealing with my problems?"

"They're nothing we can't handle together," he said, rising to slip an antique emerald and diamond ring on her fourth finger.

Their engagement delighted Gerda. She, too, had come to adore Rachel's handsome and dedicated suitor. Like her daughter, she'd seen the softer, caring side of this warrior-journalist. He was the only man who could protect Rachel from her depraved father.

Radiant, wearing a dark two-piece suit and a white blouse, Rachel married Delano with Gerda as their sole witness in a civil ceremony before the Brussels Registrar.

Gerda's heart went out to Delano. In him, Rachel had found the ideal man with whom to share her future. Looking distinguished in a pinstriped dress suit with a red rose boutonnière, his blue-gray eyes misted with happiness as he wed the woman whose life he'd helped restore.

Rachel was back, her rosy cheeks framed by the inky darkness of her waist-length hair, dark eyes liquid pools of happiness as they exchanged vows. Her short skirt and high heels displayed her recently toned legs as she stood strong beside Mike, a picture of good health holding a bouquet of red roses. There were no signs of her recent ordeal.

After the ceremony, Gerda had their union blessed by a rabbi, and the newlyweds left for the airport to start their Caribbean honeymoon on the first voyage of *Talespinner*.

CHAPTER EIGHTEEN:

CONFLAGRATION

Quinton Werner and his co-conspirators, dressed in camouflage, were in place as darkness fell. At an agreed signal, the three men pushed rubber dinghies into the murky Everglades water, then clambered aboard. With one attacker following the other, they paddled silently out into the gloomy swamp. Each had a 50-caliber machine gun and a magazine full of tracer rounds. They were in touch by radio.

Nearing an island, they heard the prattling voices of extras, the shouts of the director Stuart Cohen and his assistants, readying hundreds of cast members for the movie's climactic scene. The dinghies stopped at three points of the compass in the gloom, away from the island's voices and glaring set lights. The attackers would triangulate their fire when the moment came.

Werner had planned his revenge mission precisely to wreck Rothenberg's blockbuster production's most essential and costliest scene. The only hitch in the plan was the presence on the set of one person Werner cared about, his friend from earlier days in Hollywood, Morgan Masterson. Quinton had risked calling him that afternoon with a warning: "Get out of the helicopter scene. It's gonna go badly wrong."

"Go wrong?" Masterson had inquired nervously.

"Yes, it's going down. Crashing. Don't be on it unless you want to die."

And Werner delivered an extra admonition: "If you rat me out about this, buddy, I can't protect you. The dudes I'm working with will blow your ass away."

Morgan knew enough about Werner's criminal connections to take the warning seriously. If his badass friend said he was in danger, he'd listen. And, no, he wouldn't warn anyone of the coming disaster – Morgan didn't want a bunch of killers coming after him.

There was another component to the superstar's reaction: Masterson resented Rothenberg for making him work for nearly nothing, and he sensed his career might be on the rocks.

So what if Max had paid millions buying off Delano? The cheap motherfucker could afford it. What about the countless millions his films had earned for Paragon? Had the Boss forgotten that, too?

With his salary cut not just on this film but for an indefinite period, he was hurting for money, yet his extravagant spending hadn't changed. He spent plenty on nightclubs, drugs, and casual affairs. Plus, he had seven kids, a spendthrift wife, and staff at the Bel Air mansion to support.

Morgan couldn't see an end to money problems. On top of that, Delia was threatening divorce. She could bankrupt him. That was another concern. Worse, he feared Max would fire him once *Mission Cyclops* was complete.

But even with troubles piled on troubles, Morgan didn't feel suicidal. He rapidly decided his stunt double, Luther McIntyre, must take the fall. Shitty luck for the muscle-bound dummy.

Morgan had never liked him – and that hadn't stopped him from making moves on Luther's stunning Vietnamese fiancée. To hell with scruples, he was grateful for Quinton's timely tipoff. If Luther snuffed it, he'd be first in line to console the Vietnamese beauty.

On the set at dusk with the helicopter warmed up and waiting for him, he feigned sudden illness. Seconds before boarding, he clutched his belly, falling to the ground in apparent agony. Stuart Cohen rushed to his side.

"What's wrong, Morgan?" the director asked.

"I need a doctor, Stuart. I've got a wicked belly ache, diarrhea. Must have picked up some lousy bug working in this stinking swamp…"

"The scene's ready to shoot. We can't delay," he told Morgan without expressing any sympathy. He stood up, shouting new orders: "Luther! You do the next sequence, OK? And somebody come help Morgan to his trailer."

"Yes, Stu, I'm ready," said Luther, giving the superstar a withering look. He walked to the Huey, strapped himself into the open doorway, and then gave the thumbs-up for liftoff.

The craft rose, and the pilots circled. At a signal from the ground, they went to full throttle.

Below, unseen, three armed men in dinghies listened attentively to the whop-whop of helicopter blades slicing through the humid blackness. Their fingers tightened on the triggers of their weapons.

Perched precariously on the chopper skids, Luther didn't like this low-flying assignment. And he was sure Morgan was having one of his "yellow days."

"It's not the first time that asshole's ducked dangerous scenes. I take his place, do the risky work. I keep my mouth shut while he boasts he's a star who performs his own movie stunts," Luther thought bitterly.

While Morgan remained his meal ticket, the man disgusted him. Not a guy to rely on in a battle. You'd never know whether he'd run or stay to fight.

Looking down at the Everglades speeding past 150 feet below, he saw a moving vista of mangroves, sawgrass marshes, and pine flats.

The copter's navigation lights occasionally reflected off the predatory luminescence of an alligator's eyes. It was no comfort knowing such creatures were searching the swamp for fresh meat.

Luther wished he were safely home tucked up with beautiful, loving Hanh Nguyen. She was also working on this film as an extra. They'd wed when the shooting finished; it was all planned. Morgan had been hitting on Hanh, but his fake charm didn't work with her. The actor's moves on his fiancée maddened Luther. Any guy other than his boss, he'd have punched out.

The chopper roared out of the darkness into probing searchlight beams with Luther's eyes narrowing against the sudden brilliance, his mind concentrated on getting his next move right. The pilot slowed from 140 knots to hover at 200 feet. Luther started down a rope he had tossed from the Huey. As he swung beneath the howling rotors, dozens of upturned faces followed his every move.

He was over the island where Paragon had created a perfect replica village of thatched Mekong Delta huts. In this scene, the hero rescued a South Vietnamese general, saving him from the Viet Cong holding him hostage on the island before execution.

With the whirlybird throbbing noisily above, pyrotechnics experts below prepared to fill the sky with sham shell bursts from flack guns. Dozens of extras, clad in black pajamas to portray Viet Cong guerillas, stood amid the huts, Kalashnikovs pointed skyward to let loose salvoes of blanks.

Among them was Luther's fiancée. Hahn instantly recognized the man she loved descending the rope. Why wasn't Masterson doing the big scene himself, she wondered?

A single red rocket burst into the blackness, signaling Stuart Cohen's order to start the barrage. With Luther halfway down the rope, the Huey rocked violently in the volley of pyrotechnic blasts.

Everything was just as Luther expected until the moment live tracer rounds flashed up, snapping past terrifyingly close to his face.

A combat veteran, he recognized "hot" ammunition. Horrified, he saw tracers explode against the helicopter's rear rotor, shattering it. The shells ate their way hungrily along the flimsy vintage chopper's fuselage, coming from three directions.

"Jesus Christ, what the fuck – are they trying to kill us?" Luther screamed as the Huey spun out of control.

With strength born of terror, he clung to the rope he had intended to descend as the machine became an insane monster, bucking and rearing.

Showers of razor-sharp metal shards from the rotors sliced into the upturned faces below. A group of shocked and bloody extras ran screaming, others plunged into the swamp. Shrapnel slaughtered some where they stood.

Luther knew he was about to die. But he clung on stubbornly until the machine's vicious downward spin broke his grip on the rope. Centrifugal force flung him hundreds of feet out into the darkness, the descent rope cracking like a circus trainer's whip behind him.

With the stuntman gone, the howling wreck plunged downwards, creating a deluge of mud and stagnant water as it skimmed the swamp's surface towards a camera crew still doggedly filming, their danger unrecognized.

The Huey's 48-foot spinning blades slashed into the cameraman and his assistants, reducing them to a hail of crimson body parts. The craft's gas tanks exploded as the chopper shuddered to a halt. Its pilots, struggling to free themselves, died in burning aviation fuel.

Within seconds, the bamboo village was a blazing pyre. Shrieking extras ran diving into the water to douse their flaming black costumes.

Fifty yards from the wreck, director Stuart Cohen stood speechless as a shocked Morgan Masterson joined him. The star had heard the crash as he hid in the safety of his trailer. Now he stood next to Cohen, unharmed.

They both gagged at the pungent smell of burning flesh wafting with the smoke. For a moment, the crackle of flaming thatched huts provided the only sound.

Then a wave of reactive noise broke over the pair. The helicopter wreck hissed and steamed when water from fire hoses hit it. Set workers, cut and scorched, screamed for help. Survivors yelled into satellite phones for outside medical assistance.

Shoving her way through the babbling, bleeding crowd, Hanh knew the bitter truth: it was her Luther who'd died, not cowardly Morgan.

Her hatred exploded at seeing him. She ran at the actor, thrusting the steel barrel of a Kalashnikov against his face so forcibly he yelped in surprised agony.

Enraged by the tiny barefoot figure confronting him, Morgan tried wresting the gun from her hands but failed.

"I shoot you in the goddamned face," she screamed, eyes ablaze, finger increasing pressure on the trigger. "I spoil pretty-boy looks..."

He went rigid with terror. Blank cartridges inflicted disfiguring injuries at point-blank range and could even kill. She pressed the Kalashnikov muzzle under his noble chin, and he shuddered at the prospect of her making good on the threat.

"Quit it, bitch, don't do it," he snarled. "Remove that gun, or you'll never work again. I'll finish you in this business even as a lowly fucking extra..."

Hahn's broken English became calm and deliberate as she delivered an ultimatum: "We go find Luther. Now. He need help. You save your lousy skin. I make you pay. Big-time. Tell everyone what you try on me when Luther not home. If you not his boss, he beat you. Say you dirty coward. But he needs job."

Morgan's fists bunched. He was close to smashing her. The crazed woman continued prodding the rifle barrel painfully into the flesh under his chin. Her eyes blazed hostility. He feared she was close to pulling the trigger.

Shaken out of his inertia, Stuart Cohen jumped between them, pushing the gun away. She was right. They had to find the stuntman. If he'd survived, perhaps he knew what caused the disaster.

With so many injuries and deaths, Cohen saw massive lawsuits looming. A disaster like this could end his career if they pinned it on him. God, what would Rothenberg say? He'd blame him as the director and hold him responsible.

"Calm down," he pleaded. "We'll find Luther. Just cool it."

Cohen urgently called on two dazed grips to bring flashlights to help with the search. Their arrival eased the tension.

Led by Hahn, they waded into the swamp seeking any sign of Luther. It didn't take long. Twin flashlight beams revealed his remains. His legs, stripped of trousers and boots by the force of his downward plunge, stuck out of the muddy water like derelict white fence posts.

All four men pulled on the stuntman's limbs in a combined effort to free his torso. Velocity had buried him waist-deep in water and thick black mud. The foul ooze made resentful sucking sounds as they heaved upwards to break the swamp's muddy grip.

The look on the stuntman's dead face was one of grim determination. Hanh sobbed as Cohen felt for a pulse. There was none. When Morgan placed a consoling hand on Hahn's slender shoulder, she shook it off in disgust.

Quinton Werner and his accomplices watched from the shadows with satisfaction as the *Mission Cyclops* set became an enormous bonfire. Cancellation, or at minimum a long and expensive delay, faced the film.

Either was OK with Werner. He'd exacted costly revenge on Rothenberg for sending a killer after him. In his paranoid mind, they were almost square. The three attackers paddled quietly away, undetected by police or the paramedics who began arriving on the scene from the mainland.

* * *

The sabotage of his blockbuster movie told Rothenberg there were more powerful enemies out to destroy him and his cherished studio than he'd identified. He had contained Delano so far, but who were the others?

"Find out who's responsible," he bellowed at Liz Hightower on learning of the carnage on his Florida set. "And when we know, I want them wiped off the face of the earth. You understand?"

Worried, Liz slunk out of Rothenberg's office. The psychological blows had hit in deadly rat-a-tat-tat succession. Mentally, he was staggering like a battered boxer, reeling and about to hit the canvas. Liz had never seen him like that. His enemies had undermined his usually utterly-in-control life.

Delano's $100-million extortion had enraged and humiliated him. Worse for Max, it had cleared the way for the detested journalist's reunion with Rachel – something her father resented more than ever when he learned they'd married.

Morgan's costly decadence had threatened the studio's stellar reputation, as well as his superstar box-office appeal.

Rothenberg was casting about for ways of saving his half-finished film as actors and crew members filed lawsuits against the studio for their injuries.

It scared Liz to see the Boss so unnerved. The phone interrupted her thoughts.

"It's me," said Morgan Masterson's agitated voice calling from Miami. "I tried to get Max, but he's not taking my calls," he whined.

"What's the problem?" she asked sharply. "We're all super-busy here, trying to sort out this disaster."

"I just want to assure the Boss I had nothing to do with that crash. Anyone saying I did is a liar. I avoided the chopper scene because I was sick – no matter what that stuntman's crazy girlfriend claims."

Liz sighed, her patience fraying into anger.

Already, Hanh Nguyen had told reporters Morgan was a "chicken shit" who, despite his frequent boasts, avoided filming stunts whenever he could. "He tried getting in my pants. I think he planned this. Wanted Luther dead," she claimed bitterly.

Knowing Morgan, Liz didn't doubt Hahn's claims of harassment, but there was no proof of anything more. Morgan would vehemently deny all the woman's allegations.

"No one here's accusing you of anything, Morgan. You're getting paranoid. Stay calm," she urged. "Don't give interviews. Let our PR people handle the press. Just go home. There's nothing more you can do in Florida. The movie's on hold."

Her words gave him some reassurance. "It's just that Max blames me for everything. I'm in shock, too. I wish I'd died in that crash. Luther's such a loss to us all. We were buddies."

Liz didn't believe a word. Secretly, stunt workers called Morgan "Old Yeller Pants," and Luther was no exception. "OK, Morgan. We're all sorry. We lost many good people in that crash: two pilots, a renowned stuntman, camera operators, and five extras. You're lucky to have gotten off that set alive. I'll let Max know you called."

She was about to disconnect, but something about the way he'd spoken, the fear in his voice, made her ask, "Morgan, do you have any idea who fired those shots at the chopper?"

There was a moment of silence, then a slight wobble in his voice as he replied: "I don't know, Liz. Not a clue. Some nut job, I guess."

"I hoped you might have heard something. Why not come back home soon. Max wants to discuss your future with us if, indeed, you have one."

"What do you mean if I have one?" Morgan barked. "I can tough this out. I just need another chance, a new movie."

She'd had enough. "I can't discuss that now," she snapped and hung up.

* * *

It didn't take long for Gil Ackerman to discover someone had forewarned Morgan of the attack – and he failed to sound a warning.

When a small splinter group of terrorists in Beirut claimed responsibility, Ackerman recalled Quinton Werner's Lebanese ancestry from background checks he'd done on the union organizer years previously.

In short order, he had obtained phone records showing Werner and Masterson had talked before the attack. That was proof enough for him. Any way he could contribute to the superstar's downfall pleased the security chief.

For 15 years, he'd cleaned up after the troublesome actor. To protect the studio from lousy publicity, Ackerman had intimidated gossip writers, paid off police, and silenced starlets threatening to reveal Morgan's sexual harassment.

Now Gil entered Liz Hightower's office triumphant, ready to report the results of the investigation she'd ordered.

"I'm nearly certain Werner warned Morgan not to do the helicopter scene. I had my CIA contacts check all calls to his phone. Werner called an hour before the crash. Strange – even if Morgan didn't care about the people on the set, seems like he should've cared about endangering a movie supposed to be his next big hit."

Liz nodded, her lips tight with anger and disgust. "I know why. Morgan was enraged that he wasn't getting paid for this flic."

She knew what a scumbag Werner was, but Masterson was running a close second with his betrayal. She hadn't known they were friends.

"You're certain Werner warned Morgan the chopper would crash?" she asked.

"I don't know their exact words," Ackerman replied, "but that surely was the purpose of the call. Werner has it in for the Boss. He and Masterson go way back. They used to be roommates."

Liz wanted to be on solid ground before going to Rothenberg. When Ackerman left, she called Masterson, who'd returned overnight to his LA mansion. Maybe she could get a direct admission from him.

Masterson claimed to be tired and jetlagged after returning from Florida, but Liz overruled his objections and summoned him to her office. He arrived, seeming his usual confident self – but she saw through the pretense.

After polite preliminaries, she dropped the hammer: "Why did Quinton Werner call you an hour before the helicopter crashed?"

Morgan's hand shook as he reached into his pocket for a cigarette. How the hell did she know about that? He lit up, inhaling the comforting nicotine, hoping it would inspire the correct answers. It didn't.

"We're old buddies. He wanted to know how the filming was going. We talked about old times. How we shouldn't have lost touch..."

Liz smiled thinly. Now she had confirmation that Morgan and Werner had spoken. "You know he's on the run, suspected of murdering some black guy, don't you? Did he warn you not to do the helicopter scene? Did he tell you why?"

Morgan's composure shattered. How could she know so much? His face was ashen, but still, he was determined to tough it out. "No, of course not! I didn't get any warning."

Her icy blue eyes were Nordic drills boring into him, probing for the truth. "Don't lie to me, Morgan. I've got good information Werner warned you not to board that chopper."

Liz watched his features crumple. Whatever sex appeal he had was lost on her. Despite the air-conditioning, he sweated. Guilt pulsed from him. His cowering, perspiring presence sickened her.

The truth came tumbling out, a load he was too weak to carry any longer. "He told me I'd die if I made the flight. I didn't know what to do. He said they'd kill me if I said anything. Please, Liz, I beg you. Don't tell Max. I had no idea how serious this would get, all those people dying."

Morgan watched her blood-red nails toying with a letter opener, sharp as a stiletto. For a moment, he thought she might plunge it into him. He could tell she wasn't buying his excuses.

"You've got till tomorrow to provide a written explanation – and it better be the truth. If I'm satisfied, maybe – just maybe – we can keep it from Max. I haven't made up my mind. But if you give me bullshit, I go straight to Rothenberg. It's up to you."

Morgan stubbed out his cigarette and stood up; he needed to escape. It was useless challenging this formidable woman. Nobody got the best of her.

"You'll have what you want early tomorrow," he said, preparing to leave. "If you decide to give it to Max, I need to be there, so I can explain."

"I don't see why you shouldn't be present," she said. "It's your career on the line."

He left her office, frightened and furious. But he had one card left to play, and he intended to use it: Werner had also come back to LA.

Recording and monitoring their conversation from nearby, Gil Ackerman admired the way Liz had confirmed Morgan's guilt. Once Paragon's hottest property, the actor would soon be history. Of course, she would tell the Boss, but it was a smart move making the bastard provide a written confession.

It would be tricky making someone so well-known disappear. Ackerman figured he'd get the job, and wondered how Max would want it done – if that was what he decided.

CHAPTER NINETEEN:

PROBLEM SOLVED?

At dusk in the San Fernando Valley, bats flitted through the warm air, gorging on insects. Quinton Werner's car climbed the steep tree-shaded slope from Ventura Boulevard to Picturesque Drive in the Hollywood Hills. The call from Morgan Masterson, hours before, had sounded desperate.

"I need your help, Quint. That bitch Liz Hightower knows you called to warn me before the chopper crashed. She's going to tell Rothenberg. He'll tear up my contract for sure. You got me into this mess; you've gotta get me out of it."

Werner had snuck back into California with his new face and passport and wasn't happy about getting involved. He and his jihadi accomplices had more important work to do. Until then, Quinton needed to keep away from trouble. He was hiding out at a safe house with the twins who were anxious to plan their attack on the Academy Awards. Soon they would make their big move.

"Calm down, Morgan. I'm risking life in prison, not just getting fired, if they catch me," Werner had cautioned. "Give me her address. I'll see what I can do to shut her up."

Another thought occurred: "Who else knows? How did Hightower find out anyway? Did you tell her?"

"No, of course not. Why would I?" Morgan lied. "My guess is Gil Ackerman told her. He does the studio's investigations. He must have my phone records, saw the call, put it together.

Liz wants me to spill my guts before she goes to Rothenberg."

"Stop worrying. I'll take care of both of them before they get to Rothenberg," Werner sighed. "Wish to hell I hadn't tried to save your worthless ass."

Werner's battered Chevy slid to a halt two blocks away from Liz Hightower's Studio City home. Perched high on the hillside, 80 feet above the ground atop steel legs, it looked precarious. In reality, it was safer than properties on solid foundations. During earthquakes, the steel beams swayed, absorbing shockwaves, saving the building from falling.

Liz liked the extra safety feature. She was a woman who avoided risks. At 36, she was Rothenberg's steady right hand – a bulwark against stars pestering him for better roles, lobbying for exclusive deals, trying to get millions more added to their already generous contracts.

Liz knew who was hot in the business, who'd gone cold, which movies were likely hits, and which would flop. In Rothenberg's absence, Hightower ran the studio. She covered for him even when his deeds were decidedly criminal. She'd made herself the indispensable woman in his business life – one of the few females he trusted and respected. Their brief affair, begun when she first came to work for him, had ended amicably. Their professional relationship linked them in a way neither love nor sex could.

It was nearly midnight when she returned from a private screening and dinner party. Locking the front door behind her and resetting the alarm, she walked into her marble-floored living room. The furnishings were ultramodern, minimalist. Tall vases of flowers, delivered twice weekly, scented the room. Liz sighed with satisfaction; she loved her home.

She deactivated the alarm on the sliding glass doors and opened them to the westerly breeze blowing across LA from the Pacific. Walking out onto the red cedar wood deck, she could see Paragon's backlot with its monster soundstages a few miles to the north.

Turning her back on the view, she headed back inside to the spa room with its large sunken marble tub. The timer had started the heater, so the water had reached the ideal temperature of 101 degrees when she got home. She looked forward to a good soak after an evening of flattering and soothing the egos of actors, directors, and producers.

Her feet were killing her as she kicked off stiletto heels. Slipping out of her cocktail dress and silk underwear, she surveyed her toned body in a floor-to-ceiling mirror. Her pubic hair needed a trim, and she could spot a few gray hairs. A dye job? she mused. It should exactly match her long blonde mane. Or should she get it waxed? Oh, the pain! But baring it all was fashionable. The breasts remained firm, maybe starting to sag a tad, she noted with regret.

She'd call a plastic surgeon for a fix in the next month or so. Better catch it early. Naked, she stepped into the warm water, luxuriating in creamy bubbles, listening to Gustav Mahler's second symphony.

Werner had waited two hours, hidden on the hill beneath the house, for the sound of her Lexus pulling into the garage. Now he was halfway up one of the supporting girders. Sweat ran down his face as he clambered toward the deck. It was Quinton's lucky night; the sliding doors to the living room were open. He wouldn't have to break in or disarm alarms.

He heard music. Where was Liz? A renewed burst of Mahler and a delicious smell of soapy bubbles provided the answer. The symphony silenced the sound of his approach. With quick strides, he entered the spa room, coming up behind her unsuspecting blonde head. His gloved hand over her mouth stifled her shocked screams. He hauled her from the water backward.

Unable to see his face, she tried to beg for release. Instead, he shoved a hood over her head. Terrified but struggling to bring her renowned self-control into play, she pleaded: "Don't hurt me. I've got money, jewelry. You can have it all."

"Shut up," he answered. "I don't want your money."

Slippery in his grasp, she swung around, trying to rake where she thought his face would be, but her long nails failed to connect. In retaliation, the assailant punched her hooded head, knocking her to the floor. Dazed and gasping, she couldn't resist as he bound her ankles with duct tape. He used more tape to restrain her hands.

Uncontrollable terror took over as he dragged her into the living room, lifting and pushing her back onto the couch. Her body shook, her mouth dry with dread. Rough hands ran over her body, squeezing her soapy breasts. Then she understood: the man was a rapist. It sickened her, but she could perhaps still regain control.

"You wanna fuck me, that's it, isn't it?" She got the question out tremulously.

"Yeah, that would be a fine start to what I have to do," he answered, his fingers now between her legs, probing. "You gonna be good and cooperate, or do I have to get mean?"

"I'll cooperate, anything you want," she said as he cut the bindings on her legs so she could open them. "Then, please, you'll let me go?"

There was no answer.

Quinton thought about the many times he'd been in studio negotiations with her – and had fantasized about humiliating her by pulling her long blonde hair out of the elaborate updo she wore at work.

Now he grabbed her by that hair, getting leverage to position her kneeling forward on the sofa. He was already hard and entered her from behind. There was a fierceness to his rutting and eventual explosion deep within her. She'd never experienced such hatred in the sex act. The sense of violation consumed her. She fought not to scream and vomit.

Then the rapist turned her around, pulled the hood off her head, and she saw him for the first time. At first, there was no recognition of the surgically altered face. Then she knew: the fierce dark eyes and the ever-present dark stubble on cheek and jawline gave him away. Even the voice she could now connect with memories of facing this man across a negotiating table at the studio. It was Werner, the union troublemaker who had escaped their hitman. But he looked so different! It was confusing.

"YOU! It's YOU," she said, her voice rising to an outraged shriek. "Why are you doing this to me? Are you crazy?"

"No, it's you who must be nuts, sending a hitman after me. Don't talk, don't scream. Another scream like that, and you're dead," he snarled.

Trussed and helpless, she went silent for a moment, but she wasn't ready to give up: "You got what you wanted. I won't make a fuss. I swear it. I won't tell anyone. So help me God."

He wasn't listening, just breathing heavily and eying her as if trying to make up his mind about something. He knew she would not stay quiet about the information she had on him and Masterson. It was a pity, but she had to go.

Hightower still believed escape was possible. Somehow, she needed to defuse this savage freak. Liz understood now: Morgan had returned the favor and warned Werner she knew about his role in the Florida attack. Making one last bid for life, Liz pleaded: "I'll never breathe a word about your involvement in the crash – or what just happened here. I swear it."

"You think I believe that crap?" Werner smirked. He got a kick out of killing. The thrill was there when he slipped the noose around Liz's neck with one quick movement. She pulled away, begging, trying to push him off with her legs.

He paused for a moment, looked into her tearful blue eyes, and then steadily pulled the cord tight, so tight she couldn't make a sound. He loosened it for a moment.

"Tell you what. You tell me who else knows, and I might believe you." When she said nothing, he tightened the noose again.

It bit agonizingly into her flesh. She managed to choke out: "Wait… wait…"

"What do you have to say?" he asked, loosening it again just enough for her to speak.

"Just Ackerman," she said in a rasping whisper. "He found out and told me. We haven't reported it to anyone yet. Morgan was supposed to write a full confession before I went to Rothenberg."

That did it. That was the last favor Werner would do for his "old buddy." He had no more friends. There was no loyalty – none he would expect, none he would give.

He tightened the noose again without mercy. Blood trickled down Liz's breasts. She tried holding on, but it was useless.

Werner's strong gloved hands pulled the rope ever tighter. He held her arching body in a viselike grip. Loud drumming sounded in her brain. White mist suffused her brilliant mind until, deprived of oxygen, it sank into darkness.

Werner studied his work's results: the beautiful face contorted in violent death, a useless tongue hanging out, her lifeless body grotesque on the blood-flecked couch. He could smell urine; she'd pissed herself as she died. Most unattractive, Werner thought.

He pulled out a pair of metal cutters, snipped off Liz's ring finger, and yanked a tuft of blonde hair from her head.

Werner left her right where she lay, a grotesque goggle-eyed message to Rothenberg, his hated Paragon Pictures, and everybody who worked there.

Back in his car and on route to Gil Ackerman's Glendale home, Werner calculated the next job to be far riskier. Ackerman was a pro, not a pushover like this haughty executive bitch. But Quinton had an advantage.

Like Liz, Paragon's security chief had no idea what was coming down on him.

Werner found the house he had visited before, a ranch-style white stucco building surrounded by citrus trees and a gated five-foot-high stone wall. He drove a short distance past it. Walking back in the dark, he stopped, hoisted himself silently up on the wall, landing softly on the other side.

He went to the back door, which opened into the kitchen. He tried the knob. He could not believe his luck was holding – Ackerman hadn't locked it. The so-called security expert had left himself wide open.

Letting himself in, Werner hoped to find his target asleep, but now luck ran out. He could hear Ackerman up late, bawling out someone working the studio night shift.

"You wake me up to tell me that crap, you fool," Ackerman bellowed into the phone. He was sitting in a chair staring at numbers on a computer, his back to the door.

"If there's smoke coming from the hills behind soundstage four, I assume you've called the fire department, right? Good, then you've handled it. Call me if flames get within 200 yards of the lot."

He disconnected, slamming his phone down angrily.

Hunting knife raised, Werner charged through the door but wasn't fast enough to stab Ackerman.

Hearing a noise behind him, the former spook stood, turning sideways with cat-like agility. He grabbed Werner's arm, his fingers steel pinchers. The hunting knife clattered to the ground, kicked out of his reach.

"What the fuck!" Ackerman shouted, releasing his attacker and stepping back in confusion.

Werner remained calm and calculating, picked up a chair and slammed it into Ackerman's chest, knocking the breath out of him.

Before his opponent could recover and pull out the pistol he carried, Werner was gone, sprinting out of the front door across the lawn. He clawed his way over the wall and disappeared down the road to his car.

Breathless, Ackerman staggered after him, yelling and shouting, hoping to rouse his neighbors into calling the police. By then, Werner was speeding along the freeway.

He knew that once they found Hightower's body, Ackerman – and Rothenberg – would be on high alert. He'd blown his best opportunity to kill Ackerman. He had to get out of the country – soon, they'd be on to him.

There was no time to tell his Lebanese cousins he wouldn't be available to help with their big jihadi score. He had to look after himself.

Helping out Morgan had him on the run now. He should never have shown loyalty to the narcissistic piece-of-shit actor who only took care of himself. He was getting out of LA – and not coming back for a long time, if ever.

A few hours later, he was on the first available flight to Zurich, where he made another large withdrawal on Spike's Swiss account. After that, he looked for the most remote place he could find for an extended stay until the heat was off.

* * *

At nine the following day, the phone rang, unanswered, at Liz Hightower's home. Her mobile rang with the same disappointing result. When she didn't respond after repeated tries, Rothenberg gave up. She was usually at Paragon by eight o'clock, often before him.

Her absence was unusual. He relied on her manipulative brilliance during early morning meetings with challenging, demanding producers. Although he would never admit it, she did most of his strategic thinking. Liz was worth every penny of her $3.5 million annual paycheck.

Uneasy, Max asked Hightower's assistant Doreen if she'd heard from Liz. She looked into His Lordship's flushed, agitated face and feared trouble.

She hadn't heard from Liz either. That was unusual because Liz stayed in close touch. She always called if delayed.

"Keep phoning her house and her mobile every few minutes. Don't stop until you get a reply," Rothenberg ordered. "I've got questions needing answers now, not tomorrow. I want her here, pronto," Rothenberg grumbled. "Why don't you know where she is?"

"Yes, sir, I'll call every few minutes," Doreen said. "I don't know why she's not answering. She didn't have any outside appointments. There's an in-house marketing meeting scheduled later today. I'm sorry, sir. Don't worry, I'll find her…"

"Damn it. Just keep calling. As soon as you reach her, patch her through to me."

"Yes, sir."

It was unpleasant being around him when he was like this – spiteful and unpredictable. He fired people on the spot for giving what he considered the wrong answers. A vindictive tyrant, he wouldn't tolerate events going against him. An hour later, when no one had heard from Liz, Rothenberg knew something was seriously wrong. Rather than call the police, he phoned his fixer.

Gil Ackerman answered, trying to sound unruffled, but the previous night's attack still shook him. Sitting opposite him were two Glendale detectives, taking a report on the intruder's knifing attempt. They'd collected the knife Werner left behind for fingerprinting.

When Ackerman heard Max angrily complaining that Liz was missing, it alarmed him. Was her disappearance connected to the attack on him?

"Where the hell are *you*, anyway?" Rothenberg snarled. "Never mind, just get over to her place right now. Find out why she's not here. Be discreet. We don't want to alert the press."

Not wanting to reveal anything to the waiting detectives, Ackerman replied: "Yes, sir, I'm on it. You'll hear from me soon."

It took nearly an hour on the crowded freeway to get from Glendale to Studio City. Ackerman's black Cadillac left a trail of angry drivers hooting and giving him the finger as he passed other cars, weaving his way in and out of the line of traffic mounting the hill to Picturesque Drive. He didn't care. He knew His Lordship wouldn't brook delay.

He rang the front doorbell. No response. The lock on the side door to the garage yielded quickly to Gil's bunch of picks. Liz's Lexus was there. He popped the hood, felt the engine; it was stone-cold, not driven for hours.

He entered the house through the kitchen. Throughout the home, speakers played classical music. He went into the bedroom where the king-sized bed remained untouched; she hadn't slept there.

He found shoes, a cocktail dress, and underwear in the adjoining spa room, all in a heap on the floor. Each garment was in good order, not torn, just casually discarded. He lifted the dress, still fragrant with her perfume, to his craggy face.

At the studio, he liked being near her. She always smelled delicious. He'd fancied her in a way – even while envying her position and higher salary. He imagined her naked in the tub. His penis stirred, and he restrained a sudden urge to jerk off. Instead, he felt the water in the undrained tub. It was cold; soap scum still floated on the surface.

The towels were dry, unused. But Gil detected a faint trail of dampness leading out of the spa room and across the marble floor towards the living room. Like a tracker dog, he followed the path. The naked horror that was now Liz Hightower glared up at him from the white couch, her throat bruised and torn from strangulation. His stomach twisted in revulsion.

Jesus Christ, who'd done this to her? he asked himself.

The answer came as he connected her death to the attack on him the previous night. Although his assailant had looked different, Ackerman was sure now it was Werner.

When he heard Morgan Masterson buckle under Liz's questioning the day before, he hadn't imagined that Werner was fool enough to be back in town. Masterson must have realized his confession wouldn't save his career. The cowardly superstar wanted him and Liz dead before they told Rothenberg. The douchebag put his career ahead of their lives.

Reluctantly Ackerman called the Boss. "Max, I'm at Liz's place. It's not good," he began.

"What do you mean not good?" Rothenberg demanded.

"She's dead, murdered. I'm sure it was Quinton Werner. He broke in and strangled her. I'll have to call the police."

Rothenberg collapsed into his cavernous office chair with a leather-cracking thump, his florid face crinkling in disbelief.

"Killed her? Killed her? You say Werner did this?"

"Yes, Boss," Ackerman said. "He tried to kill me, too. Tried to knife me at my house last night. He looks different, but now I'm certain it was him."

"Why would he go after you and Liz?"

"Revenge for the hit we put out on him, and because we found out from Masterson that Werner was behind the Florida chopper disaster. He didn't want us telling you he'd tipped off Masterson to avoid the flight. Werner was helping out his buddy again, murdering us to save his film career."

"How could Morgan do this to me?" Rothenberg asked. "Why side with Werner?"

"He and Werner are friends from way back," Ackerman said. "I have phone records showing they talked before the crash. Morgan admitted to Liz that Werner warned him not to make the chopper flight."

Rothenberg turned deadly calm. Ackerman, tense in the ominous silence, waited for him to speak again.

"Werner will pay for this," he said, his voice dripping with venom. "As for Morgan, I'll devise a fitting response to his treachery."

"Yes, Boss. Whatever you decide, you know I'll back you up."

* * *

Twelve days later, they buried Liz Hightower at Forest Lawn Memorial Park. On the day of the funeral, a small package bearing a Swiss postmark arrived addressed to Rothenberg. His secretary, Sadie, came close to fainting when she opened it. A ruby ring Liz wore constantly adorned a severed digit nestled in a bed of blonde hair.

Sadie reluctantly handed the box to Rothenberg when he insisted on looking inside. He shuddered at the sight before removing a black-bordered card.

It read: "Max, you could have avoided all this ugliness if you had paid me what I asked for. Worse, you sent someone to kill me, but I killed him. Now Hightower is dead. I wrecked your Florida set. I'm a man of serious purpose. Dying is the only way left for you to settle your debt."

* * *

Lord Rothenberg's bad reaction to the destruction of his movie set and Liz Hightower's death concerned Gil Ackerman. His Lordship, usually a light drinker, was hitting the bottle and using tranquilizers to calm himself.

Some mornings the mogul arrived at his LA office disheveled and bleary-eyed after nights of partying with young hookers. These distractions led him to duck urgently needed business decisions.

Ackerman wondered how to handle this dilemma. Max was consumed with his grief and misfortune – and, for the first time since Gil had known him, was out of control psychologically.

Gil confided in his security team second in command Tony Pugliese: "I gotta get a grip on the old man, he's going nuts. He's freaked out since that note arrived threatening his life."

Pugliese agreed Ackerman's best course of action was to pack the Boss off to his Costa Rican Island, where no one could touch him. There, he might recover sufficiently to deal with critical events affecting GMI, and especially Paragon.

The biggest problem Rothenberg needed to resolve was Morgan Masterson: how to punish his treachery in not warning the *Mission Cyclops* cast and crew their set would be attacked.

Gil knew the Boss wanted to be rid of Morgan – but the question was how? He remained the studio's number one asset with millions of fans. Under more normal circumstances, Paragon would either have to pay off his contract or freeze him out, with both alternatives causing scandal.

Additionally, Rothenberg's unhinged state had led him to conflate his two primary enemies, Delano and Werner. He believed they'd teamed up to destroy Paragon and everyone associated with the studio.

However, the mogul's delusion presented another opportunity for envious Ackerman to exploit his animosity towards Mike. He knew Max bitterly resented paying another fifty million to the journalist as agreed – and was furious Rachel disobeyed him by marrying the writer.

Instead of Ackerman delivering more duffle bags stuffed with millions to Nassau, he urged Rothenberg to renege on the deal and let him have Delano killed. And he promised to personally link up with the Chicago syndicate, to help hunt down Werner and make him disappear, too.

Rothenberg embraced the idea of disposing of opponents who'd crossed him but feared disastrous repercussions that could follow Delano's disappearance.

"That swine still has disks incriminating Masterson in three bank vaults. If anything happens to him, they'll be released globally," the mogul nervously pointed out. "My part in covering up for Masterson would ruin both me and my studio. It would also spark a new investigation into the death of Masterson's maid that I wouldn't be able to muzzle."

Ackerman, expecting a multi-million-dollar bonus, presented his plan over Max's objections: "I put a couple of the best operators from the

Colombian cartel on him, men without links to you or the business. They torture Delano until he gives up the codes to those bank vaults. We collect the disks – then they dump his ass in the ocean."

Rothenberg brightened; he profoundly resented making his nemesis any richer. Nor could he condone Rachel's defiance in marrying a deadly enemy. Once he had her back, he'd punish her disobedience.

"I'm leaving for Costa Rica. You're right, don't pay Delano any more money. Get rid of him – but don't cause a stink. And make sure Rachel's not injured. When they're rid of Delano, take her back to Switzerland on one of our jets. She needs another long rest at the clinic," he said.

"Once you've made arrangements, come on and join me on the island. I need you to take charge of security there – while I ponder what to do about Morgan."

CHAPTER TWENTY:

ISLAND-HOPPING

The newlyweds had been island-hopping for two months when they dropped anchor on the calmer Caribbean side of Barbados, where they intended to stay for three weeks. Rachel continued making an impressive physical recovery from her ordeal. Running on tropical beaches, hauling sails, and swimming in warm seas had further improved her stamina.

But her emotional stability remained precarious. She suffered nightmares, leaping out of their bed, pacing around the yacht, unable to sleep. Delano feared she hadn't spent enough time with the Belgian psychologist, whom she had begun to trust. Also, the effects of clinical sedation over a long period had not entirely worn off.

These worries faded as he watched her, tanned and gorgeous in her bikini, dive overboard for a dip marking their arrival offshore from Bridgetown.

Moving through the blue-green water towards the yacht's ladder, Rachel thought how being with Delano made each day a new adventure; it was the quality she loved most about him.

She had learned to sail the *Talespinner* and proved herself a skillful angler, turning her catches into delicious meals. With Mike's unwavering support, she had worked hard at restoring her zest for life. She felt the mists lifting from her mind. But just as she had from childhood, she dreaded new and chastising contact with her father – especially as she had married a man he hated.

Rachel was also bothered by Delano's insistent belief that her father was responsible for her Swiss ordeal. It was their only significant disagreement. Even after Mike had led her step by step through all the reasons it had to be Max, she still couldn't accept that "Daddy" ordered the abortion and her imprisonment.

"Daddy didn't do it," she protested angrily. "He wouldn't do that to me. It was Aaron, that SOB. They released me after he died in Africa. I saw his signature on the papers. The hell with him. I'm glad he's dead."

Delano avoided saying her release was part of the sordid deal he'd forced on Rothenberg. He'd disclose that when her emotional recovery matched her physical healing. Rachel stubbornly gave her father the benefit of any doubt. When Mike recounted GMI's cruel acts, she blamed them on Max's subordinates, not him.

While she understood her father's anger over their marriage, she didn't believe his vengeance could become lethal. Nor did she accept Delano's assertion Max had conditioned her since childhood to please him. Her lasting grievance against the mogul remained his having kept her from becoming part of the family business.

"If I'd been born a boy that wouldn't have happened," she said. "I've discussed it with my mother and she agrees he has little respect for females in positions of authority."

They minimized these unresolved conflicts to rejoice in the honeymoon happiness they now shared. The jazz and classical music they both liked filled the boat, whether sailing or at anchor.

They were much alike: creative and disciplined. Like Delano, Rachel valued the outdoor life: yachting, fishing, and exploring sparsely populated Caribbean islands. She, too, was capable of making rapid judgments and becoming laser-focused on a problem. He admired how she worked at being the best at whatever she did: winning at sport, cooking a delicious dish, or producing fine art.

When the ocean was flat calm and the boat anchored, she got out her easel and painted, capturing stunning tropical views in oils. There, alone on the bow in a tiny bikini, she seemed happiest at her canvas, memories of the Swiss ordeal fading.

Rachel had a degree in art history, had read the classics, spoke French, Italian, and Hebrew – and shared Delano's interest in global politics, a passion he'd gained covering the United Nations.

Rachel fulfilled another of his unspoken needs: she was a companion from whom he could learn. Besides being an art expert, Rachel provided her British grammar school-educated husband insights into literature he hadn't had before.

Mike deplored ignorance in himself and others. And Rachel Rothenberg Delano was brilliant. He'd decided his next professional challenge would be writing novels, and her savvy suggestions of books to read provided him with new perspectives.

While she was a responsive and adventurous sexual partner, she also provided the unstinting nurturing and attention he craved. But despite their closeness, she was the first woman in his experience he couldn't easily read. This intrigued him.

There was a part of Rachel he'd never know. There were so many reasons he loved this woman, he couldn't count them. In moments of reflection, he couldn't believe she'd become his wife. He loved her with a passion he hadn't known existed in himself.

Alone on the boat, the newlyweds learned plenty about each other. Rachel was a pragmatist and had inherited some of Rothenberg's ruthless business attitudes. When Mike confessed to extorting millions from her father in return for "spiking" the Morgan Masterson story, it didn't draw her disapproval.

She viewed his deal with her financially slippery parent as a coup rather than an ethical collapse. She might have held a different opinion if he'd confided her release was part of the deal – that her father was her jailer.

"One hundred million," she snickered admiringly. "He really must have badly wanted that story stopped. But don't worry, he's so wealthy he won't even feel it."

And just as Delano had bested her father, Rachel said she eventually intended doing the same by securing a hold on the family business when the right opportunity occurred.

She thought Max needlessly cruel, thwarting her ambition to become a player in the company he'd built. With exceptions like Liz Hightower, few women occupied critical positions at GMI.

"I don't know how or when it will happen – maybe there will be a health crisis – but nothing will stop me from taking over from him when the opportunity comes," she vowed.

"He's chauvinist. I've suggested excellent new media opportunities – but he brushed them aside. He believes women – especially me – should be home raising kids."

Mike didn't respond. He'd heard these resentments before. Realistically, he knew her chance of running GMI died on their wedding day. It would be no surprise if vengeful Rothenberg had already disinherited her. His fortune would likely go to Israeli charities.

Wanting to keep their discussion light, he changed the subject: "I'll get you a rum and coke," he said. "Don't talk about Max. Working for him was a lousy experience. You don't want to try it."

Rachel snuggled up to her invincible husband. "Daddy picked on the wrong guy when he went after you," she murmured. "You put him in his place. No one's ever done that. Maybe it's why I love you so much."

She gave him a full, deep kiss on the mouth, then stood up before he could move, saying: "I'll fix the drinks. You make them too strong!"

The blissful honeymoon continued until a satellite phone caller delivered a warning Delano couldn't ignore. It was Laura Chesley, one of Delano's most valued contacts, an informant unerringly plugged into Hollywood's buzz.

"Mike, there's a hit out on you," Laura said with her usual bluntness. "And I know how it's supposed to go down."

At first, he was skeptical, but he heard her out. Could she be right? Laura would say or do anything for money. She hustled LA journalists for cash by dishing dirt.

When not informing reporters, her primary business line was pimping youngsters to Tinseltown power brokers, Saudi princes, anyone with the cash to buy young flesh – but Delano had found she rarely steered him wrong.

"One of my best girls was up at Rothenberg's mansion. She said he was in bad shape, couldn't get it up. Ranting about you. Boozing. Vowing vengeance. Claimed you'd stolen his daughter, extorted him for millions. Didn't know you were on the hustle, too, Mike."

Laura paused; she hated being out of the loop about Hollywood happenings. When he didn't respond, she insisted, "Hey, dude, you never told me you'd married into the Rothenberg family. And suddenly you got rich. That right?"

"You don't know everything now, do you?" Delano replied peevishly.

But Laura wasn't to be deflected. "How come you kept the juicy news from me? Don't you trust Laura no more?"

"Of course, I trust you. But it's my personal life. I wanted our marriage kept quiet. Not blasted all over town. Anyway, it happened in Brussels, not LA," Delano replied respectfully, trying to soothe her ruffled feelings.

"Well, what you don't know, smartass, is your new father-in-law wants you dead," Laura snapped back, happy to put the cheeky journo in his place.

"The big guy got wasted the other night. Booze and pills. Boasted to my gal he had contacts who'd sent two guys to blow you away. Can that be true?"

Shaken, Delano was all ears as Laura rattled out what she'd learned.

"He claimed you'd wrecked Rachel's marriage to that Israeli arms guy who got blown up in Africa."

Delano kept listening. But he was glad an ocean and a continent separated them. Mike hated sitting across a table from Laura in some West Hollywood dive. She was a perspiring 200-pound-plus chain-smoking hag with straggly gray hair as unwashed as the rest of her.

She'd done time for extortion. Burn scars from lit cigarettes pressed into her chubby arms were prison souvenirs, payback for ratting out other inmates in the joint. Her best asset was a seductive yet reassuring motherly voice.

Laura cajoled young Hollywood newcomers into the sex trade, claiming it was a stepping stone to a showbiz career. Her pimps met such innocents at the bus, rail, and air terminals the moment they stepped onto California soil.

Delano was wary of her knowing too much. If offended, she'd spread the story of his troubles with Rothenberg by selling it to print and TV, heightening the mogul's fury. Happy to buy her silence, Mike was grateful for her warning.

"I can't talk about this now. I'll fill you in later. Anything more you heard about these supposed assassins?"

"What's it worth?" she asked.

"Send one of your minions to my agency tomorrow. There'll be a $3,000 check waiting for you. Just keep quiet about threats to my life – and the marriage. Can I rely on you, Laura?"

"Make it six grand. Then you have my word, my silence too."

Delano grinned wryly.

"Ouch! OK, six grand it is. You hear any more, call me."

"Sure will," she said, a greedy smile in her melodious voice.

He clicked off, knowing he'd be foolish ignoring the tip. If Rothenberg's thugs were after him, he assumed they'd been instructed to grab Rachel again.

Delano called Ray Flynn, a source his agency cultivated within the Chicago syndicate that did Paragon's dirty work.

"Ray, pal, can you find out whether anything is going down involving me?" he asked. "Something Rothenberg's ordered."

"Ain't heard nothing, call you back if I find anything. Gonna cost you. Sit tight," Flynn replied.

Sure enough, he came back the next day, his voice bouncing loud and clear off the satellite.

"Yeah, better watch your ass. Rothenberg knows you and his daughter are on a boat off Barbados. One of our people tricked her mother into telling them. Chicago's farmed the job out to Colombians in Miami; they're closest – supposed to be a rush job. They're already on the way to Bridgetown."

"Thanks, Ray, will ten grand keep you happy?"

"Yeah, that's fair."

Delano disconnected and angrily tossed the phone across the cabin.

That afternoon he took Rachel ashore in the dinghy for safety. Ignoring her pleas to remain with him, he booked her into a Bridgetown hotel under a false name.

Before leaving, he unnerved her by saying: "Lock the door and don't open it for anyone until you hear from me."

He stopped at a sporting goods store to buy a crossbow, plus a dozen vicious-looking broad-headed arrows used for hunting, before returning to his yacht.

Aboard, he rigged a hammock in the stern. Sleeping in the open increased the odds he'd hear noises signaling approaching attackers.

For two nights, he waited, talking with Rachel by phone. She still doubted her father would send killers – and he refused her demands to return to the boat.

On the third night, he awakened to the hum of an electric motor on the starboard side. Jumping from his hammock, he grabbed the crossbow and bolts and peered into the darkness. Clouds obscured the faint light of a quarter moon. Then the noise stopped. He heard the sound of paddles stealthily applied against the tide.

His powerful searchlight joltingly revealed an inflatable dinghy with two men blinking in the powerful beam and spewing guttural Spanish curses at being all lit up.

Mike ducked when one of them rose hurriedly, getting off a hail of automatic fire. He threw himself down on the deck. The burst missed him, but it shattered his searchlight.

With their motor running flat-out, his assailants skimmed towards *Talespinner*. Closing, they fired another burst at the yacht. Bullets splintered its splendid teak trim, tore into stowed sails. The damage angered Delano, who treated his vessel as a living creature.

He moved forward, the moon showing now between the clouds. Seeing the inflatable and its occupants outlined against the horizon, he swung the crossbow up, aiming the razor-sharp bolt where he'd last seen muzzle flashes.

His first shot hit the shooter in the stomach, knocking him backward, writhing in agony as he tried pulling the bolt from his gut. When his companion opened fire, two more bolts traveling at 300 feet per second ripped gaping holes in the watercraft's air tubes.

In the stillness of the windless Caribbean night, Mike enjoyed the hiss of air rushing out and the screams of its occupants. In minutes, the inflatable crumpled into a useless sack dragged down by the weight of the still attached motor.

Both Colombians floundered in the water, one howling from his wound, the other begging for help. Delano lit the scene with a standby flashlight before he hauled anchor and started the engine. He saw one thug face down, apparently dead.

The other slimeball swam with desperate strokes against a tide sweeping around the island. It would carry him out to deep water where he'd drown.

"Good riddance, you murderous bastards. That'll teach you to shoot up my yacht," Mike murmured, motoring away triumphant.

By dawn, he was at Bridgetown, where he docked and walked through the quiet streets to get Rachel. She fell silent when told about the attack. Once aboard, she examined the bullet-ridden teak – but still found it difficult to believe Max had ordered such violence against them.

"Are you sure?" she asked. "You've made other enemies."

Delano shook his head. He trusted Laura Chesley's tip-off – it had saved them. Maybe there was another way to convince Rachel.

"Let me check with my bank in Nassau. If the second $50 mill didn't arrive as scheduled, I'd say that's confirmation your father ordered the hit."

By phone, Ralph Clark-Hall sourly told Delano his second cash payment hadn't arrived as agreed. The banker complained His Lordship's accountants were "suspiciously unreachable when I sought an explanation for the delay."

Reneging on the deal was ugly enough, but the attempt to murder him was war. Mike was quick to enact his revenge. He called his London bank's unique security number. "Code 4082 Delano procedure 999. Subject M for Masterson. Password: Lechery. Release all pictures, video, and text," he told the automated vault keeper.

For a moment, there was silence as voice recognition software assessed his authenticity, ensuring it was their client.

"Yes, Mr. Delano," said a bank executive who came on the line. "Please confirm we now have your permission to release all material held by us – according to your earlier instructions."

"Yes. Make sure everything in the digital file – text, video, and pictures – goes to my Santa Monica news agency with my instructions for global distribution."

A day later, the story of Suzanne's death following an orgy with Morgan Masterson made headlines worldwide – as did allegations that Carmelita Sanchez died to protect the debauched superstar's reputation.

* * *

The Masterson scoop was a triumph for Delano and his news agency. Parts of the honey trap sex video went viral on the web. The story was headline news everywhere.

Shocking Sex Tape Shatters Superstar Morgan Masterson's Marriage, screamed the tabloids. The story revealed how Morgan fooled fans with his "Happiest Marriage in Tinseltown" image when, in reality, he was a serial adulterer and drug user. Variations of the story appeared internationally for days. Even respectable broadsheets like the New York Times carried it. While usually avoiding scandal, this tale was too big for the "Grey Lady" to ignore.

Singing superstar Delia LaBelle stoked the furor by immediately filing for divorce: *Most Expensive Hollywood Split Ever – Country Singer Wants Morgan's Bel Air Mansion, $200-Million in Cash, Plus Alimony!*

Female actors Morgan seduced with broken promises and silenced with threats jumped on the legal bandwagon. Convinced the confidentiality agreements Paragon lawyers forced them to sign were no longer valid, they sued Morgan and the studio, too. Several earned five-figure payments from tabloids by recounting their sexual experiences with Masterson, resulting in headlines like *Lying Morgan Promised Me Stardom in Return for Sex!*

Even family members turned on their sex-obsessed father: *Adopted Teen Claims "Naked Morgan Chased Me Around Mansion When Mom Was Away!"*

Delano, banking a fortune from Masterson's downfall, celebrated his retaliatory strike at Rothenberg. Moreover, he hypocritically enjoyed proving he was the new king of the scandal business he loathed.

In a mere couple of years, Delano's stories, and those of other journalists, had boosted circulation for traditional media and a growing constellation of websites serving up sleaze minute-by-minute, creating a three-billion-dollar river of cash for newsmen exposing Tinseltown's secrets.

Now that he'd broken the Masterson story, the gutter press took down the superstar, with most of the so-called establishment press piling on, too.

They were gleeful media savages dancing around scandal's cooking pot, rejoicing in having a new victim to boil alive.

CHAPTER TWENTY-ONE:

BANISHED

Rothenberg could no longer tolerate the cascading horrors Morgan Masterson had brought down on Paragon. The humiliated superstar had sobbed and protested when Max banned him from all studio properties. The banishment didn't end there.

He suspended Morgan's contract and insisted he leave the country indefinitely. Rothenberg also forbade the actor from giving a single interview to defend his horrendous behavior, particularly that leading to Suzanne Francis' death.

The mogul hinted at a possible return if the ruinous publicity subsided. He duplicitously provided this ray of hope to keep Morgan controllable until he decided the actor's doom.

Masterson knew too much about Paragon's criminal doings, especially about circumstances leading to Carmelita Sanchez's death, to be left alive.

"If he reveals any of the incidents he's privy to, we'll all be behind bars," Gil Ackerman admonished his Boss with unusual bluntness.

"Just get him out of the country. I'll decide what to do about him later," Rothenberg bellowed, disliking being counseled as to what he should do.

"But that piece of shit will pay for the damage he's caused us, that's for sure."

Studio PR specialists tried covering for Morgan, claiming the loss of friends in the helicopter crash traumatized the star so severely he couldn't work or speak with the press. They issued a statement saying he was undergoing grief counseling and drug detoxification at an undisclosed location.

* * *

To ensure no press got to him, Gil Ackerman drove Morgan to the airport at five o'clock on a Sunday morning, a time when most reporters were sleeping. A Paragon jet waited to fly him to Bogotá, Colombia.

"When do you think I can return? Max couldn't have meant it when he said 'indefinitely,'" Masterson whined.

Ackerman was evasive. "Who can say? Perhaps six months will be long enough for the stink to fade. Be patient, man. It's up to Rothenberg when he's ready to put you back on the screen," said the security chief.

In need of a place to exile, Masterson had called his cousin, Carlos Bomba, leader of Colombia's second-largest cocaine cartel.

"I need a place to live in total privacy, Carlos. Somewhere I can escape the press. Can I stay with you, until the heat's off?"

His plea amused the drug chief, who enjoyed having a superstar in the family. Yearly, Morgan invited him to California, introducing Carlos to Hollywood stars – many of whom were addicted users of the Colombian's fine quality coke.

"You been bad boy, Morgan. Dead pussy, coca, and junk. I seen the video, you and the blonde puta. Not good for the big-deal movie star, family man," Carlos bantered with a cynical chuckle.

"Sure, you come to me. Nobody bothers you here. I promise – no big mouths yapping. I shut them permanently if they do. You're family. You like a brother, I help."

Morgan stammered his thanks in rusty Spanish. He remained determined to make a comeback and wasn't putting up with indefinite banishment.

Seated alone on the jet, he knew he'd made a mess of his fame and fortune; the divorce from Delia could wipe him out. But he agreed to everything she wanted financially to make the parting easier.

She claimed his disgrace had destroyed her career, too. Country music brass now shied away while reporters pestered constantly for her comments about their bogus "happy marriage" – and his debauchery. Delia didn't buy Morgan's pretended sorrow anymore. She believed he was glad to be rid of her and the kids, so she would take him for everything she could get.

An hour into the flight, the attractive brunette flight attendant surveyed the empty cabin feeling sorry for her sole passenger. Hunched up in his seat, he appeared lonely, depressed. He was in big trouble.

Even so, he was one of the hunkiest men she'd ever seen. You couldn't help fancying him. Colombia was hours away; the two pilots were busy in the cockpit. Their eyes met and held for a second as she offered him breakfast. Her unspoken message: I can give you something more comforting than food.

A beauty, Morgan thought as he accepted orange juice and scrambled eggs. But for once, he decided it wiser to avoid temptation.

Flight attendants were poison. He shuddered, thinking how he'd learned the hard way in New York.

* * *

Morgan's often-told tale of a youth spent running cattle on a Nebraska ranch was mostly studio hype designed to make him look rugged and earthy. He wasn't a man of the prairie, as millions of fans believed. He'd failed miserably as a cowhand.

Morgan's real roots were in Colombia, from where he'd fled as a teenager. Born Alejandro Bomba, Morgan was the spoiled only son of the late drug lord Fabio Bomba, a father who indulged his son from birth.

When Alejandro's mother Alicia died, leaving her five-year-old son behind, cartel staff took care of his every need.

As years passed, Fabio spent heavily on privately educating his heir, Alejandro. The boy learned English and business skills. The father hoped his son would run their estate sixty miles from Cali – and later rule over the entire drug empire.

Fabio's cartel supplied $400 million worth of cocaine yearly to growing markets in Europe and the States. But Alejandro showed little interest in narcotics as a business. But as a user, he became addicted to coca as a teenager.

Father and son argued when the handsome youth revealed his real ambition: "I must go to the States, Papa. I want to act. My dream is to become a movie star."

Alejandro's raging teen libido had already caused problems. Two servants, too scared to refuse the Boss's son, became pregnant. His angry father gave the young women money and returned them to their families.

When not chasing women, Alejandro spent his days reading movie magazines, watching American films and television, smoking marijuana, and bribing his father's employees to bring him cocaine.

He had never paid the price for these misdeeds until he seduced 16-year-old Anna Maria Castillo, resulting in a pregnancy. Anna Maria was the adored daughter of Ramon Castillo, one of Fabio's ambitious lieutenants.

When Alejandro, 18, refused to marry the teenager to give the child his name, civil war broke out within the Bomba cartel.

Castillo believed he should run the business instead of Bomba. Damage to his daughter's honor propelled him into making a move on the head honcho.

Early one morning, Castillo's men overran Bomba's estate with orders to shoot father and son. Isolated on the hacienda stairs, Bomba killed several attackers before shotgun blasts took him down.

As he lay dying, the last sound he heard was his son's Ducati motorcycle starting up. After seeing his father fall, Alejandro had fled as fast as his bike would carry him. Courage wasn't a quality inherited from the parent he left to die.

Shortly after that, relatives removed Alejandro to the safety of America. They provided him a new home on a 500-acre Nebraska cattle ranch purchased from the Mastersons, a debt-ridden family with their land in foreclosure.

In return, the grateful ranchers adopted Alejandro, re-naming him, Morgan Masterson. While the deal provided refuge and a new identity, the teenager was miserable. He missed his cushy life with easy access to drugs and sex. Worse, the newly-hatched Morgan Masterson hated ranch living and manual work.

He disliked rising at five o'clock in the morning to feed the stock. He loathed riding in the rain and cold to drive cattle. He fought with his adoptive parents for failing to do his share of chores, and he lost privileges for not doing them well.

The Masterson sons, 18-year-old Jeb and 19-year-old Jason, both disliked Morgan. They frequently tried knocking sense into the Colombian, but he went to pieces after a few punches, sobbing for them to stop.

"Don't hit me. My face is my fortune," Morgan protested as he ran from his rugged "brothers."

Cornered, Morgan would snarl: "You can't get away with this. My people saved you, rescued your property. You should be grateful to me…"

His protests usually resulted in the brothers getting the best of the Colombian. One day they grabbed him, dragged him kicking and screaming to the pigpen, where they pitched him head-first into the feces-laden muck.

"My face is my fortune," Jeb mimicked him.

"You're a lazy bum, a work-shy spick. Actor, my ass," jeered Jason. "You're full of shit, man!"

Squealing animals trampled Morgan black and blue in their haste to escape. When the stinking youth tried climbing out, the brothers shoved him back amidst the porkers.

Hearing the uproar from the pigsty, the Masterson parents rushed to intervene. They demanded their boys clean up the foul-smelling orphan as penance.

When the adults left, the brothers stripped Morgan, hosing him down with jets of ice-cold water chanting shrilly: "I'm going be an actor. I'm going to be famous…"

The next day, boots dangling from laces around his neck, Morgan crept out of the ranch room he shared with his snoring adoptive siblings, picked up what cash he could, and headed for the barn.

There, he jumped into their beater Ford truck, hot-wired it, and headed to California. He'd never return to Nebraska with its humiliating memories.

As Morgan climbed the Hollywood ladder using the Masterson name, they stayed silent about their connection to him, fearing the cartel would kick them off the ranch if they made any noise about how their kinship came about – or the deal they'd made with the cartel.

And, of course, Paragon's publicity department squelched any hint of their superstar's cartel connections. Their projection of Morgan portrayed him as the offspring of salt-of-the-earth American ranchers – private folks who preferred remaining in the background.

CHAPTER TWENTY-TWO:

TROUBLE-MAKER

Even on a sailboat with the woman he loved, Mike Delano couldn't escape sources looking to bleed him for cash for their stories. Their interruptions made him regret his earlier eagerness to build a show business network by being generous and widely circulating his number.

It was a breezy day, and they were running before the wind off Martinique when the satellite phone rang several times in the main cabin below. Each time, the call went to voice mail and, after seconds of silence, the phone rang again.

Looking healthier every day, Rachel took the wheel while Delano negotiated the boat's heeling decks to answer the persistent caller.

"Delano here…"

"Hell, dude, where you been? Why don't you answer your goddamn phone?"

It was the abrasive Laura Chesley again. "Mike, I got more good stuff. Hope your checkbook's available at the agency back here in sunny California," she said.

"Depends. What you got?"

"It concerns Paragon again. That officious blonde cunt, Liz Hightower, who runs the show. She's dead. Someone strangled the bitch."

Delano sounded disappointed. "That's been all over the wire services."

"Screw the wire services, I've got better shit than them, Mr. Smartass. There's much more…"

"OK, tell me what you got this time."

"Rothenberg's hunting that union fixer, Quinton Werner. Put a price on his head. He believes Quinton killed Hightower and caused the Florida disaster. Cops already want him for offing some Black dude whose body turned up at Werner's ranch."

This interested Delano. If his LA reporters could confirm it with LAPD sources, it could make a good follow-up story.

"You got anything juicier than that?" he inquired.

"Yeah, Rothenberg's canceled Morgan Masterson's contract. Your sex and drugs yarn and his divorce scandal busted his balls with everyone, especially his fan base."

Delano smiled with satisfaction.

"Where's Morgan now?"

"He's in Colombia, hiding out with his druggie cousin. Paragon's claiming he's traumatized, in rehab – the usual PR bullshit."

"Where's Rothenberg?"

"With Hightower gone, he's panicking, leaving for his Costa Rican retreat. My airport guy says they've reserved a studio jet for a trip to San José."

After agreeing to another generous fee, Delano hung up. It was useful knowing Masterson was in South America and Rothenberg was retreating to his private island.

Delano had a spy, Enrique Garcia, who worked for Max in Costa Rica. He crewed the mogul's deep-sea fishing boat and doubled as a waiter at Max's island mansion. He kept Delano briefed about activities there.

Laura's intrusion into his honeymoon bliss got Delano thinking about contacts, how much a journalist depended on them. Laura was the best, he had to admit. Few Hollywood bigwigs evaded her network of informers.

In LA, the worst scumbags – and Laura was among the nastiest of them – made the best informers. She was a spider sitting at the center of a gossip web spun over the city.

A return to prison held little fear for her. She blithely broke the law in her scramble for cash and scoops. But her main racket involved pimping. She befriended unfortunate boys and gals trying to break into show business.

When promised acting opportunities didn't materialize, selling their bodies became a survival strategy. For a 40 percent cut, Laura helped hard-up youngsters get clients and negotiated the best prices. Sex and youth were hot commodities in an industry that worshipped both.

She worked with Beverly Hills procurer Madame Julia who catered to movie bigshots and, occasionally, Saudi royals. Madame Julia sent her hookers to hotels and Hollywood homes.

They serviced customers in Europe, the Caribbean, and the Middle East for more significant fees and better profit cuts.

Delano knew Laura's hustlers could sneak through showbiz doors usually closed tight. The stacked young beauties and brawny boys she ran placed her in a position to blackmail clients, especially cheating husbands and rich gays with a taste for youthful studs.

Her wealthy clients included closeted men hiding behind unloved "show" wives. As well as providing Laura cash for services rendered, they compensated her by confiding dirt on rival celebrities. Delano knew that among scandal writers, his generosity made him Laura's favorite.

Mike returned to his bride topside, regaining the helm from her. Surrounded by the freshness of the ocean, he felt sickened by this intrusion of Hollywood sleaze.

While he didn't show it, the call left him feeling soiled. For the umpteenth time, he wondered why he was in this business. Bargaining with Laura always heightened his dislike of Hollywood and the gossip trade.

Nor did big money erase his distaste for the celebrity beat. People sold their souls for fame and wealth. The realization he'd become one of them didn't make him feel any better. Rachel noticed his frowns and, concerned, asked who had called.

"Just story tips I've got to pass on to my news agency to check out, nothing much," he replied.

She sensed his evasion and wondered if it had anything to do with her father.

"Does anyone know yet we're married?" she asked

"Sure, it's in the trade papers – also a short bit in the LA Times.

"So, Daddy knows?"

"You bet he does. He knew before it became public. That's why he took out a hit on me."

Delano watched her face to gauge her reaction. She looked worried, her expressive brown eyes full of tenderness.

"He's raging mad at both of us," he added. "You, he may forgive. Me? That's a different story."

He put the boat on autopilot, pulling her to him, their mouths meeting. Lovemaking usually remedied their fears.

CHAPTER TWENTY-THREE:

"SQUAW-MAN"

Banshee wind moaned around the stone chimney stack. Fierce gusts occasionally blew wood smoke back down into the fireplace. Outside, the temperature was 30 degrees below zero. Snow piled high against the cabin's stout pine timbers and began covering its one double-glazed window. Moonlight reflected off ice frozen three feet thick across the 400-mile surface of God's Lake in Manitoba, Canada. An occasional wolf cry floated mournfully in the distance.

Quinton Werner was hungry for fresh meat and wished he, too, was out hunting for moose and caribou, but he wouldn't survive in this icy wilderness. In truth, wolves or bears would likely eat him.

He knew the blizzard outside closed off opportunities for him to hunt or fish. Instead, he huddled in front of the fire, thankful for its life-preserving heat. Sparks flew when he poked the glowing logs for added warmth. Thick clothes and the blazing hearth were barely a match for Canada's savage winter.

He'd been in this icy prison too long; months felt like years. But it was preferable to facing a murder charge back in Los Angeles. While police were looking for him for killing the Spike, Rothenberg sought vengeance for the murder of Liz Hightower and destruction of the *Mission Cyclops* set.

A dark beard covered Werner's cosmetically altered face. Long hair spilled over his shoulders, and he could smell his own stink. He needed to bathe but couldn't face undressing in the Arctic chill.

When forced to flee, he'd angered his jihadist co-conspirators, the Hakim twins; his unexpected departure forced them to postpone their plan to bomb the Academy Awards. A note he left at their LA safe house merely said: "I'll return when the police stop looking for me. That may take a while, but wait for me."

His message gave no clue as to where he was going. When he wrote it, Werner didn't know where he'd hide, just that he had to escape. Abisha and Basheer Hakim had no choice other than await his return. They needed his expertise in Oscars' security. He had convinced them that only he could smuggle bombs into the premier celebrity event.

Quinton's agile mind ached from boredom. He'd read a stack of magazines, watched – and re-watched – a basket of videos. He would have played them again, but the generator ran out of gas. It left him without lights or the use of his satellite phone.

Now he relied on the few remaining candles and blazing pine logs to provide light and heat during the long winter nights of the far north, yet he dreaded daybreak. He'd have to force himself outside, to get more wood and risk hypothermia by boring new ice fishing holes to catch the fish needed to augment his dwindling food supply.

Werner had been in Canada for two months, arriving in Winnipeg from LA via Switzerland. In Geneva, he'd withdrawn $300,000 in cash from the Spike's bank account. The dead hitman's money made him feel secure. Forcing his victim to sign over his savings had been a smart move. Over $3-million was still available in the account.

To go with his surgically altered appearance, his cousins had provided him with a forged US passport and a California driver license in Roberto Costello's name. Relying on his new face and credentials, he hoped to evade investigators when he eventually returned to LA.

The short summer was ending when he reached Manitoba. After studying local maps, he found God's Lake about 500 miles northeast of Winnipeg. Barely populated, the location was an ideal place to disappear. Werner had taken a floatplane to Moose Island Lodge, claiming to be on a fishing trip. There, he bought a boat and outboard motor for cash from Nattah, a rugged Cree widow with whom he began an affair.

A fishing and hunting guide working for the lodge, she lived with her two children at the reservation 20 miles across the lake. Despite her backwoods heritage, Nattah was a canny businesswoman. It didn't escape her attention that this greenhorn had plenty of hard cash. When he said he wanted to winter in Manitoba, she rented him a cabin she owned on one of the many small islands in the middle of God's Lake.

She vowed to bring supplies and stay a few occasional days with him during the worst months. Nattah liked rough sex, and Werner, with his sadistic streak, enjoyed providing it. He rewarded her orgasmic clawing with stinging face slaps and bites that left red teeth marks. In return, she sank her nails into him as he went at her with the vigor of a rutting stag. Struggling to dominate this hard-muscled woman of the woods turned him on. Often, they were both bloody when they'd finished.

That she had no fear of him was challenging, something he could barely tolerate. That challenge wouldn't be over until he controlled her. If she wouldn't yield, thoughts of torture and murder arose in his warped mind.

He complained about the price and usefulness of the weapons and supplies she provided. Nattah believed she'd done everything to ensure the backwoods survival of the man she knew as Roberto Costello. She sold him an old Canadian Army Lee Enfield rifle and a vintage Ruger pistol for twice their worth. She advised they'd be essential for shooting animals for food and warding off marauding bears. She also set him up with ice fishing gear, teaching him how to use it. The lake was full of big trout, walleye, and northern pike, but he found these fish harder to catch than Nattah claimed.

Werner disliked the hand-numbing act of punching holes in the thick frozen surface with an auger. Quinton figured he burned more calories shivering on the windswept ice than he gained from eating the few fish he landed.

Poor fishing and hunting skills meant Werner had gone through most of his canned goods. He'd been unsuccessful in shooting moose and caribou. The big game rarely came within range of the cabin, and when it did, his clumsy movements scared nutritious elk and deer away. Nattah had claimed shooting them would be easy, but for him, it wasn't so.

And, if he succeeded, he dreaded gutting and dressing the carcass in the bitter cold. The woman's survival competency and his lack of it humiliated him. His resentment of Nattah mounted over the lonely days and nights she wasn't there. He grew suspicious she was abandoning him to starve when she didn't show up as expected with the promised paid-for supplies. Beating her to death and pushing the body through the ice became a recurring fantasy.

Werner kept telling himself not to risk that line of brutality. When Nattah came with the needed goods, she left her two children with relatives. If the single mother didn't return, tribal police would come searching for her. Plus, he needed her help to make it through the winter – if she ever showed up. But he became determined to make her suffer when she did arrive. No one disrespected Werner without paying the price.

* * *

Quinton's resentment of Nattah grew more unreasonable as his third snowbound month began. Only two cans of baked beans remained, and frigid hours spent by a hole in the ice yielded one small walleye, barely enough for a meal.

The next day, he tried stalking a pair of caribou from downwind. They scented him and bolted before he could raise his battered rifle. At dusk, he trudged wearily on snowshoes toward the cabin.

He stopped and pulled his cap off his ears when he thought he heard a faint engine noise far out on the frozen lake. Hallelujah! In the distance, he saw a pinpoint of light approaching. It became a beam, then a headlight. Eventually, Nattah's snowmobile crunched to a stop in front of the cabin. Wearing furs, she swung her sturdy body off the machine. Werner waded into the snow, taking her roughly in his arms in belligerent greeting.

"Thank Christ you got here," he growled, his breath steaming furiously. "I've been waiting for you for weeks, running out of everything. Thought you'd forgotten me, you fuckin' bitch."

She responded by pushing her hooded face into his, kissing him on the mouth, biting his lip until it bled to shut off his anger-tinged words. The pain felt good, creating a lustful expectation. It was a relief to feel the heat from another human again.

"Who you calling curse names, city man? I no your bitch. I'm hunter, my people proud," she retaliated, unbowed by his ugly reproach. Nattah mouthed the words awkwardly. She mostly spoke the Plains Cree language. Releasing her, Werner walked around the snowmobile to the sled it towed across the ice.

She'd loaded it with boxes and a ten-gallon drum of diesel fuel. Cutting the restraining cords, Werner unloaded the welcome supplies. The boxes contained cans of pork and beans, bags of rice, dried fruits, nuts, Spam, dried beef, flour, butter, honey, pancake mixes, canned stew, and two bottles of Canadian Club whiskey.

"It's good, Nattah, just what I needed. Thanks," he said reluctantly. "I started thinking I wouldn't see you till spring – if I was still alive," he said.

Now she was angry. "I keep my word. Not let man starve. I showed how to get meat, fish. What wrong? You got the gear. Not my fault, you lousy hunter."

Her scornful remarks rekindled his irrational rage towards her. Relying on this hard-as-nails woman for his existence hurt his pride. He didn't wish to argue; that would come later. He watched her fueling the generator tank. Her strong arms yanked the pull cord several times, and the machine came reluctantly to life, lighting up the cabin. Even that annoyed him; all her actions underlined his helplessness and her superior survival skills.

They carried the cartons into the cabin. With the supplies stowed, they sat at the rickety pine table. Nattah, with a taste for liquor, poured them both triple shots of Canadian Club. She shed her furs and parkas, contentment spreading across her moon-shaped face. It was handsome in its roundness, lined prematurely at age 31 from a life spent mostly outdoors. Relieved to be in the warmth after a grueling 20-mile trip across the frozen lake, she released the pins holding her coiled thick black hair, and it cascaded free.

Her dark slanted eyes surveyed Werner; they were calculating, measuring him. She liked this guy. He looked skinnier than the last time she saw him. He'd been having a hard time. She wanted to make life right for him again. The air of menace about him remained; she detected that, too. Her instincts were those of a hunter: sharp, aware of the danger. He was tough but not as rugged as he thought. Not like Nattah's late husband, Abooksigun, torn apart by a bear five years ago. Drunk when he tried skinning it, he didn't realize he'd merely wounded the animal, not killed it – until it grabbed him.

They'd wed when Nattah became pregnant at 13. Abooksigun, too, tried to break her spirit but couldn't. When he was at the bottle, they had bloody battles that usually ended in brutal sex. From girlhood, Nattah learned to give as good as she got with aggressive males. Years later, several white men regretted trying to force themselves on her after Nattah left them bloody and beaten out in the woods. She picked her own lovers, and hadn't had sex since she last bedded this mysterious city man. Sex with him was good, no tender stuff. They got right at it. A man who couldn't satisfy her didn't get a second chance.

"Get under covers, make warmer than out here," she suggested hungrily.

She was horny as she slipped out of her clothes. Her breasts, never restrained by a bra, swung enticingly free as she slid between sheets and beneath blankets covered by the balding bearskin that acted as a comforter.

Werner stood in the glow of the big stone hearth undressing. He didn't feel like participating in the sexual marathon she expected. She might be burning for him, but he'd cooled off.

He was weary, fed up with everything: his helplessness, the confinement, the freezing environment – and especially her. The Cree whore constantly ordered him about, telling him what to do, how to do it.

He walked to the table, picked up the bottle of whiskey, and took a long swig. Returning to the blazing fire, he took another swig. In bed, Nattah watched indignantly, dark eyes narrowed above the bearskin, making her seem as if she'd become part of the animal.

"Bring the bottle," she demanded as he continued warming himself. "I want...come here. I warm man up with my body."

More than a month of Werner's pent-up rage expressed itself in a torrent of verbiage.

"You can't order me around. I'm not any fucking squaw-man. Get it yourself. Or I might drink it all," Werner snarled, taking a defiant swig.

Now the liquor was talking, bringing out his violent, resentful inner self.

"I'm sick of you telling me what to do—calling me a lousy hunter. You don't know me. I hunt men, destroy them. I'm a killer. And I'll kill you if you don't shut your fuckin' Indian trap…"

She looked at him, eyes crinkling with mocking disbelief. "How many men you kill? You don't kill nothing. Not moose, not fish. You no fire gun straight. Not hook fish good. Big-talk guy. Bet you get sick slitting caribou belly, cuttin' meat, dick shrivels when you cut meat."

His rage burst from a shattered psychological dam at the last insult to his courage – and his manhood.

"Here's the bottle, cunt," he bellowed, hurling it at her head.

Nattah ducked out of the way as he bounded towards the bed. The killer in him was drunkenly roaring for release, ready to inflict injury, even death. She tried warding him off, but he had the advantage of crashing down on her. She was rapidly breathless after his hands locked around her throat, beginning a lethal squeeze. He didn't care anymore. He wanted to see the lights go out of those mocking eyes. Once done, he'd get rid of the body, take the snowmobile, go to Winnipeg and, forgetting the risk, fly back to the States.

Nattah's head sank back into the pillow as his fingers dug deeper, everything going fuzzy. The crazy man meant to kill her. Thoughts of her kids left alone sent a surge of adrenaline through her muscular frame.

Her frantically groping right hand found the still intact half-full liquor bottle. Knowing it could be her last action, she swung it in a vicious sideways arc into Werner's head. The glass broke, soaking them both in alcohol.

His killer rage faded into a pathetic look of surprise. His cruel hands lost their grip. Like a slowly toppling tree, he collapsed away from her. Blood streamed from his brow.

Gasping, she struggled upright. She grabbed the Ruger pistol from the bedside table, keeping it with her as she dressed. Then she got the caribou hide rope from the stores.

When he came to, Nattah was pulling him by the legs off the high bed. He couldn't move a muscle. His naked body hit the rough cedar planks with a bone-jarring crash. He groaned in pain and anger, trying to regain his feet. Before he could stand, a rough pine chair smashed down on his head, opening a second bloody wound.

Nattah wasn't taking any chances with this madman. She bound his arms to his sides, then his hands together. She dragged him naked out to the windswept cabin porch. Once outside, she used her remaining energy to heave his limp form inch by inch onto a log table. There, she lashed him down like he was a load on her sled.

Deep down in his guts, Werner felt terrible fear. It prompted him to wail for mercy, but Nattah wasn't buying it. This son of a bitch had tried to kill her, to make her children face a motherless future. She smiled like a victorious hunter about to give an injured animal the coup de grâce.

Not believing this tenderfoot was dangerous had been a near-fatal mistake. There was something in his eyes that told her he'd done this before, murdered a woman. Now she'd be rid of him in the traditional way Cree warriors disposed of evil-spirited enemies, letting them die in the clutch of nature's icy hands. He would join the legions of tortured ghosts roaming the woods forever in search of salvation.

Nattah spoke rapidly, her words intoned like those of a medicine woman: "Evil spirit dies slow, knows punishment. Evil spirit froze. Bears, wolves find evil spirit. Drag him off. Take flesh, guts, gnaw on bones. Nothing left – just bones."

She closed: "Now I go back to my babies. Not tell Mounties evil spirit want Nattah dead. No men here until the thaw. Long time away. Tenderfoot, he gone. No trace by then."

Tears of humiliation froze as soon as they left Werner's eyes. His body shook furiously in the icy blasts. Now Jack Frost was his fate, not the bullet or knife he'd always expected, not the lethal injection he deserved. The woman had won. Instead of breaking her, he'd become her bitch. Like the people he'd murdered, Werner frantically sought some escape from unexpected death.

"Don't leave me. It was the whiskey. I lost control. I beg you, don't go," Werner pleaded. The chill was already eating into him. His teeth chattered, his limbs were turning numb and blue. The ropes binding him bit his limbs painfully. He heard the snowmobile motor roar to life.

"You can have all my money if you free me! There's nearly $300,000 in the cabin. It's yours," he shouted hoarsely.

Nattah smiled. These would likely be his last words. She slammed the snowmobile grindingly into gear and drove out onto the frozen lake, snickering mercilessly at his plight as she faded into the whiteout. Above the howling wind, Werner could make out her response to his plea.

"Fuck you, *squaw-man!*"

CHAPTER TWENTY-FOUR:

THE MALCONTENT

Morgan Masterson lounged by a rush-bordered lake forming part of his cousin Carlos Bomba's 1,200-hectare Colombian estate. Stretched beside him on a brightly-colored beach blanket were two teenage prostitutes, one on either side. A mostly-consumed two-ounce bag of cocaine lay atop an ice chest near several empty wine bottles.

The actor and his hookers were nude in the warm sunshine, recouping from a wild threesome. All were glassy-eyed-high from the coca washed down with sparkling Prosecco.

The young women gabbled admiringly in Spanish about Morgan's libido, complaining he'd exhausted them, claiming they deserved a cash bonus. But Morgan wasn't listening to drugged-out prattle.

Despite the comforts of his Colombian stay, he desperately wanted away from this place, to be back in California. Living with cartel thugs depressed and scared him, his displeasure showing after a few weeks. He yearned for LA glitz, fans, and fawning Tinseltown minions.

Most of all, he missed starstruck beauties throwing themselves into his arms. Isolated in this drug kingdom, he hired prostitutes. Cartel wives, mistresses, and family members were off-limits. Their murderous partners threatened death for merely flirting with their women.

These fearless gangsters considered Morgan a conceited fop, one who'd piss his pants at real danger. They mocked him for not being the hero he portrayed on the screen, for being the coward who ran out on his dying father. Oh yes, they remembered that story. And so did most of the drug trade people.

But being the drug chieftain's beloved cousin saved him from the beating all agreed he so richly deserved. Terrified by their hostility, Morgan prayed his stay would be brief, that he'd soon reclaim celebrity life amid the California palms.

He fingered his cell phone, unsure whether to make the call that had been on his mind most of the day. Eventually, he stood up and walked along the lakeshore, away from the high, chattering women. Standing knee-deep and naked among the lily pads, he dialed the personal satellite number only he and a few Paragon executives knew.

"Hello, Morgan," Max Rothenberg groaned unenthusiastically, deeply displeased at hearing from his banished superstar. He had been napping in a hammock strung amid the cool breezes on the balcony of the main suite at his Costa Rican island estate.

"What's your problem now?"

Fortified by wine and cocaine, Morgan unloaded, his words tumbling out: "I'm going crazy down here. I want to come back – and soon. You must give me a role in one of the two big movies I know Paragon's making this year."

Rothenberg sighed heavily. This spoiled man-child disgusted him, but Morgan was still a danger to Paragon, so he reluctantly placated him.

"Come on, Morgan, we've been over this before. You've been away just a few weeks. It will take much longer before fans give you a serious second look portraying a hero."

Masterson's voice rose to a demanding druggie shriek. As of now nobody said no to him, not even this nasty prick of a British kingmaker, whose billions allowed him to flit between London, LA, and all over the world, screwing with other people's lives.

"Don't give me excuses, Max. I'm your hottest property. They worship me. Women fantasize about me when they're fucking their ugly boring husbands…" he said, sniffing indignantly through cocaine-clogged nostrils.

Rothenberg grew impatient, his voice sharp enough to cut glass. "Our PR people tell me your Q rating is down the tubes. Fans don't see an action hero anymore when they look at you. They see the sex- and drug-besotted coward who ran away from a dying woman. Research shows they have nothing but contempt for the heartless fool who allowed her to over-dose on the heroin he supplied."

Rothenberg paused to let this bitter reproach sink in.

"You're just another Hollywood star shown to be a louse. You made fools of your so-called fans. You're an especially nasty reminder that movie people sell phony images they can't live up to."

This frank assessment shocked Morgan. His frustration made him desperate. He waded out of the lake and up the sandy beach, pleading, "Don't give up on me, Max. Get your PR people working on it. They've cleaned up worse problems. I'll do interviews with the glossy magazines, with the lousy tabs if necessary. I'll follow whatever advice the PR folks come up with."

Rothenberg sighed. Would this fool never learn? He struggled out of his hammock. He looked out at the blue ocean far below his mountain-top home, wishing he hadn't picked up this call.

"That won't do you any good. You're toxic," he interrupted. "This is no minor problem you've created. Confession and rehab won't be enough this time."

The mogul knew if Morgan got on his knees to confess his betrayal, it wouldn't bring Liz back to life or repair the damage Werner's Florida attack had done. Nor would it offset the noxious scandal stories Delano had spread around the world.

"Bible-belt dummies may feast on that remorse stuff," he concluded. "But not this time. Morgan. Your professional image is at the bottom of the cesspit. It stinks to high heaven with everyone."

Despairing, Morgan recklessly played his trump card: "Remember, Max, if I go down, you go with me. Your links to the Chicago mob, nannies with their throats cut – all kinds of nasty shit. Remember, too, my cousin leads an army of drug dealers. They've got pictures of your stars doing blow – partying with teenage hookers. I think you're in some of those snaps, too."

Right then, Rothenberg decided to get rid of Morgan – forever. The fool was making threats on an open phone line. The National Security Agency could be listening in, probably was – especially as the idiot was calling from a Colombian drug czar's compound.

Mindful of possible eavesdroppers, his tone warmed while his words became more cautious: "Morgan, you're talking total nonsense. I don't know where you're getting all that ugly stuff. None of it's true. None of it."

He paused and then continued in a more consoling tone: "I know you're miserable. Sit tight a while longer. I care about you. But you can't return yet. You'll be back, I promise. But not now."

Max disconnected, as was his habit, without a good-bye, leaving Morgan looking at his phone indignantly. The actor was just beginning to like what he heard. Then silence – Rothenberg was gone.

"Arrogant pig, what the fuck?" he said to no one, spitting out the words, stamping through the lake shallows. "Can't say goodbye like a civilized person. Money-grubbing son-of-a-bitch. I'll fix him. Kick his fat ass publicly. See how he likes that. I hope he dies in agony from cancer."

Cocaine-wild features twisted with hate, muttering menacingly, he reached the young women. "Put your clothes on. Get out of here. Get going. Fuck off!" Morgan bellowed, throwing down his phone. To hurry them, he yanked the blanket out from under their bare asses. Raging, he picked up the empty wine bottles, one in each hand – and flung them far out into the lake as if they were the cause of his problems.

Shaken, the girls scrambled into their tops and jeans, eager to escape this madman.

"I'll show that bastard you can't mess with Morgan Masterson," he bellowed at the fleeing prostitutes.

Getting their nerve up, they screeched back: "What about our money?"

"I paid in sex, cocaine, and wine…now leave before I have Carlos's men kill you," he warned.

Frightened, they disappeared into the distance without further protest.

* * *

His morning spoiled, Rothenberg sank into the big leather sofa in his study, ready to think. Morgan had done too much damage and now dared to threaten him. He'd allowed him to get too close, to know too much; there could be no "comeback" from the turmoil he'd created for Paragon.

He called Ackerman to his suite, telling him: "I've decided what we do about Morgan. We'll bring him here. We'll give him a pleasant welcome, but it will be more of a farewell party."

The security chief nodded approvingly, glad his boss was finally ridding them of a major liability.

It was a different Lord Max on the phone when he surprised the Hollywood idol with a call an hour later, inviting him to visit Costa Rica to discuss his career prospects.

"I know there's been bad blood, but we've always been friends, and shared many successes. I've been rethinking your future – and I have ideas you'll like," the mogul said, his voice honey-toned.

Morgan, down from his drug high and brooding in his bedroom, became faint with relief. Giving the Boss a piece of his mind had paid off.

"Oh, Max, I knew you'd come through for me," he said, choking back deep, emotional gratitude.

"When do you want me there? I can get a flight to LA tonight."

"Not LA," said Rothenberg. "I'm on my island. You can fly to San José. I'll send a boat to bring you here from Playa Jaco."

"I can do better than that. My cousin has floatplanes," said Morgan. "He'll be glad to fly me directly there. That way, I can arrive the day after tomorrow, the latest."

"OK, sounds good. Looking forward to seeing you," said Rothenberg.

"Can't wait," said Morgan.

"Yes, we'll have fun – just like old times," the mogul promised.

"What you got in mind?" Morgan asked, hoping Max had brought some starlets down with him, like on past trips to the island together.

"You'll see. After we've talked about your career, the fun begins," Rothenberg hinted mischievously.

His Lordship hung up, again without saying goodbye.

But this time, Morgan didn't resent his rudeness. Instead, he hurried to see Carlos, whom a guard said was in the basement counting room. It was off-limits to people not working there.

"It's forbidden to disturb him," the man warned.

Ignoring the caution, Morgan ran down the stairs and knocked loudly on the door. When there was no reply, he pressed a security buzzer.

* * *

Carlos Bomba was sipping a half-tumbler of 18-year-old single malt scotch as he watched fourteen of the cartel's financial specialists prepare the take for counting. They had piled the cash high on the twenty-foot-long polished mahogany table.

Some bills were old and tattered, others spanking new as the specialists fed them into a battery of counting machines. Drug revenues from Europe and the Americas neared three hundred million in hard cash. They represented months of cocaine sales.

The sight of a colorful mountain of bills always made Carlos feel good, proud of his cartel's success. When the buzzer sounded in the secure room, it startled the drug boss out of his self-congratulatory thoughts.

He sprang to his feet, stepping back from the table, a .45 Taurus in his right hand. The cash counters grabbed machine pistols. There was silence. A lock of Carlos's unruly dark hair fell across his brow as he nodded to the head counter.

The jittery little man pressed a button, and a steel security door swung slowly open. Every muzzle pointed at the entrance. Standing there was Morgan, awed at the sight of so much cash, unnerved by so many guns aimed at him. He regained composure when they lowered their weapons.

"What's up?" Carlos asked, irritated by the intrusion and escorting the actor out of the counting room.

"I've got great news, *primo,*" Morgan replied, smiling.

"What's that?"

"Max has invited me to join him on his island to discuss my career revival. He needs me back in Hollywood. Can one of your pilots fly me to Costa Rica?"

"Yeah, I can arrange that," Carlos said thoughtfully.

Running a drug empire made him wise. Far brighter than his peacock cousin. The savvy gangster smelled a rat. Carlos looked at the gloating actor with pity for his naivete.

"That fat *chocha,* I no trust him. He's a tricky one. He wants you on some island. Why not LA where he runs movie business?" he questioned.

Blind to anything other than restoring his former glory, Morgan scoffed at Carlos's skepticism.

"Don't spoil this for me," he pleaded. "This trip could be my only chance of salvation."

"OK, cousin, you know best. But I do not allow you to go alone," Carlos said, thinking that Rothenberg behaved like a drug lord, a man more like himself.

"You go on my plane, a couple of my guys, and I come, too. Yes?"

Morgan thought it needless but agreed. It was useless resisting Carlos's decisions. He returned to his bedroom suite, where he could speak on the phone privately.

He wanted to share his news with one of the few Hollywood people he considered a true friend. He called Stuart Cohen, director of the delayed *Mission Cyclops*. Under studio pressure, Cohen had exploited the fatal helicopter crash, splicing it into the final cut.

But the news about Morgan's involvement in the flight attendant's drug death broke before the movie's release, so it remained on the shelf. The leading man was too toxic.

"Hey, man, I'm getting back in good with Max. He's setting up a meeting at his place in Costa Rica," Morgan blurted out as soon as Cohen answered.

Stuart Cohen disliked Morgan intensely. He feigned friendship because it was politically expedient. The actor's news shocked him. Summoning up all the phony camaraderie he could muster, he pretended enthusiasm.

"Marvelous news! The whole town's wondering where you've been. We've missed you, Morgan."

Thrilled to be talking to someone who'd recognize the importance of what he was saying, Morgan couldn't help bragging.

"I'm coming back big-time, Stu. Big-time. You can take that to the bank. Those folks who wrote me off, they'll be sorry. I'll make sure of that."

Cohen, who owed his directing success to Morgan's films, didn't believe any comeback possible. Morgan was the new poster boy for Hollywood debauchery. On the other hand, Cohen wasn't taking chances. In this business, you were up one day, down the next–but that didn't mean you couldn't rise again, even from career suicide. Cohen knew how to play the game; he was a master at it.

"We'll have a huge party, a real celebration when you get back. All your pals will be there," he said. "I'd love to direct your comeback movie. You'll make it big again, brother – thrilled to hear the news."

Choking up, Morgan was glad there were people he could still count on to wish him well.

"I love you, man," Morgan said before hanging up.

Perplexed and wondering why Max hadn't told him about this development, Cohen put down his phone. It was hard to believe Rothenberg could make such a colossal blunder.

"Stupid asshole, he's out of his mind," he said. "I never wanted to see that self-serving douchebag again. Christ knows how he's managed to bring Max around."

"Who are you talking about, Stu?" his bedmate asked lazily.

"Morgan Masterson. He's meeting up with Max Rothenberg – on his private island, no less. Says Max promised him another gig. Can't believe Rothenberg's such a schmuck."

The boy, a gorgeous blonde 18-year-old from Arkansas, smiled, pretending not to understand the value of Stu's words. But this was insider stuff, a chance to make some money.

He went by the name Van and was one of Laura Chesley's boys. She'd usually hand him a couple of hundred extra bucks for good information.

His clients, most of them closeted gays and bisexuals occupying the upper levels of Tinseltown, paid $1,000 a night to sleep with him.

The next day he went to see Laura, to pass over her cut of Cohen's fee. She shocked him by pressing four crisp hundred-dollar bills back into his hand after he related the conversation he'd heard. Then, to his dismay, she kissed him.

Laura's first call was to Mike Delano. Sitting in the cabin of his boat, the journalist picked up.

"Morgan Masterson's getting a second chance from Rothenberg," she said. "They're meeting on the big shot's private island. It sounds like a good story for you. You got sources in Costa Rica, right?"

"I just might," Mike replied. "And thanks for the info. I'll have my office send you a check for $3,000. OK?"

"Fair enough," she said, thinking what an easy profit she'd turned even after allowing Van to keep her commission.

CHAPTER TWENTY-FIVE:

RESURRECTION

It was difficult seeing ahead as Nattah gunned the snowmobile over lake ice into biting wind and billowing snow. Eager to be home with her kids, she was going too fast for the conditions. Clouds blotted out the stars, rendering them useless for navigation, making her unsure of her exact direction.

The outside world matched the swirling confusion in her mind. Fuck that white man. He was hiding a big secret, and she hadn't a clue what it was. He'd tried to kill her; he claimed to have killed others. After what he'd done to her, she believed him. It quieted any guilt she might have experienced for abandoning him to die.

Werner's last desperate words stuck in Nattah's mind, however, as she sped through the swirling whiteness. Was there three hundred thousand dollars stashed in the cabin she'd rented him? Or was it just a pathetic try at saving his miserable hide?

What if searchers discovered the cash in the spring? If they were tribal police, she knew they'd keep it for sure. The thought of losing such riches nagged at her. Opportunities to make big bucks never came her way. This was a fortune. Enough to get the family off the reservation. That much dough would buy a winter place in Winnipeg for them. Or maybe she would build a summer hunting lodge, get a bigger boat, and the new fishing and hunting equipment she needed.

If the money was there, she reasoned, why shouldn't she have it? The cash wouldn't do him any good after critters ripped his pathetic carcass apart, she thought nastily.

Nattah brought the snowmobile to an abrupt halt – she had to go back, she had to know. She'd never sleep nights if she didn't uncover the truth. Nearly an hour would have passed when she got back to the cabin. Hypothermia would be getting to the man she knew as Roberto by then; the cold would soon turn him into a block of solid ice.

Snow flew behind her in a perfect rooster tail as she opened the throttle wide, circling back until the cabin's lights came into view again. As she got closer, she could hear the generator still running. No doubt, the engine noise and light from the open cabin door had discouraged any prowling predators. She was glad not to deal with hungry bears. Walking with cougar-like caution, she climbed the three steps up to the porch.

There was no movement from the naked man lashed to the picnic table. The cruel face remained motionless with eyes closed. His dark beard and hair had frosted. She looked closer. Hell. Faint wisps of breath rose as he breathed out. There was still life in him, but not much. She jumped back, startled when the frosted lids cracked open, the eyes gazing, pleading.

"Help me," he said in a barely audible plea.

It horrified Nattah. The evil one was hanging in. What should she do? The thought occurred of shoveling snow over him to speed his departure. She'd killed many animals, but never a man. She put that idea aside. It would defeat her purpose.

"Where's the money?" she whispered menacingly into his frozen ear. "You tell, or I gut you like walleye. Where'd you put it?

"Get me inside," he begged. "Then, I'll tell you..."

"You lie," she said, leaving him and entering the cabin.

Her search revealed nothing. She looked under the bed, in the two cupboards, up in the ceiling rafters, in two travel bags. Nattah's blood was up. He'd hidden the fortune outside or under the cabin. Had to be. Only he knew where.

The Cree woman was angry and frustrated. Was this a wasted return journey? She went back to the porch, unsheathing her long hunting knife as she bent over him.

His dark eyes stared up at her wide with alarm. Was she about to stab him?

Instead, Nattah cut the ropes binding him. She heaved, and he came off the table with a thump.

As strong as she was, Nattah already ached from the effort of dragging him onto the porch, and now she was lugging him back inside.

She dropped him in front of the hearth. The fire was flickering low but still had plenty of glowing embers. With fresh logs, it roared back to life. When she abandoned him, in her haste to leave, she'd left the cabin door open. She reckoned just enough heat reached him through the opening to temporarily ward off death.

Now the added warmth would revive him. To speed his recovery, she pulled the bearskin off the bed and covered his shaking body.

The gash in his head was bleeding again from her rough treatment. She applied bandages from the emergency medical kit. She kept his hands tied.

Nattah would never trust him again, not even in this sorry state. He was a crazed animal; she knew that now. Three hours passed, and he'd improved enough to beg for something to drink. Nattah opened a can of beef broth and heated it on the propane stove. She propped him up with pillows in front of the blazing logs. She hated reviving this monster, but it was the only way to get what she wanted.

Mouthful by mouthful, she fed him the warm broth. Little by little, color returned to his face. His nose and ears were frostbitten, his legs and feet numb. He was coughing, too. Nattah suspected pneumonia would set in, that he wouldn't survive the winter without medical treatment.

That was good. His death fit her plan well. Better he dies alone in the cabin. When they found him, there'd be nothing to connect his death to her. Just a tenderfoot unable to handle a backwoods winter.

Glad to be alive, Werner felt no gratitude towards this Indian cunt. Werner viewed her with unrelenting hatred. Given the opportunity, he'd kill her. He looked at the knife in its sheath at her side, wishing his hands were free.

If only he had the strength to wrest it from her, to stab her to death. He felt ashamed that, again, his survival depended on her. The bitch was feeding him, nursing him. The lure of money had earned him a reprieve. Piss her off, and she'd reinstate the death sentence.

She was a dangerous woman, something he'd sensed and liked when they first met. But not anymore.

Nattah opened the second, untouched bottle of Canadian Club she'd delivered earlier and poured herself a shot. She walked over to the hearth, looking down at the wreck of Roberto Costello.

"You wanna drink? Make you feel better," she suggested, hoping the alcohol might loosen his tongue.

"Yeah, mix it with some hot tea and some of that canned milk," Werner murmured.

Nattah heated the water, filled half a mug with whiskey mixed with tea and condensed milk. With her help, Werner gulped it down. Feeling the fiery warmth spread through his body, he asked for a second drink. Nattah poured another mug full, adding more whiskey this time.

"Now, where the money you promised, big mouth," she said, prodding him with the barrel of the old Ruger pistol she'd sold him months previously.

"I'll give you fifty grand," he said, the booze starting to slur his words.

"You liar, you say $300,000."

"You get the cash when I'm well, and that's gonna take a few days."

Werner didn't expect what happened next. A rope went around his neck. She pulled back sharply, making him gag up tea and whiskey, yanking him out from under the warmth of the bearskin.

"You want me to haul your ass back outside, killer-man?" Nattah snarled, her face glowering into his, her right hand simultaneously twisting his frostbitten nose until, despite the frostbite, he wailed at the sudden pain.

"Stop, stop," he sobbed. "I'll tell you…"

"That's better, you do not fool Nattah second time. Once enough. I make you die fast, you lie. Tongue tells big lies all times."

He tried to compose himself. The rope was still around his neck. He couldn't tolerate the thought of being out in the bone-freezing cold again. His nose throbbed. Nattah's thumb and finger had left white prints on its ruby tenderness.

Suddenly, she was all sweetness and light: "You don't need to suffer no more. Just say where the money is hidden. Then Nattah nurse you up good – and go. You get well. Return to big city…"

He looked at her, defeated now. He must give her the cash. This bitch always succeeded in making him feel like a failure. He wished they'd never met. More than anything, he wished he'd killed her. Another sharp jerk on the rope, and he was telling her what she wanted to know.

"There's a stone at the far end of the hearth away from the heat; I dug it out. Money's behind it," he said in a thin, peevish whimper.

Out came the big hunting knife, and Nattah probed where he pointed. The stone moved. She pulled it out, setting it on the hearth. The black leather bag inside was weighty. The dirty liar was telling the truth – finally.

Sitting at the table, she unzipped the bag and turned it upside down. Packets of cash cascaded out, all $100 bills in many thousand-dollar wads.

Her eyes widened; she'd never seen so many American greenbacks. Her heart sang.

Despairing, Werner's head fell to his chest. If she took it all, he'd be left stranded in the wilderness, sick and needy with barely enough supplies to last until spring. Then, not even the cash for a return ticket to LA. At the table, Nattah was busy counting. It surprised her; he hadn't lied. There was nearly $270,000 here.

"OK, I bring in more logs, put whiskey bottle near, canned food and opener, a jug of water. Then I'm outta here with my money. I did like you say. I come back and save you. Deal's done. I'm gone."

Then, what sounded like the squeal of a wounded animal stopped her as she scooped the cash back into the moneybag. "Please, please, don't take it all. Gimme a chance. I gotta get back to civilization. You can't take it all. Leave me half."

Nattah's laugh was harsh, like the growl of a wolf bringing down a fawn. "Half? You make a big joke, yes?"

"I'm talking about you taking more than a hundred grand. That's good—more money than you've ever seen. I'll send you more when I get to where I'm going. I swear it."

"You liar, cheat. No trust words from twisted mouth. Because I'm a good Cree woman, I leave you $3,000." She counted the bills onto the table, zipped up the bag, and said, "That gets you where you from. Don't return. My people or I see you near our village, we kill you."

Werner tried getting to his feet, but a quick jerk on the rope sent him sprawling. Dressed in her winter gear, she stood ready to leave. With the Ruger in her right hand pointed at his head, Nattah reached down and used the knife in her left to cut his wrists free.

Grabbing the cash bag, she was out the door in three long strides. Clad in her furs and humming some happy Cree ditty, she started the snowmobile motor. Quickly, the sound of its engine disappeared into the oceans of whiteness. Quinton was alone with his anguished thoughts until the spring thaw.

But she'd left him a few bucks; he had the means to get home. It wasn't all bad. He was inside, not lashed to a table naked and freezing. It had been expensive, but it was so good to be back in the warm cabin, hoping for a future. He'd make it through. Thinking about the $2 million left in the Swiss account cheered him up.

He could still help his cousins with their murderous Oscars ambitions – and complete his revenge on Lord Maxwell. He picked up the newly charged satellite phone to call the Lebanese terrorists to assure them of his return.

CHAPTER TWENTY-SIX:

BIG GAME FISHING

The vintage Catalina flying boat came in over the island, landing gracefully on the bay's mirror-smooth waters before taxiing toward the floating dock. The aircraft was one of three World War Two-era amphibians Carlos Bomba used to ferry dope from Colombian jungle rivers to boats on the ocean.

Morgan sat with Carlos behind the pilot during the flight. Behind them were two of the cartel's best *sicarios*, hitmen who could shoot the whiskers off a running rat. The actor thrilled at seeing Max Rothenberg standing on the dock with two guards waiting to welcome him. It was a good omen, the great man coming personally to greet him.

Stepping out of the Catalina, he hurried into the studio chief's welcoming arms. They held Morgan in a bear hug as tears of relief and gratitude ran down Morgan's handsome face. The actor's hand stayed on Max's arm, squeezing hard as he tried to find the right placatory words to soothe the mogul.

"God, Max, I can't tell you how good it is to see you again. I hated our rift. I've so wanted this moment. Please, let's settle the problems between us. I swear I'll never step out of line again," he said, struggling to control his overwrought emotions.

"Yes, that's right. I want to settle our problems," Rothenberg replied with a thin smile. "I'm hoping you've learned your lesson. If not, there's no future for you with us or anywhere else for that matter. I hate to think I've wasted time and money on a useless investment."

Morgan nodded in servile agreement, resentfully accepting blame he couldn't dodge. This meeting would decide whether he'd ever appear in front of a camera again. He was desperate to save his tattered career.

With their minders in tow, Rothenberg guided Morgan into a cable car. It ran up the side of the mountain for those arriving by sea. The mogul usually flew in by helicopter from San José, landing on a special pad close to his grand mountaintop mansion.

The trolley glided up smoothly to the summit. There, Max and Morgan stepped out to be greeted by Gil Ackerman, whose unexpected presence set the superstar's heart pounding with fear and suspicion.

Relief flooded the actor when Gil offered a handshake and welcoming smile. Morgan realized he must have been wrong in thinking it was Ackerman who told Liz about his prior knowledge of the Florida attack.

Max wouldn't have wanted to discuss Morgan's future if Ackerman had revealed his cowardice. No way would he be getting this second chance.

Leaving Ackerman behind talking amiably to Carlos and his men, Morgan and Rothenberg walked towards the grand mansion.

"Too bad you've brought your cousin and his men with you. I wanted our meeting uninterrupted," Rothenberg remarked as they entered his home. "I hoped you'd talk Carlos out of making the trip. I thought they'd drop you off and return to Colombia. Having him here will just make things more… complicated."

Morgan flushed uncomfortably. He, too, suspected his cousin's presence would sour their reconciliation.

"He insisted on coming. I kept telling him it was unnecessary, but once he'd decided on making the trip, I couldn't change his mind," he apologized.

Rothenberg's reaction was an irritated grunt. Even under different circumstances, he would dislike Carlos being there. Cocaine was a problem with many Paragon employees, and he knew Carlos ran their supply chain.

Morgan sought to soothe Max. "He won't get in our way. I'll see to it. Please accept my deepest apologies for the problems I've caused."

"I'm trying, but it's difficult," Rothenberg remarked dryly.

An elevator took them to the mansion's second floor. There, the mogul showed Morgan to a suite with adjoining bedrooms for him and Carlos.

"Bomba's men can eat and sleep in the staff wing with my guards," Max said firmly.

When Carlos entered Morgan's bedroom for a chat, his mood was dark. He disliked separation from his *sicarios*. Still, with a knife strapped to his leg and a pistol in a shoulder holster, he could take care of any threat to himself or Morgan.

The actor hastily brushed off his cousin's suspicions about Rothenberg's motives. "Don't start causing trouble," he said. "Max and I have difficult decisions to make. It doesn't help, you sewing doubts about him in my mind."

Carlos left in a huff. At least his room adjoined Morgan's. He didn't trust Rothenberg; he thought his cousin stupid for doing so. His sense of survival was ever-active. The rumor was he slept with one eye open. Anyone sneaking up on him in the night died suddenly.

With Carlos gone, Morgan threw himself down on the king-sized bed. The 600-mile flight over land and sea had wearied him. The first meeting with Max left him tense.

Morgan again vowed to rein in his degeneracy. He determined to get more professional support. Amy, his shrink, wasn't helping enough; he would replace her. His addiction to sex and drugs would be hard to quell.

He would tell Max he was willing to spend time in a rehab clinic. That had far more appeal than returning to South America and isolating with a bunch of murderous drug thugs. The contempt shown by Carlos's men terrified Morgan. He could tell they saw him as weak, cowardly, and self-indulgent.

It was good to be back on the island. He and Max had partied here in better days. He hoped this wouldn't be his last visit to Rothenberg's off-shore complex. Thirty-five construction workers had labored for six years erecting this impressive retreat – all the building materials delivered by boat and helicopter from the mainland.

The island was one mile long, most of it a large mountain rising straight from the seabed. The mansion comprised three wings, one for the Boss, another for guests, and the third for staff. The center was an open lounge, a beautiful wood-paneled dining hall, and a fully equipped media room.

All around, the views were of the Pacific and sheer cliffs descending to surf-pounded rocks. Rothenberg's yacht, a 50-foot Viking Sports Fisher, awaited his use.

Nobody approached this fortress without detection by guards with powerful binoculars. A mile-wide bay with a narrow inlet facing south was the only way in from the ocean. Only a man worth billions could afford such tropical privacy, Morgan thought jealously. He regretted blowing his wealth on divorce and wild living.

Carlos's raucous arrival from the adjoining room jolted him out of his rare and disagreeable introspection.

"You no ready yet, cousin? I need to eat. I could eat a cow. See what's on the fat guy's menu. He gets an extra good share of the best food, by the look of him," he said, grinning.

"I wish you'd stop insulting Max," Morgan snapped. "I'm here to mend our broken friendship and business alliance, not to make him angrier by mocking him …"

"I help you, don't worry. I get it," Carlos said, unruffled by the criticism.

They joined their host in the dining hall, where a white-coated bartender poured perfect chilled martinis. Over drinks, Morgan tried to launch discussions about his stalled career, but Rothenberg airily rebuffed him.

"Relax, we can talk about that after dinner," was his response.

Hiding his impatience, Morgan struggled to keep the atmosphere agreeable, but as the evening went on, not so Carlos. He rolled his eyes in silent mockery of the movie chief's comments. He became drunker by the minute. Tensions mounted.

The actor was helpless to calm the fundamental hostility between Rothenberg and Bomba. Sitting at a large oak dinner table designed for 14 guests, they were a chilly threesome, Max at the head of the table, Morgan, and Carlos on either side.

The dinner was superb: reef-caught Cubera snapper, fresh-baked bread, tropical fruit soufflés with cream, aged cheese, and wine. Over coffee and brandy, Rothenberg was finally ready to discuss business. But first, he wanted the annoying cartel boss gone.

"Carlos, give us privacy to talk, please," he commanded as he gestured toward the door.

Carlos's face flushed. He didn't take orders from anyone. The effect of three martinis and his share of a bottle of vintage red wine at dinner took over.

"You not my Boss. Don't tell me what to do. I'm no *campesino*. I'm a boss, too. Nothing you say to my cousin I can't hear. *Comprende*?"

Throwing Carlos a warning look, Morgan tried to silence his aggressive relative.

"Max means no disrespect, Carlos. Do as he says. Let us talk alone," he pleaded.

Rothenberg's guards watched apprehensively, hands on their weapons. Unperturbed, Max surveyed drunk Carlos. "All right, you may stay. You won't like what I must say – so please remain silent. I won't tolerate any interference."

Slumped in his chair, Carlos snorted defiantly. He was angry but listening.

Morgan didn't wait to hear what Max had to say. He spoke eagerly: "I want to return. I know I need to rebuild my image. But, Max, just let me come back."

"Not until I'm satisfied you're under control," Rothenberg declared bluntly. "Let's face it, Morgan, you've fouled your nest; left us covered in crap. For that reason, no more major roles."

He paused, relishing the shock on the superstar's face, then continued: "I might allow a slow comeback doing some low-budget features and supporting roles. That's it. Maybe, a few years from now, I'll change my mind. It depends entirely on how the press and the public respond."

His words were a stiletto through Morgan's heart – and he could see Rothenberg enjoyed twisting it. But he suppressed his bitter disappointment.

"Max, if that's the only way, I'll do the minor roles. I'll prove you still need me. You won't be sorry…"

But this offer was too much of an insult for Carlos. The contents of a large brandy snifter slopped on the polished oak table as he leaped up, waving his arms in protest.

"What kinda fuckin' deal you offering?" he objected. "You say he's not big star no more. Then he don't work for your cheap-ass studio. He don't want shitty little parts; he's superstar. You disrespecting him. Sticking finger in the Bomba family eye, too."

Morgan again tried silencing his enraged relative, shaking his head to indicate Carlos should shut up. This embarrassing reaction made it seem like a drug deal gone wrong, not a Hollywood negotiation.

"You don't understand our business, Carlos," Morgan explained. "He's preparing the way for my eventual return. It's what I need, a gradual reintroduction. Please, apologize to Max…"

Outraged at having come so far to hear so little, Carlos howled his displeasure. He glared at Rothenberg and gave him the finger.

"Apologize? I say go fuck yourself, fat man!"

He pounded the table again, this time so forcefully, porcelain cups and cut crystal jumped about hazardously. The sound of guards cocking weapons was also audible.

Carlos flung down his napkin, pushed back his chair, and staggered around the table to confront his quaking cousin.

"You got no balls, that's your problem, Morgan," he hissed. "You worthless coward. Get a better deal before we leave the island tomorrow. I take you with me, whether you like it or not. *Comprende, Alejandro?*"

Morgan nodded weakly, furious at the mention of that name—the name of the youngster who ran, leaving his father to die. He felt relief when Carlos staggered out, slamming the door behind him. Rothenberg's guards followed close behind.

Now Morgan was alone with Rothenberg at the big table. Morgan was about to apologize again, but Rothenberg spoke first, his voice low and hostile.

"So, do you agree with Carlos? Do you believe I'm doing you a disservice? Now is the occasion to speak…"

Morgan swore he approved his new career plan. He condemned Carlos as an ignoramus who knew nothing about the business and begged forgiveness for his boorishness.

"I want to work again. You've never steered me wrong, Max. I know you won't now. I can wait for the big roles to come back later," Morgan conceded meekly.

Rothenberg nodded his approval. He had enjoyed his game of psychological torture.

* * *

Carlos awoke the following morning hungover but in slightly better humor. He and his men ate breakfast, laughing and joking about Rothenberg's sissy guards. Better still, the drug king had decided they would leave the island that day and take his loser cousin with them – by force, if necessary. Picking up the house phone, Carlos called Morgan, who was still sleeping.

The dispirited actor answered groggily: "Yeah, what's up? I need more shuteye…"

"Get your stuff together. This guy, he make fool of you. Bit parts! I called for the plane's return hours ago. We leave soon." Carlos said. "This place, bad deal. I get you a good contract in Colombian movies. You don't need to eat shit from Max. Forget past. Start again in Colombia."

Morgan, now alert, registered utter disgust. "Are you out of your mind? I couldn't work there. I have to return to LA. It's where I belong, not in some sweatbox studio in the fucking jungle."

Morgan's ungrateful put-down stung Carlos. "Don't be a prick with me. Be on the patio where the trolley goes down the mountain in one hour," Carlos ordered, "or we come get you. You know what that means. Good thing you got the thick skull, cousin, 'cause you need it when we bang your fuckin' stupid head…"

An hour later, intending to let Carlos leave without him but afraid to face him alone, Morgan was waiting near the upper terminal of the cable car with Gil Ackerman.

The security chief's presence irritated Carlos as he and his men approached. The Colombian considered Gil a lackey. Any one of his men could take him out. Not wanting to reveal his hand, Carlos nodded in a friendly fashion and drew level with Morgan and his new protector.

"Why you here?" Carlos asked Ackerman. "You not invited…you not needed."

"Mr. Rothenberg would like you gentlemen to stay a while longer," Gil countered coldly, ignoring Carlos's question.

Carlos's voice assumed an equal chill. He wasn't letting some Yankee flunky push him around. They were leaving, and no one was stopping them.

"Tell Rothenberg, go fuck himself. I wanted to say *gracias* for hospitality. But not no more. He show no respect. Push me around. Bad way to treat an important guy like me," he said menacingly.

Ackerman grinned nastily. "Important guy? You're kidding. You're a drug-running punk. The best parts of you ran out of your mama's pussy when daddy finished doing her in the slum where they lived. Important? No fuckin' way. You're an asshole."

Carlos moved like lightning for his .45 but not fast enough. Red laser dots appeared on him and his men, followed by a shatteringly loud volley of gunfire. Squawking birds rose from the mountainside palms. One sicario pitched forward dead; the volley had blown the top of his skull off.

Blood and brains spattered Morgan and Ackerman, both of whom had dived to safety. The other Colombian gunman lay writhing, shot through the groin, his face masked in agony. Carlos hit in the shoulder, his gun dropped, cursed the hidden shooters.

Rifle smoke drifted up from different parts of the dense foliage. Ackerman's CIA training showed. He'd had his marksmen cover the location from all angles. They'd zeroed in before the Colombians arrived.

Carlos's mind raced as he lay on the ground in agony. They'd suckered him into a trap, and it seemed his filthy traitorous cousin was in on the ambush. Morgan and Ackerman had dived to safety before bullets flew.

Bitterly, Carlos asked himself why he'd never accepted the warnings: Morgan was a rat. As he lay injured, the drug boss hated being outmaneuvered, especially by a family member's betrayal. Overhead he heard the roar of the approaching Catalina amphibian.

As his shoulder bled and throbbed, he accepted that he and his men wouldn't be making the journey home. Morgan and Ackerman were back on their feet. Above him, Carlos heard Ackerman on his walkie-talkie, reporting to his master.

"Yeah, no problems, Boss. Bunch of amateurs. They walked right into us. I killed one of them outright. I'm about to take care of another one. Carlos is still alive. You want him gone, too?"

"No, keep him going. We want him on the boat, don't we?" Rothenberg responded over the wireless link.

"Of course we do – sorry, Boss. I'll patch him up. You go down to the dock. I'm bringing Morgan and the others down too…"

"I'm already aboard the boat," Rothenberg said.

"OK, Boss, good."

Ackerman had disarmed Carlos while he was on the ground, shoving him back down as he struggled to rise. Now he sent up to the house for bandages to stanch the Colombian's wound. While waiting, he walked over to the groin-shot *sicario*.

"Time for you to go, boyo. Figure I'm doing you a big favor," Ackerman said, pulling out his Beretta and pointing it dead center at the wounded man's forehead. He squeezed the trigger twice, and neat holes appeared in his skull.

The retorts set the jungle slopes echoing with bird cries again ringing out across the water. A few feet away, Carlos cursed in Spanish and English, warning Ackerman the cartel would eventually make him pay for this slaughter.

The gunshots had alerted the Colombian pilot to stop taxiing the seaplane towards land. Thirty yards from the dock, the flight deck window still partly open, he turned the amphibian around, giving her full throttle for a fast takeoff. He'd had a hunch this mission would turn to shit. Everyone around Carlos had been saying that Morgan brought bad luck to anyone who cared about him.

Ackerman's shooters, out of their jungle cover, fired at the rapidly departing seaplane, but the Catalina was a difficult target from their positions on the mountain.

Bullets punched holes in the fuselage but missed the pilot. Nothing could stop the plane now; the man at the controls was determined not to stick around and become a better target.

He was rapidly airborne, heading for Colombia. The cartel would soon choose a new leader. It would be up to the new boss to avenge the deaths of Carlos and his men.

* * *

The cable car rattled gloomily down the mountainside, halting near the dock. Carlos staggered out, Ackerman's pistol prodding him in the back. Morgan Masterson followed, blood-splattered and shaken by the shootings. The actor hadn't known Ackerman's men would kill the Colombians. He'd only sought Gil's help to remain on the island when Carlos threatened forcible removal.

The dispirited star had hoped for more career concessions out of Rothenberg before leaving. He hadn't foreseen the bloody crisis he would provoke. Real bullets whizzing past his head and seeing the Columbians gunned down shocked him.

"You never warned me you were gonna kill them," he complained to the security chief.

Ackerman didn't respond. It was as if he was in on a secret joke, a joke about Morgan only he knew.

"Listen, this isn't some movie set with fag actors," Gil sneered. "Those guys were killers. It's no good griping to me. Blame Max. He said shoot them if they pull weapons – and that's what happened. They're druggie scum. You shouldn't have brought them here. Big mistake."

Suffering intense pain, Carlos listened to their conversation. He stared at Morgan, muttering through gritted teeth: "You idiot, cousin. Shit for brains. Trust the wrong people. My men not wrong. You're a rat. This all because of you. If I had a gun, I'd blow your fucking brains out…"

Ackerman's pistol prodded Carlos in the back, silencing him. The last remark scared Morgan. The hate in his cousin's eyes terrified him. Maybe it was better if Carlos died; he wouldn't beg Rothenberg to spare him. Morgan had to think of his future – the hell with his thuggish relative. He didn't want to spend the rest of his days fearing retaliation from Carlos.

Ackerman shoved Carlos onto the yacht. Morgan followed. He hadn't the slightest doubt Carlos was going to a watery grave. Rothenberg's men started the engines, cast off the dock lines, and the boat sped towards open water.

Among the four-person crew was Enrique Garcia, a small-time San José scammer who snitched for Delano. He'd inveigled his way into Rothenberg's trust at Delano's suggestion. The mansion had been a gossip gold mine. Enrique provided information about actors and dignitaries Rothenberg brought to his island as guests and lovers.

Already, Enrique had called Delano reporting the tension at dinner the night before when he waited on the rancorous party of three.

"There's going to be trouble. This Colombian drug boss, says he's Morgan's cousin, detests Rothenberg, thinks he's ruining Morgan's movie career…" he told Delano in a snatched satellite phone call after going off duty. "I'll be on the boat tomorrow. They're all supposed to go on a fishing trip."

Enrique realized it was no ordinary fishing trip when he heard shooting ashore. He watched when Ackerman shoved Carlos aboard, bloody and wounded. Enrique guessed the other two Colombians were already dead.

The boat's twin diesel engines combined into a harmonious purr. Gil Ackerman was at the helm, pushing the throttles forward. The vessel was soon riding a foaming white step, its bow high at 40 knots heading for an opening in the reef surrounding the island.

Morgan went astern where Carlos lay, dumped on the deck, his hands and feet bound. Rothenberg stood nearby, watching. It was clear Carlos was going overboard. An uneasy Morgan walked to where Rothenberg stood. He wanted to assure the Boss he agreed the shootings were Carlos's fault – that his cousin reached for a gun first.

"Killing them doesn't offend me, Max. Carlos asked for it. And, of course, I'll forget what I've seen," Morgan promised.

He wasn't precisely blackmailing Rothenberg, but Morgan figured knowing about these killings would apply extra leverage on Max to give his career recovery a more significant boost than the Boss had offered.

"Are you trying to pressure your way into better parts, Morgan?" Rothenberg asked, smirking at the actor's implied threat.

"Of course not, Max. I just want us on the same page. I didn't want Carlos here. I don't care what you do with him. I never liked him, a low-class thug. Toss him overboard. He deserves it."

Max smiled grimly. Morgan felt fear; something wasn't right. He tried to read that smile, but it revealed nothing.

Meanwhile, Carlos lay listening, helpless but still defiant. "You traitor, Morgan. You sold out our family. Ran out on your Papa when he was dying. Run out on me. You Judas bastard."

Morgan and Rothenberg ignored the angry ravings.

"Good, glad you agree, Carlos must go. So, let's get on with it," Rothenberg ordered.

The boat went through a gap in the reef. It rode into swells over water so deep the bottom wasn't visible. Ackerman throttled back, leaving the vessel wallowing in slow waves and a robust southern current.

He descended from the captain's station, joining the group at the stern. He ordered two crew members to wrestle the cussing and swearing Carlos onto the boat's swim platform, the ledge where swimmers climbed on and off the vessel.

"OK, Bomba, let's have a look at that wound of yours," Ackerman said, ripping the Colombian's shirt open. Heartless, he pulled off the dressing that had prevented the gunshot wound from bleeding.

"My people kill you," Carlos snarled at this painful new assault. "They get you someday...you see..."

"It'll never happen. I'm too smart for you South American monkeys. I make fish bait from tree-dwellers like you." Ackerman sneered.

Carlos learned the fish-bait taunt was no joke. They put a cork vest around his chest, cut the cords restraining his legs and wrists, and pushed him overboard attached to the boat by a rope.

"We're after big-game...and you're the bait," Ackerman shouted down at his victim, struggling in the yacht's wake. "You bleed well. Blood attracts predators. You should know. You spilled plenty of it. You're a predator, too, right?"

Rothenberg joined in, jeering at the helpless man in the water: "Yes, the big fish here are quick on the scent. I've seen it before. They take offerings in one gulp or just carve them up piece by piece. What's your preference?"

"Fuck you, man," Carlos screamed back. "My people come. Kill your fat ass..."

The boat drifted for ten agonizingly long minutes towing the bleeding man. Soon he was at the rope's extremity. His brown face and mop of black hair bobbed rhythmically as breaking waves washed over him. All the while, he defiantly cursed his tormentors.

Blood from the wound now stained the green water around him brownish-red. Fathoms below, a tiger shark tasting Carlos's DNA swam up to investigate. It circled cautiously. Noticing the predator, Carlos prayed to the Virgin Mary as fast as he could get the words out.

He knew what was coming. Ackerman and Rothenberg cheered as the shark circled. Three of the four crew members also stood nearby the Boss, watching. Soon, more fins appeared. They left it to the biggest among them to start the feast. The tiger struck first, lunging up from below to take a chunk out of Carlos's thigh. Then the others flashed in on their hapless prey.

His screams grew fainter with each slash and twist. They tore off chunks of flesh and bone with each attack. The water turned ruby red as Carlos died. Still attached by the rope, the sharks hadn't consumed his upper torso.

Ackerman pulled the remains out of the water for morbid amusement. Strangely, the Colombian's face looked peaceful, his eyes closed as if asleep. Finally, Ackerman cut the rope, the head and torso sinking slowly into the depths.

The manner of Carlos's death horrified Morgan, but he didn't have long to think about it. Muscular arms seized him in an unbreakable grip as Ackerman and his men pushed him out onto the swim platform.

"What in hell's name are you doing?" he screamed. "Get your goddam hands off me! Stop it! Let go. I've got millions of fans around the world! They'll be asking for me. You can't do this to me. I'm a superstar. Are you crazy, Ackerman? Max, tell him to stop!"

Rothenberg looked into Morgan's pleading face, enjoying seeing the actor become a shuddering, wailing wreck of a man, pinned on the stern by Ackerman and a burly crew member.

"Yes, we can do this to you," he intoned, "And we will. We'll say you fell overboard – a terrible accident. Don't worry; we'll arrive at a reasonable explanation. You made me money. I thought you'd make more. Instead, you tossed fame away, so now we're tossing you away."

"Max, Max, don't, don't do this to me," Morgan sobbed. "Please, please, I'll do anything. Don't kill me. Not like this. Pleeeeease!"

A wolfish smile creased Rothenberg's face as he pronounced the sentence: "Sorry, Morgan, I can't help you. It's punishment time. I wanted something with a little bite in it for your final grand performance."

He nodded to Ackerman and the deckhands. They fought to break Morgan's iron grip. Like a giant leach, he clung to the nearest crew member, then to the stern rail. He shrieked when they used a mallet to break his grip, the repeated blows crushing his fingers. Pain and terror caused him to lose bowel control as they shoved the writhing, stinking, screaming superstar overboard.

When his head bobbed up, he took several desperate strokes towards the boat, but the sharks were waiting. A big swirl and most of the actor's right leg was gone. The next tiger shark sank its teeth into his waist and swam off near the surface with its screaming, hemorrhaging prize. Other big fish converged to join in the feeding frenzy. He was gone, ripped and torn to pieces.

A few bits of expensive khaki cloth and ragged squares of bloody shirt fabric floated away on the surface. Rothenberg, Ackerman, and three hands were all transfixed by the actor's last moments.

No one noticed the fourth crew member high on the flying bridge, filming with his cell phone.

CHAPTER TWENTY-SEVEN:

TAPED

On *Talespinner*, Mike Delano and Rachel awakened to the satellite phone's persistent buzz. Delano staggered out of the captain's suite into the main cabin to answer.

"Yeah, who is it?" he murmured through a hangover from the night before when they attended a boozy party on another yacht anchored nearby.

"It's me, Enrique Garcia. I've got something big for you, real big. Morgan Masterson's gone. And I got pictures of him dying. You've never seen anything like it. All I can say now. When can we meet?"

"Masterson's dead?"

"Yeah, right, you won't be seeing him no more. Rothenberg sent him on his way..."

"How'd he die?"

"We got to meet. I'll show you the video. We got to get together. Otherwise, I'll take it to someone else."

Delano's aching head cleared rapidly. This news could be the game-changer he sought. "For Chrissakes, man, I'm on a boat in the Caribbean. Just tell me what happened to Morgan?

"Not until we meet in person," Enrique insisted. "How about LA? I fly there once you send me a ticket."

"All right, we'll meet at my Malibu place. My office will book you a round-trip ticket."

"Don't want no round-trip," Enrique answered quickly. "I'm done with Costa Rica."

Delano hated another breach of what was becoming an idyllic life, but what little Enrique had said so far intrigued him. He wasn't about to pass up a blockbuster story.

Delano returned to their cabin, explained what he could, and told Rachel to pack for LA. They moored *Talespinner* in St. Lucia, and they flew back to Tinseltown.

* * *

"Man, this is beautiful," Enrique Garcia sighed, looking around the living room of Delano's Malibu beach house while accepting a glass of iced tea from Rachel. It was an impressive home Delano had bought and decorated with the profits from his news agency.

The interior was inviting, with Persian rugs, towering green plants, antique furniture imported from Europe, and the colorful impressionist paintings he collected.

Outside, waves crashed on rocks, and seagulls screeched for scraps. Seeing such opulence, Enrique decided he wouldn't accept anything but the highest payment. This story and video were his shot at the good life, and he intended to take it.

What Enrique offered was huge. Delano, generous in the past, would have to pay top dollar plus significant side benefits if he wanted this scoop. He looked at Enrique thoughtfully, knowing any show of eagerness on his part would drive up the price.

"OK, Enrique, let us see what you've got; better be good, making me interrupt my honeymoon."

The informant reached into his rucksack, pulled out his phone, and turned the screen toward Delano. A video played, portraying the ugly deaths of a Colombian cartel boss and his cousin, the Hollywood superstar.

It was breathtaking in its steadfast focus on the horrific scene. Delano whistled appreciatively. He could imagine how stills taken from the film would appear in newspapers and magazines globally.

The video was sharp, good enough for the most demanding television broadcasters. It showed Carlos's death and how Morgan was carried away and torn apart by tiger sharks. Perhaps most astounding was how it captured Rothenberg's amusement and delight at the horror.

At last, Delano had his arch-enemy in the crosshairs. All he need do now was pull the trigger.

"My God, this is great," he said, forgetting his need to bargain. He wanted this material, no matter the cost. He also wanted Enrique's first-person account of the horror. With it, he'd put the media mogul away for life–maybe make him face the death penalty.

"What's this worth to you, Enrique? The video and your eyewitness account?" Delano asked softly.

"I've given it much thought, Mike. There's no going back to San José once this is released. Rothenberg will have me killed. I'll need cover under a different name, someplace out of the country."

Intent on negotiating with Enrique, Delano had forgotten Rachel was standing behind him, watching the video over his shoulder.

She was ashen, having seen her father's enthusiastic involvement in a sadistic double murder. Many of Delano's past accusations against Max now screamed like noisy unwelcome guests through her head.

Rachel was close to vomiting. She sat down, shocked by the gruesome images, speechless. Eventually, she found words barely adequate to express her sorrow and horror.

"I'd never have believed Daddy could be so cruel," she murmured. "What could have happened to involve him in such horror?"

Delano stood to put his arm around her, holding her tight. He could feel her shaking. The journalist wished he had shielded her from seeing the ugly reality of her father unmasked.

"He's not the father you knew as a child," he said gently, "and we can't let him poison our future or continue harming people. He'll have to face justice. Everybody does at some point. Karma."

Tearful, angry, and confused, Rachel shook off Delano's embrace and walked out of the room. She sensed hypocrisy in his soothing words.

When it came to destroying Max, her thoughts and feelings were of little importance. Delano was a predator going in for the kill.

Captivated by the prospect of bringing Rothenberg to book, Mike continued making his deal with Enrique.

"OK, what do you want in return for the video and the story. All first-person – and, of course, told only to me?"

Enrique's demands were heavy. He wanted a $1.5-million cash payment, an apartment bought for him in Cabo San Lucas, and a new identity that Rothenberg's investigators couldn't crack.

"You've got a deal," Delano agreed without hesitation. "You can stay here until after we've wrapped the story and you're ready to leave for Baja."

Delano's hospitality had a purpose. It would keep other journalists away from Enrique before and after his latest blockbuster appeared. He could stop Enrique from getting greedy – and doing follow-ups with media rivals. They'd all be after him with fists full of cash for a piece of this yarn.

The two men shook hands to seal the deal. The images Garcia had captured on his phone had earned him a deal that would change his life. They would transform Delano and Rachel's lives, too.

CHAPTER TWENTY-EIGHT:

THE WHITE WHALE

In the days that followed, Delano became so involved in the story that he overlooked the disastrous effect his blockbuster scoop continued having on his wife.

After he had spent hours polishing the piece and selecting grisly pictures to go with it, Rachel shocked him when she appealed for cancelation of the gruesome tale.

"If you love me as much as you claim, you won't destroy my father's life," she begged. "He'll surely go to prison. They'll charge him with murder. He'll be detested for his cruelty everywhere – all of which will reflect badly on me as well."

Rachel's objections and conclusions were correct. And she wasn't buying Delano's thin pretense that this story was an unbiased journalistic scoop, rather than the coup de grace he'd sought against Max for years.

She became even angrier as he stubbornly defended his position on ethical grounds. He denied he was exploiting a tragedy with what she called cheap sensationalism.

"People need to know about Max's murderous excesses. He's a criminal. Moreover, I've spent several million dollars locking up this piece. My reputation's riding on it. Someone will get this story. I'd be a laughing stock if I let it slip through my fingers now."

She shook her head in disbelief. "So, the money and your already tawdry image mean more to you than disgracing my family name? I know Daddy's done unspeakable things. I felt sick watching that video. But it's not him alone I'm concerned about," she insisted.

"There's a giant corporation with thousands of employees to take into account. His downfall will do incalculable harm to them and the GMI conglomerate."

Delano had brought their conflict to a boiling point. Rachel stormed out of the room to their bedroom upstairs when he refused to budge. Disgusted, she threw herself on the bed, sobbing and cursing his intransigence.

Disturbed, he followed, taking her in his arms, but failed to soften her rage and frustration.

"Don't you see how important this is to me," she implored. "Drop that story and we can resume our love, our life on the boat. And all will be well."

But he refused even that appealing offer. "I must publish. I can't hold a story like this. Innocent people are dead, not just Morgan and a lousy drug boss, but the mother of two children – and others we likely don't know about. Murder means nothing to him. Hell, he tried to kill me. Look what he did to you – and our unborn child. He's a monster."

Angrily slipping out of his arms, Rachel turned, facing him defiantly. "You're the damned monster. You won't rest until Daddy's in prison."

"Isn't that where he belongs?"

"No! You're destroying a global corporation my father spent his entire existence creating. It's my heritage, too. I made a big mistake trusting you, marrying you, believing in you."

Her words stung. It was a side of her Mike couldn't placate – a side rooted in wealth, privilege, and loyalty to family, imbued from birth. She would never accept his reasons for publishing the story were genuine.

Delano was disgusted to his core by Max's depravity. Moreover, and perhaps more self-serving, he felt bringing Rothenberg to justice would wipe away his own ethical collapse into yellow journalism.

For him, there'd be no more compromise with the Rothenbergs, not with the father or the daughter. He'd done it before; he refused to do it again – not even for the woman he adored.

"I can't kill this story. CSI has alerted our print clients to reserve space for a major newsbreak. TV stations have cleared blocks of time. Promotional material's already gone out. There's no way for me to keep a lid on this," he insisted. "Failing to deliver would ruin me, be forever on my conscience. I'm sorry it's your father, but exposing him will save lives. He'll kill again. I'm certain of that."

Rachel's dark eyes blazed with contempt at what she considered his opportunistic hypocrisy. "So suddenly you're a yellow journalist with a convenient conscience," she sneered. "Don't feed me your pious platitudes. It started as revenge and continues as such. You've lost your way. Cash and acclaim mean more to you than I do. Why can't you see how serious this is? Drop that story, or we're over."

"Sorry, I can't do it," he told her. "Do you need reminding how Max wrecked my career, branded me a thief, tried having me murdered? No one can blame me, least of all you, for being unforgiving."

"But I do blame you," she insisted. "You extorted millions from my father; made your reputation writing ugly stories about Paragon stars. You can let this one go. Pay Garcia off. Give him what you promised, send him back to Costa Rica. Then our problem's resolved."

"Do you really not know how this business works? He'll just take the story elsewhere and make me look ridiculous when rivals publish – and accuse me of backing off because I'm married to you," Delano snapped.

Rapid footsteps on the stairs brought Enrique Garcia to them, his face pained as he stepped uninvited into their bedroom.

He'd heard what was said with raised voices. He understood Delano's dilemma and Rachel's misery. It made no difference to him if the journalist didn't publish – as long as their deal remained in play.

"Look, Mike, I understand the problem. You don't have to worry about me going elsewhere. That's the truth; I swear it. Stick to our deal. That's only fair. The money, the apartment, and a job in Mexico, and I destroy this video recording. Then I won't be looking over my shoulder, worrying about Rothenberg coming after me. Far as I'm concerned nothing ever happened on that damned boat."

Rachel leaped from the bed, hugging the snitch. "That's right, Enrique, you get the money, an apartment, a new life – you give us the master recording, we destroy it and everyone's happy. It's a wise decision."

Silence, then Delano spoke slowly and firmly. "That's not the deal. I have the recording – and I'll publish. It's my story. I'm sorry, but that's the way it is."

* * *

The TV and print account of a superstar thrown to sharks by his studio boss became a global sensation.

It earned Delano and CSI enormous acclaim and millions in payments. It turned Max Rothenberg and Gil Ackerman into international pariahs.

Police in Britain and America sought them, but the pair vanished before any authority could bring murder charges.

For Rachel, Max's disgrace and disappearance were unbearable – especially as Delano had brought them about.

As much as she loved him, this was unforgivable. It hurt profoundly seeing her renowned parent made a despised global figure. Her concern for GMI mounted as the share price plunged, and financial writers forecast the conglomerate would disintegrate, falling apart without a Rothenberg in charge.

For days, there was silence between her and Mike. She had never imagined he'd find such a hideous way of bringing Max down.

Thus, when a GMI executive contacted her offering a senior management role, she accepted. She claimed doing damage control at the New York headquarters was her family duty.

Packing to leave, she sorrowfully told Mike: "I want a divorce."

Shaken, he stood on the deck, inhaling one of his daily three cigarettes, as his wife brought her suitcase down, ready for when the limo arrived.

She joined him. They stared out at the waves breaking on the beach, unable to face each other.

"I'm sorry Mike, I didn't want it to end this way," she said, her brown eyes glistening, holding back tears. "But you've become like the people you write about, little different from the stars you've delighted in destroying these past few years – addicted to fame and wealth."

Delano bristled at what he inwardly conceded was a partial truth. He wanted to tell her he'd change, that he planned a return to serious journalism, to write novels, and leave Hollywood behind.

But he was too hurt by her departure to say the words. The hell with it. She wouldn't listen anyway. Worse, he knew there was some validity to her accusations.

He'd come to California determined to destroy Rothenberg and to save her. He had succeeded in the first part, but not the second. He'd saved Rachel only to lose her again.

Now he couldn't stop her from fulfilling a long-delayed ambition. Seizing the GMI opportunity was more important to her than their love – no matter how much he disapproved.

There was irony in their romance falling foul of ulterior motives: his desire for revenge on Rothenberg, and hers for corporate power. He detected a heretofore unseen ruthlessness in her turning Max's comeuppance into her chance to step into his shoes.

He walked with her to the waiting limo, where she had one final question: "What will you do, Mike, now you've harpooned your white whale?"

Likening Delano to Melville's mad captain was unexpected. Mike smiled, thought for a moment before answering:

"Well, if I'm Ahab, my white whale's still out there, living large somewhere."

"I know, thank God," Rachel murmured. "Sadly, there will never be peace until one or both of you are dead. I can't spend my life trapped between two men I've loved so much – it's too painful."

CHAPTER TWENTY-NINE:

DANGEROUS BLOOMS

Quinton Werner luxuriated in the warmth of LA sunshine after the icy misery of Manitoba. He'd re-entered the US from Canada without problems. His new face and forged passport got him past officials in both countries.

Basheer and Abisha Hakim met him at the airport. The twins were sullen in their greetings, still sulking over Werner's extended absence. But their resentment softened because he was essential to their jihad against Hollywood.

Both were educated men, careful and detail-oriented, who spoke several languages, including English. The pair had spent their time well during Werner's absence, studying how best to attack the Academy Awards extravaganza.

They'd learned that more than 300 guards were present at the auditorium on the big night, hired from two contractors. Leading up to the event, security personnel would inspect all packages and equipment that entered the building.

Besides private security, the LAPD would be on high alert, studying every movement picked up by strategically placed cameras. The surveillance system was activated in the week before the ceremony and recorded everything inside and outside the auditorium.

Expert control room personnel constantly watched for unusual happenings. On the awards night, their cameras homed in on individuals, their faces, their clothes. With a billion TV viewers tuning in for the big night, officials were susceptible to any possible threat.

With regret, the Hakims had decided the main Oscars ceremony was too vast a target for a successful attack. Instead, they wisely selected a secondary location: *Fabulous Living* magazine's awards night party. Striking there would achieve their objectives, presenting a lower risk of failure.

"The magazine party's the right place, my brother," Abisha explained to Werner, who listened with interest as they discussed the plan on the ride from the airport to their Encino safehouse.

"That hotel ballroom holds about 500 to 800 of the top people," Basheer gloated. "Our bombs will kill or maim many of them. Slaughtering that many infidels will draw maximum global attention."

The prospect of the enormous notoriety they'd achieve within the Muslim world delighted the twins. They enjoyed the righteousness of their cause, having identified many movie bosses as supporting what they considered the Zionist crusade against Islam.

Werner broke the silence abruptly: "How do we hide the bombs?" he asked.

The Hakims took his question as acceptance of their plan. They had expected Werner's positive response. Year after year, the Oscars party drew fame and acclaim for Quinton's hated enemy, Max Rothenberg, who owned the glossy magazine, *Fabulous Living*.

"We'll hide the explosives in the huge floral planters at the party location," Basheer said. "We'll bury the bombs beneath the plants supplied by your friend at Beverly Hills Flowers."

Quinton now understood how essential his Hollywood connections were. The twins knew he had ties to Martin Petrescu, owner of Beverly Hills Flowers. He had introduced them to Petrescu when they were studying film making years earlier. Their planning research revealed that the "florist to the stars" supplied floral arrangements for the party annually.

"We believe you can get the bombs in without arousing suspicion. It all depends on you getting Petrescu to give you a job at his store," said Basheer. "Then we load the bombs the night before the event."

"You won't let us down by disappearing this time," said Abisha pointedly.

Werner nodded in agreement. He was wary of the twins, having enraged them by hiding out for months in Canada. If he failed them again, they could well kill him regardless of family ties.

"Yes, I know enough about the florist to compel him to employ me. I can make your plan work," Werner agreed.

Basheer smiled grimly. He liked the method of bomb concealment; it had symmetry. From innocent floral beauty would come death and disaster.

Hollywood infidels would pay with their lives for their part in perpetuating centuries of Muslim persecution.

* * *

Martin Petrescu was a man with dark secrets. Most people considered him a family man, unaware of his expensive dalliances with whores. Nor would they have believed he used his prestigious flower business as a front for a drug distribution racket.

When Quinton Werner entered his shop, he tried to make himself known to Martin through his knowledge of their shared past of women and drugs. Then the renowned florist recognized the voice and became apprehensive. The former movie union thug knew too much about him.

During his friendship with Werner, he became hooked on narcotics and kinky sex, vices that continued even after his marriage to a prominent Beverly Hills lawyer.

In need of additional cash to finance his weaknesses, Martin had for years been using his flower shop as a convenient cover for dealing drugs, mainly to Hollywood's rich and famous.

Only select customers knew that floral displays conveniently delivered to their mansions could include packets of cocaine, heroin, and opioids once they let Marty understand their requirements.

Petrescu greeted Werner warily after getting used to his former friend's surgically altered face and blonde hair.

While tempted to brush off this unwelcome visitor, the florist feared doing so.

Werner could easily take revenge by exposing Martin's sexual dalliances and his financially necessary narcotics business to the person he feared most – his wife, Alessia.

What did this low-class criminal want from him, anyway, Petrescu wondered? Quinton always had hidden motives.

"What can I do for you, my friend?" he said, extending a hand made clammy by nerves. Werner responded with a bear hug. The embrace did nothing to ease Petrescu's suspicions. Quinton was far from a touchy-feely guy.

"Good seeing you, Marty, it's been too long," Werner said, releasing the flustered florist from his firm grip.

"Truth is I need a job, and I figured with the Oscars coming, I'm just the man to help with your business at its busiest time."

Shocked, Petrescu was about to speak when Werner mouthed seemingly innocuous questions.

"How's the divorce lawyer wife. Is Alessia still practicing? Did you have any more kids, or just the three?"

Petrescu detected the menace in the inquiries about his family – a reminder of how much he had to lose if he didn't do what Quinton wanted.

Trying to smother his suspicions, he took a deep breath, saying he had no job openings. Martin knew he'd been right to fear his visitor's menace when Werner got to the point.

"Come on, Marty. You wouldn't want the missus to hear about your whoring. Worse, someone could tell the cops about your drug deals with clients."

Seeing his world about to collapse, Petrescu didn't need to hear more. Werner didn't make idle threats.

"OK, Quinton. You're in," he said. Fear made him generous: "I'll pay you $1,000 a week. It's all I can afford."

As a frown formed on Werner's altered face, he hastily added: "And with a cut of the 'other' profits, it should come to a couple of grand a week. You happy with that?"

Werner nodded his satisfaction. "It's good. Play this right, and there'll be no problems. I won't be here long. I need the cash for a trip I'm planning."

He was glad Petrescu hadn't given him trouble. The Oscars were three weeks away. The Hakims had started building their bombs.

"By the way, I'm using another name, Roberto Costello. Remember it, Marty, if anybody asks questions. And don't you go calling the cops, or I'll be calling Alessia, telling her things that'll come as a surprise. Let's avoid that. Right?"

* * *

Martin poured out his woes to Jenny Daniels, embarrassedly admitting he could no longer afford his $1,000-weekly liaisons with the luscious young blonde.

"I've had to hire this guy as shop manager," he bitched. "He's threatened to wreck my life with Alessia if I didn't employ him. It's a tough problem."

Perturbed at the dent in her income, Jenny asked, "Who's this jerk?"

Martin knew he shouldn't blab, but his grievances came tumbling out. Who could Jenny tell that mattered, anyway?

"Quinton Werner. We used to party together. He's changed his face. I think the law's after him. Calls himself Roberto Costello now. Looks different; dyed his hair. Listen, don't tell anybody – could be trouble. Says he's not staying long. Then we can get back to normal."

Jenny phoned her madame to explain why her cut from Petrescu's payments would be stopping.

"He claims this asshole's blackmailing him into letting the dude run his shop. He's squeezing Marty for more cash than he can afford, a couple of grand a week."

Irked by anyone interfering with her cut from Jenny's liaisons, Laura Chesley indignantly asked: "Who's this blackmailing fucker?"

"Some asshole on the run called Roberto Costello, but used to go by Quinton Werner."

Laura didn't blink. She knew the name well, and that knowledge would soon compensate for any cash shortfall she'd suffered.

There was no advantage to telling Jenny more than she already knew; she hurried to brush the hooker off.

"Thanks for letting me know about the problem. We'll talk soon," Laura said, disconnecting and hitting speed-dial to Delano.

She could sense big money here.

* * *

Werner's return to LA surprised Mike. He knew the LAPD and FBI were after the former unionist, but the trail had gone cold. The Los Angeles police had connected Werner to the murders of Liz Hightower and a Chicago hitman with a memorable nickname, the Spike.

238

Delano's sources claimed federal investigators also sought Werner for aiding unidentified terrorists suspected of destroying Paragon Pictures' *Mission Cyclops* Florida set.

So far, investigators had kept Werner's name out of the press. His capacity to evade capture after committing capital crimes embarrassed them.

Knowledge of the thug's whereabouts, plus naming him as a terrorist and murder suspect, promised to be a final scoop for Delano before his planned departure from Tinseltown – and he latched on.

"Keep this under wraps, Laura, until I discover what he's up to. Are we agreed?" he cautioned Chesley. "You get a bonus fee, no matter whether the story goes big or small, so don't let the cops know Werner's back," Mike demanded.

Indignant at his implication she would work with LAPD, even if it was true, Laura snapped: "Why would I tell the goddamned pigs? Those motherfuckers don't pay my bills."

Delano hung up, grinning. He knew Laura paid police informants for tips, then jacked up the price by reselling news to reporters.

Mulling Werner's return, he dialed Dave Fuller, his partner at CSI: "Remember that racketeer, Quinton Werner? He's working at Beverly Hills Flowers. Do you believe the balls? He's a killer, maybe a terrorist. Suddenly he's a florist. What do you make of that?"

Dave considered for a moment.

"Beverly Hills Flowers. Aren't they famous for supplying those huge displays to the *Fabulous Living* party every year, the night of the Oscars?" he recalled. "The owner's always bragging, making sure he gets lots of press about the 'magnificent' bouquets he sends to that celebrity zoo."

A bell rang in Delano's brain. Murder, terrorism, extortion – all hallmarks of Quinton Werner. Could he have his sights set on blowing up a bunch of celebs on Oscars night?

If so, Delano intended to stop him. This could be his final block-buster – not a scandal yarn, but something of which he could be rightly proud. He looked forward to leaving town on a high note.

* * *

Dave Fuller parked CSI's stakeout van across the road from Beverly Hills Flowers. Delano parked his rental car in the alley behind the store before joining him. For three days and nights, they watched, seeing nothing unusual.

Fortunately, the tricked-out van was comfortable. It provided a microwave, a toilet, and side windows with one-way glass. Journalists inside could see out, but no one outside could see within. The van had swiveling bucket seats, a table, a couch for catnaps, and tripod-mounted cameras on both sides.

Publicly, it innocuously declared itself the property of Beverly Hills Best Sparkle – providers of "tip-top cleaning services."

Inside, they snapped customers and florists arriving and leaving the flower shop. With old pictures for comparison, the pair also photographed surgically altered Quinton Werner while he worked.

From across Bedford Drive, Delano and Fuller had an excellent view through their telescopic lenses. They could see into the store, watching what was taking place.

It wasn't until the fourth night that Werner made his move.

He arrived at three o'clock in the morning, driving a Toyota SUV. He was in a good mood, even as he strained to pull a heavy canvas bag out of the vehicle.

It contained three bombs sheathed in protective bubble wrap. He intended placing them in the floral containers for delivery to the big party at the Sunset Grand Hotel later that day.

Knowing the layout of the shop, he did not need to turn on the lights. He went straight to the cold room where the floral artists stored their stunning arrangements. A chilly blast of 34-degree air hit Werner as he entered. He left the door wide open and switched on a powerful flashlight.

What he saw took his breath away. Three large ceramic planters were a blaze of color, lush with flowers and plants from five countries.

There were blue hydrangeas, light pink tulips, Peruvian lilies, white orchids, hot pink carnations, orange ranunculus, purple Matsumoto asters, lavender, orange chrysanthemums, and Australian wax flowers in various shades. Ferns and moss highlighted each display.

Unexpectedly, Werner took a perverse pride in the florists for creating these works of art. In a moment of dark thought, it pleased him to know such beauty would soon have a role in killing some of Tinseltown's so-called beautiful people.

These wealthy fat cats had always rejected him – slights for which he'd never forgive them. Blowing up a Rothenberg event made the venture especially sweet for him.

He got to work. The explosives were easy to hide in the large planters destined to beautify the ballroom party location.

Quinton would insist to Marty the blossoms were of such delicacy he'd handle the delivery himself. The Hakim twins, dressed as GMI security guards, would meet him at the Sunset Grand Hotel delivery entrance.

The three of them would put the heavy pots on a small forklift, placing them at strategic points around the big room—a simple plan.

Werner's knife cut through the moss surrounding the plant stems. The openings allowed him to force his explosive canisters beneath the green floral foam that held moisture to keep the blooms fresh. He cleaned up a few broken roots, turned off the lights, and locked the front door.

Working unseen with a long lens and infrared camera, Delano and Fuller had unchallengeable incriminating footage of Werner shoving explosives into the planters.

When Werner drove off, Dave slipped out of the van and into Delano's car. He followed the Toyota at a distance to Encino, where Werner and his accomplices were hiding out.

Waiting until morning, he witnessed the Hakim twins leave the house dressed in matching uniforms and drive off. Consulted by phone, Delano agreed Dave should follow them.

Around the same time, Mike watched through his long lens as Werner returned to the shop to load the bomb-laden planters for delivery. He then followed the thug as he drove to the hotel where Fuller had the place staked out.

As they watched, two apparent GMI security guards greeted Werner. He and the twins moved three giant planters, one at a time on a forklift, into the Sunset Grand ballroom.

"Get ready for your closeup," Mike muttered to himself as he videoed the terrorists unloading their deadly blooms.

CHAPTER THIRTY:

RACHEL STEPS UP

Lord Rothenberg's jet landed in the 106-degree heat of Dubai's international airport. It taxied to a select enclosure where VIPs parked their planes.

The mogul descended from the rented Learjet 75, followed by Gil Ackerman. Both were taking their first unwilling steps into exile. They were criminals on the run seeking sanctuary in a country where they would be safe from extradition.

The pair climbed stoically into the air-conditioned frigidity of the awaiting Sikorsky S-92 executive helicopter outfitted with satellite phones, a bar, and a paneled workstation. They sipped glasses of chilled fruit juice handed to them by a flight attendant.

The machine rose smoothly in the hands of its two uniformed pilots. It flew over Dubai's gleaming towers, a city of magnificent malls, stunning apartment blocks built into the clouds, and homes on artificially created ocean islands.

Rothenberg owned one of these islands in the Persian Gulf and the luxury mansion on it. As the chopper neared his island's helipad, Max swallowed two Valium tablets.

The man he hated more than any living person had turned the full fury of his hostility on him and Ackerman – and Lord Max vowed to get even with him.

Delano's latest story branded them both as power-obsessed murderers. Rothenberg had no choice but to flee, abandoning the cosmopolitan life he once relished.

Two miles offshore in the Gulf, he was safe from criminal charges, but running his far-flung media empire from there sparked problems of both logistics and loyalty.

His disgrace and absence led to boardroom fights at GMI's New York and London offices and Paragon Pictures. Power struggles broke out all around the empire he'd so painstakingly constructed.

Ackerman's successor in LA, Tony Pugliese, had taken charge of studio security but didn't have the authority or political savvy to stop the disputes. More than ever, Rothenberg missed the steadying hand of poor Liz Hightower.

Maddening him were the moves underway to cancel his seat on the studio board. Worse, a group of executive plotters sought to merge Paragon with a rival studio. Enraged, Rothenberg was in no position to save his beloved studio from such a move designed principally to make the grasping directors and shareholders wealthier.

Max was a bitter man. While safe in the Middle East from Western law, his luxurious exile didn't compensate for what he'd lost. He'd never see London, New York, or Los Angeles again. His palatial homes were in the hands of caretakers who had covered his splendid possessions with white dust sheets.

The threat of extradition would always hang over him. A single misstep and authorities would force him back to America where he would face trial and a life sentence. His billions could not buy him out of this fix.

Rothenberg mourned the glittering world he once dominated. Time and distance similarly challenged his business acumen in ways he couldn't counter. He knew the heartless, savagely ambitious men he had surrounded himself with had turned on him, taking maximum advantage of his plight. Power was bleeding out from him like a dying man.

Then, after weeks of gnawing frustration, Rachel provided a lifeline.

"Daddy, I've left Delano. I can't accept what he's done to you, the shame he's brought on us. I tried to stop him but couldn't," she said.

"I know, sweetheart. Thank God, you warned me before he published. I'm so grateful..."

She interrupted him: "I'm at Paragon on a trouble-shooting mission. I know you wanted to keep me out of the business. But your absence surely changes that sentiment. Am I correct, Daddy?"

"Of course," Max assured her, his mind racing with ideas for pulling the power balance back in his favor.

"I'm sorry Rachel. It was a bad mistake excluding you," he said with apparent sincerity.

Suppressing her lingering displeasure, Rachel knew it was now or never to get what she wanted from her disgraced parent by making vital business decisions in his absence.

Even before this phone call, she had blunted Paragon's merger discussions with a rival Hollywood studio – gratifying news to Max, the principal shareholder. Now, with him on her side, she could stop the negotiations dead.

"I'll be visiting New York and London next. There's a lot of bad shit happening there, too," she said after receiving his thanks for ending the merger talks. "I'm extremely proud to fly the Rothenberg flag, Daddy. Now, I need your approval of my joining the board. I require authority over all the companies in the group."

Stunned at her audacity, Max recovered rapidly. She could be the answer to the power vacuum his exile had created – allowing him to hold the reins behind the scenes. She was, perhaps, the only person he could trust to help him regain control of their sprawling empire. He said a silent prayer of relief that she was out of Delano's bed.

"I'm delighted, darling, on both fronts – that you're divorcing that swine and you've proved our business means so much to you. I'll make sure your elevation to chairwoman is rapidly approved," he said, his voice shrill with excitement. "I still own the company, although they're trying to steal part of it. What I say still goes. Everyone will know you're my eyes, ears, and spokesperson. We'll run GMI together. They won't like it, but that's the least of my concerns. As for Delano, I could save you the trouble of divorcing him."

Rachel heard the threat. As much as she didn't want to believe her husband's accusations, she'd reluctantly come to accept her father had tried to kill Mike – and was willing to try again.

She reconsidered Aaron's sudden death, too. His demise at the hands of supposed terrorists had been convenient to Max. He could continue to blame her dead husband for the Swiss clinic nightmare once Aaron was no longer around to defend himself.

"Daddy, even though we'll soon be divorced, Delano remains important to me. You may hate him. That's your problem, not mine. But if anything happens to him, I'm out of your life, out of the business. Are we clear on that?"

"Very clear," Rothenberg grunted reluctantly. "I hope you're not going along with his tales, blaming me for every unexplained death and attempted murder."

Rachel responded with facts he couldn't wriggle out of: "What about Morgan Masterson and his cousin? You were responsible. I've seen the video, listened to a witness. It was horrific."

Max's anger flared: "That putz Masterson deserved what he got. He could have stopped the Florida disaster, prevented all those deaths – and the enormous cost to Paragon. And he was directly responsible for Hightower's death."

Rachel decided against arguing over whether shark-feeding was an appropriate punishment. She was beginning to understand the terrible lengths her father would go to in dealing with those who crossed him.

"Never mind all that. I'm just glad we've settled that revenge against Mike's off-limits. Let's worry about GMI, how we can keep the business intact. We'll have video meetings several times a week, daily if necessary. Rely on me to help take care of our mutual interests."

CHAPTER THIRTY-ONE:

IGNORANCE IS BLISS

After following Werner to the Sunset Grand, Delano knew he had proof of the man's involvement in a terrorist plot to attack the Oscars party. Now his conscience told him he should sound the warning to save lives.

His first call was to Ralph McKenzie, famous for his bold and innovative editing of *Fabulous Living*, a magazine noted for its flattering interviews with celebrities and ingratiating front-cover pictures of stars.

McKenzie's condescending New York assistant, Fiona Watson, became immediately disapproving and suspicious once she heard who was asking for the editor. She knew all about Mike Delano – and didn't approve of him.

"Mr. McKenzie's in LA. I'm certain he's too busy to speak to you," she huffed.

Mike sighed impatiently.

"Ms. Watson, I'm trying to warn you of a bomb plot. Terrorists have placed explosives among the floral arrangements at the party location. Many people could die. Just give me McKenzie's number and I'll warn him myself."

Fiona, who relished her position as the editor's gatekeeper, considered Delano's information phony, a sensationalistic reporter's irresponsible and disgusting trick.

"You're trying to drum up a phony bomb-scare yarn," she observed scornfully. "We're not falling for that one. Tony Pugliese inspected those flower arrangements this morning. He found nothing wrong with them. He's our security expert. I'll pass your message along when I speak to him later today," she said before abruptly disconnecting.

Delano couldn't believe her stupidity. Angry, he called Pugliese.

"I inspected those planters earlier today and there was nothing abnormal," the security man snapped indignantly. "You publish anything about a bomb scare, and we'll sue your ass. You've caused GMI and the Boss more than enough trouble already. Why don't you just leave us alone."

Delano took a deep breath.

"I'm warning you, there will be a slaughter. My partner and I both witnessed bombs placed in those planters by a wanted criminal. You missed them."

The implication of negligence enraged Pugliese.

"I've done this gig at the Oscars party for years. I always check the floral displays. This year was no different. All was in order. I'm not causing a panic because I don't believe a word of it. And I won't call in the bomb squad and create delay."

Delano wrestled with the problem. Should he call the police himself and have them swarming over the place? Doing so would cost him and Dave the scoop they'd worked so hard to get. He resented rival media cashing in on their enterprise.

He decided they'd deal with the threat themselves. "Terror at the Oscars" would be a splash story everywhere – and now he was determined not to share it.

They had it all, the location of the bombs, video of them being unloaded. They'd also be miles ahead on follow-up stories, thanks to Laura Chesley's tip about Rothenberg pointing the finger at Werner for the terrorist attack on his Florida movie set.

None could match such material or be able to pump it out like them. But one call to the bomb squad and the story was in every paper and all over TV. Delano called Dave and said he'd tried to sound a warning, but nobody believed him.

Now they must gate-crash the *Fabulous Living* party to save lives and land their exclusive. Fuller was unsure of the propriety of what Delano was proposing, but as usual, went along with his partner's usually clear-eyed judgment.

They were crossing an ethical line and possibly committing an offense by not calling the bomb squad. But Mike's approach was "anything for a headline" – he'd whatever it took to beat rivals on this scary but extraordinary drama.

CHAPTER THIRTY-TWO:

WERNER'S INFERNO

A blitzkrieg of TV floodlights and paparazzi flashes at the entrance to the Sunset Grand Hotel transformed the California night into daylight brilliance. Fifty camera crews and a hundred photographers recorded Oscar-winners arriving with their golden statuettes.

Superbly gowned invitation checkers crossed names off their official *Fabulous Living* guest lists as celebrities and Hollywood power brokers entered the party. Bouncers stood ready to eject interlopers.

On Academy Awards night, it was the hottest ticket in town for 850 guests. No one entered without the haughty editor Ralph McKenzie's coveted personal invitation.

Mike Delano and Dave Fuller, both old hands at crashing parties, knew better than to try breaching the event head-on. They slipped in through the kitchen, disguised as uniformed waiters, beating security by passing themselves off as paid help.

A $1,000 bribe to a catering company clerk put their phony names on an exactingly inspected wait-staff list. Once inside, the catering manager set them to work carrying champagne flutes on silver trays into the ballroom.

"Don't slop the wine on the trays," the manager cautioned before they circulated among hundreds of VIP guests to serve their cargo of vintage bubbly.

Inside was a pageant of beautiful people: acres of white teeth, superbly toned flesh, and flowing manes of costly hair extensions. In an industry based on the relentless pursuit of fame, a flawless image was vital – especially with the world watching.

Stars wore gorgeous gowns they didn't own. Fashion houses paid fortunes to celebrities for promoting their exorbitant labels for a few globally seen hours. Magnificent necklaces sparkling around famous throats were on loan for the night, too.

Paragon Pictures' set designers had given the ballroom a 1920s nightclub atmosphere, complete with backlit translucent bars, overstuffed couches, and dim lighting. A jazz trio provided background music. Large glass panels on the ballroom's south wall opened out to airy, torchlit gardens, parts of which were tented. Guests wandered out, away from the press of the crowd inside.

Looking around, Delano saw no sign of Werner or his accomplices. Yet he sensed they were nearby, predators ready to pounce. Helped by the dim lighting, he moved toward the first of the planters, recognized from his surveillance at the flower shop. It was at the north end of the room.

He had come prepared for the job, with a slim metal rod and wire cutters hidden beneath his waiter's jacket. With the ballroom lights low, he was in the shadows and hard to see as he probed the planter's dark soil until he struck metal.

Digging down with his hands, he found the bomb. He pulled gently until it came free. With the canister top exposed, he unscrewed the cap. A penlight held with his teeth showed red and green wires between a wireless receiver and a detonator. Holding his breath, Delano cut first the green and then the red wire – completing the job.

Bomb disposal wasn't altogether new to him. While working in the Middle East, he had watched experts disarm roadside bombs that relied on pressure plates to detonate. A similar weapon had wounded him.

He could see these bombs were different – set off by a wireless signal. Immobilizing the internal receiver disarmed them. He rendered the first of the three Semtex-laden canisters inert.

Looking at an actual bomb, he had guilty second thoughts about not alerting the authorities to the danger much earlier – plus, with a bomb in hand, he now had evidence proving his warning was no exploitive tabloid scare tactic. He phoned Dave Fuller at the other end of the ballroom to call the police.

Guests were still arriving. Presumably, the jihadists were waiting for the room to fill before exploding their weapons to achieve maximum carnage.

During their hurried phone communication, Delano told Dave to give police a description of the attackers disguised as security men. Now he prayed the cops arrived in time to make arrests before any killing began.

Meanwhile, Delano would continue his mission to disarm the other two bombs – while hoping they didn't explode before he got to them.

Picking up his tray of glasses again, Delano saw *Fabulous Living* editor Stewart McKenzie mounting a stage at the room's south end. He tapped a microphone for attention, but the room's hive-like buzz drowned him out.

Show business sycophants were busily fawning over Oscar winners and consoling losers. In this town, it paid to be friends with everyone – even those you detested.

Delano's sharp eyes combed the crowd as he moved towards the second planter. Fifty feet away, it was near the entrance that he got his first glimpse of Quinton Werner – now dressed like his co-conspirators, as a security guard.

Nearby stood the two men Delano had seen Werner with that morning. All three peered intently through the open double doors leading into the ballroom.

The journalist's heart lurched at seeing Werner begin punching numbers into his phone. With seconds to save himself, Delano flung aside his tray of champagne flutes, bursting into a desperate sprint, shouting as he went: "Get down…bomb, bomb! Get down!" Only Dave Fuller heeded the warning, flinging himself flat.

Party guests stood bemused, questioning this bizarre behavior, watching a crazed waiter dive behind one of the small cocktail bars set up around the room.

The answer to their puzzlement came in an ear-shattering roar as the planter Delano had been heading for exploded. It sucked the oxygen out of Delano's lungs, deafening him, and rocked his refuge.

Jagged chunks of metal scythed through bodies. Delano heard piercing screams and groans of pain rising all around from dozens of injured men and women.

The hail of nuts, bolts, and nails had slashed through unprotected flesh, leaving gaping wounds. People known and worshiped globally were dead or bloody, grievously injured.

The biting smell of spent explosives enveloped the smoldering room. Behind the bar, Delano shook in terror; later, he would weep. He blamed himself: he had failed to prevent this bloodbath.

He felt weak with shame. He should have sounded a persistent, early warning to the authorities. He realized his silence, motivated by a craving for another exclusive headline, had been an enormous mistake.

But there was nothing he could do to correct it now. More and more, he knew he must leave this form of journalism. But for the moment, he was determined to disarm the last bomb before more people died.

The shocking sight when he crawled out from behind the bar and struggled to his feet heightened his anguish.

Party gowns hung ragged, revealing lacerated bodies. A superstar and her husband lay crushed by the weight of a crystal chandelier crashing down.

Dazed men in gashed tuxedos frantically sought the exits. Gashed corpses lay all around as survivors staggered about, pawing in disbelief at their wounds.

Eyes shone weirdly out of faces covered in white powder from blasted roofing plaster. The floors were slippery with blood. Couches nearest the explosion were ablaze, adding thick smoke to the nightmare scene.

Moving towards the last bomb, Delano saw Fuller. He was alive, bloodied with cuts to his face and the back of his head. His partner looked shaken but alive, ready to help with the third bomb. Together, they crept along the wall towards the remaining unexploded planter.

It was then Werner and his men locked the room's double doors behind them. They immediately opened fire with automatic weapons on any partygoers unlucky enough to be near the doors. Bullet-riddled bodies piled up in front of the locked doors.

Delano knew Werner was seconds away from detonating his final bomb. His activating phone was out of his pocket, the number keyed in. But he delayed pressing the button, providing the time needed to allow his fellow jihadists to leave through the garden exit, away from the blast area.

While his partners in terror hurried outside, Werner rampaged. He delighted in reducing Hollywood power players to whimpering curs. It fulfilled him knowing his final blast would kill and maim many more.

Delano, creeping along in the shadows, saw people clustered around the small stage. There, battered and bloody, Ralph McKenzie had regained the microphone and bravely sought to calm the wailing crowd.

Furious at the unintimidated editor, Werner marched towards him, firing his gun into the ceiling for attention, sending down more showers of white plaster. McKenzie represented everything he hated: power, wealth, success.

Ignoring the gunshots, the editor instructed his surviving guests: "Be calm, help is on the way. Get out through the garden doors at the end of the ballroom, if you can."

An imposing man, McKenzie surveyed Werner contemptuously, urging a few of the uninjured men: "Stop this madman. He's a cowardly terrorist. Bring him down."

His words went unheeded as those male guests still standing backed away, too frightened to tackle the gunman.

The "cowardly terrorist" epithet pricked Werner's inferiority feelings. How dare this artsy-fartsy fool try to belittle him. Glowering menacingly, he reached the foot of the stage.

McKenzie's china-blue eyes blazed down at him defiantly. Werner could have killed him instantly. Instead he stared back, his face contorted by anger as he spat out retaliatory insults:

"You and your kind are parasites, degenerates. The whole industry's run by Jews who don't pay us what we're worth. We're the victims of their greed. They exploit the entire world, and you're just one of their lackeys. You think you rule. But soon, you're history. Tonight's a taste of what's coming on a massive scale."

McKenzie's microphone picked up this manic outburst. Werner's tsunami of hate flowed from the loudspeakers. More bedraggled celebrities edged towards the doors, discovering them locked.

Others tried fleeing through the gardens – but Abisha and Basheer, waiting with guns leveled, shot them as they approached.

"You – 'victims' – what a laugh," McKenzie responded fearlessly. "You're loathsome killers—disgusting losers with guns. We're not responsible for your evil. You're cheap, murderous thugs who…"

He never finished.

Werner shot him through the right temple. The editor stood for a moment, contempt still written large on his bloody aristocratic features. Then he toppled down onto people crouched below the foot of the stage.

Werner clambered up to take his place, grabbing up the microphone from the floor.

"Look at you cowardly rats searching for bolt holes. You won't escape, none of you bastards," he screeched, his hysterics producing hideous feedback.

"There's no hiding place here," Quinton roared.

For emphasis, he callously fired into the whimpering crowd hugging the floor face down. Satisfied, Werner surveyed an ocean of trembling tuxedoed backs, bejeweled female partners in the rubble with them.

Delano had by now crept to the third unexploded planter. His steel rod probed until it hit metal. If Werner pushed the button now, it was over for him. With shaking hands, he pulled the bomb up. Like the first bomb, two leads led to the detonator.

He sighed with relief after cutting both wires – now he'd deal with Werner. If he died doing so, he didn't care. It would be justice for his failure to bring in the authorities earlier.

It would be his punishment, also, for setting up a situation that would remain on his conscience for the rest of his days.

Sneaking back, he climbed onto the stage behind the raging gunman. His only weapon was the steel probe.

Lifting it high, he brought it down like a spear with all his strength into the back of Werner's bull neck.

The metal lance missed the killer's spine by a fraction. The force of the blow snapped off the probe's top, leaving several inches of metal in Werner's flesh.

Agonized and surprised, Quinton Werner swung around, eyes blazing. Who dared attack him?

Fists raised, Delano jumped in close to hit Werner. Recognition dawned on Quinton as he tried to dodge.

"You're that fucking dirtbag reporter," he snarled, bringing up his pistol for a shot to the head.

Mike's fist smashed into Werner's gut at precisely the moment he pulled the trigger.

A bullet creased the top of the journalist's skull. Velocity spun him, knocking him flat, bleeding profusely seemingly from a lethal head wound.

The brawl on the stage emboldened people to start rising from the floor and crawling out from under tables. They hoped a rescue effort had started.

Believing Delano dead, Werner focused on potential attackers. If they rushed him, they'd tear him limb from limb.

"Stay down, or die!" he bellowed. Two shots into a burly director who'd gotten to his feet underlined the order.

On hearing loud banging against the ballroom's locked double doors, Werner knew he must escape. A SWAT team was breaking in – time to get out.

No matter what the future, he felt exultant. He'd murdered and injured dozens of the Hollywood glitterati – and he'd killed Mike Delano, a celebrated journalist.

He leaped from the stage, running for the gardens. The wound in his back throbbed as he lurched awkwardly towards palm trees at the gate. There was no sign of his partners.

They'd fled in the Toyota to their agreed meeting place. Werner had a fast and maneuverable motorcycle parked for his escape.

Now to detonate the final bomb, to destroy the remaining bigwigs and most of their rescuers, too.

Quinton quivered in anticipation, his cell phone at the ready. Hearing doors caving to battering rams, he smirked at the babble of relieved voices as medics and police swarmed among the injured. Many would die. Fiendishly gratified, he pressed the button.

Nothing.

Desperate, he punched in the number a second time, making sure he got it right. No explosion. He entered the number yet again. Still no explosion.

"What the fuck?" he growled.

An intolerable answer came quickly. The ballroom speakers crackled back to life. He heard a calm British voice, more intense than the dead McKenzie's, speaking slowly.

"It's OK, everyone. We'll get you out of here and take you to hospitals. I'm Mike Delano. The remaining bombs have been disarmed. The attackers have gone. Thank God, we're safe now. Help the injured…"

Shaking with rage, Werner flung the useless phone to the ground as he headed for the rear gate. Police were coming through with guns drawn. They looked at him suspiciously, but seeing his bloodstained security guard uniform, they offered medical aid.

"No, I'm OK, officers, thanks. I can get myself to the hospital," he replied politely.

And he added helpfully, "One terrorist's still in there. Hurry, before he kills more of those unfortunate souls…"

Werner started his motorcycle and, with a roar, headed for the North Hollywood safe house, where the Basheer twins would be waiting.

* * *

Delano filed yet another scoop: "Inside the Oscars Horror," first-person accounts of how he and Dave Fuller tracked the terrorists, disarmed bombs, and tackled the jihadist leader.

The superstar journalist and his partner became instant talk show darlings; popular media anointed them the heroes of Hollywood's darkest night.

But Delano knew the truth. Again, he'd placed money and ego above integrity. Beating everyone to the story had become an addiction, but dozens of lives were lost or ruined this time.

This behavior would have been unthinkable in his past life as a respected and trusted foreign correspondent when he'd done everything conscientiously – and denounced ethical failures in others.

Under Rothenberg's tuition, he'd abandoned honor and gone for the jugular in landing stories that promised to be global media sensations. Selling their souls became a way of life for Max's employees until it was too late to stop. Delano recognized it had happened to him, too.

He vowed it was the last time he'd compromise his integrity. This latest success piled more shame on a conscience silenced since the day he drove the Rev. Francis Morley to fling himself in the Thames and drown. Then there'd been the murder of his source, Carmelita Sanchez, and the overdose of Suzanne Francis as part of the honey trap he'd set.

The number of deaths he felt responsible for was mounting. He carried little guilt about Carlos Bomba's demise. But as much as Delano detested Morgan Masterson, the actor hadn't deserved to end as shark bait. Now he'd played into the hands of terrorists and had innocent deaths to torment his already troubled psyche.

As media chronicled the misery suffered by Tinseltown's most renowned men and women, Delano and Fuller got maudlin drunk at the King's Head in Santa Monica.

Both knew they should have sounded a strident warning about what was coming well before the jihadists had a chance to plant bombs in the ballroom.

Slopping down their drinks, they agreed they'd joined the gaudy tabloid circus, marching behind the ragtag band of noisy sensationalists, tumbling with the corrupt clowns of pop journalism – and they must change their ways or be damned.

CHAPTER THIRTY-THREE:

AN INSULT AVENGED

The Colombian cartel's new leader, Joaquin Gallardo, had a nagging problem. He had done nothing to punish Rothenberg for killing Carlos Bomba. With his *sicarios* whispering their new boss was wimpish, Gallardo needed to make a bold move proving them wrong.

More than a year had passed since the movie mogul fed Carlos and his actor cousin to the sharks after ordering valuable cartel men gunned down. Too occupied consolidating his leadership, Gallardo had neglected vengeance on Max for his grievous insult.

The drug lord was indifferent to Morgan Masterson's death. He got what he deserved. But the loss of Carlos and two of his men had to be avenged. Without action, the cartel appeared feeble, and in the cocaine business, weakness invited attack.

While considering what move to make, Gallardo put Rothenberg's Dubai island under surveillance. He wanted to know every detail about how the tycoon and Gil Ackerman lived in exile.

Gallardo's spies included the courtesans Max helicoptered in for his and Ackerman's pleasure. On the cartel's payroll, these women had supplied details of the mansion's staff, security, and layout.

More valuable information came from Colombian *sicarios* on a supposed Arabian Gulf fishing boat, working waters close to the mogul's island home. These assassins listened daily to Rothenberg's satellite calls – mostly made to the daughter running her father's empire.

"Daddy, I'm not the most popular figure around here since you named me chairwoman," Rachel complained during a call from her Manhattan office. "There's all kinds of jealousy and resentment."

"That's to be expected, just give me the names of the troublemakers – and I'll make sure they behave," Max reassured her.

Listening to reports from his men, it was evident to the drug chieftain that Rothenberg was still GMI's boss, working through his daughter.

For this reason, the wily Colombian had a second spy team watching the daughter in Manhattan. They knew when the limo picked Rachel up in the morning and returned her at night to a Fifth Avenue penthouse home.

Both teams prepared to strike against father and daughter simultaneously once they received the order from Gallardo.

* * *

The setting sun colored Rothenberg's island in a rosy glow. Still wet from his evening dip in the warm ocean, Max punched in Rachel's number. This call had become his thrice-weekly ritual while stewing in exile. Rachel answered, her voice cheering him up.

"Daddy, glad to hear from you. How are you?" she inquired.

"I'm OK, stir-crazy on this island. There are only so many books you can read, so many films to watch. I need to see people, new faces besides Gil and the staff. I'm thinking of traveling in disguise."

Rachel was immediately alarmed. "If they catch you, it's all over. You go to prison for life. Is that what you want?"

"No! But you don't know what it's like, locked up on a sand bar, surrounded by water. It's hard to take, especially after the life I've lived."

Rachel smiled wryly. Her father hadn't been keen to answer her pleas for release when she was a prisoner in Switzerland – but she said nothing.

The public's memory of his criminality was fading. If he were captured, deported, and tried, it would renew the unwanted spotlight on GMI.
Company stock prices would plunge again – an eventuality she wanted to
head off.

Rachel enjoyed the corporate life Max had previously denied her.
Global media power had magically transformed her into one of the world's
most influential women; she'd soon be one of the wealthiest. And in Max,
she enjoyed exclusive access to a genius business brain available to be consulted any time.

"Now tell me about the company," he urged.

Her voice reflected the satisfaction she felt. "I've reviewed the annual
report; it looks good. I've dealt with the troublemakers. Fired three directors, and paid them off to keep quiet. Profits are up by hundreds of millions. Should be billions next year. Stock value's increased by ten percent
since I took over."

Max mumbled approval. That he wasn't sharing in the credit for
these achievements rankled him.

"I'm proud of you," he said.

Ignoring pangs of professional jealousy, he nevertheless enjoyed
seeing his daughter succeed, especially now she was free of Delano. His
pride swelled at the proof that she was a worthy successor. He was grateful
that, through his talented daughter, he remained a powerful influence on
GMI executives.

"Never thought you had it in you, but you've shown that you do," he
said, unable to hide the resentment in his tone.

Such reluctant praise had taken a lifetime coming, but it still thrilled
Rachel. "Thank you, Daddy. I'm enjoying the challenge."

"What about Delano? What are you doing about him?"

"The divorce will be final soon. We'll meet in New York next week to
sign the papers. He's hurt, but he's not causing difficulties."

Rothenberg's face darkened. He sensed her underlying emotional connection to the man he hated. He remained determined to destroy him, but that could wait until, hopefully, Rachel lost interest in protecting him.

He would not risk angering her. She could easily cut him off from the day-to-day running of his beloved business– a challenge that kept him sane and gave him reason to live.

"You're smart to divorce him. I hear he's back on his boat."

"Are you spying on Mike?" Rachel asked, her voice rising toward annoyance.

"No, no – people just call, tell me stuff, you know," he answered, quick to soothe. "I've left him alone. He's been quiet since his showboating heroics at our *Fabulous Living* party."

"Don't knock him, Daddy. He's gutsy. Not many journalists take such risks. They wounded him; he saved many guests. I've no complaints since we parted. He was good to me. I miss him – but I couldn't stay married to a man who nearly destroyed you."

Rothenberg wished he'd never mentioned his nemesis. "I don't deny he's got guts, but it's better that you parted."

Fearing he'd overstepped boundaries with talk of Delano, he turned to placatory praise again.

"Well, a beautiful woman like you should soon find somebody else. And you're respected now for your business success. Keep up the good work. I'll have more suggestions for you, maybe after I see the annual report."

"I look forward to hearing them. I'm glad we're working together, Daddy. Meanwhile, I'm not looking for any replacement for Mike," Rachel said.

The last remark didn't please Max.

* * *

Several miles away from Rothenberg on a wooden fishing boat, Sebastian Martinez removed his headphones, turned off his recorder, and prepared to call Joaquin Gallardo.

An English-speaker, Martinez was second to Gallardo in the cartel's chain of command. He and his *sicarios* had listened in to Rothenberg's calls since they arrived in the gulf weeks previously.

"We've got to do it tonight," Martinez told his boss. "He's talking about travel. He might do it, no matter what the daughter says. I say we go for it tonight."

Gallardo agreed, reminding Martinez that the goal was abduction, not assassination.

Martinez, in turn, cautioned his thuggish crew:

"Rothenberg and Ackerman must arrive in Colombia alive, so go easy taking them. That's an order from the chief. Don't get trigger-happy. They'll die later. Joaquin wants to see them pay for the deaths of Carlos and our men."

* * *

It was a starlit night. The black inflatable cruised at 20 knots towards Rothenberg's island, slowed, bumped gently onto the sandy beach behind the mansion.

Martinez's men carried tranquilizer guns and chloroform-soaked pads as they moved across the dunes and onto the mansion's paved terrace.

They forced the lock on the utility room and neutralized the alarms and security cameras, cutting power at the breakers. They then picked a sliding door lock, silently entering the main building.

They anesthetized the staff in their rooms to avoid interference: two sleeping cooks, a housekeeper, and a maid. One of the visiting hookers in the Cartel's pay had bribed the security guard not to put up any resistance.

On the second floor, a tranquilizer dart immobilized Ackerman before he could reach for the shotgun beneath his bed. The way clear, the Colombians entered the main bedroom where Rothenberg snored loudly, oblivious to his danger.

"Get up and don't make a sound, or you're a dead man," Martinez growled in his ear while prodding an automatic into his fleshy gut.

"What's happening. Who are you?" the angry mogul demanded in the officious voice he reserved for bungling servants and underlings. "Get out! Don't you know who I am?"

Sebastian Martinez grinned. The nerve of this jerk, believing he could order people around, even with a gun poking in his belly.

"Yes, we know who you are, Mr. Bigshot," he said in accented English. "One wrong move, and you'll be food for the fishes. I hear you're good at feeding our people to the fish. Now get up."

Rothenberg arose in dread. Now he knew. They were from the cartel, there to take revenge for the deaths in Costa Rica. He stood, shaking in his undershorts, and tried bargaining.

"Please don't kill me. I can make you rich. I'll give you more money than you ever dreamed of, much more than whoever's paying you…"

"Stick your filthy money up your ass," Martinez jeered. "We're not here to kill you, but we'll hurt you if we have to. Just do as I say, or I'll break your stupid gringo face. Or blow your kneecaps off. Now you understand?"

His pistol again prodded Rothenberg into shuddering obedience. "We're going down the stairs and walking outside. Don't try to run. There's nowhere to go. I'll be right behind you."

Rothenberg wanted to scream for Ackerman but didn't dare. Was he already dead? He silently cursed his locally hired security guard and household staff who hadn't raised the alarm or stopped these ruffians.

He stumbled across the sand, the way lit by flashlights. At the water's edge, the kidnappers taped his mouth shut and bound his wrists.

Martinez ordered him into the rubber boat bobbing a few feet from the beach. Another armed man waited at the tiller. He tied the mogul's feet together so tightly he yelped in pain.

Back at the mansion, two *sicarios* had hauled semi-conscious Ackerman out of bed, bound his hands and feet, carried him down the stairs grunting and puffing. They sledded his muscular frame, wrapped in bedsheets, across the sand.

He regained consciousness as they tossed him into the inflatable next to Rothenberg.

"Why are you doing this? Where are you taking us?" the security chief complained seconds before they gagged him.

Martinez answered his question with a vicious punch to the side of the head: "You'll see. Cooperate if you want to live."

Trussed-up, the mogul and his supposed protector looked at each other desperately. They shared a new understanding: Piss them off and they'll kill us.

Dumped like sacks of potatoes in the stern of the fishing boat, there was no escape. The vessel headed for an isolated pier on the mainland. They were then loaded into a car and driven to a remote runway where a cartel Gulfstream G150 waited.

Twenty hours and one refueling stop later, the plane landed at Joaquin Gallardo's estate. Hard braking brought it to a wheels-smoking halt near the end of the short runway. Armed guards watched workers move stairs to the forward exit.

Sebastian Martinez and his men pushed their prisoners out, hands tied behind their backs. The pair were dirty, their clothes rumpled, their chins covered by stubble. Dazzled by the cloudless sky above them, brilliant and blue, they blinked nervously in the bright Colombian afternoon.

Moved to the shadow of the wing, they watched as Gallardo welcomed Martinez with a grateful embrace.

"You did a spectacular job grabbing the gringos. There's a bonus coming for you and your guys. I want everyone to know I'm punishing this pair for killing Carlos and his men."

The ride from the private runway to Gallardo's fortress home quelled any hope the prisoners had of escaping. Electrified fences encircled critical sections of the residential estate.

Security cameras and guard towers looked out over miles of Gallardo's land beyond the barriers. Within the manicured garden areas were fountains, vibrant green lawns, flowers, and fruit trees.

The estate administrator, Alejandro Mendoza, Gallardo's 80-year-old uncle, greeted the group as they entered a magnificent hacienda.

Mendoza escorted Martinez and his men into the living room with its bulky oak furniture and thick hand-woven carpets.

While the boss and his uncle sat at the big table talking about the kidnapping success, the *sicarios* left with three women who'd been waiting for them.

With Gallardo at the head of the table, they celebrated their success while eating local delicacies and drinking chilled wines. Joaquin and Alejandro talked of the past, of days when drug-running was more straightforward and when rivalries between (and within) cartels weren't so vicious.

Rothenberg and Ackerman remained standing at the back of the room, hungry, thirsty, and badly frightened, hands tied behind their backs.

With only Gallardo left at the table, Mendoza nodded towards the prisoners, asking: "Will you settle your business with them downstairs, Joaquin?"

"Yes, take them down now," he said. "Don't kill them yet."

Mendoza pressed a button, activating a wall panel. The panel slid open to reveal a staircase. The older man pushed another button, and two burly men in leather butcher's aprons responded.

They grabbed the prisoners and hustled them down to the interrogation chamber. Gallardo followed. Many enemies had died in his basement, a place designed for torture.

The soundproof walls were thick enough to withstand bursts of gunfire and smother screams. In one corner was an oil-fired crematorium for disposing of bodies. This place of pain and death proved to be the last stop for most who entered. Executioners took their ashes outside to fertilize the roses.

While his henchmen stripped Rothenberg and Ackerman of their clothes, Gallardo pronounced his verdict: "You're going to the hottest corner of hell. You'll pay for killing Carlos and his crew."

* * *

Two of Joaquin Gallardo's men followed Rachel Rothenberg's driver, George Roberts, home after he finished his shift. Outside his Queens apartment building, they forced him at knifepoint into a van and drove him to the rundown Brooklyn building where they were rooming.

The following day, under threat of having his throat slashed, the Colombians forced Roberts to call in sick, then drugged him so he couldn't raise the alarm. Rachel had no hint of danger when the Cadillac with a substitute uniformed driver arrived for her at the usual hour.

On route to the GMI tower on Park Avenue, the driver closed the partition between them before releasing Fluothane gas into the rear compartment. Rachel had no idea anything was going wrong before she slumped semi-conscious to the floor.

The *sicario* drove the limo with his comatose passenger straight into a shipping container to be immediately loaded onto a ship due to leave Staten Island Container Terminal for South America.

Once at sea, terrified Rachel was taken from the container to a locked cabin by two armed men. They told the sobbing heiress she'd come to no harm – as long as she cooperated.

Studying the brawny Colombians, she had no choice but to agree.

* * *

In New York to sign divorce papers with Rachel, it didn't take Mike Delano long to deduce the fate of his estranged wife – whom he'd still had hopes of dissuading from ending their marriage.

He had waited for hours at the lawyer's office, but she didn't arrive. Phone calls to GMI, her cell phone, and her apartment failed to locate her.

Manhattan police eventually contacted Delano to tell him his wife had been reported missing by her staff. When he questioned them, they confided they were interviewing her driver, who complained of being attacked by three foreigners the night before.

Hours later, Mike heard news reports his adversary, runaway tycoon Max Rothenberg, and a security man were missing from their island refuge in the Arabian Gulf.

Shocked, Delano carried out his own investigation, interviewing Rachel's friends and business associates, and her driver once the police were done with him.

"They held me at knifepoint overnight and drugged me," the man said. "They spoke Spanish. They made me call in sick and give them the keys to the Escalade."

So far, the authorities hadn't made the connection between the abductions in Dubai and New York. Delano, however, guessed Max and Rachel were almost certainly in the hands of revenge-seeking Colombians. He was sure the cartel had snatched them in retaliation for the murder of Carlos Bomba and his men.

Mike's mind raced to form a plan, aware of the vicious treatment drug gangs inflicted on prisoners. They could do what they wished with His Lordship, but they weren't going to hurt Rachel. The thought of the woman he loved being tortured, raped then killed filled him with dread.

While remaining angry that she'd chosen corporate ambition and family loyalty over him, he figured there must be a way of recovering her from the cartel.

He punched the speed dial for Dave Fuller in California. For the second time, he'd need Dave's help on a dangerous mission.

CHAPTER THIRTY-FOUR:

FINANCING JIHAD

After their vicious Oscars attack, Werner and his Muslim cohorts sought refuge in Beirut. Quinton enjoyed his position as an essential asset in the Bashir twins' war against the West.

But having paid for three terrorist attacks and financed an expensive year on the run, he'd tightened his grip on what remained of the Spike's millions. That made him less valuable to the jihadists – until they heard his proposal of a new Middle Eastern drug scheme.

"We need a fresh source of cash," he told his compatriots. "The best way to get it fast – and keep it coming – is drug dealing. And I mean big-time drug dealing. For example, there's a huge new market for cocaine right here in the Middle East."

The twins looked at him in shocked disbelief, even disgust. They shunned all intoxicants, considering them evil.

"Muslims don't use drugs like Christians," Abisha Bashir said scornfully. "The Koran says it is *haram* – forbidden."

"You should know better than most we can't become involved in anything like that," added Basheer. "It's why the decadent West is falling apart."

Werner was unfazed by this expected reaction, knowing it would not be difficult to change their minds. He smiled as he made his pitch.

"Who said anything about feeding junk to Muslims? There's an untapped gold mine here: 25 million infidels working on $2.7-trillion worth of Middle Eastern construction contracts. And these fools are flush with cash, ready-made customers for dope."

Quinton had done his homework on the supply and demand sides of the business. He'd learned, with coca production rising, all the cartels were desperate for new markets. Western countries, with 17 million cocaine users, couldn't absorb much more blow. Suppliers, anxious about the surplus, needed new outlets for their products.

In privately delivered proposals and follow-up phone calls to Colombia, Werner pitched his business plan to Joaquin Gallardo, one of the most successful Colombian drug bosses.

He told Joaquin he planned to set up a Middle Eastern distribution network involving Hezbollah and al Qaeda groups.

Such groups, he claimed, had enthusiastically welcomed his drug plan. The prospect of exploiting unbelievers staying in their countries pleased them.

They were also hungry for the hundreds of millions of dollars needed to continue their struggle against the West. The money would come as a gift from Allah.

It didn't take long for a smooth talker like Werner to win his cousins' approval to move ahead with his proposal. They agreed to go with him to negotiate the final terms with Gallardo in person.

As Werner had predicted, they found the drug boss enthusiastic about a proposition that could open a vast new market, producing millions more in profits and absorbing the cartel's surplus dope.

CHAPTER THIRTY-FIVE:

RESCUE MISSION

"I don't know why I listen to your madcap ideas," Dave Fuller moaned huffily from behind *Talespinner's* wheel. The splendid yacht, heeling before the wind and nobly climbing breaking eight-foot swells, was sailing well on the eleventh day of its voyage to the Colombian port of Cartagena.

"You listen, my friend because you make big bucks off my good story ideas," Delano joshed as he handed his partner a steaming hot mug of coffee, which, because of the rough seas, had just made a jittery journey from the galley below.

"Good ideas? Dangerous ideas are more like it. And this latest one beats all the others," Fuller said, running a rueful finger over scars on his broad chest, souvenirs from their clash with Werner and the Bashir twins the night of the Oscars.

Lucky to be alive, both journalists had recovered from their wounds. Doctors had dug shrapnel out of Fuller's body. They had stitched up Delano's bullet-plowed scalp wound. His thick hair mainly had grown back over the scar.

Fuller had misgivings about the reasons for the new mission but hadn't talked about them. He judged Rachel harshly for callously trading the man who loved her for the promise of business success. He supposed family loyalty went into her calculations, too. Now Delano had polished his dented armor, intent on rescuing her. He knew his friend wouldn't rest until he won her back.

Dave prayed that all three of them would get out of Colombia alive. Delano had determined sneaking into Cartagena by sea was their best shot. He and Fuller had high profiles after their Oscars night intervention and the resulting press and television appearances.

The cartels had spies among airport staff and customs officials. Paid-off officials provided details of people seen as threats to the drug bosses and their interests. Arriving by private boat was the best bet to avoid detection – and even then, they were running a significant risk.

"We'll hire a panel truck to drive to Medellin. It should take about six hours. Gallardo's estate is about a hundred miles from there," Delano shouted above the freshening wind.

"I'm told the place is like a fortress, covers several thousands of acres of the Abura Valley. They've surrounded the living quarters with guard towers and electric fences."

What he heard from Mike heightened Fuller's uneasiness about the mission. What unspoken danger awaited them?

"How are we going to spring her, then?" he asked, handing the yacht's wheel over to Delano, who made a minor course correction, ensuring a nightfall arrival.

Mike looked pensive. For once, he lacked a ready answer.

"I don't know. We've got to find a way of making them release her. No use in us going up against an army of killers."

"You're right about that," Dave said, relief in his voice. "You know anybody there?"

"I have a contact in Medellín. His name's Nicolas Sánchez," Delano responded. "He's a friend from my London days when he covered for a Colombian news agency. Now he's the chief investigative reporter on

Bogotá's *El Tiempo*. I've been in touch with him. He filled me in about Gallardo's compound. He'll meet us in Medellín. He may be able to help us."

Having moored the yacht in Cartagena and made the tricky mountainous drive to Medellín, the pair found a backstreet dealer willing to sell them guns. They left his dingy home with two Glock 19s, ammunition, and an AR-15 semi-automatic with boxes of cartridges.

Their meeting with Nicolas Sánchez took place that night and was a success on all levels. The Colombian journalist delighted in seeing Delano again. During his past life as a British tabloid editor, Mike had tipped the Colombian to significant scoops.

Over dinner, they caught up with events in both their lives. More importantly, Nick promised to cooperate in saving Rachel. He provided additional intelligence on the cartel gathered from his sources. Most valuable was his offer to introduce Delano to Rafael Agosto.

"He's a tough guy, a scrap metal dealer who hates the cartel. They murdered his favorite uncle and the uncle's wife. Someone falsely accused them of being police informers," Sánchez said.

"Rafael wants cash for his help, but he'll grab at any chance of harming Gallardo. I'll call and explain your problem. He'll be in contact once he's checked you out. He's a cautious guy. You have to be, in this town, if you want to stay alive."

While Delano and Dave waited for the call from Agosto, the Colombian journalist provided another valuable tip.

"There's an American and two Middle Eastern types staying at the Hilton. They're negotiating with Gallardo, setting up some Middle Eastern drug deal. They've been out to Gallardo's ranch where my informant says they were treated like royalty."

Intrigued, Delano sent Fuller to the Hilton to eyeball the mysterious strangers. He returned with mind-blowing news: "It's Quinton Werner and those guys we identified as the Hakim twins after the *Fabulous Living* attack."

There was no mistaking who the three men were. The picture Dave snapped from across the hotel lobby, using his phone, confirmed their identities.

"We'll go there tonight, see if we can sweat some information out of them about Rachel," Delano decided. "We'll go in disguise. Don't want them recognizing us and panicking. I'll pick up some wigs and mustaches from that theatrical costumer down the block."

Dave smirked, "Always wanted to be blonde."

"Yeah, better than that shaggy brown mop you rarely comb," Delano agreed, grinning.

They were in the Hilton lobby near the reception desk sipping cocktails by early evening, one a 200-pound muscular giant with long blonde ringlets, the other with an afro and a bristly dark mustache.

It wasn't until late in the evening that Werner and the twins stopped by the front desk to pick up their room keys. The twins went up to their rooms, turning in for the night. Werner went into the bar where several attractive women sat alone, waiting to turn tricks.

When tipsy Quinton and a young woman entered the elevator an hour later, Fuller rode up and exited along with them on Werner's floor. Following at a distance, he noted the room number as he passed.

"Room 306," he texted Delano, who hurried to join him. Minutes later, they drew their Glocks and knocked loudly on the door.

Pretending to be hotel security, Dave shouted: "*Seguridad! – Seguridad del hotel!*"

Nothing happened until Delano banged with the butt of his gun. The door opened slightly. They kicked it open all the way. A woman screamed as she fell backward, releasing the towel she'd been holding to shield her nakedness. Werner, also naked, reached under a pillow for a weapon.

Delano's Glock cracked down on his head, stunning him, opening a bloody gash. Then the barrel prodded his chest, stopping all resistance, pushing him back on the bed. Dave took over, pinning him down.

Delano hustled the woman into her clothes. He pushed a hundred-dollar bill into her hand and told her to leave, warning her to keep her mouth shut.

She fled, relieved to be out of whatever trouble these gringos had brought with them. Werner, breathless from Dave's weight pressing him into the mattress, was speechless. Shocked recognition dawned when his attackers ditched their wigs.

"Not you SOBs again," he groaned. "I got serious backup here. People who'll kill your asses if anything happens to me."

Delano grinned, delighting in the moment. He pulled out a razor-sharp knife, grabbed Werner by his unprotected scrotum, and cupped his balls in his right hand.

"Hello again, Quinton," he said. "Last time we met, I stuck you in the back. You creased me with a bullet. This time, it's more personal. I'll deball you if you don't tell me what I need to know."

CHAPTER THIRTY-SIX:

HOOKED

Lord Rothenberg looked like a hog hung up for slaughter. Cowhide straps attached to his arms hung from ceiling hooks, suspending the mogul's naked bulk. Powerful arc lights illuminated his degradation.

Frantic, he pushed his toes against the slick cement, seeking to relieve the strain on his joints. Bulldog clips with wires attached to them led to various body parts – one to the flab under his double chin, the other to an inflamed scrotum beneath his fat belly.

The connections led to car batteries and a switch. He hollered in blind misery as electricity pulsed through his body whenever sadistic jailers completed the circuit. Agonized shrieks from the jolts had reduced his usually refined British voice to a harsh croak as he begged for mercy.

Gil Ackerman similarly hooked up, emitted agonized shrieks from a few feet away. He sounded like a woman in distress when electricity pulsed through his genitals. The shrill hysteria of his screams amused the otherwise bored jailers who kept the current on longer for him.

Joaquin Gallardo stood watching, indifferent to their wretchedness. He'd already decided their fate. Torturing the prisoners displayed his control and silenced any among his gang who doubted his leadership. He was finally punishing the foreigners responsible for slaying Carlos Bomba and his men.

He nodded curtly to the torturers, signaling them to lower Rothenberg. The drug boss moved closer to the broken media baron, now seated on a rough wooden box, shaking.

Joaquin's cold dark eyes stared into those of the petrified billionaire.

"You want to live? Or perhaps you'd prefer remaining strung up while we burn your balls until your black heart bursts?" Gallardo hissed.

Tears ran down Rothenberg's fleshy face. "Please, no more. I can't stand it. What do you want? Just tell me."

"For a start, I want your island off the coast of Costa Rica. I hear it's pleasant to visit and will make a useful refueling stop for my seaplanes."

"It's yours. Just stop the pain. Let me go. Let me return to Dubai."

"Possibly – if you cooperate. But you don't think all I want is that little island, do you? I need more from you before you can leave."

When the negotiation ended, Rothenberg had given up a majority share in the ownership of Paragon Pictures as well as his cherished island. He had also made a rash promise involving Gallardo's adored only son, Miguel. He'd agreed the 22-year-old film enthusiast would join Paragon Studios as a senior producer and director despite his complete lack of movie-making experience.

Another part of Gallardo's strategy remained veiled for the moment – his intention to finance his cartel's expansion into the Middle East with some of the mogul's millions.

Nor did he mention he had Rachel locked in another part of the mansion's basement.

First, Gallardo had a harsh lesson in loyalty and obedience for Rothenberg to learn. It came the following day when cartel jailers turned fire hoses on their captives, cleaning them up for transport to a remote part of the estate.

Hustled into their soiled clothes, Rothenberg and Ackerman boarded an SUV with three rows of seats. Joaquin, pistol out, sat behind his quaking prisoners.

"I thought we had a deal," Rothenberg whined. "Where are you taking us?"

"Silence, Max, you're not dying. Not while you're useful to me. I'm having legal papers drawn up, to seal our deal. You must sign them tomorrow. Only then may you return to Dubai."

Leaving the manicured gardens, the SUV bounced across two miles of scrubland before stopping. Armed men surrounded Rothenberg and Ackerman as they got out.

A mound of dirt freshly dug from a six-foot deep hole greeted their frightened gaze. A single coffin built of rough-hewn planks stood near the grave. Several workers watched, leaning on shovels.

Gallardo, crewcut and muscular, walked toward them with purpose, merciless eyes focused on Gil Ackerman, his lean, goateed face relentless.

"You, Ackerman, are going to die. You enjoyed tossing my friend Carlos to sharks. You shot his men like dogs. Now you pay the price. I bury you alive. You have plenty of time to consider your sins."

Ackerman fell to his knees begging Rothenberg to do something. Instead, the man he'd served for decades quickly backed away.

"There's nothing I can do, Gil. They want revenge for what you did to Bomba."

"You liar!" Ackerman screamed. "I followed your orders. The sharks were your idea."

Before he could say more, two husky laborers slammed him to the ground. His hands and legs bound, they dragged him to the box. They placed their struggling victim inside and nailed the thick lid down tight. Screams came as they lowered it into the ground.

Rothenberg shook. He heard more muffled groans from the bottom of the grave. Next came the thud, thud, thud of dirt shoveled in until the hole filled. Gallardo walked over the grave in his embossed cowboy boots, stamping down the last bits of rough ground, completing the barbarous burial.

"He'll last a while, maybe an hour, before the air runs out," he said as he led Rothenberg by the arm back to the SUV. "You fulfill my commands, or you'll die the same way – gasping for your last breath in the blackest darkness."

It pleased Gallardo to see Rothenberg's reaction, his face contorted by terror. He would do anything to avoid a similar fate, no matter what it took to survive.

"I'll give you whatever you want. I'll make you wealthier than you ever dreamed. Let me go."

"It all depends on you," Gallardo interrupted. "I don't want anything to happen to my son in LA. I know how you make 'difficult' people disappear."

Now the drug king casually played his trump card.

"Incidentally, I have Rachel. We grabbed her when we took you. Anything happens to my son, your daughter dies."

Max looked horrified, stuttering out his words: "Joaquin, she must be released to get back in her position as my proxy. Without her, there's no guarantee we can give Miguel the position he wants."

"I'll consider it," was all Gallardo would say. "After all, if anything happens to Miguel, you will die. You know now that I can make that happen whenever I wish. Maybe that's enough."

He paused, then continued: "One more thing you need to know. Quinton Werner's here. Doubtless, you have cause to remember him? We had an interesting talk over dinner a couple of nights ago. He told me how he blew up your Florida set, killed one of your executives, and attacked your big fancy party."

"Why would you bring that swine here? He's my worst enemy," Rothenberg spluttered.

Gallardo laughed.

"Well, you and I are not exactly best friends, are we? Werner and I are in business together. The time has come for you two to end your feud. You know what happens to those who anger me. I can always have my men dig another grave."

"How are you in business with Werner?" Rothenberg asked, appalled.

"He's setting up a new marketing venture for me, one you'll help finance."

Gallardo, who enjoyed deflating this stuffed shirt, paused again before adding: "You and Werner will return to Dubai together. He'll stay there with you, to ensure you honor our agreement. Consider him your new security chief – you need a new one."

CHAPTER THIRTY-SEVEN:

TAKEN FOR A RIDE

Werner howled in outrage when Delano's knife nicked his ball sack. Dave Fuller slapped a hand over the former union fixer's mouth, silencing him. Fortunately, the hotel rooms on either side were vacant.

Even with Fuller astride his chest and Delano threatening castration, the incensed thug couldn't believe this pair of amateurs had jumped him.

He was ready to fight to the death if he could escape from under his attacker, who had him pinned to the bed. Desperately shaking his face free from Fuller's ham-sized fist, he challenged: "You cowardly fuckers. You wouldn't pull this shit if I were on my feet, facing you *mano a mano*."

Delano smiled, delighted to accept the challenge. He detested this depraved degenerate.

"Get off him, Dave. Let him up. You want to try your luck with me, Quinton?"

Werner, still naked, leaped off the bed, fists up, ready to do battle, but he didn't see the right hook that flashed under his guard and slammed into his jaw. He staggered, spraying blood and snot, yet unbowed. Delano moved in with a series of short sharp jabs to his face and body, knocking him flat.

As his opponent rose unsteadily to his feet, Delano demanded, "Answer some questions – or take another beating."

"Fuck you, asshole, I got nothing to tell. I got people coming here any moment to blow your sorry asses away."

Both reporters knew it was a bluff. The Hakim brothers were asleep in their rooms on another floor, unaware of Werner's plight. Delano was confident the cartel was so far unaware of their presence.

Fuller drew close, staring menacingly into Werner's hate-filled face. "You're a liar. And disrespectful, too. I'm going to teach you some manners, the most important one being it's better to be truthful."

Werner looked at the bulked-up former rugby player and figured him slower than Delano. Ducking under Fuller's guard, he landed a hard blow to his gut. His fist met a stomach that felt like concrete. Fuller barely blinked. Grabbing his opponent by the throat, he shook Werner like a terrier shakes a rat.

Releasing Quinton, Fuller's fists became steam hammers, delivering a succession of vicious blows to his victim's chest and face. The first broke his nose. The second knocked out two front teeth. Punches to the stomach left Werner gasping on the floor again.

Remembering their horrific experience at the Oscars, both reporters were tempted to kill him but restrained themselves. Delano pulled him upright by his hair, shoving him into a chair.

As he brought his knife up under the broken, bloody nose, Mike experienced the same compulsion to cut he'd felt before beheading the perverted jailer in Iraq.

But he suppressed the urge to mutilate this murderous thug. His warning was ominous: "You'll get no mercy unless you answer my questions," Mike said. "I'll cut you – badly. When I'm done, not even your dear old mother will recognize you. And if you're wondering if I'll feel bad about it, don't bother. You deserve worse – and you'll get it unless you tell us what we need to know."

Werner experienced the same fear he'd inflicted on the Spike, seeing a blade hovering close, ready to slice into him. His mouth was bloody with broken teeth. His swollen nose throbbed. It was difficult to see through fast-closing eyes. He was one big, aching agony.

"What you wanna know?" he muttered, spitting out tooth fragments.

"Where's Rachel Rothenberg?" Mike asked, beginning the interrogation.

"Joaquin Gallardo's got her in his basement. They're gonna hold her hostage."

"A hostage? For what?"

"To protect Miguel."

"Who the hell's Miguel?"

"Gallardo's son. They forced a deal on Rothenberg for Miguel to work at Paragon, making movies."

"Rothenberg's still alive?"

"Yes. Gallardo's squeezing him for cash and property. They're gonna kill Ackerman – bury him alive – put the fear of God in Rothenberg."

"Why are you here? What's your connection?"

The blade pressed painfully under Werner's nose prompted another surprising answer.

"I'm setting up a drug network in the Middle East. I got a deal with Gallardo. They'll let Rothenberg go if he coughs up the cash to finance it. They'll keep Rachel to make sure Max stays in line."

Understanding this sequence of events brought Delano no closer to saving Rachel. He helped Dave pull Werner from the chair. Together they gagged and dressed him in the tracksuit he'd discarded earlier.

It took their combined strength to drag the stumbling man down the hotel fire exit to the panel truck parked outside. There, they bound his hands and feet for the long drive to the coast.

Dave would keep Werner captive in *Talespinner*'s forward cabin. Delano stayed behind. The reporter Nicolas Sánchez, had called with the news that Rafael Agosto was ready – for a price – to discuss ways of helping Mike.

* * *

Delano and Rafael Agosto were two of a kind, rebels willing to cut corners to get what they wanted. Mike had arrived by cab at their meeting place, an old warehouse in a compound covering several acres.

High metal fencing topped with razor wire surrounded the property. Dogs growled and snapped unnervingly as the reporter paid off the worried-looking driver and walked through the gate, trying to look unconcerned.

Armed men greeted him and removed the Glock he carried. He was markedly grateful when they restrained their attack dogs from taking chunks out of his legs. Led into Rafael's office by one of his lieutenants, Delano shook the scrap metal dealer's hand, trying not to cringe at the man's steely grip.

With a shock of dark hair over a thickly bearded face, the Colombian was of medium height with a wrestler's shoulders. Muscular arms bulged from under an oil-stained T-shirt. His voice was gruff, his accented English surprisingly good. He wasn't anyone Delano would want to alienate.

Rafael knew about Delano's mission to get his wife back and admired the journalist's courage. Over straight shots of fiery Colombian liquor – the anise-tinged *aguardiente* – Rafael revealed he had important insider information. One of his men had a cousin who was a notary public. She worked in a law office that handled business – legitimate and not so legitimate – for Joaquin Gallardo.

"She says Gallardo, his son, and some important foreigner are coming to the law office this Sunday morning. They told her, be there to notarize important papers for Gallardo."

Based on Werner's information, Delano guessed this was the deal that would sign Rothenberg's assets over to Gallardo and his son. The fleecing of the media mogul amused Delano; his hated father-in-law usually conned others.

"Does she know what the papers she'll notarize are about?" asked Delano.

Rafael looked pleased with himself. He'd make this guy pay plenty for his help.

"She says it is about ownership of a big American movie studio and some property in Costa Rica."

"When will they come in to sign?"

"Sunday morning, she says. They want her there early – not usual, working Sundays."

Delano got to the point. "I intend to be there, too. With your help, we'll snatch Gallardo's son."

A mean smile crept across Rafael's face; his predatory green eyes narrowed in anticipation at the thought of hurting Gallardo.

"You crazy, man. Gallardo will kill you. They have bodyguards with them. No chance for you alone."

"I won't be alone if you're with me, will I?"

The smirk never left Rafael's face. "That cost much money. You willing to pay me big bucks? And keep your mouth shut about my help?"

"$100,000 if we get Miguel Gallardo – and I'll need a panel truck to transport him to my boat. An old clunker will do, as long as it gets me back to Cartagena. Have you anything like that around here?"

"Sure, we got something for you. I want $50,000 up front, the rest when the job is done. That is just for my help. I give you truck for nothing."

Delano agreed and ordered his Bahamian bankers to wire the hundred grand to a Medellín bank where he'd opened an account.

He delivered the $50,000 to Rafael on Saturday afternoon, the day before making their move. It's good to be rich, Delano thought on his way back to the hotel. He hoped he'd live to enjoy his remaining wealth.

* * *

Delano and Agosto sat in an old black panel truck parked in the underground garage of a recently built Medellín office tower. Gallardo's lawyer had a suite on the 18th floor of the modern glass and metal building. It was early on a Sunday and only two other cars were there.

The place was echoingly empty compared with weekdays when it held hundreds of cars. Once in position, they waited. Rafael saw Delano struggling to light the first of the two daily cigarettes he was down to.

Delano was nervous, and it showed. His hand shook so much the match slipped from his fingers. If this failed, he knew his chances of saving Rachel went to zero. He waved away the vial of cocaine Rafael offered as a courage restorative. He'd already seen the Colombian take several hits.

Amused at Delano's reticence, Rafael turned away, busying himself loading cartridges into a pump-action shotgun. Having succeeded in his second try to light up, Delano inhaled deeply on the Marlboro – and felt better. He racked the slide on his Glock, wanting Rafael to know he was a standup guy, ready to fight.

He still hoped to avoid bloodshed and had asked the Colombian for similar restraint. The journalist suspected Rafael intended to kill Gallardo, given the opportunity, from the way he smiled at Delano's cautionary words – and there would be nothing Mike could do about it.

Watching Delano draw on his second cigarette, Rafael decided he liked this Englishman. Delano was a man to respect. Few guys dared to take on gangsters for the sake of a woman.

"You calmer now? Having the gun ready helps, yes?" he said, slipping a black hood over his head. He tossed a similar garment to Delano, signaling him to put it on.

"We do not want them to know who we are," he explained, his cat-like green eyes gleaming through the two slits. "Otherwise, the cartel tracks us down. They never give up."

They slid their seats back. From the outside, the battered panel truck looked unoccupied.

They waited until midmorning to see Gallardo's armored black Mercedes with tinted windows pulled into the garage. It stopped at the door leading to the elevators.

Delano and Rafael raised their hooded heads just enough to see Joaquin Gallardo, his son Miguel, and Lord Max get out and head for the elevators. A mean-looking bodyguard escorted them, his right hand hidden inside a jacket bulging with weaponry. Rothenberg looked pallid, bedraggled, and desperate – thinner than the last time Delano saw him.

Gallardo's driver remained in the parked car. He opened both front windows, lit a petit corona, and, angling his face toward the driver's side window, blew the smoke out.

As the elevator rose with its four occupants, Rafael slipped out of the panel truck. He crept silently from the back to the passenger side of the Mercedes.

His silenced pistol popped twice. The man at the wheel slumped over dead, the cigar still stuck to his lower lip. Rafael reached in for the car keys. After stamping out the petit corona, he dragged the driver out and stowed him in the trunk.

Delano foresaw more deaths. He had to accept his inability to control Rafael. Nor did he want to alienate the Colombian. Delano was grateful to have him on his side.

An hour later, they heard the hum of the descending elevator. Rafael and Delano exited the panel truck, still hooded, with guns drawn. Unsuspecting, the Gallardos, Rothenberg, and the bodyguard emerged when the elevator doors opened. Delano and Rafael were in the shadows on either side of the door leading into the garage.

The bodyguard came through first, followed by the others. Rafael brought down the barrel of his shotgun on the man's head with a thud, cracking it open, knocking him out or killing him; Mike couldn't tell which as he lay still, bleeding.

Gallardo bellowed at his son to follow as he scrambled back towards the elevator, where he frantically punched the button to open the doors.

Miguel tried to join his father, but they were out of luck. The elevator had moved to another floor. Gallardo fumbled for his gun as Rafael caught up with him and shoved the bloody shotgun barrel in his face. The drug boss knew Rafael would blow his head off unless he dropped the pistol. He let it clatter to the ground.

Delano shoved the Glock back inside his jacket and picked up Gallardo's Beretta. He pointed it at Miguel, who appeared ready to make a run for it. The young man froze, then threw himself flat on the floor, begging for mercy.

"Shoot the jerk," Rafael ordered.

"No, no, don't," Gallardo shouted in Spanish. "Don't kill my son. We surrender."

A moment later, the elevator arrived, and its doors opened right behind Gallardo. He turned around and jumped in, frantically pressing the button to secure himself and ascend.

Rafael swung around as the doors were closing. Joaquin crouched to the left as three bursts of buckshot blasted through the decreasing gap.

The pellets snapped and buzzed around the car biting painfully into Joaquin's flesh. From outside, they heard squeals of pain and fury as the door closed and the elevator rose.

Rafael delivered a string of curses, wishing he'd shot his enemy immediately. As Delano suspected, he had been out to murder the drug lord, but his best chance of vengeance had gone.

His blood still up, Rafael sought a target. He swung around and saw Rothenberg, who had been cowering in silence, glad to escape from Gallardo.

Wanting the mogul left alive, Mike jumped between them, shoving away Rafael's threatening shotgun barrel.

"Don't shoot," he warned. "He's mine. I get my kicks when I turn him in to face a life sentence."

Gallardo reluctantly lowered his weapon. He disliked living witnesses. Better to put them in the ground.

Still hooded, Delano and Rafael pushed Miguel and Rothenberg into the panel truck. Tires smoking, it left the garage with Delano at the wheel.

Rafael was in the back, holding the prisoners at gunpoint. At his compound, they bound both men securely and blindfolded them. The success of the mission was a relief to Delano. Now for the next phase of the rescue plan: trading Miguel for Rachel.

Mike handed Rafael an attaché case with another $50,000. They hugged, said farewell.

Before getting on the road to Cartagena, Delano phoned Dave Fuller and dictated a message for transmission to Gallardo: "Miguel dies if anything happens to Rachel Rothenberg. We'll be in touch again soon to discuss terms."

"What about Lord Max?" Fuller asked.

"He's in the back of the truck, trussed up with Gallardo's son Miguel. Gallardo got away. I'm leaving now. I should arrive after dark. Stand by to help bring them aboard. It will be late; I doubt the cartel spies will see what we're doing."

He added as an afterthought: "You got plenty of canned food? There'll be five to feed now."

"We got plenty, but the grub's boring. Baked beans and Spam mostly."

"Sounds better than these jerks will get in prison," Delano sniggered.

CHAPTER THIRTY-EIGHT:

PRISON SHIP

It took hours for a skilled surgeon to pick the buckshot out of Joaquin Gallardo's body after the garage shoot-out. Each ping of a pellet into the stainless steel bowl – dozens of them taken from all over his anatomy – made him angrier.

More than the pain of being peppered with lead, he felt humiliated and furious. They'd kidnapped his son and Rothenberg. Now Quinton Werner was gone too, the other key player in an excellent plan to sell cocaine in the Middle East.

Worse, with his bodyguard murdered, his cowardly flight into an elevator had drawn derisive amusement among his men.

Added to that, his abandonment of Miguel to the enemy drew bitter scorn. Joaquin knew he must act soon if he was to remain leader much longer.

He was aware any of his *sicarios* would have risked their lives, staying to shoot it out with the abductors. Their contemptuous whispers again made Gallardo look weak and blundering. It didn't bode well.

Gallardo's Cartagena spies hadn't missed the night-time arrival of Delano's panel truck. They described two men resembling Rothenberg and Miguel being loaded onto a yacht moored in the local marina.

Further inquiry showed it registered to the notorious journalist, Mike Delano. By the time Gallardo had identified his enemy, the *Talespinner* was long gone with its captives.

After the painful session with the surgeon, Gallardo returned to his fortress home to find a message waiting for him from Mike Delano.

"If you want Miguel back, put Rachel Rothenberg on a plane to St. Thomas. If you don't agree to the exchange, you won't see your son again," it warned. "He could tragically disappear mid-Atlantic, and I'll expose your plan to pollute the Middle East with narcotics."

With rebellion simmering in the cartel ranks, it worried Joaquin when Sebastian Martínez offered unwelcome advice. Gallardo already suspected his second in command of ambition to take over the leadership.

"We must get Miguel and the others back," Martínez urged. "We can't let these gringos get away with such an insult. We're becoming a joke. Rivals see us as weak. They'll move on our growers, steal our business."

"So, what do you suggest?" Gallardo asked sharply.

"Let me have one of those small subs we use running coca. I'll catch up with Delano's yacht, board it, kill him, and get Miguel and the others back."

While Gallardo liked the idea, he was paranoid about Martínez again becoming a figure of heroic rescue and revenge. His cartel's *sicarios* already admired Sebastian's bold capture of Rothenberg and Ackerman from their Dubai island hideout.

The Hakim brothers represented another pressure point to Gallardo. Still in Colombia, they demanded urgent action to recover Werner and Rothenberg. To finance continued jihad, they needed Werner's know-how and ability to squeeze millions out of the mogul.

"All right, but I'll lead the rescue mission. The Hakims can come along if they want to help," Joaquin agreed. "You, Sebastian, will run the submersible. I'll be in command. That understood?"

Sebastian saw menace in Gallardo's eyes and hastily answered, "Yes, of course, boss. You're in charge, as always."

* * *

The *Talespinner* had transformed from comfortable yacht to prison ship.

Not much happier than their captives, Mike and Dave alternated guard duties. They spent long hours either at the wheel or below, guarding prisoners who were increasingly rebellious despite the risk of a beating if they turned on their captors.

Each of the three captives needed escorting separately to the head and meals twice daily. Either Delano or Fuller unbound their hands while the other kept a gun on them. It was a strain on the journalists, who also shared navigation and sailing responsibilities.

Werner, still not recovered from the thrashing he'd received, was a constant problem. With little to lose, facing life in prison or a death sentence, he needed careful watching. He was like having a dangerous animal aboard, ever alert for the opportunity to jump his captors.

"You try anything, mate, and I'll beat the living daylights out of you–again," Fuller warned him. Mike feared Dave losing control and murdering the union extortionist-turned-terrorist before their voyage ended.

Rothenberg simmered just below the boiling point. Out of Gallardo's clutches, he was docile and cooperative at first. But when he learned Delano intended handing him over to the authorities once they reached a safe harbor, he regained his previous hostility.

"Just let me return to Dubai. Rachel will never forgive you, Mike, if they put me away for life," he pleaded. "I'll pay you millions more if you let me return to the Gulf."

But Delano couldn't be bought off, this time. Nor could his failed marriage be used as a bargaining chip. He refused to let Max evade justice again.

Miguel Gallardo was less of a worry. He sulked in the forward cabin, miffed over the delayed start of what he believed could be a meaningful movie career.

"My father will get you bastards. You'll both die horrible deaths, and I'll watch," he said in a rare outburst. "He'll never forgive you. If anything happens to me, he'll hunt you down, no matter where you hide."

A stinging slap in the face from an increasingly offended Fuller left Miguel sobbing in the cramped forward cabin.

Both "jailers" considered him a spoiled brat who actually would be better suited to the wiles of Tinseltown than the Colombian drug racket.

Talespinner had been heading north at five knots. But the breeze had fallen away. She was running at top engine speed over a glassy-calm ocean powered by her diesel motor.

Delano, concerned about using so much fuel, prayed for the wind to come up as he headed for the US Virgin Islands.

If all went as planned, he would hand over Rothenberg and Werner to the authorities there. But before that, and more importantly, he would exchange Miguel for Rachel.

He also intended to file his account of capturing the runaway mogul Lord Max and the Hollywood jihadi Quinton Werner. It would be his final scoop, one that would end his wretched filmland sojourn.

Delano hoped it would also foreshadow his return to mainstream establishment journalism and rehabilitate his reputation.

While his show business stories had distinguished him as a journalist had no fear of the rich and powerful, he'd used shameful, at times unethical tactics to get them. Nor had the big-money blockbusters provided the fulfillment he'd felt in his earlier career as a war correspondent.

In the next phase, maybe he'd spin the raw material of his life into fiction, with hopes of a best-selling novel in his future. He wanted to distance himself as far as possible from delusional Tinseltown.

CHAPTER THIRTY-NINE:

TWO FATHOMS DOWN

The helicopter came in low over the jungle tree line. It landed close to a dense mangrove swamp hiding three miniature submarines for running dope to North America. Joaquin Gallardo, Sebastian Martinez, and the Hakim twins left the chopper carrying automatic weapons and backpacks.

Basheer and Abisha remained stunned by Werner's disappearance. When he didn't answer their repeated calls, they had demanded hotel staff open his room. The sight greeting them was of smashed lamps, bloody sheets, and a glass-littered floor.

At first, they feared a rival drug gang had discovered their Middle Eastern drug proposal and kidnapped Quinton. In a panic, they called Gallardo. He told them Rothenberg and Miguel had fallen victim to kidnappers, too.

The brothers' outrage mounted when the Colombian said their scourge, Mike Delano, had pulled off the abductions. He had Werner, too, and intended handing him and Rothenberg over to the authorities. Gallardo thought it best not to mention Delano's offer to return Miguel in exchange for his Rachel.

"I'm taking one of our subs to go after that yacht," Joaquin announced. "Come with us. I'll let you have the pleasure of killing that reporter swine."

The twins, eager to recover Werner, embraced the opportunity to destroy their nemesis. Delano had thwarted much of the destruction they'd hoped to inflict during the Oscars rampage.

But once at the mangrove swamp submarine base, they started having second thoughts about this mission. They watched apprehensively as cartel hands fueled the 60-foot vessel with diesel, then loaded it with compressed air canisters, food, and water. The prospect of spending days underwater in the tiny sub unnerved them.

Gallardo's spotter planes had provided coordinates for *Talespinner* but kept losing the yacht when forced to return to refuel. Their last report said it was under full sail heading north after a becalming. Cartel pilots saw only one man on deck and asked permission to rake the vessel with automatic weapon fire. Fearful they'd hit his son or sink the boat, Gallardo refused.

"Let's get going," the drug boss barked at Sebastian Martínez. "They're two hundred miles ahead of us. We must make up the time."

The tiny craft was soon out to sea, with Sebastian running its twin diesel engines flat out. It plowed through the water at maximum surface speed, just short of ten knots. Gallardo, his bearded face poking out of the tiny conning tower, shrank back in annoyance when waves slapped his face.

Below, the twins vomited into buckets as the sub pitched and seawater sprayed through the open hatch, soaking them. The reality of this voyage was far worse than they had ever expected.

"Wouldn't it better if we dived?" Gallardo demanded of Sebastian, an expert in running the cartel's miniature subs. "These Arab assholes won't be worth shit as fighters if this pounding continues."

"Yes, boss, but we'll be at half speed running on batteries. We can only stay down two hours at a time. We must surface to recharge our batteries. Don't blame me if we lose the yacht."

Gallardo, detecting a note of disdain in Sebastian's voice, was beginning to despise his second in command. He'd dispose of him when this job was over – or at the next opportunity.

Joaquin looked down at the wretched Hakim twins. The cramped vessel that usually carried eight tons of cocaine stank of their vomit. The stench made him and Martinez feel ill, too. Their condition concerned Gallardo. He wanted them strong enough to fight when they caught up with Delano.

Werner had boasted to Gallardo the jihadists were proven fighters, but he feared they were becoming useless under these conditions.

"OK, take her down," he said reluctantly, shutting and latching the hatch. The hot diesel-contaminated atmosphere worsened without fresh air coming in, but it was calm twenty feet down where the buffeting subsided.

"Sea conditions above should improve," Sebastian said hopefully. "That's what the forecast says."

"They'd better be fucking right," Gallardo growled. "Can't we go faster? We must catch up."

The drug boss knew it would add badly to his loss of face if his attackers escaped. He suspected overly ambitious Sebastian of hoping for that.

It would be shameful for Gallardo if Delano's account of snatching Rothenberg and Werner from the Colombians appeared in the international press.

He would look like the inept boss of the drug gang that couldn't shoot straight. Not only must he get the kidnapped men back, but he also had to stop Delano from filing that story.

* * *

They had kept Rachel locked in a dimly lit room below Gallardo's hacienda for what seemed an eternity. Each day she feared she might die – the woman who brought her food and water as much as told her time was running out.

"They'll turn you over to the men as a sex toy before cutting your throat," she maliciously warned her gringa captive. "I've seen it happen. Poor bitches were glad to die."

Rachel spoke enough Spanish to understand the frightening words. During the first days of her imprisonment, she'd heard screams from another part of the basement.

Realizing those heart-stopping cries came from her father and Ackerman demoralized her. It was hard to believe, they'd captured them, too.

"I'm cutting a deal with your father. You'd better hope he keeps his word. Otherwise, I'll kill you both," Gallardo had said at their first meeting.

The drug boss was pure evil, the devil incarnate.

During another visit, he boasted how he'd plucked Rothenberg and Ackerman out of exile. He also revealed part of his grand plan to make his son Miguel a movie producer at Paragon.

When the agonized cries stopped, Rachel feared Max already dead and figured she could be next. Barefoot, in a nightdress soiled from constant wear, she now knew there was no chance of escape.

As the silence continued, paranoia set in. Rachel suspected her devious parent of negotiating his way out of his misery, leaving her behind as security for whatever deal he'd made. As much as she cared for her dad, she knew he was ruthless enough to save himself at her expense. He was the supreme survivor.

In this dismal state of foreboding, Rachel shook on hearing heavy steps along the tiled corridor. She cowered in a corner, irrationally praying the approaching men wouldn't see her there. Was this it?

She hoped for a quick bullet, not the long, drawn-out agony of gang rape. It wasn't easy accepting her privileged life may well end this way.

If she could magically return to that pivotal moment at Delano's beach house, she'd choose love over career and family loyalty. She should never have abandoned Mike for an ill-considered role in her father's corrupt world.

The men outside unlocked the door and entered. Suddenly she had courage; Rachel would fight. Fueled by rage, ready to scratch, kick and punch, she looked up, defying their intimidating stares. But they weren't carrying weapons – and didn't look threatening. What did they want?

The older man appeared to read thoughts. Having power over a beautiful woman aroused him – but he would not do anything to anger the boss.

"Rápido, rápido. Wash up. You fly home today. We're letting you go," he said beneficently.

Had she heard right? "You're letting me go?"

"Yes, orders come – take you to the airport."

The handsome younger *sicario* carried her black business suit, panties, bra, and a white shirt, all washed and neatly ironed. He passed them over with her high heels and purse. Glancing inside the bag, she could see everything was there: money, credit cards, and mobile phone, all untouched from the moment they'd seized her.

Locked up for weeks, maybe a month, Rachel had lost track of time. Why were they releasing her now? Had Max arranged it? It must be him.

She felt guilty for distrusting Daddy. Depraved though he may be, a beam of light occasionally shone through his darkness, especially for his only child. Whatever the reason for her release, she was grateful.

"Dress quickly. You go on a plane," said the first man. "We leave in 20 minutes."

She turned her back on them– all the modesty they allowed – as she struggled into her underwear. She was past caring about humiliation as she slipped on her bra.

All that mattered was getting out of here. If it was possible to be more scared, Rachel was for a moment when the older thug pulled her close, peering into her face. He had a message to deliver in broken English. He wanted to ensure she understood.

"When you in America, you not talk. Got it?" he said. "Boss says no hiding place safe for big mouth. You not say what happens here. Talk, and you spend life waiting for bullet or knife, all because Rachel no keep mouth shut. Understand?"

She put a single finger to her lips like a frightened child, signaling her eternal silence. Having found her once, she knew they could do it again. Next time, there would be no reprieve.

He smiled and repeated the message for emphasis: "You beautiful smart lady. You forget what happened here. You got one chance, right?"

She nodded frantic agreement, willing to meet any requirement for freedom. Faithful to their word, they took her to the airport.

The older man handed her a ticket to St. Thomas. She wondered why St. Thomas rather than New York where they'd captured her, but asked no questions.

Flying 30,000 feet above the Caribbean, she shuddered at memories of Medellín – and wondered what happened to Max. But she was ecstatic to be alive and among ordinary people again.

Earlier regrets resurfaced. How different life might have been if she'd stayed with Mike. They had been on the verge of signing divorce papers when the Colombians took her. What had he made of her disappearance? Had he written about it?

Her heart still raced when she thought of him. Was he down below sailing on that vast blue sea? Or was he abroad, chasing some crazy yarn?

He was happiest sailing, fishing, or chasing stories. Rachel smiled at the fanciful idea he might be far below, skippering *Talespinner* and thinking of her.

The plane's engines slowed, its undercarriage thumping down for the landing. Rachel breathed a sigh of relief when the jet pulled up to the airport gate in St. Thomas.

She would stay one night there to rest before continuing to New York—and picking up her previous life.

Reveling in unexpected freedom, she wondered, what was next?

* * *

Dave Fuller was waiting when Rachel walked out into the humid Caribbean heat. While they'd never met, he had seen photos of her. Following her from the airport exit, he mimed a silent whistle. She was a curvy, raven-haired beauty, a woman not easily missed. He understood why Delano had fallen so hard and risked so much for her.

As Rachel moved towards a cab rank, he fell in stride with her. When he gently took her arm, she pulled away, startled. For a moment, she feared the burly stranger was from the cartel, sent to take her back. His face was friendly, almost familiar, but she could not place it amid the panic-inducing fear rising in her chest.

"It's OK, I'm not here to harm you," he whispered as his rugged features creased into a blue-eyed smile that partly allayed her suspicions. "I'm here to help you, not hurt you, Rachel."

"Who sent you, then?" she demanded, puzzled he knew her name.

"Someone you'll be glad to see," he said mysteriously. "It's a surprise."

"Did my father send you?"

"I'm not at liberty to say, but if you come with me, you'll see your father soon. That much I can tell you."

Max must have gained his release from the cartel, she thought. Of course, it was Daddy who'd arranged her liberation, just as she had guessed.

Dave told the driver to take them to the Compass Point Marina, and they left the airport for the short ride to the ocean.

At the marina, her eyes searched eagerly among the boats – and her heart lurched as she saw Delano walking towards her, a big grin on his determined face.

Tanned and muscular from weeks at sea, he engulfed her in the loving embrace she remembered so well and had missed so much. She should have known. Only Mike could have pulled off her seemingly impossible release.

Rachel was in for another shock as they walked down the dock to where *Talespinner* was moored. There, Lord Rothenberg stood beaming, waiting to greet the daughter he'd not seen in person for over a year.

Max held her close, his usually chill eyes misty at the warmth of their reunion. He kissed her cheeks lovingly, and she responded with joy in her father's embrace.

"I'm so relieved at seeing you, darling. I know you've had a miserable time. I'm so sorry. It's been bad for both of us. Now you're here, let's hope we can look forward to better days."

"I'm praying that's true, Daddy," she said, holding back tears.

They boarded the yacht and entered the salon. There, the warmth of reunion faded when Fuller escorted Max to the forward cabin.

Rachel caught a glimpse of a bruised and battered man seated through the open door, staring out balefully at them.

They had shackled him to one of the sturdy teak bunks. A second chain lay on the decking. Fuller closed the cabin door behind him – and Rachel knew he was shackling her father, too.

Rachel eyed Delano quizzically. Her questions followed rapidly:

"What are you doing to my father? How did he get here? Why is he locked up with you, someone he detests?"

Delano, uncomfortable, made known the unpalatable truth to the estranged wife he'd saved and wanted back.

"I'm sorry, Rachel, Max is my prisoner. He must answer for his crimes."

"Your prisoner?" she asked incredulously.

"Yes, Tomorrow I'll hand him over to the authorities. They'll send him back to the States for trial and sentencing."

"Who's that other man you have chained up?"

"That's Quinton Werner, also my prisoner," Mike said. "I'll hand him over, too. He's wanted for murder and terrorist attacks on your father's film set and Oscars party."

"How did Daddy become your captive? Did the cartel pass him over to you?"

"Far from it. We took Max and Werner by force. Grabbed Gallardo's son at the same time we got Max. I exchanged Miguel Gallardo for you – it was the only way I had of getting you out of Colombia, away from them."

Rachel, overwhelmed, willingly took a glass when Fuller opened a celebratory bottle of Champagne. After toasting her new freedom, the journalists told the whole story – how together they captured Werner and how Delano later mounted the attack that yielded Max and Miguel.

"You did all that for me?"

"I couldn't leave you there. I knew those assholes would torture you, maybe kill you. I still love you…" Delano said.

"I was lucky to get Max, too. They'd have killed him eventually, once he'd been financially sucked dry. You wouldn't have wanted that would you?"

Rachel sat down, amazed at what she was hearing. She downed her Champagne and held out her glass for more.

"Of course, I'm supremely grateful for what you've done so far, but I can't stand by and let my father go to jail for life," she said stubbornly.

Dave Fuller decided it was time to leave and said he was going on deck for a smoke. He needed relaxation when he could grab it. This harrowing voyage was not over yet.

As partners, Rachel and Mike fascinated Dave, who'd listened with interest to their verbal jousting. Both were tough negotiators with calculating natures – which would make compromise difficult.

He left them haggling over His Lordship's future, glad not to be there when their discussion turned into a full-scale argument.

Delano had opened a second bottle of bubbly. They needed something to ease the rising tension between them. The third glass of wine loosened Rachel's tongue.

"You can't turn my father over to the authorities. If he goes on trial, he's done for. If you still love me, let him return to exile," she urged. "Confinement on a tiny Gulf island is punishment enough. Let's face it, Mike, you set him up. Of course, I know why you did it, but directly or indirectly, it was you who put in motion all the ugly events that followed."

Delano had feared this. As much as he wanted her back, he would not allow Rachel to dangle a possible reconciliation as a bargaining chip.

She'd seen the video – Max ordering Masterson and Bomba thrown to the sharks. She had heard how he had the cartel men gunned down. And she still wanted to save his evil ass?

More wounding, he suspected Rachel of again putting her business ambitions ahead of their marriage. She wanted to keep Max available to exploit his brilliance in running GMI.

From his Gulf island, he could support her corporate moves. GMI would continue to prosper with his backing, and Rachel now relished the fame corporate success attracted. Imprisoned, he wouldn't be as useful.

"Daddy won't bother you once he's back in the Gulf. I'll see to that. I run the company now. I have the power." Then the expert angler baited her hook: "You and I can be together again, start a family. Write your books, or I'll appoint you the editor of any publication in the group you fancy."

Rachel's tempting – and eerily familiar – offer made him uneasy. He flashed back to Lord Rothenberg's luxurious 747 and the compelling job offer laid before him then. She sought to buy him like Max had when he dangled wealth and the editorship of the Sunday *News of the Planet*.

Regardless, the possibility of a reunion got to him. The idea of saving their marriage had been with him since the day she walked out on him in Malibu.

He needed more time to think through the Max problem. Perhaps he should delay handing him over. It would take a week sailing to Miami. By then, he'd have decided his best course of action. He might also be able to win Rachel over to the right side.

Besides, if he handed over the prisoners in Florida, the story would get far more "play" than if he did it in St. Thomas. Delano wanted this story to get maximum attention – the better to increase Max's suffering for his sins.

"OK, Rachel, I'll consider it. We sail on the first tide tomorrow. I'll make up my mind what to do about Max before we reach Miami."

She walked over to him and placed her lips on his. Their tongues met, tentatively at first, then passionately. When they drew apart, she had the last word:

"I hope by then you can see it my way. I want us to start a new life together."

CHAPTER FORTY:

TENSE TIMES

Four days out from St. Thomas, heading for Miami, the tension aboard *Talespinner* had ratcheted up. Tentative steps toward renewed romance had turned into ugly confrontations.

Rachel didn't want her father chained up with Quinton Werner. Why couldn't Daddy enjoy the comfort of the main cabin with her? Why wouldn't Delano allow her to cook kosher meals for Max with fresh supplies they'd taken on in St. Thomas?

And now, halfway to Florida, Rachel badgered Delano to know if he'd decided her father's fate: island exile in the Gulf or a cramped prison cell?

"You're in Daddy's debt for your own wealth and success," she reminded him. "You were just another hack covering foreign wars when he made you top editor on a leading London paper. Then you turned around and extorted millions from him. You owe him – big time."

There was weight to such ugly assertions, and Delano didn't like it. He had relented by letting father and daughter spend time together in the main salon, but he remained firm about handing the mogul over to the FBI once they reached Miami.

Not wanting the others to hear their ongoing disagreement, he insisted they go to the boat's bow to thrash it out once and for all.

With *Talespinner* nosing into the waves of an approaching storm, they hung on to rigging lines, spitting caustic accusations at each other.

Mike wished for old times when they were alone at sea, moving around naked in the sun when they resolved their differences by making love.

Now, he worked like a dog on this prison ship, and his estranged wife had returned only to become a nagging scold.

But looking at her now, wind whipping dark hair around the face he adored, he gave in to the urge to pull her into an embrace.

She responded to his kiss with all the passion he remembered, wrapping warm hands around his neck.

He was ready to tear off their clothes right then and there when she suddenly wriggled out of his arms and pushed him away.

"You swine, I know what you're about," she bitched. "You just want to turn Max in because it's another big fucking story, one that glorifies you."

"No, Rachel, that's not it. Max is a murderous goddamn criminal. He deserves to rot in jail for homicide. With the problems it causes between us, I wish to hell I didn't have to do this."

With the wind puckering her angry face and the yacht plunging into whitecaps, Rachel again used her most potent weapon against him.

"If you truly want me back in your life, then let daddy go. Hand Werner over. He'll provide your goddamned story. Isn't that enough? Don't you want us to be together again?"

"Of course I do, but you're being unfair. Imprisoning that rotten pair is nothing to do with getting a story – it's about justice," Mike countered. "Max destroys everyone he touches. He killed our baby, drugged you, branded me a thief, threw people to sharks, and had a woman's throat cut merely for talking to me – and there's plenty more."

"I've heard all that before – many times over," she snapped. "I know those words by heart. He's still my father. Do what you want, but I won't believe you still love me."

Delano hated being the cause of the wind-whipped angry tears now flooding her face. Despondent, he couldn't imagine mending their marriage on this voyage, or maybe ever – not without a miracle.

"How can you defend such a man?" he demanded to know. "How can you dismiss all the horror he's caused so unfeelingly?"

"Because he's my father. I need him in my life. I admire his brilliance. And I believe you provoked many of the events that led to his brutality. You wouldn't stop harassing him and his actors – not even on our honeymoon."

Her final reproof caused Delano to think twice about the advisability of handing Rothenberg over to the authorities.

"What happens now if he brands you an extortionist?" she asked spitefully. "Tells everyone how the high-minded hack blackmailed him for a hundred million to shelve the Masterson story. Won't they say you share responsibility for sparking murder?"

Mike knew there was no defense against this truth. Rothenberg could ruin him, publicly accusing him of extorting a massive bribe. And he knew once Max went on trial, all the dirty details would explode in court.

Lawyers would label him a fraud and a cheat who stashed unlawful wealth in the Bahamas. Ironically, he, too, might face legal charges – even jail time – if he couldn't cut a deal with the authorities.

The yacht lurched sickeningly, distracting him from such dire eventualities. He hurried to the cockpit and pulled hard on the wheel. He put the boat back on course and reset the autopilot before returning to Rachel.

"You wanted to know what I'd decided," he said. "This time I must do what's right, even if it brings me down, too."

Looking at the worsening storm clouds, he told her: "Let's go below. You can't stay up here. It's getting dangerous, you could be swept overboard."

"Wouldn't you like that?"

"Don't be ridiculous."

They went below in angry silence.

* * *

Fear gripped the occupants of the minisub as it navigated the heaving surface. They were hundreds of miles out from St. Thomas and had again lost sight of the yacht.

Eight-foot waves broke over the vessel. The men inside were tossed around like pebbles in a long skinny can. The rolling and pitching were torture and made all four occupants seasick.

It smelled like a sewer within the fiberglass Kevlar-sheathed hull, reeking of urine, feces, and vomit. Much of the foul mixture slopped from the bilges over their feet, splashing onto their pants legs.

Joaquin Gallardo didn't know which was worse, running on the surface or underwater. Submerged, they avoided the buffeting but must accept the stinking, damp, claustrophobic atmosphere.

Rundown batteries forced them to remain on the surface longer than they wished, charging the cells. Currently, the batteries were at about fifty percent of their capacity.

Fully charged, they'd provide eight hours of underwater running time – about what they needed to launch their attack once they sighted the yacht again.

Miguel Gallardo had called his father by satellite phone the previous day. He reported his exchange for Rachel went smoothly. He repeated what he'd overheard during captivity: Delano was heading for Miami with his prisoners – and Rachel was urging him not to hand them over to the law.

"He'll give them to the cops as soon as they arrive. You've got to stop him, Papa. Kill the son of a bitch. You must get Rothenberg back. He's my way into the movie industry."

In the cramped conning tower, Miguel's movie ambitions were of minor consequence. Gallardo's primary concern remained to prove his leadership, to be known as a boss the cartel could count on to annihilate enemies.

Hours later, he hooted with joy, catching sight of sails on the horizon four miles distant. Wiping saltwater out of his eyes, he slammed down the hatch, growling: "She's a few miles to the north. Take her down now, Sebastian. Give her full power so we catch up undetected."

This order worried the skipper because they hadn't fully charged the batteries– but he obeyed Joaquin, shutting off the diesel engines and switching to electric power.

Compressed air hissed out of the buoyancy tanks replaced by weighty seawater. They submerged to periscope depth and hovered with Gallardo peering out through the scope.

He noted high wind had forced Delano and Fuller to reef their mainsail. The yacht was limping along on its storm jib, barely moving.

"Good," he told Rafael. "We'll be on them soon."

Two hours later, as they closed in, Gallardo shouted: "Keep those engines flat-out. I'll tell you when we're close enough to surface."

The Colombian turned his attention to the twins. "Get up, cowards," he yelled in Spanish, a language they barely understood.

He switched to English: "Out of your bunks, pick up your guns, make sure they're loaded. We board the yacht, kill that bastard who took Werner and Rothenberg."

Both twins felt faint with fear and nausea as he shoved automatics into their unwilling hands. Bruised and battered, they could barely stand upright in the noisome, plunging vessel as Gallardo gave the order to surface.

Bracing against the slimy, condensation-wet hull, they prayed to Allah for salvation from this watery nightmare as the sub knifed through foaming breakers.

All fight had departed the Lebanese pair. Both had come to loath the demanding drug boss. They wished they hadn't agreed to help rescue Werner and Rothenberg – they weren't worth this ghastly voyage.

Terrified, they cowered from Gallardo, who had his pistol trained on them as they prayed in Arabic. Gallardo crossed himself and kissed the crucifix hanging on a chain around his neck; he didn't want to hear their Muslim claptrap. He'd made a stupid mistake bringing them along.

He should have used experienced cartel submariners. They were experts in handling these tiny vessels no matter what the weather. They made long runs, delivering cocaine to North America, Mexico, and Caribbean islands. They shot it out with coast guard and navy patrol boats.

Gallardo, looking with contempt at the pallid, flinching twins, screamed: "Fight or I kill you!"

* * *

Mike watched the ocean ahead intently as he wrestled the heeling yacht's wheel against wind gusts reaching 50 miles per hour. GPS showed them off-track for Miami, and that bothered him.

Then shatteringly, he felt a sickening bump and heard high-pitched squealing and grinding noises at the stern.

His mind raced; had they hit a drifting wreck or something worse, perhaps a shipping container fallen from a storm-tossed freighter?

He lashed the wheel, yelling down to Fuller on the intercom: "Dave, get up here pronto. We've got a big problem with the boat."

Looking astern, he got a heart-jolting fright. The bow of what looked like a mini-submarine had plowed into them, bending the handrails and becoming lodged on *Talespinner*.

"What the fuck…" he exclaimed.

Then two men appeared, struggling to clamber aboard the storm-tossed yacht, having slammed grappling hooks into Mike's beloved boat's already bullet-scarred teak.

Delano, who'd left his Glock below with Dave, ran toward them with the yacht's hooked docking pole.

But one man, already aboard, pointed a lethal-looking AR-15 at his chest. His companion wasn't so nimble. He still fought the bucking stern for a grip to board the yacht.

Delano's brain reeled in disbelief. He recognized the thug pointing the weapon at him as drug kingpin Joaquin Gallardo.

He backed off when the Colombian ordered: "Put the pole down, Delano, before I shoot the fuck outta you…"

Mike prayed the gangster, readying to attack as he staggered on the pitching deck, wouldn't get off an accurate burst.

But the drug boss didn't intend to shoot if he could avoid it. He needed Delano to run the yacht. Still determined to save his Middle Eastern drug deal, Joaquin must rescue Werner and Rothenberg – and grab Rachel as a hostage again.

Believing further resistance would prove fatal, Mike threw down the pole and put his hands up. Just then, a terrorized cry from the stern followed by a splash and pleas for help grabbed their attention.

Sebastian Martínez lost his battle to board and fell into the sea. Without a life vest, he disappeared rapidly beneath the breakers.

More alarming, dark smoke poured out of the minisub. Its overtaxed batteries were afire. The screaming Hakim twins now fought one another to escape through the cramped hatch.

But there was no escape for them.

Dragged partly under by the forward momentum of the yacht, the submersible flooded quickly. The trapped twins wailed like banshees for help as water flooded in, and the vessel broke free of the yacht's stern with a grinding jolt.

Water rushed over Basheer stuck in the conning tower, knocking him and his brother back into the filthy bilge. Within seconds, the sub capsized and sank, taking them down with it.

Delano and Gallardo had trouble taking in the rapidly unfolding events. They watched, hypnotized by the disaster.

Unseen, Dave Fuller had moved closer and fired two snatched pistol shots at Gallardo's head but missed.

Hearing the shots, the drug chief swung around and fired a long burst from the AR-15. It opened a gaping hole in Fuller's broad chest. He fell backward with a grunt, dead before he hit the deck, his blood running into the scuppers.

Gallardo trained his gun on Delano again. Mike kept his hands high. Stunned speechless by Fuller's sudden death, he stumbled back into the main cabin, the AR-15's murderous barrel prodding him along.

There, Gallardo found Rothenberg and Rachel crouching under the galley table.

"Where's Werner?" Gallardo barked.

Rothenberg nodded nervously towards the locked rear cabin; he'd no idea how Joaquin had boarded the yacht, but he wasn't asking questions. For now, at least, he wouldn't be heading to prison.

"Thank God, you're here," he sniveled. "Delano's planning to turn us over to the authorities when we reach Florida. I thought it was all over for us."

Ignoring him, Gallardo ordered Delano: "Open the door. Let Werner out."

"I can't," Mike said. "I don't have the key."

"Where is it?"

"On the man you just shot."

"Get up on deck, Rothenberg. Get the key," the Colombian told him.

Max nodded servile agreement, lurching out onto the open deck. He returned with the key, hands bloody from searching through the pockets on Dave's bleeding body.

"Open that door."

Rothenberg obeyed and undid Quinton Werner's padlocked chains. Werner pushed past Rothenberg to step out with a sinister smile on his ashen face.

"Let me kill this motherfucker," he said, gesturing toward Delano.

But Gallardo, gun trained on him, remained cautious and in charge. "Not yet. We need him to run the boat. Can either of you navigate or sail?"

Werner and Rothenberg regretfully shook their heads.

Werner took a pistol Gallardo offered and shoved it in Delano's face.

"See this, asshole? It's just a matter of time."

Mike obeyed as they pushed him at gunpoint toward the yacht's cockpit.

"Forget Miami," Gallardo ordered. "Set a new course for Ft. Lauderdale."

Pleased by their reversed positions, Werner shackled Delano to the binnacle using the same padlock and chain previously used to lock him to the forward cabin bunk.

"Give me your fucking sat phone," he demanded. "You don't need to talk to anyone, do you?"

Werner cut the cord on the ship-to-shore radio microphone. "Nor do we want any distress calls going out."

Delano could move only a few feet either way. He had just enough length of chain to manage the automated sails and run the boat. As instructed, he set a new course for Ft. Lauderdale.

He mourned the loss of Dave, whose body Werner had been so happy to shove overboard.

At least, Mike thought, I'm still alive. He didn't know how it would happen, but he'd make sure these filthy thugs answered for his partner's untimely end.

* * *

With Mike chained, Werner took malicious advantage of his enemy's misfortune.

Ordered by Gallardo to oversee Rachel's trips to her husband with food and hot drinks, he used the opportunity to abuse the journalist.

On the third day of their yacht seizure, Werner went too far, pressing a lit cigarette into Delano's neck.

Howling in rage and pain, Delano turned to grab his persecutor. Anticipating the move, Werner kicked the journalist's legs out from under him.

Weakened by sleepless nights steering the storm-tossed vessel, Delano crashed over backward.

Rachel exploded: "You lousy coward, torturing a man who can't defend himself."

"Shut your mouth," Werner ordered. "Do you know what he and his pal did to me? Knocked my teeth out, tried to cut my balls off. I'm in charge here. I'll crack your skull if you say a single word to him. Understood?"

Rachel remained helpless, watching the vindictive jailer kick Delano repeatedly as he struggled to rise. Werner hadn't forgotten the beating in Medellín or his Oscars night agony with a probe stuck in his back.

Now he longed for the moment Gallardo let him kill Delano.

"That's just a taste of what he's got coming," he sneered at Rachel. "I'll cut him up and toss his bits overboard one by one. You can watch, then we can get it on, Rachel," he said, now leering at her. "If you're good to me while daddy's sleeping, maybe I'll make hubby's death fast, a little less painful."

When he produced a knife taken from the galley and moved as if he was about to cut Delano, Rachel lost control and pitched hot coffee intended for Mike into Werner's face.

He howled in scalded rage. Before Rachel could retreat, he grabbed her and rained blows on her body and face. She fell hard, bleeding and bruised.

Delano struggled to his feet and lunged at Werner, but the chain around his waist jerked him to a halt. Now he was looking down the barrel of the Glock, leveled at a spot between his eyes.

"One more step and you're dead – her, too," Werner sneered.

But before he could pull the trigger, Gallardo and Rothenberg appeared, stumbling along the pitching deck, ordering him to stop. They'd heard Rachel's screams and the sound of bodies falling.

"Put the gun down, fool," Joaquin warned, poking his AR-15 into Werner's ribs so hard he yelped. "It's you who'll die if you disobey orders. I warned you, we need Delano. When we land, you can do what you want with him."

Rothenberg helped his battered daughter to her feet. Angry and shocked by the violence against her, his eyes blazed hatred at Werner.

"Touch her again, and I swear to God, I'll kill you," he snarled in his first display of defiance since emerging from Gallardo's torture chamber.

"What you gonna do?" Werner sniggered contemptuously. "Fat fucker like you. No Ackerman here to do your dirty work. Right?"

Gallardo stepped between them, pointing his weapon at Werner's chest.

"Max, take her down below. Disobey me again, Werner, and I'll blow you away," he said, relieving the thug of the Glock.

Humiliated at being unable to protect his wife, Delano could do no more than watch.

It shocked him to see Rachel's lips bleeding, one of her eyes swelling shut. Her wounds hurt more than his injured ribs and burned neck.

Rothenberg put his arm around his daughter's shoulders and led her below. Werner followed like a whipped cur.

Silently, he vowed retaliation on the entire Rothenberg family – the cause of all his problems from the beginning, he thought indignantly.

* * *

Alone, Delano considered the final card left for him to play and prayed it was a winner. Soon, Fort Lauderdale's lights would blink on the horizon. They'd be there the next day.

Time was running short. A few hours and he'd die an ugly death. His three enemies below – each wanted him dead – and each had reasons to make him suffer before murdering him.

Werner, back on deck checking on him, warned: "Keep her on course. Don't be a single degree off the GPS heading to Lauderdale. Any tricks and I'll fuck you up big time."

Delano heard the sound of the stereo booming below soon after Werner left. The terrorist and the drug boss were celebrating; they'd soon be ashore. They'd gone through most of the boat's liquor supply, but enough alcohol remained for a final drinking session.

Good, he thought, let them get wasted. They felt safe in the knowledge he was chained and helpless. Better still, if they passed out for a few hours. Meanwhile, the loud music provided cover for his next move.

He switched on the custom-built weather radio, his last and undiscovered method of communication. His captors believed it merely a receiver – unaware it was also a transmitter.

Delano pressed a button for channel 16, raising the US Coast Guard distress frequency. He withdrew a microphone from an unnoticed compartment in the side of the set.

"Lauderdale Coast Guard, the yacht *Talespinner* here. Mayday, Mayday, Mayday," he broadcast.

The call received an immediate answer from the Coast Guard night operator.

"I read you, *Talespinner*. What is your problem, and who's the captain? Over."

"Wanted international criminals have boarded my yacht. They've commandeered the vessel by force. I'm the skipper, Michael Delano. Over."

"You say criminals have control of your vessel, Captain Delano? Over."

"Roger. Three wanted men, armed and dangerous. Over."

"Do you know their identities? Over."

"Yes. Quinton Werner, Max Rothenberg, and Joaquin Gallardo. Over."

In the ensuing silence, Delano worried whether the operator got all the names.

"Operator, did you get those names: Werner, Rothenberg, and Gallardo? Over."

"Affirmative, *Talespinner*. I have the names. Confirm again. They boarded your vessel and have control? Over."

"Roger. Send a cutter urgently. They'll kill me before we reach Lauderdale. ETA tomorrow, early morning. Send immediate help. I can't transmit again. Over."

"Hold on, skipper, speak to my duty officer...hold..."

"This is Captain Douglas Joss. Max Rothenberg and Quinton Werner have boarded your boat? Over."

"Roger that, and Colombian drug runner Joaquin Gallardo. The FBI seeks all three. I need help. My wife and I will go overboard when your cutter arrives. We need help soonest. Over."

"Roger. Stand by," the voice of Joss crackled.

Delano prayed his captors couldn't hear him talking over the loud music below.

Joss came back on:

"We're sending the cutter. Can you leave this link open? Over."

"Negative. If they hear anything, I'm dead. You have our position?"

"Roger. We have a fix on you and your coordinates. You have priority status. Out."

Sighing with relief, Delano hid the microphone and switched the radio back to the weather report.

The winds were holding steady, and now there was hope.

* * *

Quinton Werner lay drunk and snoring on his bunk in the main salon. Gallardo's AR-15 nestled beside his stomach.

Rachel, who lay awake on a port side pull-out bed across the cabin, viewed the gun appraisingly. Could she figure out how to turn off the safety if she grabbed it, used it?

The hatred raging in the pit of her stomach demanded action. She wanted to riddle Werner with bullets, but she feared a misstep with the unfamiliar weapon. She fingered her swollen face and flinched at the pain. She couldn't afford to make a mistake.

Instead, she'd grab a butcher knife from the galley. One quick stab to the heart and the miserable cur would be gone – hopefully without crying out.

She stood to make her move when the snoring stopped. Werner turned over, his cruel eyes meeting hers.

"What the fuck you doing, bitch?" he slurred. "You wanna come over here so I can feel that juicy ass of yours. How about a little fun? We won't wake the others."

"You'll never touch me, you filthy pig; I'd rather die. I'm making coffee for Delano. I need to take him some breakfast," she snapped.

"Food doesn't matter. Let the motherfucker starve. He'll be dead soon anyway. Coffee's OK – keep the motherfucker alert."

Still drunk from his share of a bottle of Scotch consumed into the wee hours, Werner groaned at the thought of going out into the foul weather to check on Delano. Instead, he turned over and was soon snoring again.

As she put water on to boil, Rachel silently asked why she hadn't taken her chance to grab the gun but reminded herself her best chance of survival was to work with Mike.

She crossed the salon and gingerly probed the pockets of Werner's jacket, carelessly hung from a cabin hook. Her fingers closed over the prize Mike had whispered she must get: a key to the padlock holding him chained.

She returned to the stove, prepared a flask of coffee, and slipped the key into the flask, where it sank to the bottom.

Without waking Werner again, she took the coffee and a packet of sweet biscuits up to Mike. Bleary-eyed from lack of sleep, he accepted the hot coffee and cookies gratefully.

"The padlock key's in the flask," Rachel whispered, fearing Werner might appear behind her at any second.

Delano shook the flask and heard it rattle. He poured coffee into the flask top and swigged it down. He let the rest of the lukewarm coffee run over his hand until the key dropped out.

Smiling, he unchained himself and whispered: "Good news. A Coast Guard cutter's coming. When you hear its engines, get up here, fast. We'll go overboard. They'll pick us up."

Looking at the heaving water, Rachel was dubious. "You sure we won't drown?"

"We'll have life jackets. We'll make it. What's our choice? Stay here, and I'll die. You'll be taken back to Colombia as a hostage. Better we go down fighting.

She kissed him with swollen, cracked lips and left. Delano felt a massive surge of love. Once again, he hoped for a future together – if they could get off *Talespinner* alive.

The others still slept when Rachel returned below. At dawn, she heard the pulse of powerful engines. Werner heard them too. He rose and struggled into his foul-weather gear.

"What's that noise about? You stay here," he commanded.

She nodded passively.

Werner slid and slithered to the cockpit. Delano stood there waiting, a faint smile on his face. Suspicious, Quinton immediately drew the Glock which he'd retrieved from Gallardo.

"What boat is that?" he asked.

"A Coast Guard cutter."

"What do they want with us?"

"How should I know?"

Werner's angry scowling face was close to Delano's ear as he demanded, "How far are we from Lauderdale? Let me see that fucking GPS."

"Go ahead, take a look."

Hungover, Werner bent to see the small screen. It was hard to read in the sudden brightness of dawn sunlight peeking through the roiling storm clouds.

"Give me some shade here. I can't see a fucking thing," Werner complained.

He bent closer for a better view. Delano moved swiftly, smashing Werner's head down into the screen with all the power he could muster. The force shattered glass, shards cutting Werner's face and nose.

"Son of a bitch, I'll kill you," he groaned, standing upright to level his pistol, unaware his captive was free.

Before he could fire, the end of Delano's unfastened chain whipped around his gun hand and sent the Glock flying across the deck where it lodged in the scuppers.

Werner screamed, clutching a broken wrist to his chest. Delano drew his shocked enemy close, so near he smelled the man's sour, whiskey-tainted breath.

Locked in a steely embrace, he squealed in agony as Delano shoved a rigging knife into his unprotected belly.

The journalist watched Werner's face crumble as he twisted the blade to deliver maximum pain and intestinal damage.

"How's that, Quinton? And you thought you'd kill me. Seems I'm doing a better job of it than I did at the Oscars. This time, you're going to die – and painfully."

With blood from the mortally injured man squirting over his foul weather clothes, Delano dragged his victim, sobbing and begging, to the starboard rail.

"Goodbye, Quinton," he said, violently shoving the would-be drug baron off the boat into the angry consuming waves.

Werner's head bobbed momentarily in the yacht's wake. His arms stretched upward as though seeking a heavenly explanation for some tremendous injustice. Then, he was gone.

Rachel was on deck now. She locked the salon doors behind her. The rescue cutter was 50 yards away. Its engines idling, it drifted as its crew lowered a dinghy manned by two armed Coast Guardsmen.

"Get this life preserver on," Delano told his wife, flinging his own heavy foul weather gear to the deck. She followed his lead, stripping down to bra and panties so as not to be weighed down with wet clothes.

They hurriedly donned the orange life vests and linked themselves together with a rope. Mike pulled Rachel to a gap in the rails.

Holding hands, they leaped overboard, coming up gasping at the Atlantic chill. Delano rolled over on his back, blinking saltwater out of his eyes.

Talespinner, still under sail, moved away. The Coast Guard dinghy approached, but they weren't safe yet.

"Jesus Christ," Delano moaned, spotting Rothenberg and Gallardo on the stern of the yacht.

They must have woken up to the sound of the cutter and smashed through the lock on the salon doors to come topside.

Shots from Gallardo's AR-15 snapped overhead, hitting the water between them and the dinghy. While the five-foot swells of the ocean spoiled his aim, it would be only a matter of seconds before he got the range and hit them – or their rescuers.

The next moment Delano was shocked to see Rothenberg struggling with Gallardo, pushing the weapon sideways and trying to take it away.

He was protecting his daughter – even if it might be the last thing he would ever do.

Within minutes, *Talespinner*, on auto-pilot, became a faint outline to the swimmers. The dinghy arrived, its prow lifting in the waves above them.

"Thank you, thank you," both kept repeating to the crewmen who hauled them aboard. They were swaddled in emergency thermal blankets.

Delano pulled Rachel to him and held her close as they shivered and kissed. Then a worrisome thought occurred to her.

"What are we to do about Daddy? He's still on the boat with that gangster."

"The Coast Guard will get him, if he's lucky," Delano replied through chattering teeth. "He's not our problem now."

CHAPTER FORTY-ONE:

UNHAPPY SHIPMATES

Keeping station with *Talespinner*, the cutter was a stark reminder to Gallardo and Rothenberg, if they needed one, of the lengthy prison sentences they faced.

Trapped on the yacht, they listened to orders over the Coast Guard radio to heave-to, which they ignored. To comply would lead to an instant boarding and arrest.

When the cutter drew close, Captain Joss used a bullhorn to address them across the churning gap.

"Yacht *Talespinner*, I command you to lower the sail. Heave alongside so we can board you. You're in US territorial waters. You must obey federal law."

But *Talespinner* didn't slow. Ignorant about handling the yacht, neither Gallardo nor Rothenberg intended doing as ordered – even had they had known how.

Their refusal to accept orders caused the frustrated captain to summon Rachel to the bridge.

"No one on that yacht knows how to operate it," she said, "but Mike and I can talk them through it, if they'll listen."

Joss handed Rachel the megaphone so she could appeal to her father.

Her voice quavered with concern, urging: "Please, Daddy, be sensible. Do what he says. Mike will coach you with lowering the sails."

Both Gallardo and Rothenberg were now in *Talespinner*'s cockpit, examining the electronics as if they might offer a way out.

"What the hell shall we do? We might be better off doing as commanded," Rothenberg ventured nervously.

That was not the plan Gallardo wanted to hear. He picked up the AR-15 and looked at the mogul with contempt.

"No fuckin' way. I'm not going to some Yankee prison. Stay if you want, go to fuckin' jail. I'm getting off this boat, going home."

"How? Do you intend to swim?" Rothenberg asked angrily.

Gallardo turned away in disgust to leave his sole companion alone in the wet, chill cockpit, staring nervously at the cutter, now no more than fifty feet away.

For Max, the other boat represented warmth and safety, even if that meant prison. Surrender had become preferable to drowning with a vicious drug king on a runaway boat they couldn't handle.

If indicted, he intended doing as he'd always done: throw money at the problem, get the best lawyers. The right legal team might get him off or win a reduced sentence in a white-collar prison.

Meanwhile, an infuriated Gallardo was in the main salon having a satellite phone dispute with the cartel's slow-witted Ft. Lauderdale representative. Not fully understanding the gravity of his boss's situation, the operative spoke of sending a boat to rescue him.

"Hire a helicopter, you incompetent fool. I don't care what it costs. A boat's no good. The Coast Guard's already here, waiting to grab me. The only way to get me off is by air. And understand this, idiot: you're a dead man if you don't get the right chopper. It must have a hoist. If not, it's useless."

His subordinate began to tremble. He'd been standing by to greet his boss when the yacht docked. He had a private jet waiting at a nearby airstrip to fly Joaquin and his captives to Medellín. Now he was being told to mount a last-minute helicopter rescue at sea.

"How will we find you out there in this weather?" he asked desperately. "Pilots don't want to fly into a storm."

Gallardo, furious, calmed himself. How had he ever allowed this moron to run his Florida network?

"Go to the helicopter terminal with some men. Take control, shoot a few people, if necessary. That gets instant obedience. Pick the best pilot, put a gun in his ribs. He'll fly. And make sure it's one of those big choppers with winching equipment."

"Yes, boss. Certainly, boss. But how will we find you?"

Gallardo stalked around the cabin, red-faced. This fool would die in pain once he got safely ashore.

"You want me to send up flares? You can't miss us, stupid. There's a fucking Coast Guard cutter all lit up with bright lights running alongside us. Make the pilot fly a search pattern. He'll see us. Just get me off this goddamned sailboat. Understand?"

"Yes, boss. We'll get you off; don't worry. I get it..."

Gallardo disconnected and slammed down the phone. He poured himself a slug of whiskey, the last drops in the bottle. He doubted Rothenberg would go for a helicopter rescue – he'd piss his pants at the prospect of being hoisted to the chopper. Why should I care? Gallardo thought. The fat pig had outlived his usefulness.

It was a lousy deal all around. Werner was gone, presumably murdered by Delano. Without him and the Hakims, the Middle East drug venture was dead. And with Rothenberg's daughter free, he had no leverage to launch Miguel's movie career. His son would be angry and disappointed – more sullen than ever.

And he had not forgiven Rothenberg for deliberately spoiling his aim when he tried shooting Delano and his woman before the Coast Guard rescued them. Doubtless, they were now spilling their guts about everything.

"They'd be dead now if Max hadn't interfered," he muttered drunkenly to himself. "Everything is turning to shit. Rothenberg's to blame."

But he decided it wise to wait until his escape helicopter arrived before he killed the mogul. If the Coast Guard marksmen saw him attempting murder, they wouldn't hesitate to fire on him.

He went back to the cockpit to check on Rothenberg.

"Max, don't worry," he said, switching to his best English and most persuasive manner. "My guys will find us and hoist us up to a helicopter. I have a jet waiting to take us to Colombia. Ignore that Coast Guard punk. We'll get out of this, I promise you…"

His words left Rothenberg torn between enemies. Should he trust the man who'd tortured him or take emergency sailing lessons from Delano, whose instructions would lead to prison. But at least he'd be alive.

"Screw the Coast Guard. Come down to the cabin and have a drink while we wait," Gallardo urged with phony friendliness. "I finished the whisky, but there's rum."

Rothenberg, suspicious, followed the cartel boss into the main cabin where Joaquin slopped rum into two tumblers, half filling them and handing one to Max.

"Drink up, movie-man. For extra courage, right?"

It was then Rothenberg made his decision. He'd give himself up to the Coast Guard. Killing Gallardo was his single best chance of living long enough to surrender. He wasn't betting it all on being hoisted up in a chopper with bullets flying at him.

They downed the last of the rum, and Gallardo looked out of a porthole. The cutter was easing closer. "We need to go up top again," he said, grabbing his AR-15.

Seeing the two reappear, the Coast Guard skipper was on the bullhorn again. "If you don't heave to, we'll ram and sink you."

"I have a message for those sons of bitches that'll shut them up." Gallardo drunkenly lifted his gun, aiming at the cutter's bridge and firing repeated bursts.

Glass and wood shattered. Delano and Rachel joined the captain in diving for cover. Furious and deliberate, Captain Joss again picked up the bullhorn: "Heave to or go to the bottom. We're about to sink you."

Delano cringed as he thought about his beloved *Talespinner* shattered into smithereens.

Both fugitives saw the cutter's 76mm radar-controlled cannon swing around to point directly at *Talespinner*'s hull.

"For God's sake, help me stop this boat," Rothenberg pleaded. "One blast from that gun, and we're dead."

Gallardo's answer was to turn angrily on Rothenberg and point his submachine gun at the mogul's gut.

"You miserable fucking coward. I'll blow you away – now!"

Rothenberg squealed in terror when Gallardo pulled the trigger. Then nothing. Just a metallic click. The mogul's pants were wet, but he still lived.

The AR-15's 30-round magazine was empty, its ammunition expended in futile firing at the swimmers and the Coast Guard cutter's bridge.

Disgusted, Gallardo flung the weapon and missed Rothenberg's head. He then charged the mogul, kicking and punching him. Rothenberg went down hard, crying out in rage and misery, dragging Joaquin to the deck with him.

As Rothenberg struggled to rise, a miracle happened. When the yacht pitched, the pistol Delano had cracked out of Werner's hand that morning slid across the deck toward him from the port scuppers.

He grabbed the Glock, rising triumphantly. Unnerved, the drug boss crawled away, too scared to stand while the wavering pistol variously pointed at his head and torso.

"Die, you scumbag," Rothenberg screeched as he drew a bead on Gallardo and pulled the trigger.

Like a red-hot poker, a bullet bored through the fleshy part of Joaquin's right shoulder, the pain making him scream.

Rothenberg fired again, missing and plowing up a chunk of decking near Gallardo's head. The drug king rolled over, then rose rapidly, seeking safety behind the mast and its billowing sail.

Again Rothenberg fired, and again, until the Glock jammed. Rounds had gone through the sail, pitted the yacht's mast, but nothing hit Gallardo.

The now useless gun allowed Joaquin to escape. Desperate to find another weapon, he ran into the main cabin, slamming the broken doors behind him.

He needed to buy time until his rescue chopper arrived. Somehow, he must kill Rothenberg before the cowardly pig obeyed the cutter's heave-to order.

Alone topside, Rothenberg inexpertly tried clearing the jammed round, but the cartridge wouldn't budge.

Simultaneously, he heard Delano's instructions through the bullhorn on disabling the autopilot and lowering the yacht's sails – and prepared to comply.

Gallardo also heard Delano's instructions and figured he must move fast to prevent Rothenberg from surrendering the boat. Grabbing a butcher's knife from the galley, he rushed back up on deck, intending to stab Rothenberg to death.

Rothenberg heard Gallardo's approach. At the last moment, he jumped up defenseless. Seeing the knife, he backed away, dropping the useless jammed weapon.

He made a run down the port side, headed for the yacht's midsection, where he remembered a rope ladder hung from the mast.

Spurred by desperation, he climbed with surprising dexterity into *Talespinner*'s rigging – and started pulling the rope ladder up behind him.

Driven by hatred and necessity, Gallardo grabbed the end of the ladder and, cursing from the pain of his injured shoulder, climbed slowly after the movie magnate.

With Gallardo slashing at his legs, Rothenberg kicked down spitefully at his pursuer's head. Then galvanized by the madman below, he tried hoisting himself higher, but his strength was gone.

Still more enraged by the kicks, Gallardo was oblivious to everything other than stabbing Rothenberg and knocking him off his lofty perch.

The bullhorn blared again from across the water. This time, instead of demanding *Talespinner* lower her sails, it sounded an urgent warning of danger far more threatening than their mast-top combat.

"Change course immediately, yacht *Talespinner*, change course now. You're in imminent danger of collision, *Talespinner*. You're on a collision course with another vessel."

The words "collision course" penetrated both combatants' fevered brains as a fiery red barrage of Coast Guard flares lit the sky above them, highlighting approaching disaster.

Even if they'd known how to respond to the order, now neither antagonist had the time to obey.

Clinging to the swaying mast, they froze at the sight of the looming red-painted bow of a tall ship stacked high with multicolored containers.

There was no stopping this mountain of marine steel weighing nearly 150,000 tons. It was coming at them at 17 knots despite the ship's pilot putting his engines in full reverse and pushing the wheel hard over.

The colossal vessel hung like the sword of Damocles, then sliced through *Talespinner*'s forward section, with the remainder of the yacht's severed hull bumping and grinding hideously along its massive steel flanks before sinking.

As if swatting an irritating insect, the ship's enormous impact had catapulted Rothenberg from the mast top into the ocean. Seconds later, he emerged gagging and struggling toward the only piece of the yacht's forward section still afloat.

Gallardo, a ridiculous figure trussed in rigging cable, lay precariously atop *Talespinner*'s mainsail.

It had billowed out amid the waves, holding the last gasps of wind it would ever capture. Horrified, Joaquin realized the sail was his death shroud.

"Help me," he screamed illogically at Rothenberg, bobbing in the swells 25 yards away after clambering onto a piece of floating debris.

The media chief wasn't listening. His eyes focused upwards, searching for the source of rotating blades pounding the air as they got closer.

He silently prayed it wasn't the cartel's chopper. He mouthed a Hebrew prayer of gratitude when he spotted the Coast Guard emblem. The crew saw him and lowered their rescue basket.

Saltwater stinging his bloody legs, Rothenberg still had enough will to live though barely the strength to clamber in.

As he was winched up, he looked down with unforgiving eyes on Gallardo's last moments. He smiled with malicious pleasure at the pathetic figure below.

"Damn your conniving soul. I'm alive. You're going to drown," he bellowed with sheer loathing.

Beneath the howl of the chopper, he couldn't tell whether Joaquin heard him or not. The Colombian's eyes widened with terror. His refuge atop the sail was failing, spilling air, deflating.

He'd sent many people to terrible deaths without a second thought, but how could it happen to him? He was a drowning rat, no longer a drug king.

The rescue basket was on its second trip down when Gallardo, wrapped in *Talespinner*'s mainsheet, was dragged screaming to his fate beneath the waves. Like his predecessor, Carlos Bomba, he'd feed the fishes.

Aboard the helicopter, an FBI agent read Lord Maxwell Rothenberg his rights and snapped on the handcuffs.

CHAPTER FORTY-TWO:

RELUCTANT BARGAIN

Max Rothenberg reluctantly accepted 25 years in prison for the murder of Morgan Masterson and his cousin, Carlos Bomba. It had taken all of Rachel's powers of persuasion, plus a team of top criminal attorneys, to convince him: plead guilty, cut a deal, avoid the trial.

"Face a jury and they'll either sentence you to death or put you away for life with no possibility of parole," Rachel had warned her father. "At least this way, Daddy, you'll have hope of getting out some time in the future. I'll have lawyers working constantly on parole possibilities."

He'd planned shifting blame for the murders to Gil Ackerman, whose body now rotted in an unmarked grave near Medellín. His decision to accept a stiff sentence was forced on him when former boat crewman, Enrique García, came forward with damning video and eyewitness evidence.

García told prosecutors: "I heard and saw everything. It was Rothenberg who ordered those men tossed to sharks, not Ackerman. Gil was only doing what the Boss ordered him to do."

Rothenberg's day in court to hear his sentence read aloud was shattering for his daughter who, despite everything, continued to care deeply about her father. Still, she had not yet dared tell him she'd halted divorce proceedings and was three months pregnant with Delano's child.

Rachel's love for Mike was rekindled. She had finally reconciled herself to the reality that her father's wicked deeds must be punished. She was forever grateful for Mike's steadfast love and bravery in rescuing her from the cartel. He'd even compromised to save their marriage, supporting her decision to continue her GMI career after the baby arrived.

Rothenberg scowled at them from the defense table in LA Superior Court. He'd spent five miserable months in county jail while prosecutors built their case against him.

The mogul finally agreed that the plea deal was his only chance of eventual release. Still, He remained determined to take down Delano with him.

Disregarding legal advice against attacking Delano publicly, when the judge asked if he had anything to say, Max stood. His distinctive British voice boomed jarringly around the courtroom: "I've done wrong, but I'm not the only one here who should be jailed."

Pointing at Delano sitting a few feet away, he said, "He's a damned corrupt and manipulative scoundrel. He stole from me, ruined my daughter's marriage, extorted me for millions after setting up one of my stars in a drug orgy that cost a young woman her life."

This distorted summation of Rothenberg's grudges against Delano sent a buzz of astonishment through the courtroom, with many jealous reporters enjoying these headline-making allegations against a renowned rival.

Mike shook off Rachel's restraining hand. Unsurprised, he stood angrily to rebuff Rothenberg's twisted charges.

"I never stole from you. You slandered me as punishment for loving your daughter. You drugged, abducted her, and had our child aborted. And because her first husband knew too much, you had him murdered. After I married Rachel, you tried to kill me, too. Allow me to list more of your crimes…"

Despite bailiffs insisting he sit down and the judge gaveling him to silence, Mike stubbornly continued: "Yes, I wrongfully took hush money from you, but I've not kept it. Most of those millions have gone to the families of journalists killed in war zones – and I can prove it to the court. I'm trying to atone for the corruption Lord Rothenberg led me into."

Fearing being dragged to the cells for contempt, Mike sat down. Rachel was ashen as he took her hand.

This public clash between her husband and father had once again shaken her to the core. Now the world knew just how much they hated one another.

Minutes later, newly-sentenced Rothenberg glared at them defiantly as bailiffs led him away to face decades behind bars.

Rachel held back tears and remained silent as they left. She still resented being trapped between two alpha males, both essential to her happiness and success.

Would a future with both of them wanting her love and support be bearable? At least, she thought, with her father in prison he could not spawn further death and disaster.

* * *

Not only had Delano brought Rothenberg down, but the trial had put an indelible stain on his reputation as an exceptional journalist.

Besieged outside the courtroom, reporters demanded to know if he was, indeed, an extortionist. Deeply embarrassed, he admitted his ill-fated financial deal with Rothenberg. "But I've tried making amends by donating most of the money to charity long before today's hearing," he said.

Moreover, this means of conscious-clearing was his way of ducking extortion charges – which prosecutors were prepared to overlook. They were grateful that Delano had served Rothenberg up on a plate to them.

Mike felt relieved when Rachel snuggled up to him in the GMI limo driving them to LAX airport for their return to New York.

"Mike, you did the right thing avoiding prosecution," she said. "It's bad enough having Daddy locked up. I wouldn't want our child to be born with a father behind bars, too."

CHAPTER FORTY-THREE:

A TRIP WEST

Months had passed since Max Rothenberg's sentencing, with Mike and Rachel eagerly expecting the arrival of their firstborn, having been told it would be a boy.

They had bought a luxurious penthouse atop one of New York's most exclusive Park Avenue high rises, where they excitedly turned one of the five bedrooms into a nursery suite.

A limousine collected Rachel daily for the short journey to GMI's headquarters, where she worked at solving the corporate problems that had arisen in her absence.

She still received Rothenberg's counsel weekly by phone. His wealth bought prison privileges – including the cell phone smuggled into him – at Pelican Bay in California, where he was serving his time.

Mike and Rachel had grown closer, rejoicing in their renewed love for one another. He used the hours when she was at the office to work on his second book – a novel – which was developing nicely.

His time as editor of a British Sunday tabloid four years previously and his more recent ugly experiences had left Delano distrustful of anything resembling popular journalism – and he wanted to put the bad memories behind him.

It had been a Faustian deal he never wanted to repeat. He'd surrendered personal integrity to the pursuit of wealth and luxury, leaving a trail of dead bodies from Hollywood to Costa Rica to the Caribbean.

Above all, Delano was guilt-ridden over the loss of Dave Fuller. His partner and friend had paid with his life helping pursue Mike's lethal blockbuster stories.

Mike was in a sorrowful, reflective mood when Rachel said she needed to visit her father with essential documents requiring his signature.

"Will you come with me?" she asked.

"Why can't the lawyers take care of it?" he replied.

"For one thing I must tell him I'm expecting your child and we're remaining married – and that will not be fun!" she replied sharply. "For another, I want to make sure all is in order for me to inherit everything should anything happen to him – and that any children we have are beneficiaries, too."

Delano's ears went up.

"You've heard something I should know about?"

"Well, yes. Last time I phoned he said there was a million-dollar price on his head. That got me worried. Doesn't it worry you?"

Delano answered carefully. If he made ill-considered remarks about her father, Rachel became manic; in her present condition, she was incredibly jumpy.

"I'm sure he'll be OK. The last time you asked me to check, he had an eight-man team guarding him night and day. They go everywhere with him, to meals, to the showers, the toilets. He has some of the toughest hombres in the joint on his payroll."

"Yes, I know, but he says the Colombians blame him for the deaths of Joaquin Gallardo and Carlos Bomba. I'm scared," she said, her eyes getting glassy.

Mike took her in his arms, kissing her cheeks, stroking her lustrous hair, running his hand lovingly over her burgeoning belly.

"I love you more than anything in the world, baby. I won't let you face him alone. I'm coming with you."

It was what she wanted to hear. Mike was always there when she needed him. It was one reason she loved him so much. No other man could ever replace him – and she was convinced he would make a wonderful father.

"All right. We'll go next week. I'll book one of the company jets to fly us to San Francisco," she said. "I'll have a rental car waiting there for you to drive me to Pelican Bay."

CHAPTER FORTY-FOUR:

PELICAN BAY

They arrived at Pelican Bay Penitentiary after a tricky trip up the fog-en-shrouded coast. All along the twisty road, pregnant Rachel had complained how Mike's speedy driving made her queasy.

Delano pulled into the prison parking lot with a sigh of relief for their visit, looking around with an apprehensive shiver. The jail, housing 3,000 prisoners in maximum security, radiated menace and misery in equal measure.

Rain spattered the windshield as Rachel, in a sour mood, lingered in the Porsche Panamera, summoning up the steel needed to face her angry, overbearing parent.

She'd spoken to His Lordship over his smuggled cellphone earlier to make him aware of her impending arrival. She remained increasingly concerned about his safety – especially as threats had turned to actions.

"My protectors foiled a man who tried to knife me. They say he was after the million-dollar price the cartel's put on my head," Rothenberg said apprehensively.

"I live in daily fear of being stabbed, strangled, or bludgeoned to death thanks to Delano – why couldn't he have allowed me to return to my island in Dubai where I'd have been safe?"

"Daddy, please don't talk like that. What's done is done. I can't undo it," she countered.

"Why do you want to come here?" he had asked suspiciously.

"I have important documents for you to sign."

"What documents?"

"Because of the threats, I want full control of GMI for myself and any children I may have."

"Haven't I provided you enough authority?" he asked, ignoring her mention of children. "What are you trying to do, squeeze me out completely?" He ended the conversation by abruptly clicking off.

Now, outside the prison, she felt scared, especially as her pregnancy was evident. Not exactly the time to seek control of a giant corporation for herself and the heir fathered by a man Max detested.

"Stop worrying. Once he calms down, he'll see the logic of your proposal," Delano said, trying to be reassuring. "Tell him I'll have nothing to do with GMI. I don't want to work for it, or to be part of management."

Aggravated by his blandishments, Rachel left the car, slamming the door behind her. After all, it wasn't he who had to deal with her paranoid parent; no easy task.

Mike followed, hastily catching up with her as she neared the visitor's entrance.

"Relax. We'll be home soon," Delano soothed. "You can kick back then. Low key the corporate work until the boy arrives and you're recovered."

Rachel grunted, not liking him telling her what to do, how to feel.

Heavy with child, she resented losing her figure at age 32. And she knew Mike wanted more children – certainly not one of her immediate priorities.

They moved past the high fences. She prepared to enter the visitor's hall.

"You've got an hour, Ms. Rothenberg. No physical contact," the unsmiling guard cautioned after inspecting her briefcase and its contents and phoning ahead for their most notorious prisoner to be brought down.

Before going through the swing doors, she surprised Mike by turning back a few steps to kiss him lovingly – a welcome gesture considering her sour mood.

He paced outside, smoking the one daily Marlboro he still allowed himself. He wished he could have gone with her. But his presence would have been decidedly unwelcome – and only one visitor was allowed at a time.

Swallowed up by the jail's sanitized vastness, Rachel noticed it was quieter than expected.

One other guard was on duty across the hall – and he barely looked up from his paperback.

She sat nervously, midway down the hall, at one of many small metal tables.

Spreading out her documents, she wondered if Max had somehow ensured privacy for their meeting; they had the place to themselves.

Across the hall, a heavy door opened noisily, and Rothenberg entered alone. His posse of convict protectors, reluctantly left behind thick viewing glass, stayed watchful.

She knew her billionaire father provided these rough-looking men unheard-of benefits: cash paid to their families as well as the use of his phones and a share of luxury foods and liquor he had smuggled in by correctional officers on the take.

Rachel barely recognized her once corpulent parent as his slimmed-down figure approached. Hunch-shouldered, he'd aged ten years since his sentencing.

Gone were the $10,000 suits, silk shirts, hand-crafted shoes. Rothenberg looked pitiful in prison garb: a stained white T-shirt, orange jacket, baggy pants, and shabby sneakers.

His face, partially covered by straggly grey hair, was cracked parchment. Lined deeply, it radiated fear, desperation, and depression. He was a man fighting hard not to give up.

Rachel's heart went out to him in a pang of sympathy. It was hard to believe he had been one of the richest and most powerful men in the world.

Max squinted at her through shrewd accusing eyes that lingered on her swollen belly. He flushed in anger, sure the baby she now carried was Delano's – and there would be no interfering in this pregnancy.

Irrational fear of him emerged before either of them spoke. Rachel had seen that chilling look of parental disapproval through childhood and adolescence, and often as an adult. It came when her behavior was what he called "unacceptable."

"You promised you'd divorce him, now you're giving him a child," he said by way of a greeting. "You sicken me; how can you do this? That man was the instrument of putting me away. Of sending me to this hellhole. I'll punish him yet – I still have power beyond these walls."

Rachel's face reddened at the prospect of another significant promise broken.

"You swore not to threaten Mike when I took over your responsibilities and kept the company together," she snapped. "Your own murderous deeds put you in here. Anything happens to Mike, it's me you'll reckon with. And I can be just as awful as you."

"Yes, you're a chip off the old block. Don't know how I missed that in you. God knows what you're capable of," he mumbled ruefully. "What are these papers you're bringing? I already gave you power of attorney. What are you asking me to sign now?"

"Daddy, be reasonable. I'm looking after our future. Our lawyers have prepared a trust. Should anything happen to you, complete ownership goes to me and any children I may have. Your direct heirs."

"What about Delano, is he part of the deal too. Did he put you up to it?"

Rachel's long red nails drummed the table angrily. "Mike wants nothing to do with GMI. He's busy writing books. I swear, he'll have no role in the company as long as I live. But I'm hoping the son I'm expecting will have."

"What if I don't sign. How can I trust you? You married outside the faith – to my worst enemy. To the bastard responsible for my incarceration."

She stood up abruptly. "Then there is no further discussion. I'll call a meeting of major shareholders to inform them we're breaking up the conglomerate. The most valuable individual GMI companies will be sold off – including Paragon Pictures."

"You'd do that. Destroy my life's work?"

She looked at him steadily, her jaw thrust forward uncompromisingly. "Yes, I'd do that. Your criminal mistakes came close to wrecking the company. I'm left with a horrendous mess to clean up if you die here."

Her heart fluttered with relief as his face softened into reluctant acceptance of her assessment of the problem.

"All right, give me the damned pen," he growled. "Don't sell out. One day I'll be out of here."

Not sharing his optimism, Rachel pushed the documents across the table before he changed his mind.

One by one, he put a shaky signature to them, sliding them back to her. Relieved, she returned them to the safety of her briefcase.

Suddenly, his mood had changed; it was a relief. It felt to Rachel as if the sun had burst through snow-laden clouds on a bitter winter's day.

"I'm proud of what you've achieved. I should have provided you an opportunity long ago," he said, standing. "I hope to live long enough to see my grandson succeed you. Will the boy bear our name?"

"Yes, Mike's agreed to him being known by both our names." Emotion flooded Rachel. Finally, having a successor to the family fortune pleased him. Getting him to sign was excellent, but his acceptance of her child, even though it was Delano's, was a phenomenally unexpected victory.

Disregarding prison rules against contact, she walked around the table into his outstretched arms. He held her in a tender, harmonious embrace.

Neither reacted to the sound of footsteps. Nor did they see the brown-skinned man in a correction officer's uniform who pitched the fragmentation grenade at them.

But they heard his cruel words: "Here's a message from Colombia: die Rothenberg devils."

The missile bounced shoulder-high from the metal table, its explosives blasting apart their final loving embrace, shattering tissue and squashing the air out of their lungs – ending all their differences.

* * *

Delano was looking wistfully at the parking lot pavement where he'd ground out his cigarette butt when he heard the explosion and felt the concussive wave. He knew from experience it was a grenade.

Desperate for Rachel's safety, he ignored the swarthy corrections officer nearly knocking him down in his rush to an escape car that sped away unchallenged.

As Mike tried entering the building, more prison workers spilled out, shoving him back, screaming for him to stay outside. Part of the visiting hall was smoking and on fire.

"My wife's in there," he moaned.

No one listened until the prison fire rescue team reached the only two people known to have been in the hall when the explosion shook the place.

When they carried Rachel out, Delano's heart leaped in hope. Her eyes flicked momentarily in his direction; she was bleeding from a head wound. Her mouth hung open, gasping from damaged lungs.

Two firemen brought Rothenberg out next. His head lolled lifelessly; his sides were bloody, burned, and torn, having taken most of the blast. Prison staff appeared shocked by the death of their VIP prisoner.

The local ambulance arrived to transport Rachel to the hospital. The prison doctor remained in attendance as paramedics attached fluid lines.

Delano, devastated, put his face close to hers, straining to hear faint mumbled words. All he could make out was, "Save our baby…"

"Pulse is very weak," said the doctor as they sped along, sirens screaming.

"You must do everything you can. She's pregnant," Mike wailed at no one in particular. "Can you save the child?"

Ignoring him, they continued ministering to her. The nearest hospital was 14 miles away.

When they arrived, Rachel was comatose.

CHAPTER FORTY-FIVE:

A CRUEL CHOICE

Delano faced a cruel choice with his wife clinging to life – and feared the result of any decision he might make. Rachel had suffered brain and organ damage with little chance of recovery.

Miraculously the baby remained unscathed in her womb. Neonatologists, specially trained to handle complex pregnancies, advised an immediate cesarean operation to remove the child prematurely.

"We cannot guarantee your wife will survive," they told Delano. "The outcome for the child is doubtful, too."

When Mike asked if any other procedure could save mother and child, obstetricians reluctantly offered a rarely taken last-resort approach: keep Rachel on life support while the baby continued to develop.

Delano chose this risky alternative, praying he was giving them both a chance. At least it offered the possibility of his son reaching full term. There was little hope for Rachel, who appeared brain dead.

With feeding tubes and a ventilator pumping air into Rachel's lungs and the baby growing, he visited daily, sometimes staying overnight, hoping for miraculous signs of improvement – but they did not come.

Nurses came and went, bringing him cups of tea and words of encouragement. Otherwise, the only sound in the room was the rhythmic pumping of the machine keeping mother and child alive.

Ultrasound scans provided better news: the infant boy was doing reasonably well, even while Rachel's heart grew weaker daily.

During this mournful time, Delano received frantic calls from GMI lawyers. They had recovered Rachel's briefcase containing the signed trust documents.

They advised Delano he was the sole heir to the Rothenberg fortune – at least until the child might be born. Without Rachel and her father, the conglomerate would become a rudderless behemoth.

"You have to decide what part you want to play in running GMI should Rachel succumb," the senior legal adviser told him.

The unimaginable prospect of becoming a media billionaire was strange news for Mike. Once, it would have been the ultimate fulfillment of all his former ambitions – but not now, and not at the cost of losing his beloved wife.

Without her, he had no incentive to pull together the warring factions within Max Rothenberg's sprawling media empire. It had always been a group of corporations rife with conflict and power struggles – the way Max intentionally built it for total control. Mike detested office politics.

What happened at GMI was of far less concern than the crises he faced daily. More than once, the baby's heartbeat fluttered, and surgeons prepared for an immediate cesarean. Worries mounted when the infant stopped gaining weight, became sluggish, rarely moving. The time had come, the doctors decided, to remove him from his mother's failing body.

Though under-weight, he otherwise appeared healthy once separated from Rachel's womb. Delano's heart raced with joy and nervousness when they handed the baby to him for the first time.

Before the Pelican Bay attack, they had decided to name him Daniel Rothenberg Delano. They made a point of including Rothenberg believing that, as an adult, he would restore honor to Rachel's badly tarnished family name.

After seconds in his father's arms, Daniel opened his eyes. They were pale, and almond-shaped like Rachel's. No doubt they'd turn liquid brown like his mother's as he grew.

When Mike visited the hospital the following morning, he made the dreaded decision to turn off the machines keeping his wife alive.

Later, bending to kiss her cold cheek, he could not believe her brave spirit was stilled.

Nurses had combed their astonishing patient's long dark hair and dressed her in a white gown. She looked beautiful, peacefully asleep, relieved of all her woes.

Mike looked at her for the last time – and sobbed.

"I'll never forget you," he promised. "Thank you for Daniel. I'm so grateful. You will always be with us."

Rachel, even in death, had once again changed the course of his life, propelling him into a fatherhood role he never expected to fulfill alone – and the unexpected stewardship of GMI.

True to form, he intended to excel at both. Rachel would have expected no less.

A company jet collected him and his son for the return flight to New York. There, he hired a team of three nannies to care for Daniel day and night while he reluctantly took up the reins of corporate responsibility so suddenly forced on him.

CHAPTER FORTY-SIX:

A USEFUL GIFT

The bright lights of the Rainbow Room made the blizzard of descending snowflakes hypnotic, their crystalline beauty dancing past the 65th-floor windows, painting the grimy Manhattan pavement below brilliant white.

Thirteen years had passed since Rachel's death. Delano had taken her place in running GMI – and held onto it against the odds. Now he was getting out, retiring at a relatively young 51 from his unwanted post as chairman.

His natural combination of toughness and insight had made him a surprisingly good fit for the corporate world, despite hating every moment of his involvement.

The old guard, loyal to Rachel and her father, hadn't wanted him as boss – but came to respect his success and judgment.

Under contract and generously compensated with millions for his work, Mike had surprised everyone by refusing to assume ownership of the company that would have made him a billionaire many times over.

He insisted on acting as steward on behalf of his son. Daniel would inherit the fortune his mother and grandfather left behind, becoming the principal shareholder and owner of GMI at age 18.

Delano had honored his murdered wife's wishes by keeping the Rothenberg family's vast media group intact for their son. More than a caretaker, he had ensured the company moved with the times and remained prosperous.

He had put together top-flight management, quieted internal disputes, launched new publications and TV networks globally, and kept the conglomerate's value soaring.

Surveying this gathering of cutthroat media executives, Mike would have preferred to be sailing his new yacht, the *Talespinner II*. Equally tempting would have been a hunting and fishing trip with Daniel.

During school breaks, father and son were closest, enjoying a shared love of the natural world. They took floatplanes to the wildest Alaska forests. Just the two of them in the woods, they maneuvered boats along whitewater rivers, fishing and hunting for survival.

They caught salmon and trout to roast over open fires. They shot game birds and Arctic hares, which Daniel learned how to dress. Together, using pepper spray, they fought off the bears that attempted to raid their camp larder.

When not in school, Daniel often traveled with his father on business trips abroad. From the earliest age, the boy learned how media worked. Delano liked to think Rachel looked down approvingly from heaven at how he was raising their son.

The Rainbow Room, packed with GMI executives, was getting rowdy. Senior VP Julia Thornton stood up, tapping her glass for silence.

"I'd like you to spare a few moments for the person who knows Mike Delano best. May I introduce Daniel Rothenberg Delano. He's here representing the board, to present our gift to his father on the occasion of his retirement."

Julia signaled to the back of the room, where a door opened. Daniel, a tall and muscular 13-year-old with a shock of dark wavy hair, entered carrying a gleaming new Purdy double-barreled shotgun.

Slung across his shoulders, bandit-style, hung a hand-tooled leather cartridge belt loaded with 12-gauge shells. Calculating eyes were on him. A few years hence, he would be their boss.

He looked mature and confident beyond his years, wearing a well-cut sports jacket and tan trousers. Daniel was a striking combination of Rachel's dark beauty and Delano's sturdy athleticism.

Glowing with pride, Mike beamed down into his son's bold brown eyes, so like those of his mother. He was delighted to take hold of the splendid shotgun, snapping it open and squinting along the barrels with expert familiarity.

"My gratitude to everyone for this magnificent sporting piece. It's a Stradivarius among shotguns. The finest of its kind, a wonderful choice." he said. "And having my son present this gift makes my night complete."

With a knowing wink to Daniel, he added: "A few more years and I just may let you use it on one of our hunting trips."

As the celebration wound down, Delano moved among the tables shaking hands with old and new colleagues, wishing them well.

Outside, a foot of snow had drifted onto the ice rink across the plaza. Father and son paused for a moment, craning their necks to gaze up at the chilled flanks of the towering building. After the overheated party, they enjoyed the frigid breeze-driven whiteness swirling around their faces.

"We must learn to ski," Mike said, breaking the snowy silence.

"Really, Dad? When?" he said, sounding like the young teen he was.

"Soon," his father replied.

* * *

The company Daimler sped along Manhattan's East Side Drive, the heater blasting, with father and son nodding off in the back, exhausted after their long night of celebration.

A slight fishtailing of the big sedan on the packed snow woke Delano, making him alert.

"Take it easy, George," he told his fearless heavy-footed driver. "We don't want to wind up in the Hudson, do we?"

George, an exceptional chauffeur, nodded agreement. The ex-Royal Marine also acted as an armed bodyguard. Delano still had enemies. As Daniel's sole parent, he wasn't taking chances. George, ever-vigilant, had twice stopped attempts on his life.

Away from Manhattan and awake now, father and son were kids with a new toy, removing the Purdy from its case to study it carefully.

It was, indeed, a unique beauty, top of the line. The stock, etched with game birds, was also carved with Delano's initials. Now, nearly free from corporate responsibilities, Delano spoke happily of his plans.

"How would you like to live in England, go to a British school?" he asked.

"You mean leave America for good, Dad?"

"Well, not exactly, son. The way I see it, you'd want to come back here for university. Maybe Harvard or Yale. You've got the smarts and the grades for the Ivy League. Then you might want to return to Britain and study at the London School of Economics. You'll need to know stuff to run GMI."

Daniel grunted non-committedly, thoughts of future responsibilities far from his mind.

"What about our skiing lessons? They got snow in England?"

"Yes, in Scotland. Better yet, we can go to Switzerland and Austria. Skiing the Alps – they say it's the best in the world," Delano answered, smiling.

"Why do you want to live in England, Dad?"

"It's where I was born, a different culture. And keep this to yourself for now: I'm in talks to buy a British paper, *The Daily Chronicle*. I worked for the *Chronicle* when I was a foreign correspondent. It looks like folding. I want to save it."

"Why?"

"Because it's a fine paper. Just needs bringing into the modern age. I want to take it online while preserving the print version. I'm tired of being a businessman running an empire. I want to return to the form of journalism I once enjoyed."

"Where will we live? What about school?"

"I've bought a fine home in Central London near Hyde Park. You'll be at boarding school, in the country, but I can send a car to collect you, bring you home at weekends."

"Sounds OK, I guess."

Then came a question that surprised Delano.

"Dad, will you ever get married again?"

"Maybe, if I meet the right woman, but I haven't found her yet."

Daniel secretly wished his father would settle down. The single most important thing missing from his charmed life was a mother. He wanted a family with regular parents like most of his friends. He often sat looking at Rachel's pictures in his father's study and wished he could have known her.

There were videos, too, made on his parent's honeymoon voyage aboard the *Talespinner*. Viewing them upset Mike – although he had played them for Daniel on rare occasions. Rachel was beautiful and looked like she could be challenging as well as fun, Daniel thought. The boy was sad his father had paid scant attention to his own emotional needs.

One of New York's most eligible bachelors, Mike wasn't looking for another wife. Greying, fit, and handsome, his occasional romantic trysts with stunning women never lasted.

Ladies visiting their Manhattan penthouse, or spending weekends at their Connecticut estate, prayed in vain for a permanent role in Mike's life. But Mike avoided commitment to anything other than his son and the business. He had yet to meet a woman who made him want to settle down again.

Engrossed with the new gun and talk of a future in Britain, they barely noticed when the car turned off the main highway, taking the less-used local road.

The Daimler crunched to a stop at High Trees, the waterfront estate with a trout stream running through 15 acres of oak-enshrouded land. Snow hung from oaks and pines, bending branches to near breaking point. The cold night was clear and silent.

George jumped out first to open the rear door.

"We're home, gentlemen," he said, "Don't slip on the ice…. it's…"

They were his last words.

A rapid popping sound shattered the icy stillness. He pitched backward, a surprised look on his handsome, square face. A crimson halo spread in the whiteness where his head rested.

"What the hell," Delano growled, instinctively crouching lower in the backseat but not low enough.

The next burst of automatic fire chewed through the Daimler's flanks, hitting him. A bullet pierced his left shoulder, shattering bone and splattering bloody fragments across the leather upholstery.

"Get on the floor, now! Lay flat, Danny," Delano gasped through his shock.

The boy's eyes widened in horror at the sight of his father's bloody tuxedo. Chaotic evil had entered their warm, orderly world. He feared George, a friend and mentor most of his life, was dead.

Daniel began to shake uncontrollably. He cowered back when the Daimler door opened, and the muzzle of a Bushmaster rifle pointed inside. Cold air rushing into the warm car carried an oily scent from the still-smoking weapon.

"Come with me, Delano," ordered Miguel Gallardo, malignant resolve thick in his Spanish-accented words.

"What is it you want? Is it money?" Delano implored, at first not recognizing their assailant.

"Fuck your money, fool. That's not why I'm here. Get out, or I knee-cap your son, make him a cripple right now."

Delano now recognized his attacker. Looking back at Daniel, he maneuvered painfully from the car, staggering a dozen yards to stand bleeding pitifully in the snow.

"Don't worry, son, I can deal with this," he shouted back, displaying a level of confidence he certainly did not feel.

"Stop, Dad, don't go," the boy begged while attempting to follow. He flinched. The gun's hot muzzle, pressed against his right knee, had burned through his trousers. Smothering a pained yelp, he fell back resentfully silent.

Chilled from hours of waiting, Miguel was impatient. He would slaughter Delano first; he represented an immediate threat, while the kid did not.

"Kneel!" he ordered, putting the rifle barrel an inch from Delano's head. "This is the moment I've been waiting for, motherfucker," he sneered.

Mike flashed back to the moments after the explosion at Pelican Bay – and his heart sank. "It was you! I saw you running from the prison," he said.

"Yeah, it was me. I bribed my way in, and one of Rothenberg's protectors was on our payroll. So was the entrance hall guard," he boasted. "They tipped us your wife was visiting the old man. I knew the exact day and hour to be there. That was a good start on payback for kidnapping me and killing my father. Now I'll finish it."

Delano knew there was little chance of talking his way out of this, but he had to try if only to save Daniel.

"For Christ's sake, man, that was nearly 14 years ago. Wasn't killing my wife and her father enough vengeance? I released you from the boat unharmed, didn't I? Why kill us?"

"You got rich running the company. You ran stories that cost our organization millions; some of our people are still in prison as a result. And I lost the movie business I dreamed of when my father drowned – on your boat," Miguel growled. "You set the narks on us. You killed our men. Now you gotta pay. You and your brat are the last Rothenbergs. My people want you all gone, dead and buried."

"Why kill my boy? He wasn't even born then. He's never done anything to hurt you."

Mike searched for a way to keep Gallardo talking. "You still want that movie career? I can arrange it. Just let us go," Mike said, knowing those words to be his last desperate gambit.

Miguel's scornful laugh rang through the silence. That dream had faded long ago for him.

"On your knees. Now!"

Delano knelt. His final thoughts were of Daniel. "Look, I'll give you anything you want. Just let my son live," he begged, tears beginning to wet his face.

"Shut up," the Colombian sneered.

Touching the gun barrel to the back of Delano's head, he paused for a second as his finger tightened on the trigger. He wanted to savor the delicious moment of payback.

That was his mistake. Blinding twin flashes lit up the darkness.

Miguel staggered backward as though hit by a sledgehammer. His Bushmaster pointed upwards, spraying bullets uselessly at the clouds.

Delano, struggling to rise, looked back at the Daimler. Danny stood in the glare of the headlights, popping two more cartridges into the Purdy's chambers, his face set and determined, ready.

"You OK, Dad?" he said, the quiver in his boyish voice betraying his terror. "Did I get him?"

"Yes, son, he looks dead – call 911. I'm hurt. We need help."

Danny shakily punched in the number, explained what had happened, and gave their location.

Next, he helped his injured father back into the warmth of the limousine.

That done, he left the car again, the Purdy in the crook of his arm. No one was going to kill his father while he lived.

Stumbling through the drifts, he checked the perimeter around the house.

"Are there others?" Delano asked when he returned.

"I don't think so. There's a Toyota parked around the back, behind the trees. He must have been there hours, judging by snow piled around the tires. You know him?"

"Yes. He's from a drug gang whose plans I exposed. His father drowned when *Talespinner* went down. They blamed me for that, too."

Flinching with pain, Delano hugged his boy with gratitude. The pride he felt for Daniel buffered the agony of his wound.

Out from behind the clouds, the moon shone on Miguel's body where it had fallen, revealing gaping holes in the would-be assassin's clothes.

Seeking words to lift the mood until police and medics arrived, Delano remarked dryly: "So, Danny, you got to use the Purdy first after all."

* * *

Eighteen months went by after the shooting, many of them miserable for Delano suffering through a series of surgeries for his wounds.

Doctors had inserted pins and removed bone fragments caused by two bullets tearing through his upper arm and shoulder blade.

Daniel went to the hospital to keep his dad company in his private room after each surgery.

He listened as doctors explained it could take up to a year for Mike to regain use of his left arm.

They cautioned: "There will be numbness, a lack of sensation due to severed nerves."

"Hell, as long as I can still type, that's OK by me," Mike said. "As for that ski training we discussed, Danny, that will have to wait a while yet."

"How about fishing, Dad, you going to be OK for that?"

"Yes, son, but you'll have to land the big ones for me. They're saying don't put too much strain on the shoulder for six months."

While acknowledging his good fortune in escaping death, Delano worried more about his son than himself. The after-effects of the shooting had hit Daniel hard. Regret over having killed a man nagged at him.

"I've been having nightmares about that shooting," he told Mike, who tried to comfort him. "I keep seeing him lying in the snow dead."

"It was his Karma to die at the hands of a Rothenberg family member," Delano suggested. "He killed your mother and grandfather – and if you hadn't shot him, we'd both be dead, too."

His words brought some comfort, but Danny remained troubled.

"When are we leaving for England?" he asked.

"About a month from now. I'll have finished treatment by then." Delano would have hugged Daniel, but it was still too painful. Instead, he took his hand and squeezed. "It's going to be excellent, a complete change of scene. A new school for you, and back to real journalism for me. I've been away from my true calling for too long."

CHAPTER FORTY-SEVEN:

HOME AT LAST

It took three years of dedicated work for Mike Delano to return *The Daily Chronicle* to profitability.

Under his guidance, the paper's dwindling print circulation of 300,000 copies went to a million copies sold daily; its digital subscriptions reached a record 2.5-million. Print and online versions of the Chronicle were packed with prestige advertising.

Mike delighted in taking this century-old Fleet Street daily into the digital age. Nor did he deny that the know-how he had gained while running GMI contributed massively to his triumph.

He had returned home to the business that had been his life's blood as a young man, working with journalists he respected. He had a special place in his heart for the paper's foreign correspondents. Like them, he had braved death, torture, and disease in war zones around the globe.

For the first time since accepting Lord Max's fateful job offer, he felt cleansed of the tawdry tabloid business that had come close to destroying him.

Yet there were still jealous publishing rivals who pointed disapprovingly at his scandalous past. They had not forgotten he was an editor who'd do anything for a headline. Some still insisted on the truth of the accusations that he'd stolen money from Lord Rothenberg's Sunday tabloid.

When Daniel asked why such snide reports popped up when his father was now a prominent British editor, Mike put it down to professional jealousy.

"They hate me for beating them at their own game, for exposing your grandfather's criminality. The Oxbridge media clan don't consider me one of them – a boy from South London beating them at their own game," he said.

"It's pure snobbery, son. The English find business success embarrassing. It's one of their affectations. Achieving it without private school or a university degree gets up their snooty noses."

Daniel, home from Marlborough College, a 150-year-old boarding school in Wiltshire, two hours away from London, surprised his father by asking, "Dad, can I come work in the office with you when I'm on holiday?"

His son had become a continuing source of pleasure and pride. Now Delano looked at him with delight. He wanted Danny to have the experience of working for a reputable newspaper. Soon he would face the challenges of the New York business world when he had to take hold of the reins of GMI.

Delano still enjoyed the prosperity he'd earned at the global conglomerate. He lived in a Kensington penthouse within a gated community with a pool and a gym. He had a chauffeur to drive his Bentley, plus a housekeeper, an excellent cook, and a part-time servant to cosset him.

He felt deeply the striking contrast of his current life with his boyhood in a two-bedroom London flat shared with his abusive step-father and bi-polar mother.

Mike wondered what Daisy Louise would have made of his splendid Kensington digs if she had survived to see them. He kept asking himself, how had he been so fortunate? He had never planned for the power and plenty he enjoyed now.

Even knowing it was futile, he fervently wished Rachel was with him to share this new chapter in his life. She would have been glad to be back in Britain, where she'd grown up.

Wealth brought Delano another satisfaction. For years he'd sent cash to the families of friends murdered in Iraq: the widow and children of his photographer, and the wives left behind by his murdered cellmates. He also funded endowments to ensure a good education for their children and long term financial security. At first it had been a sad duty, but now it brought him satisfaction to visit each of them in turn, checking on their continued well-being.

Now he needed to take one last action to complete his contentment.

* * *

The casket sank slowly into a specially prepared grave on what had been Viscount Clarence Hamden's Sussex estate. The new owner was the lone mourner as a rabbi read a blessing and left.

Fighting tears, no one was there to see, Mike Delano cast a handful of the rich Sussex earth onto the bronze coffin before the soil of Rachel's native country closed over her.

He had brought her back from burial in California to be close to him in England after buying the country home and land where they'd met.

Standing alone, the journalist rejoiced in the traditional Jewish belief that a portion of the soul is always present at the graveside. He felt Rachel's nearness.

Delano walked a few yards to the lakeside bench where they first kissed, where they discovered they were two rebels striving to appease her tyrannical father.

The waning sun reflected crimson off the glass-smooth water as it had those many years past when their turbulent journey together began.

As at their first meeting, Delano lit up a joint and inhaled deeply. It brought her back: vibrant, dark eyes dancing under long lashes fluttering with happiness, mischievous at being with him.

He could hear her, too, telling him she was glad he had brought her home, that it was good to be near him again.

His voice was husky with the aromatic smoke as he breathed out, whispering: "You'll always be with me. You gave me everything. You're part of me until we meet again – when our story starts anew."